VERNON SUBUTEX 1

Virginie Despentes

VERNON SUBUTEX 1

Translated from the French by
Frank Wynne

MACLEHOSE PRESS
QUERCUS · LONDON

First published in the French language as *Vernon Subutex 1* by
Editions Grasset & Fasquelle, Paris, in 2015
First published in Great Britain in 2017 by

MacLehose Press
An imprint of Quercus Publishing Ltd
Carmelite House
50 Victoria Embankment
London EC4Y 0DZ

An Hachette UK company

This book is supported by the Institute Français (Royaume Uni)
as part of the Burgess programme.

INSTITUT
FRANÇAIS
ROYAUME-UNI

A CIP catalogue record for this book is available
from the British Library.

ISBN (TPB) 978 0 85705 541 5
ISBN (Ebook) 978 0 85705 540 8

10 9 8 7 6 5 4 3 2 1

Designed and typeset in Scala by Libanus Press, Marlborough
Printed and bound in Denmark by Nørhaven

Non omnis moriar . . .
for
Martine Giordano,
Joséphine Pépa Bolivar
Yanna Pistruin

THE WINDOWS OF THE BUILDING OPPOSITE ARE ALREADY LIT. The silhouettes of cleaning women bustle around the vast open plan office of what is probably an advertising agency. They start work at six. Vernon usually wakes up just before they arrive. He aches for a strong coffee, a yellow-filtered cigarette, he would like to make a slice of toast and eat breakfast while scanning the headlines of *Le Parisien* on his laptop.

It has been weeks since he last bought coffee. The cigarettes he rolls every morning by gutting the cigarette butts from the night before are so skinny it is like puffing on paper. There is nothing to eat in the cupboards. But he has kept up the payments to his internet provider. The standing order goes out on the day his housing benefit hits his account. For several months now, this has been paid directly to his landlord, but the bill has still been paid out, so far. Let's hope it lasts.

His phone contract has lapsed and he no longer bothers to pay for top-ups. In the face of disaster, Vernon decided on a course of action: he played the guy who has not noticed anything unusual. He watched as, in slow motion, things began to collapse, then the collapse accelerated. But Vernon has lost none of his indifference, none of his elegance.

The first thing to go was his unemployment benefit. By post he received a copy of the report written by his adviser. He got along well with her. They had been meeting regularly for almost three years in the cramped cubicle where she killed off houseplants. Thirtyish, bubbly, fake redhead, plump, well-stacked, Madame Bodard liked to talk about her two sons, she worried about them a lot, regularly took them to see a paediatrician in the hope that he would diagnose some form of hyperactivity disorder that might justify sedating them. But the doctor told her they were in fine form and sent her packing. Madame Bodard told Vernon how she had been to see AC/DC and Guns N' Roses with her parents when she was young. Now she preferred to listen to Camille and Benjamin Biolay and Vernon abstained from making any offensive remarks. They had talked at great length about his case: between the ages of twenty and forty-five, he had been a record dealer. These days, his chances of finding work were slimmer than if he had been a coalminer. Madame Bodard had suggested retraining. Together they had perused the various courses open to him – A.F.P.A., G.R.E.T.A., C.F.A. – and they parted on good terms, agreeing to meet again to reassess the situation. Three years later, his application to study for a diploma in administration had not been accepted. From his point of view, he felt he had done everything he needed to do, he had become an expert in applications and prepared them with extraordinary efficiency. Over time, he had come to feel that his job was to bum around on the internet looking for vacancies that corresponded to his profile, then send off C.V.s so that they could send back proof of his rejection. Who would want to train someone who was knocking on for fifty? He had managed to dredge up a work placement in a concert venue out in the suburbs and another in an art house cinema – but aside from going out occasionally, keeping abreast of the network problems on the R.E.R. and meeting people, it mostly left him with a dreary sense of waste.

In the copy of the report that Madame Bodard had written to justify his being struck off, she mentioned things he had talked about in a spirit of banter, like spending a little money to go and see the Stooges play Le Mans or losing a hundred euros in a poker game. As he flicked through his case file, rather than worrying about the unemployment benefit he would no longer receive, he felt embarrassed for her. His adviser was about thirty years old. What did she earn – how much does a woman like that make – two thousand a month before tax? Top whack. But kids of this generation had been raised to the rhythms of the Voice in the Big Brother house, a world in which the telephone can ring at any time to give the order to fire half of your colleagues. Eliminate thy neighbour is the golden rule of the games they have been spoon-fed since childhood. How can one now expect them to find it morbid?

When he received the letter from the benefits office, Vernon thought that this might motivate him to find "something". As though the worsening of his already parlous situation might have a beneficial influence on his ability to dig his way out of the quagmire he was bogged down in . . .

He was not the only person for whom things had rapidly deteriorated. Until the early 2000s, a lot of people were doing pretty well. You still saw couriers becoming label managers, freelance hacks getting jobs as columnists in T.V. supplements, even shiftless wankers ended up running the record department of the local F.N.A.C. . . . At the tail end of the *peloton*, those least motivated by the prospect of success managed to get by doing contract work

9

for music festivals, working as a roadie on a tour, sticking posters on hoardings . . . That said, Vernon was well placed to understand the threat posed by the tsunami that was Napster, it never occurred to him that the ship would go down with all hands lost.

Some said it was karma, the industry had experienced an extraordinary upturn in the era of C.D.s – selling their clients their whole discography on a medium that cost half the price to make and was sold for twice the price in shops . . . with no real benefit to music fans, since no-one had ever complained about vinyl records. The drawback of karma theory was that if there was even a grain of truth in the notion that "what goes around comes around" people would have long since stopped being arseholes.

His record shop was called Revolver, Vernon had started working there as a shop assistant at the age of twenty, and taken over when the owner decided to move to Australia, where he became a restaurateur. If anyone had told him that first year that he would spend most of his life in this shop, he would probably have said, don't talk shit, I've got too many things I want to do. Only when you get old do you realise that the expression "fucking hell but time flies" most appositely describes the workings of the process.

He had had to shut up shop in 2006. The most difficult thing was finding someone to take over the lease, to kiss goodbye to the prospect of turning a profit on the deal, but even so his first year being unemployed – with no benefits, since he was self-employed – went well: a commission to write a dozen entries for an encyclopedia of rock, a few days cash-in-hand manning the ticket desk for some festival in the suburbs, record reviews for the music press . . . meanwhile he went online and began selling off everything he had salvaged from the shop. Most of the stock had been sold at a knock-down price, but there was still some vinyl, a few boxed sets, and an extensive collection of posters and T-shirts he had refused to sell off cheap. On eBay, he made three times what he had anticipated, without any of the fuss of having to keep accurate accounts. You simply had to be reliable, to go to the post office once a week, to be careful how you packaged the merchandise. The first year had been a blast. Life is often a game of two halves: in the first half it lulls you, makes you think you're in control; in the second, when it sees you're relaxed and helpless, it comes around again and grinds you to a pulp.

Vernon had just had enough time to rediscover his love of a long lie-in – for more than twenty years, come hell or hideous hangover, he had rolled up the metal shutters on the shop six days a week no matter what. Only three times in twenty-five years, had he entrusted the keys to one of his colleagues: a bout of gastric flu, a dental implant fitting and an attack of sciatica. It took him a year to relearn the knack of lazing in bed and reading in the mornings if he felt like it. His preferred leisure activity was cranking up the radio and scanning porn on the web. He was familiar with the entire oeuvre of Sasha Grey, Bobbi Starr or Nina Roberts. He also enjoyed an afternoon nap, he would read for half an hour and then nod off.

In the second year, he had handled the picture research for a biography of Johnny Hallyday, signed up for welfare with the R.S.A. – which had just changed from being the R.S.I. – and he had started selling off his personal collection. He did well out of eBay, he would never have guessed what fetishistic folly stirred World 2.0, everything was up for sale: merchandising, comics, plastic figurines, posters, fanzines, coffee-table books, T-shirts . . .

At first, when you start selling, you hold back, but a little incentive and suddenly it becomes a pleasure to get rid of everything. Gradually, he had cleared his home of every last trace of his former life.

He came to appreciate the true glories of a peaceful morning with no punters to constantly bust his balls. He had all the time in the world to listen to music now. The Kills, the White Stripes and sundry Strokes could release all the albums they liked, he no longer needed to give a shit. He could not bear the constant torrent of new stuff, it was endless, to keep up you'd have to plug into the Web and be drip-fed new sounds on a constant loop.

The downside was that he hadn't anticipated that it would be a gruelling slog to get girls after he closed down the shop. People say the rock industry is a man's game, but people talk a lot of shit: he had always had a string of female customers that was continually replenished. He had an understanding when it came to girls. He didn't do monogamy, and the more he tried to sack them off, the more they stalked him. When some babe came in with her boyfriend looking for a C.D., he could guarantee that within the week she would be back, on her own this time. Then there were all the girls who worked in the neighbourhood. The beauticians at the salon on the corner, the girls in the shop across the street, the girls at the post office, the girls in the restaurant, the girls in the bar, the girls down at the swimming pool. A vast collection of potential conquests that was lost to him the day he handed back the keys.

He had never had regular girlfriends. Like a lot of guys he knew, Vernon was haunted by the memory of the girl who got away. His was called Séverine. He had been twenty-eight. He was so attached to his reputation as a player that he refused to recognise that she was the one until it was too late. He was a big cat prowling the streets, wild, untameable, all his mates were blown away by the elegant nonchalance with which he moved from girl to girl. Or this was how he saw himself, at least. The one-night stand, the lone wolf, the guy who never gets tied down, the guy who won't be twisted round some woman's little finger. He had no illusions: like a lot of insecure young men, he found it reassuring to know that he could make women cry.

Séverine was tall and hyper – so hyper she could be exhausting – she had legs that went on forever, she looked like a Parisian rich bitch, the sort of girl who can wear a sheepskin jacket and make it look cool. She grabbed life by the balls, there was nothing she could not do around the house, even changing a tyre on the hard shoulder did not faze her, she was the sort of rich brat who was used to sorting things out herself and never complaining. Which did not mean that, in private, she did not know how to loosen up. When he thinks about her, he sees her naked, sprawled in bed; she loved to spend whole weekends there. She kept her turntable on the floor next to the mattress so she did not have to get up to change the record. Piled up around the bed she had her cigarettes, her bottle of water and the telephone, whose spiral cable was constantly tangled. This was her kingdom. For a few short months, he was granted access.

She was the kind of girl whose mother had taught her not to burst into tears when you find out your boyfriend is cheating on you. Séverine gritted her teeth. Vernon had been stupidly caught in the act – and had been surprised that she did not leave him there and then. She had said "I'll leave you to it", and forgiven him. He concluded that she did not have the strength to lose him and began to feel a slight contempt for her weakness of character. And so he did it again. They had had three or four screaming matches, each time she said if you keep pushing your luck, I'm out of here, you'll leave me no choice, and each time Vernon was convinced it was just an empty threat. He never saw it coming. When he found out she was seeing someone else, Vernon stuffed her things into a cardboard box and left them downstairs on the pavement. The image of her clothes, her books, her perfume bottles being ransacked by passers-by and strewn outside his door would haunt him for years. He never heard from her again. It had taken a long time for Vernon to realise he would never get over her. He had a talent for ignoring his feelings. He often thinks about what his life would be like if he had stayed with Séverine. If he had had the courage to turn his back on what he had been, if he had known that one way or another we are stripped of the things we care about, that the best thing you can do is plan ahead. She had kids, obviously. She was that kind of girl. The kind who settles down. Without losing any of their charm. Not a bitch. A bewitching woman who probably eats organic and gets all het up about global warming, but he is convinced that she still listens to Tricky and Janis Joplin. If he had stayed with her, he would have found another job after he closed the shop, because they would have had kids and he would have had no choice. And right now he would be worrying what to do about his son smoking weed or his daughter's anorexia. Oh well. He likes to think he minimised the damage.

These days, Vernon fucks less often than a married man. He would never have believed it possible to go so long without sex. Though Facebook and Meetic are wonderful tools for picking up girls from home, unless he's prepared to content himself with a virtual fuck on Second Life, sooner or later he has to drag himself outside to *meet* the girl. Find clothes he can wear that look hipster rather than homeless, find some way to avoid going to a café, to the cinema, and certainly not for dinner somewhere . . . and avoid bringing her back to his place so she doesn't see the empty cupboards, the sorry state of the fridge and the disgusting mess – nothing like the charming chaos of the confirmed bachelor. His flat reeks of socks worn for too long, the quintessential scent of the single man. He can open the windows, spray himself with cologne. This smell marks out his territory. On the whole, he picks girls up on the internet and stands them up when they arrange a meeting.

Vernon understands women, he has made an extensive study of them. The city is full of lost souls ready to do his cleaning and get down on all fours to lavish him with lingering blowjobs designed to cheer him up. But he is too old to believe that all this comes without a series of reciprocal demands. Just because a woman is old and ugly doesn't mean she is less of a possessive pain in the arse than some twenty-year-old babe. The characteristic thing about women is that they can keep a low profile for months before laying their cards on the table. He is wary of the sort of girl who might find him attractive.

Friends are different. Spending years together listening to records, going to gigs, arguing about bands, these are sacred bonds. You don't stop seeing each other simply because of a change of venue. But what had changed was that now he had to call and arrange to meet, whereas before they could just come into the shop if they were in the neighbourhood. He was not in the habit of organising dinner parties, trips to the cinema or signature cocktails and spliffs . . . Gradually, without his really noticing, a lot of his mates had moved out into the sticks, either because they had a wife and kids and couldn't go on living in a thirty-square-metre apartment, or because Paris had become too expensive and they had sensibly moved back to their home town. Once they hit forty, Paris only suffered the children of homeowners to reside within its boundaries, the rest of the population went on their merry way. Vernon had stayed. This had probably been a mistake.

He only became aware of this fragmentation much later, when loneliness had walled him up alive. Then came the chain of catastrophes.

It had started with Bertrand. The big C had come back. This time the crab was in the throat. He had had a hell of a fucking time the first time round. He thought he had beaten it. At least his friends had celebrated his remission as a definitive triumph. But this time it was all over so quickly it hit them like an uppercut, they only truly took it in after the funeral. In the three months between diagnosis and death, the illness had consumed him. Bertrand always wore black shirts with the collar turned up. He had been wearing them like that since 1988. Over time, he had a little trouble buttoning them as his beer-gut blossomed. At forty-something, he had long white hair, a pair of tinted Ray-Bans perched on his nose, a beautiful pair of snakeskin boots and a face like a thug. Blotchy from booze but well-preserved, the big lug.

It had been a shock, getting used to seeing him wearing old-man pyjamas. Watching him lose his hair was bad enough. But seeing him in those ridiculous pyjamas made Vernon's heart bleed. Bertrand could not manage to eat, and the finest weed in the world made no difference. He had lost the stature that was his defining trait. Too prominent beneath his sallow skin, the bones became obscene. He stubbornly carried on wearing the silver skull rings that now slipped off his fingers. He could see himself wasting away, day by day, he was conscious to the end.

Then came the constant pain, the frail body, the skeletal mask. He was always joking about the morphine pump because jokes were their only form of communication. Sometimes, Bertrand touched on the death that awaited him. He would say that he was woken in the night by fear, and he would say "The worst of it is, my brain is fine and I can feel my body falling apart and there's nothing I can do". Vernon could not say "Come on, you'll be fine, just hang in there, mate". So instead they listened to The Cramps, The Gun Club and MC5 and they drank beer while Bertrand still could. His family was furious, but honestly, what else did they have?

Then the news of his death, one morning, a text message. At the time, Vernon, like the others, managed to remain dignified at the funeral. Dark glasses. They all had a pair at home, and a handsome black suit. It was only afterwards that the panic took hold. The panic and the loneliness. The impulse to call Bertrand, the inability to delete his last voicemails, the reluctance to believe that it had happened. After a certain age, we do not move on from the dead, we remain in their time, in their company. On the anniversary of Joe Strummer's death, Vernon had done exactly as he would have had Bertrand been there, he listened to the Clash back catalogue and drank beer. He had never been particularly interested in them as a group. But this is what friendship means: you learn to play on other people's home turf.

That day in December 2002, they had been queuing up to buy

smoked salmon because Bertrand was spending Christmas with a Norwegian girl he wanted to impress with his culinary sophistication. He had convinced himself that smoked salmon could be bought in this shop in the fifth arrondissement and nowhere else. Having trekked here on the Métro, they were waiting to be served. The queue snaked out onto the pavement, it would be a forty-minute wait at least. Vernon had gone off to buy cigarettes, and it was on the radio in the *bar-tabac* that he heard the news that Strummer was dead. He had gone back to Bertrand. No way, you're shitting me! You think I'd joke about something like that? Bertrand had turned pale, though he still waited and bought his salmon and two bottles of vodka. They had walked back through the second arrondissement singing "Lost in the Supermarket" and remembering the time they had seen Strummer play a solo gig together. Vernon had only gone to keep Bertrand company, but once he got there, an unexpected surge of emotion made him waver, he had pressed his shoulder against his mate and felt tears well in his eyes. He had never said a word about this, but on the day Joe Strummer died, he had confessed and Bertrand had said Yeah, I know, I saw, but I didn't want to bust your balls about it. Strummer ... fuck! Who's left worth talking about?

Three months later came the turn of Jean-No. Not drunk, not speeding. A trunk road, a lorry, a hairpin bend and a patch of fog. Coming back from a weekend away with his wife, he tried to change the radio station. She came away with a broken nose. The one they reconstructed for her was a lot prettier than the original. Jean-No never got to see it.

That Sunday, Vernon was at a girlfriend's place, sitting on a folded mattress propped against a wall and covered with an Indian throw so pockmarked by burn holes from spliffs they looked like part of the pattern. They were having an "Alien" night, the complete boxed set, with a home cinema projector. The girl in question lived in an attic room near Goncourt Métro. A stone's throw away was one of the last remaining D.V.D. rental outlets. They had already watched "A Better Tomorrow" and "Mad Max", "The Godfather" trilogy and "A Chinese Ghost Story". She was a real find, this girl, totally into weed and manga. Not the kind who always wants to go out. With her, the only ball-ache was: Hey, babe, could you go down to the corner shop and get me some chocolate? Five floors, no lift. Vernon was not the kind to be a servile sweetheart. She had just brought two glasses of ice-cold Coke on a huge tray, the film was on "pause", so when his mobile rang, Vernon took the call – something he rarely did on a Sunday. But it had been a long time since he had had a call from Emilie, so he figured it must be something important. She had just heard the news from Jean-No's little sister. Vernon was surprised that she was the one chosen to ring round his friends. After all, Jean-No had a wife. In the hospital, in the confusion, maybe . . . but asking the mistress to put the word out? There had been a time when he and Emilie were very close, but they had lost touch and now was not the time to catch up.

Vernon had insisted they carry on watching the movie. Said he didn't really feel anything. This shocked him. He thought maybe he was becoming callous. But he and Jean-No saw each other every week, and they had become even closer after Bertrand's death. They lunched together in the Turkish place near the gare du Nord, always ordered the same 12-euro menu washed down with cold beer. Jean-No had given up cigarettes, it had been a real bitch. If the poor bastard had known it was all for nothing, he would have set an alarm to wake him in the middle of the night just so he could smoke more. Jean-No had married a ball-buster. A lot of guys feel reassured by being kept on a tight leash.

It was only later, during the night, that it really hit him. In that instant when sleep took hold, he felt the icy teeth sink into him. He had had to get dressed and go out – walk through the cold, be on his own, see the lights pass other bodies melt into the milling crowd and feel the ground beneath his feet. He was alive. He was struggling to breathe.

He often went out walking at night. It was a habit he had picked up in the late eighties, when metalheads started getting into hip-hop. Public Enemy and the Beastie Boys were signed to the same label as Slayer, which made the connection. In the record shop, he had become friends with a Funkadelic fan, a scabby, runty white guy who never said much, looking back he figures the guy was probably into smack but at the time he hadn't put two and two together. The guy was a tagger, he used to spray "Zona" everywhere he went. The friendship had not lasted long, Zona was tired of working on the street, "The Métro, that's where the real action is", he wanted to tag the train tracks, the depots, and Vernon had no desire to follow him into this subterranean world. He never caught the bug – he struggled to take an interest in the heroic tales of legendary crews like 93MC or the MKC, in wildstyle and throw-up . . . He could see there had to be a buzz to it, but he never got it.

His particular buzz involved risking breaking his spine climbing up onto the roof of a building and spending two hours in the silence of the spray-can, taking breaks, smoking fags, watching the people below who never thought to look up and see his shadow, a silent sentinel.

The first night of his life without Jean-No, he walked until the soles of his feet were sore, then he kept walking. He thought about Jean-No's kids, but he could not make sense of it. Fatherless. The word simply did not square with everything he knew about the three mindless little monkeys ceaselessly clamouring for attention, for sweets, for new toys.

Jean-No was happy to act the arsehole. He was arrogant. He had always been one to listen to fucked-up music, in his teens he had loved Einstürzende Neubauten and Foetus, later he had got into Straight Edge hardcore punk – he was a fan of Rudimentary Peni and obsessed with Minor Threat – which was strange given that Jean-No drank like a fish. You had to really like him to spend time with him, because he could be completely scathing. When he turned forty, in an effort to seem more posh, he started getting into opera. He dressed like a Playmobil figurine in his Sunday best and he spouted right-wing bullshit ten years before it was fashionable. At the time, it was so unusual it had a certain cachet.

Vernon now lived in a world where Ian MacKaye could start smoking crack, and Jean-No was no longer around to comment.

Then it had been Pedro's turn. Scarcely eight months later. Heart attack. Pedro's real name was Pierre, but he snorted so much coke he earned his South American name.

Vernon had been queuing outside the Elysée-Montmartre – it hadn't burned down yet – to see the Libertines. He was trying to hook up with an unlikely assistant/intern working on some T.V. programme with Thierry Ardisson, she could talk about nothing but the presenter who she claimed to loathe, though she was clearly fascinated. He had spotted a friend in the distance, standing outside the venue and waved to him, eager to show off the girl he was with, dark hair fringe skinny jeans fuck-me shoes of the sort the city was mass-producing in the early years of the new millennium. And seeing him come over, the friend started to sob. He was saying Pedro Pedro Pedro, unable to explain himself and Vernon had felt an immense weariness surge through him.

Pedro had easily snorted three houses, two Ferraris, every lover, every friendship, every glimpse of a career, his looks and every last tooth in his head. He did not do it shamefacedly, claiming that he did not have a problem, no, his shtick was narcissism, exhilarating hysteria, a passion he had completely come to terms with. He rubbed coke on his gums, got it all over his jacket, he knew every toilet in every bar in Paris and selected his watering hole based on the practicality of the toilet. He would show up at Vernon's place trailing snow drifts everywhere and disappear two days later leaving Vernon in a state of coma. Pedro was into Marvin Gaye, Bohannon, Diana Ross and the Temptations. Vernon loved being invited round to Pedro's place, the sound system was amazing, the sofas comfortable, the whiskies intercontinental – they would take turns being mobsters, gumshoes and English dandies.

Vernon had managed to dig out a photo of the four of them together. Him and three dead men. They were clustered around him, posing on his thirty-fifth birthday. A nice photo, the sort people used to take with an old-fashioned camera and make copies for their friends. Four boys in a blurry past, but thin, with full heads of hair, bright eyes and smiles not tinged with bitterness. They were raising a glass, Vernon had been depressed that night, traumatised at the thought of turning thirty-five. Four handsome lads, happy to be morons, knowing nothing about anything, and most importantly not knowing that they were living the best that life had in store for them. They had spent most of the night listening to Smokey Robinson.

After he buried Pedro, Vernon had stopped going out, stopped returning phone calls. He thought it was a phase, that it would pass. After the deaths of several close friends, it did not seem inappropriate to need to withdraw into himself.

It was around this time that his cash-flow problems really began to bite, which exacerbated his tendency to cut himself off. The prospect of going round to someone's house for dinner when he did not have the money to bring a bottle discouraged him from accepting invitations. He was too depressed to go out in case someone suggested clubbing together to buy a gram. Depressed about the price of Métro tickets. Depressed to be wearing trainers with the soles falling off. Freaking out about details he had never noticed before, brooding about them obsessively.

He stayed home. He was grateful for the times he lived in. He binged on music, on T.V. boxed sets, on movies. Gradually he stopped listening to the radio. Since the age of twenty, his first reflex when he woke up in the morning was to turn it on. Now, he found it disturbing without being interesting. He had got out of the habit of listening to the news. He had stopped watching television almost without realising. He was too busy on the internet. He would glance at the headlines. But he spent most of his time on porn sites. He doesn't want to think about the crisis, about Islam, climate change, fracking, ill-treated orang-utans, about Roma-nians getting chucked off buses. His little bubble is snug. He can survive if he holds his breath. He reduces every gesture to a bare minimum. He eats less. He has made a start by streamlining dinner. Chinese instant noodles from a packet. He has stopped buying meat – protein is for athletes. Mostly, he eats rice. He buys it in five-kilo bags from Tang Frères. He is cutting down on cigarettes – delaying his first smoke of the day, waiting longer before the second, and after his morning coffee wondering whether he really wants a third. He saves the butts so there is no wastage. He knows all the local office doorways where workers huddle for a quick cancer stick during the day, and sometimes as he walks past he slows, picks out the longest stubs. He feels like a spent coal, like an ember quickened now and then by a gust of wind, but never quite enough to set the kindling ablaze. A dying fire.

Sometimes he gets a caffeine burst. He logs on to LinkedIn and makes lists of guys who still seem to have jobs, guys he used to know, promising himself he will get in touch. He imagines his spiel, it would start off with some story about a girl. His reputation as a pickup artist makes men more well disposed to relaxed conversations. So this is what he will say – I haven't been in Paris, I've been fucking some little Hungarian who dragged me off to Budapest, or some beautiful American who's forever jetting around the world – the nationality isn't important, what matters is giving the impression he has been having a wild time – anyway, I'm back in town and I'm looking for a bit of work, anything at all really, you got something you could put my way? He'll play it a bit cool, a bit laid-back, not edgy and uptight. On the money side, he can hardly bullshit, it's blindingly obvious he hasn't got a cent. Then again, he was never exactly rolling in it. It added to his street-cred back in the day. That was long before the 2000s when people head off to gigs, casual as fuck, sporting expensive designer shoes, this season's watch on their wrist, a pair of jeans cut so you know they were bought this year. Being flat broke has lost its poetic charm since Zadig & Voltaire started exploiting thrift store chic – whereas for decades it was the trademark of the true artist, of someone who refused to sell his soul. These days it's death to losers, even in the rock industry.

But he never makes a call to ask for help. He cannot put his finger on precisely what is stopping him. He has had time to think about it. It remains an enigma. He scoured the internet in search of advice for pathological procrastinators. He drew up lists of what he had to lose, what he would be risking, and what he had to gain. It made no difference. He calls no-one.

Alexandre Bleach is dead. Seeing his name plastered all over Facebook, Vernon does not immediately grasp the significance. He was found, dead, in a hotel room.

Who is going to pay his back rent? This is the first thing Vernon thinks. He's had no reply to the emails and text messages he has been sending these past few weeks. His cries for help. He was used to Alex being slow on the uptake. Vernon was counting on him. Like every other time he was in deep shit. Alexandre always bailed him out.

Vernon is sitting at his laptop – emotions that are contradictory or alien to each other are clawing at his chest like a bunch of cats tossed into a bag by a deft and ruthless hand. The news spreads across the internet like leprosy. For a long time now, Alexandre has belonged to everyone. Vernon thought he was used to it. Whenever Alexandre released a record or went on tour, he was impossible to avoid. Not an hour of the day passed without seeing him on display, writhing somewhere, crooning some mindless rubbish in that beautiful, deep drug-addled voice of his. Alexandre was touched by success the way someone might be hit by a truck: he never gave the impression that he had come through it unscathed. His problem was not arrogance, but a savage despair that exhausted those closest to him. It is hard to watch someone get what everyone dreams of, and then have to console them for it.

No photos of the stiff in the hotel room yet. But it's only a matter of time. Alex drowned. In a bathtub. A champagne-and-prescription-meds co-production; he fell asleep. God knows what he was doing alone in a bath in a hotel room in the middle of the afternoon. Then again, God knows what made the guy so desperately miserable. Alex even managed to fuck up his own death. A hotel is too prosaic to be fantasy but not bleak enough to be exotic. He often booked into a hotel for a few days, he only had to think he had seen a paparazzo outside his place and he would go and sleep somewhere else. Alex liked living in hotels. He was forty-six. Who waits for the onset of the menopause, male or female, to die of an overdose? Michael Jackson, Whitney Houston . . . maybe it's a black thing.

Bleach liked to hook up with his old friends. It was like the need to piss, but it happened regularly. There would be no news from him for a year, maybe two, then he would be calling like a crazed stalker, bombarding you with emails, he was even capable of showing up at someone's house unannounced. It was impossible to drink with him in a bar. Conversation was interrupted every five minutes by some fan, and fans can be aggressive. Or completely psycho. In general, the sort of fan who butts in on a conversation is a pain in the arse. When Alexandre decided he wanted to see Vernon, he would call and invite himself over. They would drink beer and pretend that nothing had changed. What a joke. With one song, Alexandre earned more than a guy like Vernon in twenty years running the shop. How could this minor detail not affect their relationship?

Alex had made himself a lot of friends on the V.I.P. circuit. But he was convinced that his "real life" had ended when he became successful. Vernon had often tried to explain this was just a theoretical notion: somewhere around the age of thirty, life starts to lose its lustre: McJob or megastar, things don't get any better for anyone. The difference is that for those who don't get to ride the train to fame, there is no compensation. Just because your youth is fading does not mean you get to fly around the world first class, to fuck the prettiest girls, hang out with cool dealers and start investing in Harley-Davidsons. But Alex would not listen. In fact, he really did seem so unhappy that it was difficult to get him to see how lucky he was.

The first time he had come into the shop, Alexandre was still a kid. His big eyes with those long eyelashes gave him a childlike appearance. He would show up with some random Jenlain girl, perch on a stool and ask to listen to records. Alex always believed that it was Vernon who introduced him to the magic, the one who had first made him listen to the Stiff Little Fingers live double-album, the Redskins, the Bad Brains' first E.P., Sham 69's "Peel Sessions" or Code of Honor's "Fight or Die". Alex was still a kid, he was chubby-cheeked and did not play the hard man. His smile probably played a major part in his meteoric success – it had the same effect as watching videos of kittens on YouTube. You had to have the empathy of a psycho killer not to feel something. He strummed his axe and wailed like every other dude, playing with this group or that. As it often does, fame struck where no-one was expecting. The music scene back then had its heroes, guys that people would have bet their shirts on. And all of them, every last one, had disappeared into the ether. Alex's passion for drugs came late and swept all before it. But the guy had always walked around with an invisible knife sticking out of his chest. He could laugh at the slightest thing, but there in his eyes was a fracture that nothing could prevent becoming a yawning chasm.

A callously pragmatic thought nags at Vernon: who is going to pay his rent now? It began shortly after the death of Jean-No. They had run into each other by chance near Bonsergent Métro station. Alex had flung his arms around Vernon. They had not seen each other in an age, not since Tricky's gig at the Elysée-Montmartre. After a few awkward minutes when they felt forced to play out the peevish farce of two old mates with so much to tell each other – as though Vernon's activities on eBay were as fascinating as the tales of drug-fucked nights on Iggy Pop's yacht – hanging out with Alexandre was cool.

Alexandre had been completely out of it that day. He had the puppyish enthusiasm and the mile-a-minute chatter of a guy who has not been home in a long time and really should get around to it. The pavements were blanketed with snow, and they gripped each other by the elbow so as not to wind up on their arses. Impulsive as always, Alex insisted that Vernon come with him to his dealer's crib a stone's throw away. The dealer was a sycophant who looked like the school nerd and wrote music using Garageband. He smoked skunk from Holland so potent it gave an instant headache. He was desperate for them to listen to his "latest sounds".

They suffered through a series of synth layers laid down over jittery second-hand beats. Alex was already off his face and listened, spellbound, to this shit and told the dealer that he had been working on hertz, on split-second modulations that, when properly orchestrated, could modify the brain. He was stoked by the idea of synchronising brain waves and the dealer was hanging on his every word. But everyone knew the truth – Alex hadn't been able to write a song in years. He fixated on "alpha waves" because he couldn't string three chords together or write a hook worth shit.

It had been dark when they ran into each other on the snowy pavement. There were not many cars and the streets were weirdly white and silent. Vernon had made a joke about some actress twerking her ass on a 3x4-metre billboard. He had said something like "She's such a fucking skank, I'd rather bone a blow-up doll", and Alexandre gave a forced laugh. It was obvious that he knew her. Vernon wondered if he had had her. Women liked Alex, he didn't need to sell records to get laid. A lot of his friends were A-list celebs, the sort of people whose names and faces you know without ever having met them. He stored their phone numbers in his mobile using code names in case it was lost or stolen. The idea of his address book falling into the hands of some random freaked him out. Sometimes, when his phone rang, he would stare at it, bewildered, unable to connect a person to the name on the screen. "S.B.", for example, could be Sandrine Bonnaire, Stomy Bugsy, Samuel Benchetrit or was it some more complicated code name like Skanky Bitch or Slimy Buttfucker? He could not remember until he listened to the voicemail and it all came back to him: S.B. stood for "Scuzzy Bathroom" because that was where he had spent hours gabbing with Julien Doré. At the time, it had probably seemed brilliant. Like so many things that happen after three in the morning.

"Do you remember Jean-No?" Vernon had asked. Of course Alex remembered. They had gigged together for a bit in Nazi Whores in the early nineties. They hadn't seen each other for ten years. Jean-No despised Alex and everything he stood for – cerebral cock-rock, middle-class militancy, and above all a staggering success that could not be dismissed as nepotism – it made Jean-No physically sick. They had been a two-man team, worked in the same industry but one had been rewarded with fame and fortune while the other got fuck-all. The parallels were unbearable – taking the piss out of Alex was a hobby that took up a lot of Jean-No's time. "You know he died?" The colour drained from Alex's face, overcome. Vernon felt embarrassed by so much heartfelt emotion, but he couldn't bring himself to say "Don't look so miserable, the guy hated your guts". Alex had insisted on dropping him off in a taxi, then coming up to his apartment. Pretty quickly, they were on the same wavelength – a couple of frenzied hamsters scurrying around the same wheel. Curled up on the sofa, Alex felt like an egg. He loved Vernon's cramped apartment, he could curl into a ball and feel safe. They listened to The Dogs, something neither of them had done for twenty years. Alex had stayed for three days. He was obsessed with what he called his "research" into binaural beats and forced Vernon to listen to various sound waves that were supposed to have a profound impact on the subconscious but which, in practice, failed even to trigger a migraine. Alex had five grams with him when he arrived. They hoovered it up at a leisurely pace, like old hands. From time to time, Vernon nodded off – coke relaxed him and helped him sleep – and Alex had decided to interview himself right there on the sofa. He had an old camcorder with him and three one-hour tapes which he piled next to the television, and every time Vernon regained consciousness, he forced him to watch this preposterous performance – "It's, like, my last will and testament, man, you get it? I'm gonna leave it with you. That's how much I trust you." He was losing it a little by now. Then he would launch back into talking about delta waves and gamma waves, the creative process and the idea of making music that acted like a drug, that would modify neuronal pathways. Vernon felt wretched, Alex kept forcing him to put on headphones to listen to shitty loops.

Vernon went down to the minimart to get supplies – Coke, cigarettes, crisps and whisky – with his rock-star friend's credit card. "There's nothing to fucking eat in this place. Which reminds me, what are you working at these days? Do you want me to give you some cash?" Vernon had two months' rent arrears and was desperately struggling not to make it three because he had heard some urban myth that unless you were three months behind, you couldn't be evicted. This was how it started. Alexandre had transferred three months' rent into his account – It's my pleasure, man, honestly, swear down. And when he left, Alex had insisted: "Call me if you need cash, yeah? I'm pretty loaded, you know . . . Promise you'll call . . ."

And Vernon did. At first, he thought he would sort things out himself, but when he was four months in arrears, he called. Alex bailed him out. No questions. And a few months later, Vernon called again. It was embarrassing, but it was also like being a child again. When his parents were still alive and he knew that – *in extremis* – he could count on them to dig him out of a hole. There was something of the sheltered childhood in this stopgap solution. And Alex went on bailing him out. He added Vernon's bank details to his list of regular transfers and in a couple of clicks, he could get him out of a tight spot. Vernon grumbled, he put things off until the last minute. He oscillated between guilt and resentment, between gratitude and relief. Money had become such a non-issue for Alexandre, but it was a very real issue for everyone else. Vernon would send his landlord a cheque, then stock up on cigarettes and food, and jealously stashed away a little in a tin box so he could buy his daily beer. This was how he subsisted.

The doorbell rings. Vernon does not answer. It is probably the postman with a registered letter. He never signs for them. He no longer deals with official documents. It crept up on him gradually, this mental paralysis – there are more and more relatively simple tasks to be done which he cannot manage to deal with. He turns down the music and waits. The bell rings again. Now someone is knocking. Vernon is sitting on his bed, hands folded in his lap, he is used to this – he waits for them to go away. But there comes an unusual sound, the grating of the lock, an alert that someone is trying to force entry. He immediately realises what is happening, he grabs his jeans, pulls on a clean jumper. He is tying the laces of a pair of low-rise Doc Martens when the door opens. He feels feverish, the rush he sometimes gets with dodgy speed. Four men step inside and look him up and down. The leader of the group steps forward, "Monsieur, you could have opened the door." He stares at Vernon, sizing him up. He is wearing an elegant navy-blue scarf knotted around his throat and a pair of glasses with red frames. His grey suit is cut too short. In a toneless voice, he reads from a tablet – yada yada head office in yada yada. The landlord of the aforementioned property hereby serves notice . . .

Ten years, ten years he's been paying fucking rent. Ten years. More than 90,000 euros. Paid into the pockets of some wanker who has never done a tap of work. The landlord is probably one of those guys who inherited everything and bleats about how much tax he has to pay. In ten years, there has been no work done on the apartment – he had to hassle the landlord to get the boiler fixed. 90,000 euros. Not a single hour's work, not a single inspection, not a penny spent on repairs. And now they're turfing him out.

Vernon's eyes settle on the bailiff's trousers, just where they bulge at the thighs. Vernon waits while the four men make an inventory of his assets before they leave, which gives him time to take stock of the situation. If he were not blacklisted by every bank he would write them a cheque and send the whole process back to square one. Surely they should be able to come to some arrangement – the one he identified as the locksmith seems like a decent guy. With his thick, grey old-school moustache, he looks like a trade unionist. Vernon hopes he did not damage the lock when he picked it, there is no way to change it. After all, he might need to nip out for five minutes. There is nothing left worth stealing – even a cash-strapped Kosovar would not take the trouble to steal what he calls a computer. The monitor and tower system weigh a ton and date from the Pleistocene era. The bailiff tells him to pack what he needs for the next few days and vacate the premises immediately. No-one says: hey, let's give the guy a break, come back another time, give him ten days to sort his shit out and see how we go. The two thugs, who have not uttered a word, stand in the middle of the studio flat and advise him – without a trace of anger – to comply.

Vernon scans the room – is there anything he could offer in exchange for a temporary reprieve? He feels the first stirrings of restless anxiety in the opposing camp – the men are worried he will react violently. They are accustomed to histrionics, to wailing. Vernon asks for fifteen minutes, the bailiff heaves a sigh – but he is relieved: the client is not a maniac.

Vernon climbs onto a stool so he can reach the top of the wardrobe and take down the most heavy-duty backpack he owns. As he takes it down, a shower of grey dust balls settles on his shoulders. He sneezes. Some situations are so bizarre we cannot imagine them actually happening. He fills the bag. Headphones, iPod, pair of jeans, Bukowski's letters, couple of jumpers, boxer shorts, signed photo of Lydia Lunch, passport. Terror prevents all thought. Since he has just found out that Alex is dead, he remembers to rummage in the back of the wardrobe, behind the impeccably organised stacks of *Maximum Rock'n'Roll*, *Mad Movies*, *Cinéphage*, *Best* and *Rock & Folk* for the pack of three videocassettes Alexandre recorded on his last visit. He could maybe sell them . . . Then Vernon takes off his Doc Martens and pulls on his favourite boots. He grabs a yellow plastic alarm clock bought in a Chinese market ten years ago, which has served him well. The rucksack is heavy. He leaves the apartment without a word. The bailiff stops him as he reaches the landing; no, there's no particular storage company he prefers, yes, he will have to collect his belongings within the month, sign here, no problem. Then he trudges down the stairs, still convinced that this is not really happening, that he will be back.

On the stairs, he meets the concierge. She has always had a soft spot for him. He's the perfect tenant, single, always takes the trouble to talk to her about the terrible racket from the street work outside, about the weather, sometimes a little joke – a little harmless flirtation that charms this woman of sixty or so. She asks if everything is alright – she does not realise that a locksmith has been up to his apartment. He cannot find the words or the courage to explain. She is not surprised to see him carrying such a hefty rucksack, she has seen him on his way to the post office dozens of times. Suddenly he becomes aware of the shame he feels at his situation. The last time he was expelled was from the lycée. He had shown up to class off his face on acid with his friend Pierrot who would later hang himself from a bridge one Sunday morning at dawn – they had been sent straight to the *directeur*, who immediately expelled them. This flash of memory reminds him of the kitchen in the house where he grew up. His parents died young. Though he is not sure they would have helped him out. They were pretty puritanical. They worried about keeping him on the strait and narrow, they had never approved of his obsession with rock music. They had wanted him to join the civil service. They always said that he would never make it as a shopkeeper. As it turned out, they were right.

Out on the street, the thought of the things he should have taken but had left behind triggers a rockfall in his chest. With his fingertips, he brushes the official documents in his back pocket. His trembling hands refuse to do his bidding. He needs to sit down, to find a tranquil place where he can think, to work out how to sort things out. A thousand euros. It's a lot of money, but you never know. He is not going to lose his personal belongings – and there are more things of value to him than he thought. The wrist-watch that Jean-No gave him. The test-pressing of Les Thugs' first album that he had salvaged back when the label manager of Gougnaf Mouvement slept on his floor for a while. The Motörhead flask that Eve brought him back from a trip to London. An original print of a Jello Biafra photograph taken by Carole in New York. And the signed Hubert Selby.

The threat of eviction had been hanging over him for so long that he had ended up believing that it was nothing but an air-raid siren in a war he was always going to win. If Alexandre was still alive, Vernon would know what to do: he would go down to his apartment building and move heaven and earth to find him. He would not have felt embarrassed in the least – his old mate would have been happy to bail him out. After all, that was Vernon's role, he gave Alex's money legitimacy.

If only he had got off his arse and tracked down Alexandre instead of sending polite emails from time to time and waiting for him to show his face. If Vernon had been a freeloader and moved in with Alex, things would have been very different. They would have been doing drugs together, chilling at his place, and Alex would never have gone to take a bath in some shitty hotel. They would have been listening to Led Zep live in Japan instead.

Skint city is a place Vernon knows of old. Cinemas, clothes shops, brasseries, art galleries – there aren't many places where you can sit in the warm without having to shell out. That just leaves railway stations, Métro stations, libraries, churches and the few park benches that have not been ripped out to stop people like him sitting there for free. Rail stations and churches have no central heating, the thought of hopping the Métro with a large rucksack is depressing. He trudges up the avenue des Gobelins towards the place d'Italie. He is lucky: though it has been raining for the past few days, today the streets are bathed in weak sunshine. If he had hung on for another month, it would officially have been winter.

He tries to cheer himself up, ogling girls in the street. Back in the day, a single ray of sunshine would have girls pouring into the streets in their skimpiest skirts just to celebrate. These days, they are less likely to wear skirts, more likely to wear trainers and their make-up is more discreet. He sees a lot of forty-something women trying their best, wearing clothes bought in the sales, outfits that looked good on the rail, cheap suits they thought were good copies of designer gear only to discover, as soon as they put them on, the only thing that shows is their age. And the girls, the girls are as pretty as ever although they don't scrub up as well. It has to be said that the eighties retro look does them no favours.

On Thursdays, the library does not open until two o'clock. Vernon is already sick and tired of tramping the streets. He walks up the avenue de Choisy and sits in a bus shelter. He had thought about going to the park, but the rucksack is too heavy. He sits down next to a woman in her forties who looks vaguely like Jean-Jacques Goldman. Between her feet is a large canvas bag full of hippie food. Everything about her exudes intelligence, affluence, gravity and pretentiousness. The woman is deliberately avoiding making eye contact, but the first bus that comes is not hers. She takes a cigarette from her jacket pocket, he tries to start up a conversation, he knows she will think he is a dickhead, but he needs to exchange a few words with someone.

"Isn't it a bit ironic? I mean, eating organic and still smoking?"

"Maybe. But then again, I'm entitled to do what I like, yeah?"

"I don't suppose I could cadge one? A cigarette?"

She turns away and sighs, as though he has been bugging her for the past three hours. She needs to get over herself, Vernon thinks, she's not exactly a babe and she's a bit long in the tooth, I bet she can go shopping without being whistled at every five minutes. Vernon persists, he smiles and gestures to the rucksack.

"I got evicted this morning. I only had five minutes to pack up and leave. I left my cigarettes behind."

She is dubious at first, then changes her mind. Seeing her bus arriving, she takes a pack of cigarettes from her canvas bag and proffers it. She looks into his eyes, Vernon can see that she is moved. She must be easily upset, she's on the verge of tears.

"I can't do much for you, but here . . ."

"You're giving me the whole pack? Wow. Now I can chain-smoke. Thanks."

Through the window of the bus, she gives him a little wave that means something like don't worry, it'll be alright. This compassion devoid of contempt he inspires in her is more devastating to Vernon than if she had called him every name under the sun.

In less than an hour, he has smoked five cigarettes from the packet. Time is passing with unbearable slowness. Vernon wishes there were somewhere he could stow his bag. If only rail stations still had left-luggage lockers.

Finally, the library opens. The decor is familiar. He has been here often to borrow graphic novels and D.V.D.s. Back before you could read the papers on the internet, he used to come here to leaf through the broadsheets. He settles himself next to a radiator and opens an issue of *Le Monde*. He has no intention of reading it. But

if he were a woman, he would want to talk to a man who was reading *Le Monde*, especially one who looked engrossed, the sort of guy
who likes to keep informed but is not easily taken in.

Mentally he thumbs through an imaginary notebook, making
up an A–Z list of people who might be able to help him out. He
must know someone who has a sofa or a spare room where he can
just rock up. It will come back to him.

He spots a brunette at the next table. Her hair is tied up and
she is wearing old-fashioned earrings, gold pendants set with tiny
gemstones. She is elegantly dressed, but there is something not
quite right about her – she looks dated. She gives the impression
of being engrossed in her solitude. A number of medical books lie
open in front of her. Perhaps she is suffering from some serious
illness. They could come to an arrangement, the two of them.
Vernon imagines her, alone in a vast apartment, her children are
all grown up, they are probably studying abroad and only come
home for Christmas, she loves sex and has a thing for immature
men, she has suffered just enough to know that when you find a
good man, you do everything you can to hang on to him, but not so
much that it has crushed her completely. And maybe she is alone
because she is too caught up in her job, or she has just been
dumped by some guy who is even richer than she is who fell for
a younger model and felt so guilty when he left that he gave her a
wad of cash. Grateful to have a man around the house, she would
give Vernon a room in her apartment, he would turn it into a
music room, furnish it with odds and sods but invest some cash in
a serious sound system and sometimes the two of them would sit
there and she would gently tease him about his collection of boot-
legs but deep down she is glad he has a noble passion. Women

love men who love post-punk, it's just sleazy enough to unnerve them while being completely compatible with a bourgeois lifestyle.

These thoughts absorb and exhilarate him for a few minutes, then fade. And Vernon remembers all the times, in the Métro, he has seen those people who mingle with the commuters but never leave the platform while he watched from the carriage. At the Arts et Métiers station, on line 11 heading towards Hôtel de Ville, there was the young black guy who always slept on the same bench, his face deformed by the huge cyst on his cheek. He was there for at least two years. Then there was the Rom at République, he had seen her breastfeeding her baby, watched as the little girl learned to walk, later she would sit at her mother's feet drinking Coca-Cola.

He does not know yet who will put him up, but he knows he will not tell them the truth, it's too much of a downer. He'll come up with something a bit more cheerful. Besides, people like to be lied to. It's how we are made. "I'm living in Canada these days, I needed to come back to sort out some bureaucratic bullshit and I'm looking for a place to crash for three nights – any chance I can borrow your sofa?" Three nights. More than that is taking advantage. Canada is perfect, the sort of place no-one gives a shit about, so no-one is likely to ask him questions he can't answer. I drink maple syrup, the Hell's Angels are as violent as ever, the blow there is dirt cheap and the girls are hot, though it takes a while to get used to the accent.

Emilie! He must be truly messed up not to have thought of her straight off, he knows the way to her place with his eyes closed. The two-room, fifth-floor walk-up behind the gare du Nord that her parents bought her for her twentieth birthday. He remembers awesome parties at her place. And dozens of evenings spent with a particular group of friends, he has danced and drunk and thrown up there, he often got laid in the bathroom, he has had dinner there, smoked weed, listened to the Coasters, to old albums of Siouxsie, to Radio Birdman. Emilie used to be a bass player. She loved L7, Hole, 7 Year Bitch and a lot of the Riot Grrrl shit only girls really get into. On stage she was stiff and scornful, all New York attitude. In real life, she was sweet. Maybe too sweet. Not particularly lucky in love. The slightest thing could make her blush, he found that sexy. She wore thigh-length boots like Diana Rigg in "The Avengers" and when she was on stage, her hips traced languorous, strangely convulsive circles, the bass slung down by her knees, thumbing the strings, head twisted around to catch the drummer's eye, she looked like a greyhound bitch. She was hot shit. No-one knows why she gave up music after the band split. When she called him, in tears, to tell him Jean-No was dead, he had felt sorry for her. Sorry she was still at the stage of fucking unavailable guys. After the funeral, she called him constantly, wanting to meet up, but Vernon felt too low. He never answered. Emilie had left a bunch of vicious comments on his Facebook page. He never responded. He doesn't hold it against her, he knows sometimes people go batshit crazy.

VERNON CLOSES THE BATHROOM DOOR BEHIND HIM. SITTING ramrod straight against the back of the chair, Emilie pinches her lower lip between thumb and forefinger and stares into the distance. Noticing what she is doing, she tugs at the too-tight jumper that rucks up at the back. She has often seen her mother do that same thing with her lip, staring into the middle distance, looking as though she is somewhere else.

She pours herself a second glass of white wine, she listens to Vernon in the shower. They will have a quick dinner, then she will retire to the bedroom with her iPod and the remains of the bottle, the earlier the better. When she saw him standing in the doorway, she felt a lava flow of rage boiling through her entrails, but despite two years in therapy she is still incapable of saying what she really thinks. She is still pissed off at Vernon, she has imagined this scene dozens of times: one of the group comes to her for help and she spits in his face. Instead, she felt the corners of her mouth tug downwards when he asked if he could stay the night; her expression grew even more gloomy when he tried to talk about Alex to lighten the mood. She does not want to talk about Alex, or to rake up the past. She got out the wine glasses, set out the coasters and filled a bowl with roasted almonds, resentfully, to preserve the tense atmosphere, going through the motions of being hospitable. She made sure that Vernon did not leave glass rings on the

Swedish coffee table that cost her six hundred euros in the Sentou sale. Emilie has become fanatical about cleanliness. Time was, she didn't give a shit. These days she could happily cut someone's throat for leaving breadcrumbs under the table or traces of lime-scale on the tap. The upside is that she feels an indescribable pleasure when everything is neat and clean.

Vernon pretended not to notice the tension, he asked "I don't suppose you could cut my hair? Remember when you used to give all of us haircuts?" But instead of just telling him to fuck off, she said "Tonight, are you sure?" With the second glass of white wine, she mellowed. When he told her he had sold off all his records, she thought back to the apartment where he used to live, a box room at the back of the shop. She felt a sudden wave of empathy. Her anger flipped over. It was not just the effects of the wine, it is something that often happens. Her peremptory mood melts away and is replaced by its exact opposite.

Vernon has changed a lot. Everything about him now betrays a vulnerability. But physically, he has got off lightly. Men with beautiful eyes have an advantage. His hair is completely white now, but it is thinning only at the front. He is lucky, he is still thin as a rake. The problem is the teeth. Seeing him flash his yellow smile is slightly disgusting.

She doesn't care. It's not as if she is planning to kiss him. Vernon is not the only one who has changed. Emilie has put on – how much? – twenty kilos in ten years? She has been lying about her weight for so long, she has lost track, as though making up a figure changes the way she looks. At first, she struggled with her weight – diets exercise thalassotherapy massage creams and anti-cellulite treatments that cost a fortune and left her feeling as though she had been put through a crusher. It was worth it, she managed to keep things under control. Then she gave up. Her metabolism, quite obviously, was uncontrollable. These days she hardly recognises herself in the mirror. No matter what she wears, she bulges, there is always one roll of fat that spills out. It is when she goes somewhere where she knows no-one that she really realises how much she has changed. Given the opportunity, people talk to whoever else is standing next to them, they avoid all contact with the fat woman.

Her apartment has changed too. She registered the surprise on Vernon's face when he came in. The surprise and the disappointment. There are no concert posters. She used to have them plastered all over the walls of the living room, the bedroom; the kitchen was reserved for photos of handsome young men. Fugazi, Joy Division, Die Trottel, Dezerter . . . have given way to a framed photograph of Frida Kahlo and a Caravaggio print. The walls are painted white. As in the homes of all the adults that she knows. She has become the person her parents wanted her to grow up to be. She took an M.B.A., she works in facilities, she traded in her mohawk for a sensible bob. She buys her clothes from Zara when she can find something to fit her. She is obsessed with olive oil, green tea, she has a subscription to *Télérama* and in the office she and her colleagues talk about recipes. She has done everything her parents wanted her to do. Except have a child, which means that everything else does not count. At family gatherings, she is a reproach. All her efforts have been for nothing.

The water in the shower continues to hum. Emilie part-opens the enormous rucksack Vernon showed up with. He does not have a sponge bag. Only a razor. As he headed for the shower, he claimed that real men don't travel with sponge bags. She knows for a fact he has not arrived from Canada. Is he homeless? It does not sound like him. Vernon is a placid guy who does just enough to keep himself out of trouble, not some raving lunatic who would let things get to the point where he is chucked out on the street. A bad break-up, maybe? But Vernon has too many friends to wind up with a girl he has not seen in so long. There is something iffy, something he obviously does not want to talk about.

Subutex has always been an easy-going kind of guy, standing behind the counter of his record shop with a permanent half-smile. A joker – not a loudmouth, but someone with a quick wit. Someone who could find the funny side of any subject and milk it, a talented wordsmith. In a world of boys desperately competing in a pissing contest, Vernon always seemed quietly confident, like he didn't need to show off to prove that he was someone. He had a single quality, he was a record dealer. Not as cool as being a guitarist, but still higher up the pecking order than the average arsehole. Vernon broke girls' hearts. When he first met them, he lavished them with compliments, put them on a magnificent pedestal seven metres high and then someone else caught his eye and he left them there, starved of sweet nothings and admiring glances.

Emilie was just one of the guys in the band. When she climbed into the truck, she was lugging her amp. She was proud of how well she could hold her drink, she was funny, she had a great record collection and she wasn't afraid to go completely wild onstage. She felt like part of the gang. Then the band had split. The record shop had closed. They had all made new lives for themselves. And her friends had forgotten to call her. When they met up for a beer before a concert, when they went to a movie together, when they organised a dinner party, when they celebrated something, she was left out. Then those same friends started to seem embarrassed when she wanted to go backstage after a gig. It was an embarrassment she knew all too well – but one that had never been directed at her. An attitude reserved for a sycophantic hanger-on you don't know how to get rid of. And when she managed to get herself invited to dinner with them, she noticed that her voice no longer carried as far. No-one seemed to hear her. It was not hostility. To be hostile, they would first have had to notice her presence. When she mentioned it to Jean-No, he told her she was paranoid, that she always had to be the centre of attention, that she had never got over the band splitting up. He was not completely wrong. Sébastien, the lead guitarist, had decided to break up the band the day some guy from Virgin offered them a contract. Out of a sense of integrity. Even though Sébastien was the only one of them who worked for a major label. But as far as he was concerned, that was the whole point: he didn't want being in a band to become just like being at work. No compromise, no career path. Just music and integrity. All he wanted was something to do in the evenings after work that made him feel like a bit of a radical. So, no T.V. appearances, no booking agents, nothing that seemed too professional. He wanted it to be something raw, something between mates, a tour bus that was a G7 van with the seats ripped out with catering that was mostly tabbouleh. Like most well-behaved middle-class kids who want to come on like rebels, Sébastien had a thing for purity. He had a flash little recording studio on the rue Galande that his parents bought him. He spent most of his energy analysing everyone around them so he could point out that, ultimately, they were sell-outs, backstab-bers, phonies and con artists. It had always bothered Sébastien, having a girl in the group. It fucked up the whole feel. Punk should be a man's sport. Twenty years later, when they run into each other, she sees a guy who has held up well, professionally, for a hardcore purist. These days he presents some culture show on cable T.V., the station managers love him – he gives them a dose of macho radical-ism without the risks associated with a real radical.

When Chevaucher le Dragon split, no other group had called to suggest she might take over from someone. This was something Emilie had not expected. She was a good bassist, she never doubted her talent. She put her bass guitar in its case and moved on to other things. She had not drifted away from her old friends. She had been sidelined. It's not the same thing. Jean-No was the only one who still hung out with her. Hardly surprising, since he fucked her anytime he got the chance. In the beginning, it felt like an affair that never quite ends because there is too much passion. Later, it became more like an addiction. When you're no longer taking the drug for the pleasure, but simply to relieve the with-drawal symptoms. He had had his first child. With someone else. Emilie was friends with the other woman. She had been one of the first to find out that she was pregnant, she had had to say con-gratulations and keep smiling. The second time, she only found out months after the kid was born. When she found the baby's dummy in his carrier bag. Emilie has become the girl without a boyfriend on her arm, the girl who has been politely dumped and always shows up to work parties on her own, the sort who has lots of girlfriends because she is such a loser she is not remotely threat-ening. What's done is done, she can't relive her youth, and this is how she has spent it, waiting for some arsehole to phone or not, to lie to his wife so he can pop round and see her, make her his bit on the side and all the while she has been unable to break out of this vicious circle, to move on, she does not know what to do with the sadness she feels. Why are certain people determined to fuck up their lives while for others it seems so easy to do things the way they are supposed to be done? The truth is, when it was not him making her suffer, it was someone else.

When Jean-No died, she desperately needed to talk to someone. The fact that she was the bit on the side didn't change anything – this was the guy she had been sleeping with for more than ten years. She had turned to Vernon, among others. But he never phoned her back. As though they barely knew each other, as though she was being a pain, pestering him with phone calls when Jean-No died. He can die on the streets as far as she is concerned, she's over it, she wants nothing more to do with him. Now it's his turn.

He emerges from the shower, she pulls out a chair and lays a terry towel on the floor to collect the hair clippings, but as soon as she begins combing, she has to bite her lip to stop herself from crying. The bitter rage has suddenly subsided and been replaced by a terrible sadness she was not expecting. When she was a little girl, she used to cut her grandfather's hair, every Sunday while he watched "Le Petit Rapporteur" and her mother would roll her eyes to heaven, "She's got him wrapped around her little finger". Standing behind the chair, she would have to stretch her arms high to reach the three little hairs that fell over his collar. His skin of a mature man, the fine hairs sprinkled with grey and a certain scent.

She touches the crown of Vernon's skull with her fingertips, gently urging him to tilt his head forward. She gathers the straggling locks, trims the ends, tries to give his hair volume, but there is not much she can do, other than to get rid of the thin wisps of hair spilling like rats' tails down his back. She is overwhelmed by a tenderness that has nothing to do with desire, nor something one might feel for a child. It is the tenderness of an adult woman yielding before another person's fragility. She fights back tears. It is something she has only recently learned to do. In the first two years she was suffering from depression, she would blub at the slightest thing, the will to hold back her tears completely deserted her: just as other people's legs give out under them, her tears would flow like a form of incontinence. Then, after the summer, her willpower returned. One morning she got up and managed to decide not to cry. It did not change the sadness she felt, but she no longer needed to touch up her make-up in the lift because she had spent her whole journey on the Métro sobbing for no reason. She wept so much that the salt from her tears had damaged the delicate skin under her eyes. The damage was irreversible.

Vernon has the skin of an old man. The skin of a man his age. It is something she felt before, with Jean-No. People say men age better than women, but it's not true. Their skin loses its elasticity more quickly, especially if they smoke and drink. It feels fragile, as though it might crumble between your fingers. She has never understood how young girls could bear to sleep with older men. The soft, supple skin of young men is so much nicer. She finds men her own age repulsive, when their balls hang down and look like fossilised turtle heads. The thought of having to touch them makes her want to throw up. She hates men who pant for breath when they're fucking, or have to roll over on their backs after five minutes because they can't carry on, leaving their partner to finish herself off. She loathes their pot bellies and their scrawny grey thighs.

Women evolve with age. They try to understand what is happening to them. Men stagnate, heroically, then suddenly they regress. The older they get, the more love and sex are linked to childhood. They long to whisper baby talk to girls who look like children, to do the naughty things boys do in playgrounds. No-one wants to hear about an old man's desire, it is too embarrassing.

The more she drinks, the more she thinks that Vernon has aged well. He was always a laid-back kind of guy. All she would have to do is open a bottle of whisky and something was bound to happen. She knows that, when she's drunk she forgets about her body, about how undesirable she has become. But though in theory the concept of sex is still tempting, in practice it is depressing. She completely lost her libido a few years ago and, to be honest, she has done very well without. They listen to Kraftwerk's "Trans-Europe Express". Emilie did not know what to pick from her record collection. Looking through it to see what she could put on, she is irritated to realise that she had not listened to anything new or interesting for years. She no longer cares.

"Remember when you used to listen to Edith Nylon non-stop?"

"I don't know what became of them. I've never been able to find their records on the internet."

"Haven't you got Snapz Pro? I'll set it up for you when you're done cutting my hair."

"Did you leave all your vinyl back in Quebec?"

"I sold it all on eBay. After the shop went belly up, that's what I lived off. Besides, you can stream everything on the net these days."

"I've got some auburn dye left, do you want me to do your grey?"

"That would be great. I love it when you touch my hair."

They have dinner, sitting side by side in front of the T.V. With the cut and colour he looks much better. The fucker, his eyes are as grey and as beautiful as always. She does not wait for him to finish eating before pouring herself another glass and, muttering that she is exhausted, folds out the sofa bed then shuts herself in her bedroom. At twenty, she would have felt guilty that Vernon was living on the streets while she had a cosy flat. She would have felt obliged to suggest he stay for a couple of days. Time was, her apartment was a crash pad for friends who were quick to turn their backs as soon as they had no need of her. She's sick and tired of fucking poets. Of guys too sensitive to put in a day's work. No-one ever gave a shit about *her* vulnerability. Emilie gives thanks for therapy, it has taught her to close her door now and then, it is thanks to therapy that she is still in the game. It doesn't suit her to have him stay here, she has no need to justify herself, still less to feel guilty.

BARBÈS IS SWARMING WITH PEOPLE FIRST THING IN THE MORNING, he elbows his way through the crowds, rucksack slung over his shoulder. Bodies are on the alert, looking for money. Cartons of cigarettes, fake perfumes and handbags, people grab at his arm, eager to show their wares, he plays a guy in a hurry so he can avoid making eye contact with the men and women who try to engage him. He walks quickly, he knows that once he passes Pigalle it will be easier to move around. The Japanese, Chinese and German tour buses have not arrived yet. The Moulin Rouge looks like a cardboard film set. The Elysée-Montmartre is still a burned-out shell. The streets of Paris are a souvenir dispenser. He has always hated the place de Clichy, too much racket, too many cars.

Yesterday's sun has vanished, it is cold and he is hungry. The familiar feeling of an empty belly. When he could stay at home, it did not bother him. Emilie's idea of breakfast is girly cereals, things that keep you regular and taste like hay, he stoically ate a couple of spoonfuls, afraid it would give him a pressing urge to shit. Last night, he nipped into a McDonald's for a quick wash. But most of them have keypads on the toilet doors so that people like him don't have it easy.

Emilie's attitude is like a metal stake through his chest. Right up to the last minute, he was sure she would give him a set of keys to her place. At least for the day. She could tell he was in dire straits. On the pavement, she stuffed a couple of twenties into his hand, careful not to look him in the eye, and headed to her Métro station almost at a sprint. Seeing what Emilie has become is the saddest thing he has ever known. There is something rank in the air she breathes, something rancid that seeps into her and contaminates her energy. That said, she has become sexier with age. She is not as fresh-faced, she's put on weight, but she carries it well. Her confidence makes her attractive, she was a bit of an airhead back in the day.

He haggled like a madman for her to lend him her MacBook. He felt ashamed, nagging her like that over breakfast – but he had no choice. He needed to get online. In the end, he had to beg. He dug Alex's videotapes out of his bag and waved them around like they were Moses' Tables of the Law – "It's his last testament, Emilie, don't you get it? I didn't want to bring it up, but this is one of the reasons I came back to Paris. I'll leave them with you as security – lend me your laptop for a week, max, and when I give it back, I'll pick up the videos. I swear, they're the most important things in the world to me." She does not need the laptop, she has an iPad, an iPhone and a huge fuck-off thing she uses as a television. She was reluctant, he insisted. Eventually she gave in, disgusted to see him grovelling. He is familiar with the look she gave him – it is the same look he used to give junkie mates who came to hassle him in the record shop because they needed a little cash, "I'll let you have it back tomorrow, I swear", and Vernon would reluctantly give in, wanting to be rid of them.

Out in the street, when she took out the two twenty-euro notes, he could have said "What the fuck are you doing?", instead he looked away and stuffed them in his pocket.

She was angry with him, really angry, for not calling her when Jean-No died. It hadn't occurred to him that it would be a big deal for her. Jean-No never talked about her. Never.

Passing a Starbucks he wonders for the umpteenth time what is so special about the place that there are hundreds opening all over Paris. He goes in, it's like McDonald's but more homely, the smell of fries replaced with the scent of moist muffins. He finds everything surprising, from the baristas' outfits to the ordering system. But he realises he has just stepped into dope-smoker's heaven: sweet treats, plush sofas, soft music, subdued lighting – if weed were legal, they could turn the place into a "coffee shop" and everyone would want to live here. He talks to the young woman at the counter, there is no-one waiting behind him. She is about twenty, a pretty black girl with high cheekbones, eyebrows that have been savagely plucked, and a warm voice. Vernon wants to know everything there is to know about the coffees on the menu. She answers coolly, not at all like a girl being chatted up. She talks to him as she would to some dirty old man who's escaped from the local halfway house and is just discovering the third millennium. He wishes she found him attractive, found him unsettling, he would like to move in with her, spend the winter in her bed. But nothing about her manner is encouraging. He leaves with a serious black coffee for €2.60.

Slumped on one of the sofas, he plugs in the laptop and catches his reflection in the screen. At least Emilie made a decent job of the haircut. He looks around the café. The difference between this place and a real bar is the bar itself. What makes a bar a bar is the actual bar. Otherwise you might as well be in a tearoom. It is thanks to the counter that you feel able to walk into a bar alone, there's a space there waiting for you. There was a counter in his record shop. A place for people to prop their elbows and perch for hours, talking mostly to themselves. The antithesis of the psychiatrist's approach: standing, facing the person you are speaking to, with no time limit. God knows, he listened to a lot of shit in the twenty years he ran the record shop.

He logs in to Facebook and posts a video of The Cramps live at Napa State Mental Hospital, a blindingly solid track, guaranteed to solicit as much sympathy as possible. Posts about Alex's death have blossomed during the night. May he rest in peace, fuck him and his shitty stadium rock, may he find the end of the rainbow, and everyone is posting their personal photo, their own little anecdote – I met him in a bar, he was reading Novalis; I slept with him; I was the inspiration for such-and-such a song; he once gave me a stick of chewing gum; I was buying toilet paper, he was buying ham; I saw him one night completely smashed and bought him a beer; I saw him lying in the street in his own shit and I felt sorry for him; he was a gifted poet, my heart bleeds for him.

Choosing from his list of friends feels complicated. There are lots of them. On his timeline, he sees an amazing photo of Harley Flanagan Jr, it's a story that has been doing the rounds for three months now – Harley Flanagan Jr stabbed the guy who replaced him when Cro-Mags re-formed. He clicks "Like" like a madman. The coffee is not bad, he drinks half a litre of it and completely fucks up his stomach.

FIVE MINUTES IN MONOPRIX AND XAVIER FEELS LIKE BLOWING
the place sky high. His local Monoprix is run by fuckwits. It never
fails: they wait until the place is full of customers and then tell the
staff to stack the shelves. Doing their utmost to ensure it is impossible to manoevre a shopping trolley. They could stock the shelves
in the morning before they open, they could do it when business is
slack. No, they prefer to do it at peak hours: stack three palettes
across the aisle, make it as difficult as possible for the cretinous
customers to do their shopping.

All the retrograde fucking packaging winds him up. The
thought of guys in offices spending weeks deciding what colours
to use on a jar of gherkins . . . all that intelligence gone to waste.
Marie-Ange has been busting his balls to do the shopping – and
bitching about how he never helps out, how she gets lumbered
with all the work, and why should she always have to . . . Always
the same patter. The shopping list she texted him is so detailed
that it must have taken her more time than if she had done the
shopping herself. For God's sake, she can't really care this much
about the brand of sandwich loaf . . . Right now here he is, like an
arsehole, looking for fat-free yoghurts that contain no aspartame,
because madame is watching her figure, but aspartame makes her
fart like a gasworks.

Xavier feels like giving the fat Arab woman wearing the hijab in front of him a good kick up the arse. Would it be possible, just for once, to walk two hundred yards down the street without having to suffer their hijabs, their hamsas dangling from their rearview mirrors and their belligerent little brats? A filthy race, hardly surprising everyone hates them. Here he is doing the shopping instead of working because his wife does not want to be mistaken for a maid, and meanwhile these lazy ragheads are strutting around while their jobless husbands are doing fuck-all, taking it easy, getting fat Social Security allowances and spending their days sitting in cafés while their women slave away. If it wasn't bad enough that they do everything around the house without complaining and go out to work to support their husbands, they still feel the need to wear the veil to flaunt their submission. It's psychological warfare: they do it deliberately to make the French male realise how devalued he is.

What's even more depressing is that they've got the choice, these Arab girls. Back in the eighties and nineties, they were working everywhere and doing pretty well for themselves – though usually it was obvious that they were just on the lookout for a rich husband, they're not dumb. But they were working, and they were more successful than most women. Since then, they've backtracked. They decided to withdraw from the job market and don the veil so as not to humiliate their brothers. You wouldn't catch his wife giving up her job to bolster his sense of masculinity . . . Shit. Truth be told, they wouldn't be in the financial hole they're in if she did . . .

He is exhausted. Last night has left him completely wiped out. The little digs have festered in his head during the night. He had dinner with Serge Wergman, who suggested he might want to come on board, write a couple of episodes for a T.V. series. They both knew the whole thing was bogus – the scripts were all written years ago, but still the channel can't decide whether or not to green-light the production, it will probably never happen. The whole premise of the series is for shit – a surgeon falls in love with the drug dealer she's just performed open-heart surgery on. Wergman is a decent guy, Xavier knows he will get paid. He accepted. He'll tidy up a couple of loose ends, rework a few lines of dialogue, otherwise his job will mostly consist of suffering through endless, interminable, pointless, deathly meetings with the arse-holes from the T.V. channel . . . twenty-four-year-old trustafarians, functionally illiterate, who will run their fat fingers, their bitten nails under highlighted passages and say "See, this bit here, it doesn't work". As though the fucktards had the faintest idea of what might grab an audience. The only reason these kids are running the show is because their parents made a few phone calls.

But it's a living. He's glad to have anything. He was thrilled that Serge invited him to a high-class Italian on the canal Saint-Martin. They talked about the new collective agreement that was about to be signed and bitched about how the unions were killing art-house cinema . . . And Xavier, knowing Serge also produces low-key social dramas, did not offer the man his unvarnished opinion on art-house cinema. It had been a pleasant enough evening. Until Elsa showed up. On Jeff's arm. Xavier hadn't heard they were together. He hid his surprise, but instantly he felt a burning in his gullet, he could not stomach it.

Jeff had been another screenwriter. But two years ago he had moved on to directing. One hundred and twenty minutes of trac-tors filmed against a louring sky, of factories full of silent plebs with greasy skin and heads bowed. No music – too expensive – no script, the sort of raw film the critics love – because it's ugly and they're bored out of their skulls, they truly believe it speaks for the working classes. When the film was released, Xavier couldn't open a newspaper without stumbling on some rave review and a livid ulcer gnawed away at his entrails. He had not expected that Jeff, a complete nonentity, would pip him to the post. Not a single one of the scripts Xavier has written in the past fifteen years has succeeded in getting financial backing.

Jeff is working on his second movie. He has offered Elsa a role. They arrived together, flanked by a girl with lank brown greasy hair who introduced herself as personal assistant to the director. They all gave little yelps of pleasure at this coincidental meeting when in fact none of them could stand each other. Only Jeff's pleasure was not feigned. It must have been great for him, to run into a guy he had often worked with and crush him with his shitty little success. He was triumphant. He was not about to pass up such an opportunity to gloat. He wallowed in it, like a pig.

Xavier has never slept with Elsa. He doesn't cheat on his wife. He's not the kind to go around saying "I'm a good Christian, me, monsieur", and then go sticking his cock in some pussy other than his wife's. He has principles. He was young once and he sowed his wild oats then. These days he is a husband and a father and he keeps his nose clean. But it is more difficult with Elsa than it was with the others. It's not just that she excites him; she turns his world upside down. He feels the urge to protect her to fall asleep curled around her to ask her about her day he wants to kiss his way down her back make her read *Sympathy for the Devil* and listen to blues he wants to take the train with her fall asleep in a room with a view of the sea he wants to smell her scent in the morning he wants to go with her to audition and cheer her up if she does not get the part he longs to celebrate good news by hugging her to him. With Elsa, he wants everything. And it has not gone away. He has had moments of madness like this before, but they pass, one day you see the girl and you feel nothing. Worse, you realise her breath stinks, her complexion is sickly, her voice irritating or you don't like the way she carries herself. But fate constantly brings him and Elsa together, it never stops. He knows she feels the same. She is simply waiting, waiting for him to make a move. She feels what he feels and she knows why he is holding back. She respects that. Because, she is a decent girl – not some tenth-rate slut who thinks that being "liberated" is an excuse for screwing up other people's marriages. She is a lovely girl, much too nice to be an actress, and in fact she has had trouble getting a break despite the fact that she is much prettier than most of the cocksucking anorexics you see hanging around on film sets. And it is because of Elsa that, when Jeff said "Let's all go back to my place – I've just bought an apartment – let's go back to mine, there's not enough room here, we'll have something delivered", Xavier followed the crowd. Jeff has bought a shitty apartment. The guy is obviously hiding something, he stinks of old money and pretends he owes nothing to his family, but this apartment is obviously part of the family inheritance, even a fuckwit like Jeff would not buy such a dump. Though he insisted that it cost him 400,000 euros, just to emphasise that he has the means to pick up anyone he likes. It was a dismal evening. They sneered at Delarue, as though they had only just discovered that the guy was a douchebag who surrounded himself with servile sycophants and would kill his own mother and father to get a story that might make tomorrow's headlines. Xavier kept his mouth shut – he did not want to screw up his chances with Serge by losing his temper. Or to let Elsa see how disgusted he was. He would have liked to take her aside, to tell her what was on his mind – how attractive he thought she was, how much he thought about her even when they did not see each other for six months . . . Except that saying I fancy you is like asking Can I kiss you. There is only one way to be faithful, and that is to maintain a physical distance. Stay at least three metres from the object of your desire and the chances that things will get out of hand are considerably reduced.

Jeff spent the whole evening mocking him, with that easy-going air of his. Xavier stuck it out. He listened to the intelligentsia of French cinema congratulate each other on the brilliance of their work, smirk about going to Cannes. Cannes, thought Xavier, is a game of hide the salami with a bunch of tarts in Louboutins. Everyone stuffing themselves with caviar, snorting coke, and congratulating themselves on giving a prize to a Romanian film. Lefty intellectuals love Romanians because they get to see them suffer without having to actually listen to them talk. Perfect victims. But the day one of them actually says something, the left-wing intellectuals will find some other silent victims. Bunch of wankers, Xavier thought, their great hero is Godard, a guy who only cares about money and speaks in riddles. Yet even from this low starting point, they managed to nosedive. That takes some doing.

Xavier got home sufficiently smashed that he did not feel too bad. He had a wank in the toilets thinking about Elsa, washed his hands and then went and collapsed next to his wife. It was something he hated doing, but he would not get to sleep otherwise. It was only the following morning that he realised how difficult the evening would be to stomach. Though he has had to stomach his fair share of humiliating evenings, he has had all he can take. He spent the morning unable to focus on the script he had to write, trotting out monologues in which he tried to convince himself that of course he wasn't jealous of Jeff. Who would want to be in that joker's shoes? He could not stop himself going over and over the imaginary conversation in which he explained to Elsa that directing a feature film that gets three rave reviews is bullshit. In hindsight, it pained him to think that Elsa might find that the comparison reflected badly on him. He came up with infinite variations in which he told her exactly what he thought of Jeff, how he did not feel remotely upset that Jeff was working on a new film. Not even remotely upset.

Now, here in Monoprix, he wishes he had brought a bazooka. The fat blonde flashing her ugly thighs in a pair of tight shorts who dresses like she's a supermodel when actually she's just a cow? Bullet in the head. The little ultra right-wing Catholic couple styled by Kooples, her with her retro glasses and her hair scraped back and him with his pretty-boy face and his Bluetooth headset making phone calls are wandering around the aisles picking out only the most expensive items, both of them wearing beige raincoats to show that they're true conservatives? Bullet in the mouth. The fat piker staring at women's arses while he picks out his halal meat? Bullet in the temple. The Yid in the fright wig with the repulsive tits that hang down to her bellybutton – he hates women with sagging breasts: bullet in the knee. Fire into the crowd, watch the survivors scatter like rats and scuttle under the shelves, the whole fucking rabble who come here to stuff their faces, with their tendencies to lie, to con, to cheat, to jump the queue, to bullshit. Blow the lot of them to kingdom come. But he is a papa, he is a married man, he is a grown-up so he keeps his mouth shut and fills his shopping trolley foaming at the mouth with rage and when he gets home he will have to put everything away otherwise Marie-Ange will sulk and it will be one more day when he gets nothing written. His jaws are aching from clenching his teeth.

There is a queue at the till because it is not enough for Monoprix to bleed its customers, it has to stint on cashiers. He picks the Indian girl because he knows her: she is fast. At least there is one person who knows how to do her job . . . she doesn't waste time smiling as though she was here to suck everyone's cock, she gets through things quickly, she does not need to spend five minutes inspecting something before running it over the barcode scanner. She keeps things moving. Xavier would dearly like to beat the shit out of the short-arse wanker standing directly in front of him, with his goatee beard, a waistcoat the colour of dysentery, his greasy hair and his weasely face, he loathes young guys with beards. A few years ago it was white guys wearing Peruvian caps over their filthy dreadlocks. The sort who think they're smarter than everybody else, who look down their noses at everyone. Beardy little hipstellectual, probably stinks if you get too close, obviously never washes. Those manky tufts of straggly hair are bound to stink, probably full of food crumbs, just looking at him makes Vernon want to heave, a bullet in the back of the head, fucker, maybe that might teach you to wash and shave in the morning. Xavier smokes a pack of cigarettes a day, the last time he tried to give up, the stench of other people nearly drove him mad. As soon as they raise their arms, you can smell it, you don't need to turn round, you can smell them coming. He was forced to take up smoking again.

Xavier fishes out his mobile and opens Facebook. He half-hopes that Elsa has left him a message, but at the same time he hopes that she hasn't – what could he say to her? That it was lovely to see her? This is the sort of message they send each other. The sort that sound completely innocent but are laden with passionate insinuations. Elsa has not posted a message, but he is happy to see that Vernon has been in touch. Subutex. Now there's a decent guy. God, they were so young . . . Vernon took off to Canada with some girl apparently, but he's back in town and looking for somewhere to crash. Xavier replies immediately: Perfect timing, we've got a king-size sofa bed which cost an arm and a leg that never gets used and we've been looking for someone to mind the dog starting the day after tomorrow. You're not allergic to pet hair, are you?

He feels awkward committing himself without consulting Marie-Ange. She doesn't like people being in the apartment when they are not there. But this is different, Vernon is an old friend. He's practically family. And besides, they need someone to be there to take care of the dog. Otherwise, they'll have to cancel the weekend to Rome and Marie-Ange will go into a strop because they never do anything *fun* together anymore. He sends her a cheerful text message, telling her he has just solved the problem and asking what she thinks. She doesn't reply immediately, and Xavier relaxes – he can tell her he needed to act fast and that's why he didn't wait for her reply.

He is happy at the prospect of seeing Vernon again. Vernon is mad about music. Guys like Xavier owe him a lot, Vernon was the one who introduced them to so many bands. And he's one of those rare people you can count on to leave you more cheerful than when you met. They share a lot of treasured memories, they are gradually becoming the only ones left who remember. Parties, gigs, festivals, and bad times too. A time in his life when people didn't sweat every little thing, when a problem could be solved with a slap in the face. Vernon was a part of that life, he is witness to the fact that, when he was younger, Xavier was a stand-up guy: anyone who dared to look crosswise at him lost a couple of teeth. Afterwards, a beer at the bar was all it took to wipe the slate clean and everyone was happy. It was a different time, a different milieu. That's all behind him now.

XAVIER PULLS VERNON INTO A VIRILE AFFECTIONATE MAN-HUG, then steps aside and ushers him in, patting his paunch.

"See how much weight I've put on?"

"You're tall, it suits you – makes you look like a colossus."

In the living room, a little girl with pigtails is pedalling like a lunatic, zooming around the table on a tricycle. Her little face is ugly, but funny. It is hard to imagine that one day she might have her father's nose. Vernon smiles and gives Xavier a wink. He couldn't care less about other people's children, but he knows he should pretend to be interested. Then he crouches down and holds out his hand as the dog pads over to sniff it. He couldn't care less about other people's dogs either, but it is thanks to this bitch that he gets to stay here this weekend. And everything in the living room exudes the *luxe, calme et volupté* so dear to Baudelaire. He has landed on his feet, no question.

"Papa, can I play my video game?"

Xavier bends down and shows her that when the big hand gets to here, she will have to turn off the machine and get ready for her bath. She nods gravely, concentrating on what he is saying about the clock, then races to her bedroom so as not to waste a second.

"She's already playing video games?"

"Of course, board games are a little passé these days. But obviously we don't allow her to go on the internet on her own . . ."

"Because of the porn?"

"No, because of the games. You should see the stuff they come up with for girls – it's fucking sinister. My worst fear is not that sending my kid to school will mean them filling her head with stuff. To a parent, the internet is like having your child taken away before they can even read. You haven't got kids, have you?"

"Not yet. There's still time . . ."

"It's the best thing that ever happened to me."

"Never met the right woman."

People who have kids are constantly boring the shit out of people who haven't. But they can't stand it if you tell them the truth – when I look at your life it makes me want to do anything but. It's not the children that bore Vernon rigid, it's everything they come with: the babysick, Christmas presents, nursery school, watching the same D.V.D. ten times in a row, toys, snacks, measles, vegetables, family holidays . . . and being a parent. His friends launched themselves into the hellish world of adulthood with a certain enthusiasm. Vernon cannot count the number of mates he's seen rock up with a flower-print bag slung over their shoulder, a bottle-warmer between their teeth and a thousand-euro baby-buggy, guys who, from one day to the next, start telling you that even tough guys play horsey. It's bullshit. A guy with a baby is a guy with no future. If it was possible to raise them without their mothers, there might be some way to be a father and still be a man. You could bring the kids up in a shack deep in the forest, teach them to make fire and observe the migratory patterns of birds. You could chuck them into freezing rivers and order them to catch fish with their bare hands. There would be no hugging. Only a look that meant "Next time, maybe you'll be a bit more careful, son".

But the way things are, the only sensible strategy is to steer clear. Either you were wrong to listen to Slayer when you were twenty. Or you're living the wrong life now. And please, for pity's sake, give it a rest with the "everyone is a mass of contradictions". In the end, it's about making choices. Though it has to be said, that a kid would be pretty useful right now. Especially a grown-up kid with an apartment and a job, someone to call him dear old dad and make up the spare room.

They go out onto the balcony for a cigarette – this hell's angel doesn't smoke in the house, and Vernon would happily bet that when he hasn't got guests, he wears slippers so as not to muddy the parquet.

The front door slams and Marie-Ange tosses her bag onto the sofa, strokes the dog who goes over to welcome her, directs a curt nod towards Vernon that is chilly enough to make him feel quite uncomfortable, then disappears into her daughter's room. She is not pretty. She is thin, her face is harsh, her lips too thin. She dresses like shit. She looks as though she had been rummaging in some old lady's dustbin and dug out three ancient tattered jumpers that she wears in layers over a pair of pleated trousers cut too short at the ankles. Vernon knows it's a look favoured by rich women. He had a friend like this, damaged but endearing. She used to wear khaki dresses that looked like they had been cut from burlap sacks with a Stanley knife – and baggy brown cardigans with gaping buttonholes. He had often seen her naked, so he knew she was well stacked. But seeing her with her clothes on, you would never have guessed. From a good family, she had been a ballet dancer, tense and wiry with feet that were completely deformed.

One day when they were talking, Vernon realised that she spent a fortune on her clothes. It wasn't at all like he had imagined, she wasn't a depressive or the victim of a sexual assault so traumatic that she felt the need to hide her body, she didn't cut up curtains for the pleasure of making ghastly clothes. On the contrary, these were eye-wateringly expensive outfits chosen with care and worn with pride in the belief that she was championing the art of living. This is the problem, when women start talking amongst themselves, they come up with conclusions that defy all reason, and let's not pretend that, deep down, it doesn't stem from a profound hostility towards the masculine libido.

Xavier turns the T.V. to one of the news channels, he talks at the screen as though Elisabeth Lévy were in the room with them, and without listening to a word she is saying, he launches in:

"If you don't like it in France, just pack your bags and fuck off back home you bitch. They really piss me off, these Zionists, they're everywhere these days. This is a Christian country, last time I checked. I've never been anti-Semitic, but if you want my opinion, we should napalm the whole region, Palestine, Lebanon, Israel, Iran, Iraq, same deal: napalm. Use the land to build golf courses and Formula 1 racing circuits. I could sort the problem in no time, let me tell you . . . But it's a pain in the arse to have to listen to some half-wog Jew talking about France like this is her country."

Xavier has always been a right-wing cunt. He has not changed, it is simply that the world is now aligned with his obsessions. Vernon does not rise to the bait. Personally, he likes Elisabeth Lévy. You can tell she's a woman who enjoys sex. And coke – which is an added bonus. He decides to change the subject:

"You saw the news? About Alex? Bloody shame, he wasn't even that old . . ."

"Yeah. But he always was a stupid shit, it's a relief, really, knowing we won't have to see his middle-class M.O.R. face any longer . . . don't you think? Were you still in touch?"

"From time to time."

"I won't miss him . . . though at least he didn't play hip-hop."

Marie-Ange reappears carrying a glass of whisky, she looks more relaxed. Xavier is banging on about rap, a form of non-music controlled by Jewish lobbies in an attempt to lobotomise the African immigrant population. Marie-Ange listens to him and smiles as if to say, I love it when you come out with this shit, it makes me laugh, and suddenly Vernon gets an inkling of what makes her attractive. Her eyes, an indefinable emerald green, lend a compelling tranquillity to her face – the prerogative of the rich. There is an elegance about her wrists, the way she holds her head, a power that you sense can be brittle. Guys like him can't help wanting to screw girls like her.

She greets Vernon politely, "So you're Monsieur Revolver?" as though he has been playing with train sets until the age of forty. Then she pours herself another whisky, and holds out her mobile phone in its mother-of-pearl case to show them a photo she took of a homeless guy with a puppy. She is concerned about what happened to the pups, she wonders what happens when they grow up. Do they eat them? "They" means the homeless immigrants, the *roumis*, who are famous for their obscure dietary regime. The photo shows a man in the Marais, sitting with his back against the façade of a fashionable clothes shop, he is leaning against a huge billboard, a photoshopped image of a woman, a brunette, gorgeous. Someone has stuck a Star of David over one eye. Must have taken some doing, since it is three metres up. Either that guy was wandering around with a stepladder, or a friend gave him a leg up so he could play his prank.

It is impossible to put an age to the man sitting on the ground who seems to be sleeping in the cold. He is somewhere between thirty and seventy. Marie-Ange is not interested in the man, she is focused on the dog, she zooms in so that it fills the screen. It looks like a fox cub with long pointed ears, it really is quite cute. Vernon tries to think of something empathetic he can mumble about this puppy she is so cut up about.

Marie-Ange looks at her watch and decrees that it is almost Clara's bath time, she cuts short the conversation, lays a hand on Xavier's shoulder, "Maybe the two of you want to go out for a drink? I can put Clara to bed, then I've got a Skype call with L.A., so I wouldn't see much of you . . . But maybe you'd be happier all boys together, yeah?"

Xavier does not waste a second, he is like a kid who has just been given a day off school, he grabs his keys and his credit card. In the lift, as he buttons his expensive fur-lined jacket, he is babbling nineteen to the dozen:

"When we first moved in, the bar across the street was a complete dive full of regulars, I had such a laugh there. Marie-Ange used to come down and drag me out when she got pissed off I wasn't home, I was there every day. Now it's been taken over by a couple of queers who've turned it into a hipster joint, but I suppose we all have to move with the times, no?"

"It's such a pleasure seeing you and Marie-Ange, you seem to make a great couple."

"Long-term relationships are no picnic. It takes a lot of effort to keep things sweet. I really want things to work with Marie-Ange. She does too. You don't go round having a daughter if you're planning to split up. A child is a responsibility. But you've got to learn to adjust. So, say, when your other half is launched into motherhood, she changes. Once the hormonal whirl is over, you find yourself staring at a complete stranger. I understand now why a lot of guys get kicked to the kerb when the first kid shows up: women are really cold-blooded, up to that moment, they're desperate to please you, but once they've had the kid, you're surplus to requirements. You end up with a walk-on part. You don't know what to do, it's not your department: piss off. And when it comes to money they've got you by the balls, and don't they fucking know it? They know they'll get custody and child support. And by God you'll pay it. When Marie-Ange wanted to restrict access to our daughter's room, I didn't just roll over. Are you kidding? I know how to change a nappy, the right temperature for a baby's bottle. This is where the battle of the sexes is played out, and if you're not careful you find yourself on the ropes. Kids, that's the battleground. The moment I first saw Clara, I knew I would be a good dad. You take this little thing in your arms, and the sheer vulnerability is devastating, you're a different man. So I laid down the law. Every day, I'm waiting at the school gates – I'll still be there when she's in her final year. Marie-Ange wants another one. She wants a boy. But we're in no hurry. I'm a human being for fuck's sake, not a sperm bank. In the beginning, the sex . . . I won't give you a blow by blow, but, well, it was awesome. And I was a fucking idiot, I made sure she came, that way I could be sure she was mine. But to have a girl related to a baroness sucking my cock – hey, it was the greatest thing that ever happened to me, bro. You should see her family – every one of them down to the youngest daughter used to hate my guts, but now, they see everyone getting divorced and we're still together and that's earned me a lot of brownie points. I wore them down. Her folks have never worked a day in their lives, can you believe that? People of 'independent means' still exist in this day and age. Never lifted a finger, either of them. Papa managed the family fortune and maman helped out. They're as tight-arsed as they are loaded, they count every centime . . . But you should hear the way they talk about people on minimum wage. Now, I'm liberal and pragmatic as the next guy, you know me, I'm not some crypto-Bolshevik fantasist. But you'd have to hear them to believe them. How people with ordinary jobs are lucky. Because they don't have the same responsibilities for a start. Never done a tap of work, my father-in-law, but as far as he's concerned the unemployed are feckless wasters afraid of good hard graft. And it's sincere – they think everything is based on merit. Logically, those who have less *deserve* to have less. They're convinced that if they ended up unemployed tomorrow, with their neatly combed hair and their positive attitude, they'd find a job straight away and since they'd work hard and be deserving, they would climb the greasy pole. The rich are still banging on about merit. It's wild. Just between us, I'll tell you that things are pretty tight sometimes – as a screenwriter I'm not exactly earning what I expected to . . . when you add it all up at the end of the year, it doesn't come to much more than minimum wage. That why we got landed with the shittiest apartment in the parents' property portfolio: they reckon Marie-Ange could have made the effort to marry well. Her old man is always telling her 'For a woman, there is nothing worse than to marry beneath her station', and he's surprised that I get angry when I hear him say stuff like this. It's hard work, you know, being a scriptwriter. I got lucky when I was starting out, and because I was just starting out, I assumed that's how things would always be. I didn't realise that by twenty-five, I would already be past it. . . . But having a daughter gives me structure, I fight, I keep going."

Xavier pushes open the door, goes over and props himself at the bar. He does not greet anyone, does not pause in his monologue. Vernon has seen dozens of customers afflicted by this logorrhoea, typical of those who feel the constant need to keep a conversation going to avoid facing thoughts so excruciating they could dissolve them completely. The ex-bad boy turned blatherskite looks like a child wildly waving a toy sword to ward off evil thoughts. He's pissed off with life and he talks like a sprinter. Vernon has no objection to being a passive sponge, soaking it all up.

It has been months since he spent an evening in a bar. He had forgotten the pleasure of propping an elbow on the bar top. When you knock back a few drinks at home on your own, it's difficult to pretend you're a social drinker, a bon vivant, since you are inescapably confronted by the rather dreary nature of the enterprise. They chain-drink and Vernon is in his element. He loves the noise, the bodies moving between tables, the bursts of laughter, the flamenco music he would never have listened to at home, the smell of cold alcohol, perfume and washing-up liquid; at the other end of the room, a slim brunette stares at him from afar, it is like a dance, a flirtatious flicker of lashes as she does something else, a wavering, insistent attentiveness. She has pale blue eyes, high cheekbones and a light complexion. A tattoo of flowering branches coils up her neck, emphasising her delicate throat. He watches the girl, hoping she will get up and go out for a cigarette . . . The background drone of Xavier shuts up only when he takes a drink.

"Personally, I don't give a flying fuck about faggots. See those two behind the bar – the tall camp black guy and the short-arsed Arab poof? If they were wandering round Belleville like that, then fair play. I've got no problem. The two of them, hand in hand, I see them sometimes. It's like Femen – you know, the Russian babes who are always getting their tits out. Hardly surprising I suppose, Russian women are either hookers or porn stars. Not that I'm complaining, long as they're flaunting the flesh. You see them in the Goutte d'Or, screaming that the women in burkas should strip off. Fair play, girl, you've got balls, I'll say that. No, the ones I feel like punching are the guys who act like men when really they're homos – the ones who come on all butch in the corridors of Canal+ or at Cannes. The bad boys of the *salon*. You've just spread your arse for the producer, so give the tough guy routine a rest. If you knew what I have to go through, just because I refuse to brownnose . . . I swear, in France, being a scriptwriter is a mistake. The directors are all desperate to get their shitty little movie on T.V., but they're not so keen to share the residuals . . . art-house cinema, my arse, bloodsucking fucking leech cinema is more like it. They're not capable of writing a line of dialogue, they haven't opened a book since they left school, but there's no way they're about to pass up a scriptwriting credit. You should see them, getting a hundred grand to make a film and then running around looking for contract players, and don't worry when they get another €100k because the fucking thing has been on T.V., they don't start ringing round to divvy it up. They're all lefties, of course . . . but they'll get over it. It's simple – they want to have their nose in the trough. Now they're starting to realise that the film subsidies will soon be coming from the far right, I'll bet you they'll change their tune – they're pretty flexible when it comes to switching sides . . . give them four years, maybe five, and the same people who are churning out tearjerkers about the homeless will be making masterpieces about Jewish bankers, thieving gypsies and money-grubbing Russians . . . They'll adapt, I won't be losing any sleep over them . . . Marie-Ange hates it when I come home drunk. Have to admit that I'm an arsehole when I'm shitfaced, even I can't stand myself. When you get to our age, getting into punch-ups in bars is tedious . . . But I've never been unfaithful to Marie-Ange. Never. Things are as important as you make them, I'm not going to cheat on the mother of my child, on the woman that I married. She's a good mother. She's decent, dependable, responsible. If I dropped dead tomorrow, I'd know the kid was in good hands. Mark my words: the mother is the most important. There's no point having kids with some chick just because you want to jump her bones. The fact that your kid's mother has got great tits is not going to get you far. What's she like, this Canadian bird of yours? Does she want kids? If she's a good woman, then go for it! I've never felt more emotional at anything than I do when my little girl falls asleep on my shoulder. We're not twenty any longer, you have to build a life. Today, as Tai-Luc used to sing, my future is behind me. Hey, speaking of La Souris Déglinguée, you were saying you still saw Alex? Jesus, the guy was ludicrous right up to the day he died."

"I was pretty shocked. Yeah, I still saw him occasionally."

"In Quebec?"

"He played there a couple of times. He's very popular in Canada."

"All due respect, Canadians have no fucking taste . . . Frankly, just the fact that, of all of us, he was the one who managed to do something with his 'art' . . . he was the least talented, the least sincere . . ."

"But he was a good-looking guy."

"He was a big black guy, yeah. Say what you like, but white women always got wet at the idea of being gang-banged by the proud lions of the Cameroon."

"Alex wasn't from Cameroon, was he?"

"He was black. He was a stupid bastard. Jesus he was a stupid fucking bastard . . ."

"Actually, I was wondering if you've got any director friends who might want to make a documentary about him . . . I've got four hours of video interviews he did at my place . . . I don't know what to do with them. I thought maybe I could make a quick buck out of them . . ."

"A documentary? About that bourgeois hipster has-been? I don't think I've got anyone in my Rolodex interested in that . . . You want to sell them?"

"If anyone is interested . . ."

"I hope the fucker rots in hell."

With these words, Xavier – drunker than he seemed from his slurred diction – bites into the glass he is holding, spits out the glittering slivers with a thin trickle of blood and glares into the middle distance, his eyes unable to focus on a single point. Then there is the whole theatrical number while he tries to find his credit card, the barmen are blasé, they've obviously seen this routine before and they know he won't get out of hand. Vernon is annoyed, he would have liked to stay longer, to talk to the girl who has not stopped looking at him, he would have liked to chat with the guy at the other end of the bar in the fluorescent orange beanie, to make the most of this evening. But Xavier clung to him like a limpet, paying no attention to the people around them. Vernon has to help him across the street. He was always like this, the big guy. Sensitive and delicate. The moment he starts to spill his guts, he becomes uncontrollable. The fat fucker must weigh a hundred kilos, easy. Vernon puts his back out serving as a crutch, but finally manages to get him into the lift.

The family are setting off at dawn, they have an early flight to catch. Vernon gets up, wearing boxers and a scruffy T-shirt and tries to put on a good show – as though the massed carillon of the apocalypse were not tolling inside his skull – while, line by line, Marie-Ange goes through the interminable list she has written in a cramped, careful hand, of instructions for taking care of the dog. It is much more complicated than it seems: the animal eats at specific times, a judicious mix of fresh vegetables kibble white meat and organic dogfood, she must be taken out four times a day according to a strict protocol – the evening walk does not follow the same route as the morning walk, etc. The dog is called Colette. Vernon does his best not to laugh when he hears this. Sitting next to the suitcases, the animal watches with a mournful eye as they prepare to leave. Xavier is cradling his sleeping daughter, enduring his hangover in stoic silence. Then the door slams; Vernon waits for a few minutes to make sure they have not forgotten something, then runs into the kitchen. He is ravenous. Vernon succumbs to the temptation of the freshly squeezed orange juice, a decision he immediately regrets – it is a counterintuitive choice, one his stomach vigorously rejects. He makes do with some cheese, hacking off a chunk of Comté and eating it standing up while he studies the provisions. A corn-fed free-range chicken – close to its best-by date, according to Marie-Ange who suggested he cook it but make sure *not* to give any bones to Colette, though she loves the meat and the skin. Yeah, sure, he's going to give a €19 free-range chicken to the dog. It's right there on the pack: €19.00. Wankers. And a pack of chocolate Sveltesse yoghurts without a gram of fat. And multipacks of Kiri cheese for kids – it's all top-of-the-range stuff – and chestnut honey. He spots the price tag on a glass bottle of cranberry juice – €12.80. Vernon finishes off the Comté.

The dog is sitting at his feet, patient and attentive. "Clingy bitch, aren't you?" She tilts her head and listens. Eventually, he realises she wants some cheese. He gives her the rind, hoping it will not make her throw up. Happy to have worked out what she wanted, he strokes her for the first time. Then he goes back to sleep, the dog climbs onto the sofa and is asleep and snoring within two seconds.

Vernon is in the habit of keeping a tight control over his thoughts. The mind is a formidable craft that must be manoeuvred with caution. He manages pretty well, he is not the sort of guy to be

79

suddenly surprised by a dangerous reef. But something has weakened, perhaps it is the silence, or the comfort. He has to struggle not to give in to the masochistic temptation of self-pity. He reminds himself that, although things are shit, he is lucky. He has lots of friends. The dog-sitting gig was a bonus. The apartment is large and comfortable, he will be able to spend the weekend watching movies and stuffing his face. But he can distinctly sense something looming, something that weighs on his chest. If he were at home, he would do some tidying. He's always been the king of categorisation. He needs to avoid thoughts that begin "if I were at home" at all costs, but the words came too fast for him to police them. He feels a thunderbolt in his chest, short, sharp, a rending, followed by the bitter taste of ashes that has nothing to do with his hangover.

He opens a beer and takes a tour of the premises. It is a parents' home, full of useless objects he cannot imagine buying. Xavier has got life sussed: he needs to find a woman who's loaded. When they were younger, they wanted warrior women, sexual animals, gorgeous dreamlike creatures, they wanted rock 'n' roll, groupies and rock chicks, they wanted stunning babes, sleazy sinners, feral Amazons who had to be conquered in the sack. As you get older, you don't give a shit about such things. The most important thing, it has taken him a while to realise, is a woman with an apartment like this, languorous sunny weekends and a fully stocked fridge into the bargain.

Then Vernon dozes in front of the television. "Paris, Texas" dubbed in French, a comedy about football, a cop show, fat people on diets, a couple of trailer trash a vicious guy and his masochistic girlfriend.

Curled up next to him, the dog is snoring. Vernon thought he might have had to lock her up to stop her pestering him, but she is only interested in sleeping. He strokes her again, promising to take her for a walk, though he is not convinced that he actually will.

Trying to work out how to connect his iPod to the amplifier, he accidentally turns on the radio. The room is filled with Alex's voice ". . . And if I fall asleep in your arms, it's because another girl spurned me". He liked to sing this sort of sadistic shit, it was his teenybopper Gainsbourg routine. The speakers ooze a thick bass sound – slick, aquatic, a slapped bassline that forms bubbles, a lick borrowed from funk but tarnished with a fuzz pedal. On this first album, Alex's voice is scornful, sneering, aggressive. Sexy, even to guys. Alex didn't know yet that he was singing to an audience of millions, he would sing in the kitchen to make his friends laugh. It was genius, that first album. A shriek that made girls wet and boys want to be like him. He was a twisted, reckless, wounded dandy. Songs that seemed effortless, wantonly malevolent. This was something else he lost along the way; in time he became a heartless bastard in life and bleeding heart in his songs. How anyone could be miserable with all the attention, the travelling, the wild surprises, the fabulous opportunities, is a mystery to those around him. But Alex is hardly the first rock star to systematically tear down the castle that he built. At the end of the day, the guy was completely lost. For more than two years, he was incapable of composing a thing. Vernon did not really want to comprehend the extent of the tragedy. Had he been a good friend? Clearly not. But it seemed impossible, given his situation, for him to help some-one who was probably a millionaire. He remembers Alex's ravings about synchronising brain waves. He had given Vernon a long-winded speech about alpha, beta, gamma waves – a vast cosmogony of horseshit based on binary beats and neurodynamics . . . Unable to produce a new record, Alex had decided to reprogramme humans. Early on in the conversation, Vernon was thinking, go ahead, make hippie music, none of my business – but when Alex started talking about how the granite blocks of the Egyptian pyramids had been transported by sound waves . . . Vernon felt a twinge of alarm. But he had done nothing to stop Alex from sinking further into the depths.

Gone. Another one bites the dust. Vernon feels his body stiffen, something rumbling inside him makes him panic. The dog lays her head on his hand so delicately that for a moment he is left speechless, frozen. Every memory is booby-trapped. The tight covering he has kept over his fear is slipping – his skin is exposed. His was a hermetic, comforting, all-mod-cons bubble. He was living in formaldehyde, in a world that has collapsed – clinging to people who are no longer there. He could criss-cross the planet, smoke rare herbs, visit shamans, solve enigmas, study the stars – the dead are no longer here. Nor is anything that has gone.

Vernon whimpers. He is surprised at the sound he makes. The dog stands up on her hind legs and, in a frenzy of panic, starts licking his eyes. He tries to push her away, but she refuses. The only living creature who cares about his pain is a dog; he tries to make himself feel worse at this thought but the dog's face is so comical that he finds himself laughing. Colette has a clown's face. She bounds from the sofa and races to the front door, pawing at her leash and looking at him as though proposing some way-out plan: "Come on, take me out, you'll see, we'll have a blast."

*

Once outside, she tugs on the lead like a lunatic; he lets her guide him. She knows the way to the park.

Just inside the Buttes-Chaumont, a man sitting on the first bench is eating a yoghurt and talking to himself. He is laughing at something, his shoes are falling apart and attached to his ankles with string. The dog inspects the area, snuffling around before squatting to take a shit. There is no way Vernon is picking up anything. He glances around him casually as if to say: she's not mine. All things considered, he thinks that being seen with a lapdog like Colette is seriously detrimental to his masculinity. He wishes there was something about his demeanour that indicated that he is not her master – sweet though she is, he finds it difficult to be seen with her in public.

A man of about thirty is standing at the gates, he looks furious. A woman appears, flanked by two little girls. The eldest is wearing shoes with wheels set into the soles, the younger one is hugging a stuffed toy Noddy to her tummy. They are walking quickly, they are late. The woman hands the man a shapeless green canvas bag which presumably contains their things. The man takes the two girls by the hand and walks off without a word. The girls go with him, briefly turning to nod their goodbyes.

Vernon continues on his way. He knows nothing about dogs, he certainly did not know that this particular breed was a babe magnet. Whether they're jogging or chatting, whether they're sprawled on the grass or sitting on benches smoking cigarettes, it seems that all the women along his route are ready to be bowled over: "aw, she's so *cute*!", "look, it's a French bulldog", "I love those dogs", "see how beautiful she is". Vernon smiles, radiant, slows his pace, nods then walks on happily. His black thoughts dissolve. Colette is an aphrodisiac. He understands why Xavier is so attached to her. Vernon does not have the attention span to be a truly depressed. This has always saved him. He is no longer troubled by the gravity of his situation.

Nice pair of legs. He recognises the dark-haired girl in shorts. From her hair and her tattoo. It is the girl who was checking him out in the bar, the girl he could not talk to because Xavier was plastered and they had to leave. She is much taller and much younger than he thought last night. She is talking on her mobile, her eyes meet his but she does not react, he slows. The dog – ever a faithful companion – chooses this moment to roll around in the grass, rubbing herself this way and that. The girl glances over and smiles. Vernon bends down and scratches Colette behind the ears with the casual air of an ordinary guy who is not waiting for anything in particular. The girl is glued to her phone, making it difficult to approach her without seeming like a stalker. It would mean standing in front of her and staring until she finished her conversation, he can see how such a tactic might be off-putting. Vernon walks on past her, irritated. This was no coincidence, it was a golden opportunity: you eye each other up in the bar and next day you meet in the park, it is a pity not to make the most of it. The girl catches him up, telephone still glued to her ear, she flashes him a smile and crouches next to Colette. Her thighs broaden as she flexes, her skin is mouth-watering, she reminds him of a cake. She continues to listen to whoever is on the other end of the line, rolls her eyes to heaven to indicate that it is taking forever but if he will only wait a minute, she has something to say to him. No problem, let her take her time. He signals, pressing two fingers to his lips: she wouldn't have a cigarette? She spreads her hands helplessly, sorry, she doesn't smoke, or at least she has no cigarettes on her. He stares at the trees in the distance. Time drags on. He studies the trees with such rapt concentration that she must think it is part of his day job.

Eventually she says, "Listen, can I call you back? I'm at the Métro station and I'm about to go down – I'll call you in a little while, yeah?" From her tone, it is obvious she is talking to a boy, talking to a boy with whom she is on intimate terms. The fact that she is already lying to him is a good sign.

"We saw each other last night, didn't we?"

"Actually, when I saw you last night I recognised you. I love French bulldogs, I've always dreamed of having one. Is it a female? How old is she?"

"She's three. But she's not mine. I'm looking after her for a friend. Her name is Colette. Are you sure we've met before?"

"Yes, you used to manage a record shop just past place de la République . . ."

A minor anti-climax, a disappointment. She was not staring at him because she was captivated by the charisma of the predatory male. But a glimmer of hope too – she remembers the shop, she doesn't see him as some ageing loser but as a guy shrouded in the power of rock music. Then, with a sly ingenuousness that cannot be entirely innocent, she all but emasculates him:

"I used to go there all the time with my father. On Saturdays, when I was with him, it was like clockwork: we'd go to Clignancourt flea market to look at vinyl, eat *moules frites* for lunch and then we'd go to your shop. My father worshipped you. It's hardly surprising you don't remember me, I was, like, this big."

She holds her hand out at her waist to indicate how tall she was. Vernon pinches the base of his nose between thumb and forefinger – it is a gesture he tends to make when a situation seems complicated but not hopeless. He takes advantage of this new information to stare openly at her face, as though racking his brain for a memory. The girl tilts her head to one side, amused by his confusion. Vernon gets the impression that she is not unreceptive to the idea of being chatted up.

"Who was he, your papa?"

"Bartholemy Jagard. A cop. A heavy metal fan."

It all comes back. An affable guy with a moustache, a scientologist. A complete fruitcake. He would have Vernon special-order Finnish heavy metal records for him, knew the metal scene inside out. Another bullshitter. After a while, it was exhausting having to listen to him, he was always telling stories about grave robbers, necrophiliac romances and sacrificial killings, all offered with a beaming smile. Bartho came to the shop like he might go to a sex shop: he would rather have been interested in something else, spend his money on edifying books about the geopolitical problems of the world. But he could not do it. He would often bring his daughter, who would sing songs from "The Lion King", hunker down between the record racks and play. Her little head barely rising above the counter as her father cheerfully launched into detailed descriptions of animals being gutted on stage by grinning Vikings. Vernon looks deep into her eyes:

"I remember you now. How is your father? Still into heavy metal?"

"No. His new girlfriend doesn't like guitar music. She pretends like she's into the theatre and medieval literature, but actually she spends her life bingeing on reality T.V. and crisps."

It is not difficult to fall in love. First her eyes staring at him last night, her youth and that faint impudence – nothing vulgar, just enough to pique his curiosity. Then there is the way she carries herself, the urge to stroke her back, to press his lips against her inner thighs; there is the tone of her voice, the mischievous gleam when she talks to him, something just a little rushed about her delivery – but not enough to get on his nerves. And that unconscious ease that comes of being so young – still oblivious to the blows that will destroy parts of her. Past the age of forty, everyone is like a bombed-out city. He falls in love when she bursts out laughing – desire is mingled with a promise of happiness, a utopia of perfectly matched tranquillities – she only has to turn her face to his, to let him kiss her and he will enter a different world. Vernon knows the difference: arousal is a pulsating in the groin, love is a weakening in the knees. A part of his soul falls away – and the floating sensation is both delicious and disquieting: if the other person refuses to catch the body tumbling towards it, the fall will be all the more painful since he is no longer a young man. With age we suffer more and more, as though our emotional skin, more delicate, more fragile, can no longer bear the slightest blow.

Her name is Céleste. He does not have a clue what he is doing. She uses young people's words, says them without yet knowing how ridiculous they are. She says "swear down", she says "on fleek", she says "bae", and he recognises the fervent foolishness of people who feel the need to put the same expressions in every sentence. She suggests they walk to the nearest McDo so he can buy her a chocolate Very Parfait. He cannot read between the lines

– is she asking as the little girl who used to come to the shop with her father "Will you buy me an ice cream?" Is she asking as a young attractive woman who expects to be indulged? Vernon tells her he hasn't got a cent, no, not even for an ice cream, and if he did, he has better things to spend it on than taking her to McDonald's. What does he mean he doesn't have enough to buy a coffee? He can tell that he is losing her. He perseveres: the fact that he is broke doesn't mean he has no class, if she chooses her friends based on purchasing power, she'll miss out on the important things in life. She is dubious: sorry, but someone your age who doesn't even have enough to buy a cup of coffee, you can understand why I'm surprised. She is a filthy little slut. She is devastatingly attractive. Her exaggerated respect for money makes it seem possible that she is simply being provocative. But what she says is tinged with a terrible candour that makes it possible she is being absolutely sincere. Vernon is still trapped in the last century, when people still took the trouble to pretend that being was more important than having. And it was not always hypocrisy. He has spent his life dating girls who did not give a toss that he was black-listed by the banks. During the conversation, Colette is accosted by a huge hairy mutt that must weight at least 80 kilos sniffing her arse relentlessly – Vernon freezes, imagining the monstrous cur gobbling up the little dog, and he cannot see how he could stop it. Colette stands motionless for ten seconds, allowing herself to be sniffed, then bares her teeth and sends the Rottweiler scampering back three metres, yelping as though he were a common poodle. The huge hound keeps a respectful distance, then eagerly returns to the fray. Colette snarls again and puts him in his place. Hands in her pockets, Céleste gloats, "Very assertive, isn't she?" Vernon plays the laid-back guy who finds all this funny. He cannot understand how a dog who looks like a stuffed toy can possibly dominate anything, it can only be that for dogs, as for humans, it's all in the mind.

Céleste says that she has to go, she has to get to work. She asks for his mobile number and Vernon can tell that it is more so that she can get rid of him than so she can send him torrid text messages. "I don't have a French mobile, I don't live here. But you can friend me on Facebook, that way we can keep in touch." "Yeah, I don't really do Facebook..." "But you've got an account? My name's Vernon Subutex." "What kind of lame-ass username is that? Did you get it from *Harry Potter*?" "You know nothing, honestly, you know nothing about anything. So what's your name?" "Céleste. I'll friend you. Will you remember it's me?"

He gives her a wink and then turns on his heel all the while wondering whether he looks manly and decisive, or if he just looks like a loser.

He leaves the park, his mind filled with raw, pin-sharp images, how he would lay her across the dining table in Xavier's sitting room, how he would pull her panties down with a swift, precise gesture and unceremoniously fuck her up the arse, how he would push up her jumper to see her childish tits squashed against the table, her endearing little whimpers when he threatened to pull out as she begged him to keep going.

A PERSISTENT SENSATION, UNPLEASANT AND PRECISE, MAKES IT hard for him to breathe. A commotion between throat and chest. Laurent leaves his coat with the girl on the door and asks that they be given a table sheltered from any draughts, he catches his reflection in the huge mirror that covers the back room. He is slim. In six months, he has lost almost ten kilos. He is surprised by the image – proud and relieved that his body looks so lithe. He does not yet identify with this slim figure, his spatial awareness of himself is of the body he has had for the past ten years. He needs to put on some muscle. He has always had a woman's body. When he has a paunch, it is not as obvious – his plumpness is grotesque but masculine. But as soon as he regains his figure, his shoulders seem narrower, his buttocks more rounded, his general appearance more feminine. He thinks of Daniel Craig whom he saw in the most recent James Bond movie not long ago. He would sell his soul to the devil to look like that in a dinner jacket.

With a gallant wave, he gestures Audrey towards the banquette. She could have made an effort. She is not even wearing make-up. A baggy crew-neck jumper, a pair of trainers, her roots are showing three centimetres of dingy grey, she has not been to the hairdresser for months. The woman can hardly bring herself to smile. She is sleeping with Bertrand Durot and no-one in Paris can afford to piss off one of the grandees of France Télévisions. Laurent could not very well refuse to meet with her. He has no intention of producing her film. It would be a clusterfuck from beginning to end. Why court trouble? The movie would be lucky to sell thirty tickets. This is the new fad among women directors – stories of post-menopausal women who chain-smoke and talk to losers. He would love to be frank with her, to say, you know the reason I do this job is not to find myself on a film set surrounded by a bunch of cantankerous old cows who are about as sexy as a root canal. And, until there is evidence to the contrary, the ticket-buying public agrees with him on this point: everyone wants fantasy.

Audrey launches straight into the subject of women directors who are notoriously discriminated against in France. And even more so in other countries. What a chore. He does not point out that she seems to have no problem with the numerous advantages of being a woman when they serve her purpose. She has not even opened the menu, he wants to order quickly – to get this over with. He could easily order for her: she will choose the most expensive dish on the menu.

But it is not the director's presence that is making him feel self-conscious. He needs to think back over the events of the day and of last night to work out precisely when it started. He recognises the feeling, but he needs to concentrate in order to remember what was said and when, who it was who has made him feel so ill at ease. He sees so many people, so much happens in any given day. His Neurolinguistic Programming sessions have taught him this approach – at the first signs of breathlessness, isolate yourself from reality and centre yourself in your core. Find the nerve centre. The wrap party for the latest Podalydès. Some self-styled scriptwriter whose name he has forgotten was holding forth and clutching his glass of champagne – Fred from Wild Bunch had been talking about the death of Alex Bleach and this other guy said, "Actually, I've got this friend who has raw footage of his last interview, shit-hot stuff apparently. He wants to do something with it, but he hasn't been able to find a producer." That's it. That is where it all started. Laurent had cosied up to the scriptwriter, asked if he knew Alex personally, explained that they had worked together on a project that was never completed, an exceptional man, a terrible waste, such suffering, accidental death, the ghoulish prying media, the beautiful farewells from his true fans. He was walking on egg-shells. The scriptwriter was a fat brute with cropped hair and the face of an idiot. He said he had not seen the footage in question, but that he had known Alex well and, sensing Laurent's interest, used the word confession, "This friend of mine says the interview is pretty hardcore, Alex was off his face but he had so much to say, maybe he knew he didn't have much time left, this is his testament . . ." Though his senses were addled by the booze, Laurent decided that showing too much interest might backfire, and tried to get the scriptwriter to talk without going so far as to make an actual proposition – tell your friend to get in touch with me as soon as possible. He knew that if he were to give the guy a business card, this "starving artist" would take it as a licence to harass him. He is familiar with the type. The guy has fifteen projects on his hard drive. He is convinced that every one is a masterpiece of intelli-gence and originality. He is thrilled by his own audacity, and more so by his sense of humour. He believes that the bad feedback he gets on his screenplay is the product of the diseased minds of spiteful con artists. You can tell him the same thing fifty times, and fifty times he will reinflate his ego and start churning out the same shit. In general, the lack of talent in such men is compounded by a remarkable disinclination to make the slightest effort. If Laurent gives this guy his number to give to his friend, he will have no qualms about calling him twenty times a day to propose a project. The starving artist is utterly sincere, and therein lies the danger: he cannot see the difference between his pathetic scrawlings and the latest box-office blockbuster. Every Wednesday morning, he probably goes to the week's eleven o'clock screening for his regular bout of flagellation, he will choose the movie everyone is talking about and convince himself that ten years ago he wrote the same thing only better, that it is his idea they have stolen. But Laurent has never yet encountered a forty-something screenwriter whose talent has gone completely unnoticed. There are the unmanageables, the junkies, the weirdos – but undiscovered talents are truly rare. Guys like this distribute their brainchild on a grand scale, no producer, no fashionable director is spared. If they had even the germ of an idea worth financing, everyone in the industry would know. Laurent found himself lumbered with the guy for most of the evening, trying to steer the conversation back to his friend and Alex Bleach's one-man interview but the man was like a broken record, he stubbornly kept talking about his writing, his projects and insisted on giving Laurent a personalised lecture on film – what a treat, the jerk has developed opinions on every recent French movie he has seen at the cinema – and God knows he had enough time on his hands to sit in darkened rooms. Laurent listened magnanimously, all the while thinking: face it, you moron, if there were no difference between the shit you turn out and the gold I produce, you wouldn't need to spend half an hour tap-dancing for me. You would already be on my list, we would already know each other, we would probably have worked together.

He has not had time to think about this valedictory interview since. In the taxi on the way home, Amélie had been glacially fuming. "I'm not accusing you of sleeping with her, I'm just asking why you behave like that around her. I've never seen you in such a state." The "her" in question was a third-rate actress pitching for a film he was producing who spent the whole evening pushing her ginormous breasts under his nose without eliciting anything more than a yawn from Laurent, but Amélie has her little manias. Whenever she throws a jealous fit, the wrong woman always gets it in the neck. To reassure her, Laurent so completely demolished the actress that when he got up the following morning at seven, he immediately called the director, told him that she was a terrible actress and he wanted to hear no more about her being considered for an audition.

Ever since, he has been unable to shake off the feeling of having a long rusty needle planted in his throat. Panic is second nature to him. Sometimes the attacks are so intense that he has to shut himself away. He is in perfect health. It is the pressure. He has learned to take deep, slow breaths from his belly. His therapist sometimes gives emergency hypnotherapy sessions via Skype. Laurent locks himself in his study, leans back in the reclining chair, puts on his headphones, though he is not always able to relax, but more often than not it works, his heart rate returns to normal.

The woman director is explaining that she refuses to shoot in Luxembourg, that she has had her fill of Europudding co-productions and strongly feels it harmed her last film. Her creative vision suffered from the ludicrous constraints imposed upon her. She still thinks she is living in the 1990s. Her "creative vision". It's something people used to say back then. When Laurent learned his trade, you had to listen to directors maunder on about inventing new shots and everyone considered it normal for productions to go wildly over budget. It was considered acceptable to sink a fortune into a film that earned nothing but prestige. These days, people think about being No. 1 at the box office, no-one sees any prestige in films that make no money. And even good films can bomb. The public don't like shit. But Audrey has not noticed time passing. If she thinks that she is going to impress anyone by larding her movie with pretentious drivel, she is kidding herself.

Laurent has done a lot of work on himself. He knows why he is in this business. He is fifty years old. He is honest with himself. He enjoys the power. He is long past the age of bullshitting himself. He has flair, he is good at betting on a winning project, he knows how to pull a handsome financial package together, he has connections, he is hard-headed, he is a tough negotiator. What he is looking for is success. He likes the excitement that goes with it. He enjoys the panicked euphoria of a team when the phone calls keep coming in, he likes soaring figures, that incredible boost, the thought that anything might happen, and anything does, and it is exceptional. He likes to think that people fight for the privilege of getting access to him. Smiling at the two-faced flattery of colleagues and scorning those who dish it out. He likes coming home late, being the only person awake in the house, pouring himself one last whisky, gazing at Paris from his window and being able to say to himself "I pulled it off", trying to feel the pulsing of success through his body, through the streets of the city below. He wants to experience this feeling of power with the same intensity as he will feel the sting of failure when it comes. But he likes to lose, too, to bite the dust and feel a rage coursing through him, an unrelenting determination to exact revenge.

Those who have never wielded power do not know what it is. They think it means sitting at a desk, giving orders, never being contradicted. They imagine it is easy. On the contrary, the closer you come to the summit, the harder the struggle. The higher you climb, the more every concession costs. And the more you have to make. To have power is to smile when someone more powerful crushes your ribs. Humiliations are brutal at the top, and there is no-one there to listen to you if you want to moan. It means playing with the big boys, not staying in the sandpit with the little snowflakes. Only tinpot managers revel in their power, when you rise above that, you feel only the fear of being stabbed in the back, the fury of betrayal and the poison of empty promises.

For Laurent, the worst thing is another man's success. The release of "The Intouchables", and "The Artist" in quick succession has royally screwed up his year. Everything in his stable that has done well seems trivial by comparison. He has taken up sport – one hour, five times a week, at home with a personal trainer, a taciturn black guy who only smiles when he sees Laurent is really suffering. The important thing is not to lose sight of the fact that everyone else is subject to the same rules as he is: they are kings of the world, until the next turn of the wheel.

He knows that he should not feel so unsettled because someone at the party last night talked to him about an interview with Alex. It is magical thinking, lending credence to intuitions that are based on empty talk. He has no real reason to worry. He must look within himself, to find an anchor that will help him get through this. He controls his emotions by eating his way through the bread basket while he waits for his oysters to arrive. God, this woman is so mind-numbing . . .

Alex Bleach was a cretin, arrogant and fragile, the archetypal fucked-up poet – a little shit who only thought about money, but played the protest singer on the covers of his albums. The artist in all his glory: they think they can do what they like and they despise those who do the work, the real work. The problem with the public, often, is that they choose the most pathetic leaders. People love to be lied to. This was something Alex understood very well. He lied in every interview he gave, and the public adored him. Laurent had had dealings with him on several occasions. Not content with ridiculing and abusing him in front of an audience, Alex had managed to get hold of his mobile phone number and once, when he was completely shitfaced, he had called in the middle of the night to insult him. The guy was deranged, he knew nothing. When Laurent heard that he was dead, he was relieved. You never know how far a lunatic like that might go, and he had no desire to have that kind of enemy. They were not in the same league. But he needed
to be absolutely sure in his own mind.

"Are you listening to me?"

"Yes, yes, I'm sorry . . . I've been a little distracted lately, since I heard that Alex Bleach died."

"You were close?"

"Once upon a time. We hadn't seen each other for a while, and I was deeply affected by his death . . . But I'm listening. Please, go on . . ."

He ripples the air with his fingertips. The director does not even take the trouble to look concerned. She carries on like a bulldozer – focused only on her goal, on the sound of her own voice. At first, Laurent thinks that young directors are ill-mannered – did no-one ever teach this woman that it is polite to feign compassion when the person you are talking to feigns emotion? Then he realises it has nothing to do with manners. In his day, children were expected to become social animals, to learn empathy. To show sympathy when someone appeared to be sad, for example. If the subject was intelligent, he quickly learned that showing sympathy could pay off, especially if you wanted something from somebody. But then Facebook came along and this generation of thirty-somethings is made up of solipsistic psychopaths verging on insanity. Naked ambition stripped of any sense of legitimacy. She picks up where she left off. She wants to make a film about a woman of fifty who works at a perfume counter. She loses her mother – they were very close – and cannot bear to see her father start a new life only three months after the funeral. The poor old codger finds someone and the daughter wages war on her new stepmother. The suspense. Audrey is convinced she has written a comedy. She cannot see how she could possibly shoot it on a budget of less than three million. No, really? A fifty-something frump out for a good time who can't stand the thought of her old man remarrying. There's a subject for a comedy. If the paying public have a choice between Scarlett Johansson naked and some wrinkly old bat, they'll think long and hard before buying their ticket.

He douses his oysters in shallot vinegar. He likes this brasserie – it is his canteen, they know him here, the waiters are very attentive. It helps him unwind. He is not materialistic. Money in itself does not interest him. He would be just as happy eating in a pizzeria and going camping for his holidays. But this place is right next to his office, so it's practical.

He does not think Alex Bleach was so obsessed with him that he would have badmouthed him in every interview. He tries to reason with himself. They had a difference of opinion, it's true, but a lot of water has flowed under the bridge since then, even for a simpleton of Alex's level. In any case, who would believe the paranoid ravings of an imbecile like Alex Bleach?

Audrey is looking at the dessert menu, he cuts her short: "I'm so sorry, I don't have time, would you care for a coffee?" She orders a *café gourmand*, making no attempt to hide her disappointment. What a bitch. He stares at her intently, screwing up his eyes as though he genuinely cares about her story of the beautician who cannot bear to see her father happy because he is moving on too quickly – she does not yet know that men are incapable of living alone, how then can one reproach them? Laurent reminds her how complicated the business is these days, even for him. He pats the script with the palm of his hand, as though champing at the bit to get back to the office to devour her story of a bewildered fifty-something. "It has become so difficult to produce films of quality that I have to be extremely discriminating. And what I cannot abide is giving people false hope. If I tell you we're doing it, then we'll do it. But if I have any doubts about my ability to produce the film, I will be completely honest with you. My department is perhaps not best placed to produce low-budget films – you know how it is, technicians don't understand anything, they are not prepared to put in the same effort for me as they would for produ- cers more . . . familiar with art-house cinema. But I'll give you a response as soon as I can."

He looks at his watch, adopts a panicked expression, jumps to his feet, slips ten euros to the girl at the coat check and dashes out into the cold feeling a wave of relief. When he gets back to his office, he remembers his meeting with "la Castafiore". Today is not his day, Mercury must be in retrograde. He shakes the young distributor's limp, moist hand. Not all queers are handsome. Dressed head to foot in Prada, la Castafiore looks as though he has just clambered out of a rubbish skip. He has an unprepossessing physique. Hardly surprising he is so spiteful. Laurent wonders whether he knows that he is planning to stab him in the back. He promised to let him distribute the latest Canet movie if he was prepared to take the Bayona Laurent co-production, but he has already offered the Canet to Mars – not because they'll do a better job, just to piss off la Castafiore. If he can do anything, however small, to help this man fail, so much the better. He has seen them come and go, these people. He settles the man in his office, asks if he would like a coffee, leaves him with Justine, whose job is to take care of such things, and excuses himself. He has something urgent he needs to deal with, he will be right back.

He knocks on Anaïs' door. She is watching a film – shot on video, a piece of shit, every shot horribly framed, the youth market think it's "awesome", apparently. He asked her to do an overall survey of the genre, he needs to decide whether it is worth getting into these movies shot by a crew of four on a budget of less than €100,000 that kids on the internet are lining up to watch. It pays to be one step ahead. He can't simply depend on family-friendly movies, the old-style blockbusters. He needs to innovate, to be where he is least expected and to get there before everyone else.

Anaïs is perfect for this. She has the eye and the mindset of the youth market. In ten days, she will present him with a report on the three or four best directors of the upcoming generation – he knows he can count on her, she will make the right choice. Laurent Dopalet decided to hire someone of her generation when his own daughter got it into her head to be a "YouTube Beauty Vlogger". He took an interest in what she was doing because he was terrified that, as has happened with some of his colleagues' children, she was going to post sex-tapes of herself doing it with underage boys. And to his shock, he discovered a universe of young girls who know exactly how to pose for a camera, how to frame a shot, and how to upload "make-up tutorials" that can get up to 56 million hits when filmed in their bedrooms. He realised he was missing a trick, that he needed someone in his office to scour the web for new trends. 56 million girls can't all be wrong.

He sits on the arm of her chair. There is nothing going on between them, but he likes the closeness. He likes her composure, her smile, the manner she has of calming him. Anaïs is radiant. She is no prettier than other girls, she is simply radiant. He sighs:

"I've just come back from lunch with the queen of the ball-busters . . . and I've got la Castafiore in my office, you can't begin to imagine the toll it takes on me. Maybe I'll open a vein just so I don't have to face the rest of today."

"Shall I come and get you in twenty minutes?"

"Make it thirty. There are a couple of things we need to talk about for the release of the Bayona."

"It's bound to bomb. The film is too bleak. People don't want that kind of thing these days."

"Listen . . . Last night I met a young scriptwriter . . . well, not young, exactly . . . but there was something about him . . . I'd like you to put together a little bio on him. Can you track him down? His name's Xavier. I don't remember his surname."

"Are you really telling me you want me to track down the one scriptwriter at the party last night whose first name is Xavier?"

"Well, yes actually. Jeff told me he wrote something about ten years ago, and the movie was a hit, but I don't remember the title."

"Okay, that might help."

"I just want to find out who he is, see if you can dig up some little project he's working on . . . just to get an idea. Oh, and I'd like to know where he lives, who he hangs out with, whether he's working at the moment . . . Just a little recap."

"There were at least three hundred of us at the party last night . . ."

"Yes. It won't be easy. But you'll manage. And that's why I love you."

"But why exactly do you want to meet him?"

"I'm not sure I do want to meet him. I just want to . . . sniff him out."

THE HYENA SETTLES HERSELF AT A TABLE IN THE BACK OF THE
bar and instinctively checks her mobile to see whether she has had
any messages. Le Globe is empty, as it usually is in the afternoon.
It is a little neighbourhood bar. During the day, there are young
bearded men wearing djellabas and fluorescent trainers, cheerful old winos and a few local shopkeepers. When it is time for
the evening *apéro*, round about happy hour, the bar is transformed
into a hipster hangout for young binge-drinkers determined to
stay till closing time and ensure none of the neighbours get a wink
of sleep while they stand on the pavement smoking.

The Hyena checks the time on her telephone, irritated that her
date is unpunctual. Laurent Dopalet likes her to arrange meetings
in bars he thinks of as exotic, far from the neighbourhoods he
frequents. He takes his little moped and rides along the rue Sainte-
Marthe, if he passes three "gangstas" he feels as though he is in
the Bronx. They often meet up in strange places. Laurent does not
like them to be seen together.

She has moved into social media. For a while now, this is
how she has been making a living. It happened by accident. She
ran into an old friend, Tarek, who was eating on his own in a pizza
restaurant near Abbesses, sat down and had a coffee with him. She
had met him in the early nineties when he was working as a journalist for a porn mag – porn was fashionable in those days. Tarek

used to be invited to Cannes, to the swanky parties at Canal+, he had an entourage of actor friends. Everyone wanted to hang with Tarek, it was the last word in chic. Then the internet boom had once more revolutionised the porn industry and Tarek, unable to find a job, made the most of his contacts, reinventing himself as a press officer for the traditional film industry – no-one would have bet a kopek on him succeeding – but this was the decade when the counter-culture went mainstream, and the company was a huge success. And so she found him, in great form, still going to Cannes, but much more stressed than he had been when he was writing feature articles about the latest movie by John B. Root.

Realising that the Hyena had time on her hands – she was between jobs – he suggested she help him out on a film he was promoting, he needed someone to handle online presence. There was cash to be made. Basically, they needed to flood the web with positive reviews, supposedly written by people who had been bowled over by the film. It was a little tedious – but back then, you could still register with the same website a dozen times using different identities as long as you took the trouble to create fake email addresses. The Hyena did slapdash work, but Tarek insisted he was very happy with her services. He was no fool – the movie had been well received, "real people" had posted genuinely posi-tive comments – but he liked working with her, and he decided to believe that she was responsible for the positive buzz. They worked together on a second film. And the Hyena quickly worked out there was serious money to be made, but that writing positive reviews was not the most lucrative approach.

She bought a list of fake identities from a former colleague who was sick and tired of spending her time posting pointless comments on pointless subjects. She ended up with about fifty aliases – to be credible, messages had to be posted by people who had been signed up to the site for years, who had their own Facebook pages and Twitter accounts. People who seemed to exist, if you googled them. Otherwise, all you had to do was routinely change your IP address, and try to keep track of who said what on which site and using which voice. She refuses to use leetspeak – replacing "E" with "3" and systematically forgetting to make adjectives agree. This is her only vanity, otherwise she does what she is asked. And very quickly, what she was asked – in return for two or three hundred-euro notes, just like back in the days when she was dealing coke except that now the Feds can search her all they like, she has nothing incriminating on her – was to spread poison. On request, she will utterly destroy an artist, a government bill, a film, an electro group. All by herself, in the space of four days, she comes down like an army. She has seriously added to her catalogue of fake identities and – without wishing to boast – her bullshit rantings go viral. She can poison the internet within 48 hours: no-one in Paris, as far as she knows, is as efficient. After that, it takes on a life of its own – the journalists check out Twitter, read the tweets and feel obliged to report on the bullshit they read there. So whatever she posts is eventually carved in stone. For the rare positive campaigns she is still commissioned to do, she uses the services of old colleagues who artificially increase the number of eyeballs in the current climate of "how many likes". Her strategy is shockingly lucrative – it is a gold rush, no-one has a clue what is going on, but everyone wants to hit the motherlode. It is the dumbest job she has ever done. But it's well paid, when you consider how little brain-power it requires. She has got her clients by the balls – for those with the means to pursue the policy, destroying the competition is priceless.

Inciting a media lynching is much easier than generating a positive buzz – she claims that she knows how to do both, but cruelty makes for better clickbait in this day and age. A man who breaks things is a man who makes himself heard – it is crucial to adopt a male persona when trashing someone. The only sound that soothes the savage breast of the lunatics who haunt the corridors of the web is the splintering sound of a warder breaking a prisoner's bones. Three rave reviews for some T.V. pilot and people start to suspect they're being manipulated, thirty vicious comments and no-one thinks to question it. The casual browser can pat himself on the back and think "I wasn't born yesterday", but he has already passed on the message as intended. Scorn is as contagious as scabies.

In the village that is Paris, word quickly spreads that she is a first-class troubleshooter. People discreetly invite her for coffee in cafés they do not usually frequent and where they are unlikely to be spotted. They ask her to rough up a competitor, a friend, a rival. For two hundred euros, she will break a virtual leg, for twice that, she can ruin an online reputation, and if money is no object, she can quite literally ruin someone's life. The internet is the perfect forum for anonymous exposés, for smoke without fire, for rumours that spread like wildfire without anyone knowing where they started. Case in point: that prick Laurent Dopalet, who has not stopped calling since last night, has shelled out a small fortune for her to troll actresses who do not respond favourably to his advances, colleagues who have had – or might have – a hit on their hands, and former associates who have turned their back on him . . . He is constantly adding names to his hit list, and she is his voodoo priestess.

Dopalet is supremely self-absorbed. He can be bitter, lucid, sometimes droll, clueless or raving – he only ever talks about himself. And yet he has a very fragile ego, he is wounded by the slightest criticism, the slightest stain on his reputation sends him into a towering rage. If some other producer is praised on the radio, he immediately interprets it as an insidious way of implying that *he* is shit. Dopalet reads the newspapers, watches the television, spends time on the internet. And Dopalet suffers. The actors are better paid. The directors are more admired. The distributors are bankrupting him. The public are out for his blood. Everyone is getting public subsidies except him. Everyone is having fun, everyone is having a wild time, everyone but him, a poor little man who works like a dog and gets whipped for his pains. This tragedy is played out in a two-hundred-square-metre apartment overlooking the Seine – since he married a woman who is fabulously wealthy – but this is of little comfort to him. He is suffering. He is a first-rate client. The Hyena has become crucial to his equilibrium, something on which he is prepared to spend a packet . . . The personal trainer, the shrink, the hypnotherapist, the meditation coach, the acupuncturist, the magnetic therapist and the osteopath divvy up a small fortune every month and, between them and the weekends with his mistresses, it is a wonder Dopalet finds any time to work. The Hyena sends him extortionate invoices. From her years working as a dealer, she remembers that the junkie *needs* the seller to be hard-nosed. That is what makes the dealer a demi-god.

She specialises in the film industry. That way she can avoid getting landed with political gigs that are no better paid but require considerably more effort. In 2014, the only people interested in film are the professionals. No-one else is prepared to waste ten minutes discussing a tracking shot, defending an action movie or dissing a psychological thriller. She often works with actresses. Not all of them are spiteful and self-centred. They constantly feel insecure and they have a high disposable income. A lucrative combination. They are prepared to pay for someone to plaster the internet with love notes, photos, passionate declarations and real-life accounts about how lovely and approachable they are when encountered at the local café. But most of the time, her role is to take down the other actresses in the running for some part they desperately want. Or to stop some young starlet from making it too quickly. For the pleasure. Conflicts of interest quickly arise: can you take on a client when you are actively in the process of trashing her for another client? Of course you can. This is the third millennium, everything is permitted.

She has her notebook. A little black notebook chosen for its size and the soft feel of the faux-leather, an object she likes to cradle in the hollow of her hand. She fills it with rather cryptic messages so as not to be embarrassed should she ever be searched. Decoding it would require an effort altogether disproportionate to the value of the information it contains. The phone numbers next to the pseudonyms do not exist – the prefix 06 means that she can post messages from her own computer, 01 that she can send them from the internet café next door, 04 that she needs to be in a different arrondissement. A number that ends in a 3 refers to comments on general news items, those ending in 7 refer to comments on the film industry. The second digit corresponds to the year the identity was created, and so on. Sometimes she varies

– but, once decoded, the phoney numbers let her know which identities she can use. It is not a code sophisticated enough to stand up to serious scrutiny, but if whoever is looking does not pay close attention, it is enough to throw them off the scent.

As a matter of habit, Dopalet is precisely thirty minutes late; for him discourtesy is a precept. He is dressed as though it is Sunday and he is planning to spend the afternoon having a kickabout with his kids on a patch of waste ground. A hideous, tatty jacket, jeans that are not even his size, but his hands, as always, are perfectly manicured. Usually he comes alone. But, he announces straight off, before taking a call – gesturing to indicate that he will only be two minutes – "this time, it is a little exceptional". The girl with him constitutes the only interesting thing about his entrance. She is a smash hit, like when you hear a song on the radio that you've never heard before but you immediately recognise it, it has always existed, it runs through your head all day, and all you want to do is listen to it over and over. Now this was worth putting on some slap, facing the grey sky and dragging her sorry arse over here. The little hottie introduces herself: Anaïs. The Hyena pretends not to be flustered.

Dopalet comes back and sits down, looking glum. His eyes are deep-set, but never enough to give him a thuggish look, his nose is too turned up, his gaping nostrils are thick with hair, his lips thin, all in all he looks like a wimp. He is a tubby little guy. Even when he loses weight he moves like a ball, his arms held away from his sides. Anaïs takes the floor. As he listens to her, Dopalet shifts his jaw from right to left and stares into space. At regular intervals, he makes vague expressions to indicate that he is listening, that he agrees.

From what the assistant is saying, it seems the producer is trying to track down "some guy" in Paris whose name and address he does not know. But apparently this "guy" told another "guy" – Xavier, whom they describe as "a screenwriter" – that he could lay hands on some unseen footage. The boss wants to see this footage. He needs to find this "other guy", who weighs about 100 kilos and has close-cropped hair. So they called the Hyena. She stares at them, wondering if they are joking.

"And how precisely do you expect me to go about it?"

"My words exactly," says the wondrous assistant, throwing up her hands in defeat. Dopalet is beginning to get irritated, he is squirming in his seat. The Hyena rubs her eyelids, making no attempt to hide her helplessness:

"What sort of footage is it?"

She is expecting that this question will calm Dopalet, that he will fumble for words to explain that sometimes he discusses geopolitics with young boys and he does not want anyone to find out. He knows the great unwashed: they do not know the first thing about the sophisticated passions of his management team. It is the assistant who speaks:

"It's an interview. I don't know if you've ever heard of the singer Alex Bleach. It seems this may be a recording in which he might have been manipulated . . ."

The Hyena interrupts Anaïs and addresses herself to the boss, forcing him to meet her gaze.

"I don't see the connection with the work I usually do for you."

"Everyone knows what you used to do before."

"I've had a career change . . . and if it were still my job, I would regretfully inform you that your little plan is mission utterly-fucking-impossible. I'm not going to try and track down some random guy in Paris called Xavier . . ."

". . . who's a screenwriter."

"If he were a screenwriter and you'd met at a party, you wouldn't need to pay someone to find his name . . . So no-one knows who he is, this guy?"

Anaïs pipes up again, she sits like a schoolgirl, back straight, hands flat on the table.

"I've tried calling some of the guests who were at the party . . . but it didn't lead anywhere. I don't think he moves in the same circles."

"There are, what, fifteen of you in the business? Which means he's a screenwriter the same way I'm a lacemaker. So, in a nutshell, you're telling me that you're looking for a fat, bald guy called Xavier who lives in Paris. Great! I know exactly where to start."

Anaïs raises her eyebrows, worried to hear anyone speaking to Dopalet in this tone. But all in all, the expression means that she gets the picture: it is not much to be going on with. Dopalet slips his iPhone into his jacket pocket – as far as he is concerned, the meeting is over.

"You may not know where to start, but I'll tell you why you want this job: you can name your price. Secondly, you're not scouring the city for 'some guy called Xavier', you're looking for someone who knew Alex Bleach."

"You didn't mention that."

"The bit about the price or the bit about Alex Bleach?"

"Either."

"They knew each other. And the guy who has the footage was still seeing him shortly before he died."

"Alex Bleach . . ."

"He despised me. He was obsessive. Absurdly obsessive. I don't know why. Maybe I helped him out once too often . . . I want to pre-empt matters and find out what is in this footage before it ends up in the public domain . . . and I have good reason to think that you are the best person to help me."

He does not know why Bleach nursed a grudge against him . . . The Hyena studies Dopalet intently: how many times has he hired her to deal with the Bleach problem? If Alex's hostility was an obsession, then it is fair to say it was mutual. She knows the guy's reputation better than anyone – rapist, thug, anti-Semite, guilty of fraternising with Islamists, of embezzling public funds. She should know: she is the source of these rumours, they were launched in various stages. If Bleach had lived, all that remained was to brand him a paedophile. She knows the dossier, knows it well. If Alex Bleach ever guessed who was orchestrating the nebulous attacks against him, he had ample reason to want to see Dopalet's little empire destroyed.

Alex was the perfect target – famous enough for the slightest rumour about him to set people talking, but defenceless enough so that there was no risk in taking him down. Journalists had a field day. Alex represented everything about the last century they wanted to destroy, what they call *la pensée unique*, a neoliberal conformism that claimed to combat brutality by raising a few ethical objections or making a small donation . . . the same neo-liberalism that no-one in the entertainment industry would defend these days, except for a handful of deluded beatniks like Alex Bleach. You could count them on the fingers of one hand, they put out a new record every five years; it's called tyranny. The media are quick to jump on anything that might tarnish their image. It pissed them off that this big black guy got an easy ride. It has to be said, with his angelic face and his deep, husky voice, he had probably fucked more women than all the editors in Paris put together. Nor were the accusations of rape or violence likely to put them off, everyone knows these things are a turn-on for nice straight girls. Now that he was dead the journalists rushed to praise his talent, but the relief in every obituary was palpable. One down. Alex Bleach was among the tiny minority of artists who have no friends in the business.

Dopalet looks into the eyes of the Hyena and baldly lies in front of a witness, as though they have never discussed the subject of Bleach before now.

"Bleach used to call me up, insult me, send me threatening emails . . . I considered filing a restraining order, but because he was famous, it was too complicated . . . Can you imagine if the media had found out he lost the plot?"

"And yet, it's fair to say you never let it drop."

Insolence, even in homeopathic doses, is something Dopalet cannot abide. She can see it in his eyes: "You'll get what's coming to you, but right now he knows that he needs her. He gets to his feet and, without looking at her, declares: "I want this done quickly."

Then he stalks out of the bar, without paying the tab or saying goodbye, his mobile phone already glued to his ear. Fuckwit. The Hyena would happily confide her thoughts to the assistant, but all she can see in the girl's eyes is her pride at having such an assertive boss.

SITTING CROSS-LEGGED IN THE LARGE OFFICE CHAIR, SYLVIE IS reading her horoscopes: Rob Brezsny, the *Village Voice*, the *Huffington Post*, *Figaro Madame*, and lastly Susan Miller. It is something she has been doing for years. As regular as clockwork. Now, all that will have to change. She used to get up at 6.00 a.m., make a pot of black tea and turn on her computer with the radio playing softly. She would log into her various Facebook accounts – she has three. The two fakes exist so that she can make comments she does not want associated with her real identity, check whether her lovers are being faithful or catch out friends. She created the first fake profile in order to get revenge on the boys bullying her son at school. Having completed that mission, she kept a taste for shifting identities. At 7.30 a.m. she would prepare a cup of Ricoré and a toasted bagel with cream cheese for Lancelot and go into his room to wake him. She would throw open the curtains and the day would begin in earnest.

Lancelot having left for university, she would play games on her computer. Candy Crush, Ruzzle, Criminal Case occupied the remainder of her mornings. Her afternoons were devoted to her appointments – Pilates, manicure, aqua gym, the hairdresser . . . She would make sure she was back by the time Lancelot came home, she did not like the idea of her son coming home to an empty house.

He left home two weeks ago. He enthusiastically packed up his boxes – a boy who had to be asked a dozen times before he would sigh and do the smallest chore. He sorted out his clothes, piled up his books, threw out papers that had been lying around for years. She did not need to help him; his efficiency broke her heart. Worst of all was his excitement. Logical, understandable, predictable. But difficult to stomach.

When he was little, there was no more powerful consolation for her than her son's kisses. The memories of his childhood are so crystal-clear that she would not be remotely surprised to open the kitchen door and find Lancelot teetering on a stool searching the cupboards for a piece of chocolate. Sweet things had to be hidden away in high cupboards, otherwise he would have gorged until he made himself sick. All that is over now. That little body she used to lavish with affection. His tiny feet, the Dragon Ball Z duvet covers. Things became more difficult when he turned sixteen. She never stopped loving him but there were times she could have killed him, what with the football and the macho bigoted bullshit he came out with all the time. She felt hurt and betrayed, they had always got along so well. Three years of friction, then it was over. Her son is right-wing. At first she thought he did it simply to needle her, but eventually she had to face facts: intelligent young people are no longer routinely left-wing.

He is in love. With a vapid young woman who likes to play wife but is incapable of taking a pizza out of the oven. The girl is a practising Christian. As long as she doesn't saddle him with a kid right away . . . They have found a two-room flat in the nineteenth arrondissement. The sort of bleak, miserable neighbourhood where no-one would want to live. The lovebirds are very sensible on the subjects of Islam and Judaism, so they should enjoy themselves in the quartier Crimée. Lancelot showed her around the apartment with the half-witted happiness he has exhibited since falling in love. He knows he has to make a break from her. Boys do not kill their mothers, they leave them. She has never been as generous to any other man, because no other man made her so happy. Nor so bereft, in leaving her.

Vernon showed up at just the right time. So many memories have flooded back since he has been staying with her. When she used to go to the record shop, he would let her use the back office so she could discreetly roll a spliff. She would close the door and snort lines of smack – she had not started jacking up yet. She did not talk about the fact she was using, on the rock scene you could do anything you liked, except for the best of all drugs. She knocked it on the head while she was pregnant but was back on the junk by the time she was warming the first baby bottles; she only finally kicked the habit, in a Swiss rehab clinic, when Lancelot was learning to read. It is difficult, being a high-functioning addict, not many people can manage it. Good addicts, like good alcoholics, are those who are able to control their consumption. It is a happy medium that is difficult to strike – controlling the substance that you love because it is making you lose your head. She was a member of that select group. But at the age of thirty, she realised that managing her intake of skag was not enough: she was ageing more quickly than others. She got clean. Fifteen years later, she still dreams of scorched teaspoons, of dealers showing up late, of wads of cash. When it comes to the menopause, she'll see. If it's as tough as people say, she can imagine going back to hard drugs – after all, Lancelot has left, and besides she has already lost her looks – why not have a little fun? She has always dreamed of retirement homes where you could choose your own medication: M.D.M.A., coke, hash, morphine, crack . . . since everything has gone tits up, why not go out with a bang?

Back in the days of Vernon, the name Revolver daubed in red letters on the black shopfront. It was a different life. She was not yet a yummy mummy. If someone had told her back then that one day she would fall for Vernon Subutex, she would have shrugged . . . in those days she was stunning, she was funny, all the boys were head over heels. She liked the guy at the record shop, but she had other priorities. She had a thing for musicians. Groupies get a bad press, but it's only because they can do things that boys dream about but would never dare to do: suck off the whole band in the back of a van.

If Alex had not died a few days earlier, she would probably never have given Vernon a chance. She only vaguely recognised his name. But on her Facebook page, she has seen a link to the film "La Brune et moi", clicked "Like", he had P.M.'d her and she had thought that was sweet. When she heard that he was looking for somewhere to crash for a few nights, at first she had hedged – my son has just moved out, I'm having work done . . . But Vernon had still been seeing Alex when he died, maybe he could help her understand what had happened.

Alex Bleach was a mistake that had left its mark. She had never been the same, afterwards. Over time, she thought about him less often.

But she was convinced that they would see each other again some day, that he would apologise, that they would have a chance to clear the air. It was unimaginable that two people who had been so close could stay angry with each other. But Alex was dead, there would be no happy ending now. She would never get to tell him to his face: you know I loved you so much, I don't feel bitter, but that break-up, it almost killed me. He would not get to say I've always regretted the fact that it ended so badly. I was never as happy with any girl, not like I was with you. She will never know. The moment when he began to lie to her. Sylvie is convinced that he did not leave her for another girl. He left her for a line of smack, for a crack pipe. He left because she would never have allowed him to destroy himself as he did. His lover had no body, no phone number, no libido, she was a baggy of white powder. It is a love Sylvie knows at first hand. Nothing quells anxiety like a drug, no woman is as faithful or as tender as smack.

Alex was the sort of guy who reacted to the news his latest single had sold a hundred thousand copies by plummeting into a cavernous depression. He was a real son of a pleb, success scared him shitless. He was a man who felt shame. It was what he called integrity. Anything with a whiff of sophistication offended him. To invite him for a drink in a palace was to court disaster – he would weep with rage. Everything upset him. Sylvie had taught him what she knew of the world. Feeling at home everywhere, not allowing yourself to be overawed, never showing your vulnerability.

Sylvie had loved Alex uninhibitedly. She gave herself without imagining that he might betray her. But, being Alex Bleach's girl-friend was not entirely positive. Certain aspects were amusing – being able to go to the front of every queue, watching faces change the moment they stepped into a room, not having to even mention your name for the most luxurious rooms to become available . . . but her true moment of glory was when he would come off stage and look around for her, to see what she had thought. Was it good? It was great. Until she had given her opinion, those of everyone else – the thunderous applause echoing around a hall like Le Zénith – meant nothing. Being indispensable to him was a drug. She revelled in the massed camera flashes of the paparazzi, the envy of the pretty girls, the heckling calls of the journalists, that feeling that was special, dangerous. She never complained about her position – she pretended not to hear the sleazy comments people feel entitled to make about a girl who is thrust into the spotlight for being the favourite of the hero of the moment. She would never have imagined that the status of "official girlfriend" would invite so much hostility – a star's entourage argue about everything, they agree on only one point: his girlfriend is no good for him. She gritted her teeth and smiled, ignored the rumours and the reproaches whispered into the ear of the prince. She was there to support him. From the moment he woke he would be sobbing, as she got up she would muster all her strength to get him on his feet, like a coach moving restlessly around a boxer. No-one had ever seen a monster so fragile. No-one could have guessed that this arrogant brute who trashed every stage in France was transformed into a whimpering puppy the moment he stepped out of the spotlight.

He had disappeared overnight. Dumped her by leaving a message on her answering machine. She saw the new girl's face in the pages of the gossip rags. They never saw each other again. She never understood exactly what had happened. She had to invent a plausible story so that she could move on. As best she could – when you're young you believe that time heals; she learned that you have to amputate to survive.

Gradually she thought about it less often. Until the death of Alex. And the reappearance of Vernon Subutex. It happened naturally. From the moment she opened the door to him, she knew it was inevit-able. But she never thought things between them would happen so quickly. He came to her bedroom that first night, two weeks ago now. They have not been apart since.

Sylvie is having the girls round tonight, it was arranged ages ago. The moment she mentions it, Vernon takes off. He does not want to impose. He takes his rucksack – there is a friend he wants to catch up with – he won't come back until tomorrow. He laughs when she insists he come back and sleep next to her and asks how late he can come home. He gives her a long, deep kiss before he leaves. She turns to jelly at his touch. It is something she hasn't felt for a long time. That taste of battered leather and blasphemy, of a wild and dangerous bad boy. Vernon is gentle, Vernon fucks divinely, Vernon is a little disturbing. Vernon has got everything going for him.

She goes downstairs to catch a taxi from the place d'Iéna. The Somali Embassy is under siege, as always, a queue extending along the pavement. The Eiffel Tower seems so close that you could simply reach out your hand and touch it. She feels her stomach heave as she climbs into the cab, it smells of unwashed male. She taps little messages to Vernon on her Samsung. He does not answer immediately. She worries. She had forgotten how foolish you become when you're in love. Winter sunshine, late morning, the area around the Madeleine is deserted, the streets are vast; Sylvie never tires of the beauty of the capital. She has never lived elsewhere for long – a few months in New York, a few weeks in L.A.; like everyone else, she loved the States in the 1980s. But she does not feel the same eagerness to go back now – September 11 was the bell sounding the end of playtime. She loves Rome, she likes London, she enjoys spending time in Andalusia. But nothing can compare to Paris. Through the taxi window, Sylvie watches three girls walking side by side. Three little Romanian girls. She sees one of them slip a hand into the backpack of a Japanese girl, but they are too far away for her to try to intervene. As she passes Marcolini's, a group of Russians is photographing the chocolates in the window. At Au Printemps, tour buses are disgorging a gaggle of Chinese tourists. Sylvie no longer hangs out in the designer departments of the *grands magasins*.

At Lafayette Gourmand, she buys a huge box of Sadaharu patisseries: she knows that tonight she and the girls will exchange half-amused, half-outraged looks when Laure can't help but stuff her face with them. Like her arse isn't big enough already . . . When Laure comes to dinner, Sylvie discreetly steers her towards the sofa for fear that her gigantic arse will break her favourite armchair. When they talk about guys, Laure joins in as though she were one of the girls. But with a face like the back end of a bus and the manners of a trucker, her only hope of getting fucked occasionally is the rise and rise of functional alcoholism. It must be awful to have a figure that no amount of dieting, exercise or surgery could make attractive.

Marie-Suzanne will probably monopolise most of the evening reading out all the text messages she gets from Bernard. For years now she has been having an adulterous liaison with an ageing beau and saves every email, every text message on her phone so her girlfriends can vie with each other to come up with the most brilliant textual analysis. They cannot bring themselves to tell her that they know all there is to know: you're being used, girl, it's obvious that he's screwing anything that moves.

When Sylvie described her friends to Vernon, he stopped her, palm thrust forward, singing "*Stop! In the name of love*", then said, "Do you actually like any of these women?" Sylvie is a bitch. She's a Parisian. What she most appreciates about her girlfriends is the ability to rip them apart as soon as their backs are turned. If the conversation isn't catty, no-one would be likely to find her interesting. In a way, it suits her that Vernon is not staying over. She wants to tell her friends she has a new lover, who has more or less moved in with her because he's living in Quebec these days – to her friends, she will pretend she believes him, though she knows he is lying. He knows nothing about Canada. She thinks it is more likely that his last girlfriend chucked him out and that he made up the story to find a place to sleep . . . When he comes to trust her, he will tell her the truth. It's not important, all guys lie.

She is willing to bet that, as soon as they arrive, the girls will say, "My, god, you're looking *fabulous!*" Because it shows – a good fuck is a lot better than thalassotherapy for the complexion, so two weeks of frantic fucking has taken ten years off her. It completely realigned her chakras. She'll tell them that he is almost the same age as her – she knows, because she has been discreetly told, that these tarts all pretend they're shtupping younger guys because they're terrified of mature men . . . It's simple, if one of them said she was getting it on with Brad Pitt, the other would say that he's not half the man he used to be. But the truth is, she is planning to make them sick with jealousy about her wild yet gentle rock-star boyfriend.

She will wait until they all arrive, set down the bowl of roasted almonds in front of Laure, and when the girls start to get impatient – *Come on, out with it! What's your secret? You look amaaazing!* She'll tell them that he's been in love with her since he was twenty but waited all this time to declare himself. She thinks he has aged really well, and she wants to make the most of being single now that Lancelot is away at university, Jesus, girls, what do you want me to say, I've never had a better fuck in my life, how could I not fall in love with the guy?

It is not completely untrue. He's good in bed. He's an old hand, but he suffers from the faults of men who have screwed too many women, guys who are always moving from one girl to the next end up losing their instinct. What they gain in technique, they lose in passion. These are minor quibbles she does not plan to mention. Instead, she will advance a theory about the biological clock: there comes a time when the body realises that it has only a few short years of splendour remaining and makes itself available for one last fireworks display – she is having orgasms like she has never had before. Or at least that is what she will say.

She is happy that Vernon did not want to stay tonight, if only so she can feel how keenly she misses him after only a few hours. And she will feel more comfortable if she has time to send him to the dentist for a vigorous scale and polish before introducing him to anyone. Otherwise, he is fine. Physically, he is very presentable, and he can be charming in conversation. The next time she has the girls over for dinner, she will be only too pleased to introduce the beast.

She will be wary. She herself has slept with most of her girlfriends' regular partners. The guy would have to be hideous or have serious personal hygiene issues for her not to at least make the attempt. What could be better than sleeping with the boyfriend of a best friend? Especially when they seem so happy together. A quick blow job in the lift cures the jealousy brought on by other people's happiness.

Sylvie stops in front of Eres, her eyes drawn to the embroidered yellow satin lingerie in the shop window. Though it was unplanned, when she thinks about it, it seems only decent to buy some underwear she has never worn for anyone else. Having someone else constantly in your head. His movements as he screws her. The memory is almost more troubling than the thing itself. The constant background heat, the flickering, almost pornographic images are all the more arousing as she remembers them here in the street. How long has it been since she had a fling with a man she finds attractive who is actually available? How long since she made plans to go on holiday with any boy other than her son? She'll suggest they spend a week by the pool in the Château Marmont – at least Vernon will know what she is talking about. Rent a car, stroll down to Amoeba Music with him. Guys always make like they hate being "kept men", but her experience has taught her that the opposite is true. They like being indulged by the woman they're sleeping with. A pimp fantasy, maybe, but they like to be spoiled.

She chooses several outfits and locks herself in a changing room. A month ago, she would have hastily tried things on, but Vernon's passion has helped her to accept her body. Today, when she looks at herself in the satin two-piece, she sees a very pretty girl. All the exertion has paid off. Her triceps and her pectorals are firmer, her breasts are better supported. Her belly is perfect, her buttocks firm, her calves shapely enough to accentuate her slender ankles. Sylvie does a twirl, looks at herself – a fine specimen. She is still not prepared to linger on the face. The first Botox injections worked miracles, but the effects did not last. The hair extensions help to disguise the slackness in her oval face. She has not had any serious cosmetic work done yet. She is waiting until she is ten years older.

When you're young, you don't realise the cruelty of what is inexorably happening. You know it is happening, you simply don't realise. Like most girls, Sylvie thought of her beauty as something that was *hers*: she might grow old, but she would still be beautiful. Being trapped in this skin has become a tragedy, a terrible injustice, one she cannot complain about to anyone. For a long time, she believed that, if she kept herself fit, everything would be fine.

That had all ended one summer. She had been in the shower, cooling her sunburn and washing the salt from her skin. As she had been towelling herself dry, she was surprised to find some sand under her breasts. Then it struck her. She was pierced, transfixed, stunned by an invisible arrow. Straight through the heart. The penny had just dropped: once they start to sag, you have to lift them up to wash them. She remembered the pencil test – it was something women used to talk about when she was a girl: if a pencil placed under the breast doesn't fall, you're past it. She raised her head, stared at herself in the misted mirror – she had not seen herself naked in a very long time. Only in lingerie or in a swimsuit. That was when it had begun. And the summer in question was not last summer.

But now, she plans to make the most of her body: she will fuck with a fury far more intense than when she was young and still unaware of the urgent need to make the most of it.

She wants to be with Vernon all the time. In fact, she wishes she had cancelled the dinner with her girlfriends – when you're single, you pretend you could never bear to be joined at the hip to someone 24/7, that you find such relationships puerile and pathetic, but you only find them pathetic in others. She tries on different outfits and takes selfies in the changing-room mirror, posing to show her good side, glad that, for once, the lighting is flattering. And before she goes to the checkout, she sends the best shots to him via private message on Facebook. Then she writes "I so wish you were coming home to bed tonight, I should have given you a set of keys. Are you sure you don't want to come back?" She wants his cock, his hands, his jokes, she wants to watch television with him, she wants his smell, she wants his brashness . . . She had not realised that she was ready for such a grand affair.

LET HER DUMP HIM, FOR PITY'S SAKE, LET HER DUMP HIM! HE is listening to Johnny Cash on his headphones and drinking cans of beer. He breathes. Ten days, she has been on his back non-stop. The girl blathers on from the moment she opens her eyes. She gulps in air. The first night, he found it cute, but he quickly tires of her guttural croak, leaning over his shoulder, watching his every move. And it's impossible to let her rant on and think about something else. She can't stand it when he daydreams. There are lots of things she cannot stand. He smokes too much, he eats like a pig, he is moody, he is getting a paunch, he spends too long in the bathroom, he hasn't read enough books . . . how many beers have you had; God you smoke a lot, at least open a window, go on quick; close the window, it's freezing; you make so much noise I can't get to sleep; could you put your dishes in the sink when you've finished eating . . . Are you really listening to that shit? You're not telling me you actually *like* Stromae? I should introduce you to my son, you can listen to shit music together. Give me a hand here, I'm about to make dinner so get into the kitchen, you can peel this, and take out the bins, do you know how to fix a wardrobe? No? That mocking little smile of hers: men, they're all the same – useless. And the little-girl face she pulls when she kisses him – for fuck's sake, woman, you're a hundred and seven, stop acting like a child when you kiss me, and stop kissing me all the time, I'm not a fucking teddy bear . . .

At first, he accepted everything good-naturedly. He so wanted to believe things were going well. In fact, when he first showed up on her doorstep, he had almost panicked: Sylvie was stunning, she looked just like a Hitchcock heroine in a little black dress that fell just below the knee, high heels, and hair tied up in a chignon. Sylvie had been one of the great fantasies of his youth. Her apartment was pretty grim: shag-pile carpets, tacky gold highlights, framed landscapes – it was like visiting a staid maiden aunt back in the 1980s. But the sofa was comfortable and the flat-screen T.V. was gigantic. Money becomes women, and the fact that she was a little weathered by time made her all the more sexy, gave her a touch of vulnerability. She kept crossing and uncrossing her legs, looking up at him coyly, laughing at his every pronouncement, leaning forward to listen, pretending to be utterly fascinated. He had forgotten how alive you feel in that moment: when you sense that something has begun, and every gesture simply confirms the impression. He had felt his veins swell with a strange, distinctive euphoria: the delicious intoxication that comes before the first kiss.

Sylvie has a good memory. Vernon had been flattered that she remembered the parties and the gigs where they met up. Sylvie soothed an ache he had not known was so profound. He had not realised how lonely he had felt of late. They had listened to John Lee Hooker and Cassandra Wilson. There was some talk of Alex, she was clearly upset by his death, he realised that her pain was still raw and politely avoided saying that Alex rarely mentioned her, that she was not one of the girlfriends who had left an impression. Then she had said, it's so late, you must be hungry, let me see what I have in the kitchen. Vernon had got up and was scrolling through her iPod looking for Thee Oh Sees – they found themselves face to face, she took a step forward, he leaned down and after that there was no talk of dinner until four in the morning.

The first night had been bliss. He had undressed her gently, between embraces. His every gesture was sensual, moving in slow motion. Between her pubis and her navel he discovered she had a little tattooed panther in black ink. Their flesh synchronised, in the darkness Sylvie's voice became more guttural. Vernon had not fucked in years – when he got up to fetch his cigarettes, he caught his reflection in the hall mirror and saw that, without realising, he was smiling like a half-wit. And the funniest thing was that he could not get rid of the smile. He felt an ancient force stirring in him.

They got along well. There was a place for him in this house. She liked to cook for him, he loved her vast king-size bed, the little heart-shaped red metal box always full of weed, she liked him to choose the music, to take the remote control and decide what they should watch on television, they liked the same T.V. series and spent whole days with the curtains drawn lying in each other's arms. He felt as though she had come to lick his wounds and he could bandage hers. He treated her with a gentle roughness, manhandling her body, he sensed her orgasms become less and less fake, more and more intense. Yet he knew from experience that you should be wary of women who feel the need to tell a man they love him ten times a day. It tends, as a rule, to hide something ugly.

But very quickly, the constant salvo of negativity demolished him. Her critical mind, which had made him laugh at first, crushed his natural good humour. Only old-school things – Billy Wilder movies, the music of Coltrane, Flaubert's novels – did not prompt a furious barrage of criticism. And a few select designer labels. The rest of the time, regardless of the subject, and without pausing for breath, she reeled off a litany of phonies, hypocrites, morons, poseurs, genuine arseholes and fake stars . . . Vernon had started to lock himself in the toilet. Every half-hour he felt the need to go, just to get a bit of peace – but she would press herself against the door and continue to pester him. He no longed dared lift a finger – the fear of being bawled out left his back muscles in knots. Vernon would get up at six a.m. so he could have a quiet cup of coffee before she appeared.

Not only is Sylvie negative like a fine drizzle that can chill you to the marrow, she can quickly become nasty when roused. One afternoon, finding her crying after a visit to her son's new apartment because it was "too much", the way he treated her almost like she was a stranger, Vernon had tried to make light of things: "Yes, but remember how we were at his age, how much time we spent with our parents." She had whipped round, her face contorted with hatred and hurled abuse at him – what the fuck did he know about being a mother? Why did he have to stick his oar in? – before giving him a few vicious kicks intended as an invitation to leave the room. He had left her to calm down and went to look in the medicine cabinet in the bathroom where he found some tranquillisers. From that day on, he took one every morning when he heard her getting up. He reminded himself of a girl whose blog he used to read who always swallowed half a temazepam before taking it up the arse. He no longer offered an opinion, on any subject. Sylvie had hit her stride: she would shift between periods of blissful infatuation and bouts of unhinged aggression, then insist on tenderness and sex as though nothing had happened. Vernon adapted himself to her demands, with the growing feeling that he was shrivelling up inside and feigning good humour simply to avoid hassle. He counted every thrust, careful to protect his lower back muscles – fucking had become a chore, the only way to keep her quiet for five minutes.

Now, holed up in a hotel room, €40 a night, Vernon can finally breathe. He does what he used to do when he still had a home. He visits websites and makes a list of the new records being reviewed, then listens to them while knocking back a few beers. There's no-one to say how many beers have you had today, don't keep your socks on in bed, they're filthy.

He does not have much time left if he is to get his belongings out of storage. He has not succeeded in discussing the problem with Sylvie. At first, he was waiting for the right time, but then he realised that if she gave him the money, it would be as if she were buying a puppy: she would never let him off the leash. He wonders whether the bailiffs packed his things into boxes or tossed it all into bin bags. All his worldly goods, what little he possesses – the Laguiole knives he took from his mother's, the saucepans he bought at Ikea one day when someone drove him there, the genuine goose-down quilt he has been lugging around since he was thirty. The things he has cleaned, preserved, used. And the paperwork he has spent his life sifting through. A few photographs. His voting card. Never used. The letters he has kept. All this in strange hands that are neither hostile nor benevolent, hands whose job it is to flog off the lives of those in debt. It is being dead while still alive, his confiscated past. He is so vulnerable that he has the impression that an invisible thread ties him to these objects and, when they are scattered to the four winds, he will crumble to dust.

If he had talked to her honestly about the situation, Sylvie could have paid the thousand euros as easily as he might pay for a café crème. In her world, a thousand euros is a pair of shoes. A handbag costs more than that. She is always saying "I don't give a toss about money" as though this were an exceptional quality. But she has never been without – after her divorce, she got the apartment, an alimony settlement equivalent to double the minimum wage while still spending the money generated by her parents' property portfolio. Who would give a toss, in such circumstances? Vernon too would happily be a poet if he had never had to worry about paying the rent.

He could reply to her Facebook message: "Hey babe, thinking of you, can't wait to see you again", then leave her to stew and show up tomorrow morning with a couple of croissants, put on a hangdog expression and confess I've been lying to you, I don't have an apartment anymore, I didn't know how to tell you. Then sit back and let things take their course. She would take care of everything. He will have to discreetly replace the volumes of the Pléiades he "borrowed", not to mention the gold watch he assumes belongs to her son. He grabbed everything he could, and cleared out while Sylvie was taking a bath. He tries to reassure himself, tells himself he will buy it all back as soon as he can. He reasons: it wasn't premeditated. She mentioned this dinner she was having, he knew he was going to do a runner, pictured himself on the streets without a cent in his pocket so he swiped a couple of things. An act of revenge that was petty. But pragmatic: he sold the five volumes from the Pléiades – two volumes of Stendhal, three of Karl Marx – at Gibert Jeune for €100. Cash. The baseness of his actions in no way detracted from the pleasure he felt as he walked back down the boulevard Saint-Michel looking for a cheap hotel where he could spend a peaceful night. He is getting by.

The cheapest available hotel room with free Wi-Fi was round the back of Bastille. He knows this street. Céline used to live here. That was the year of "Groove is in the Heart". Céline had a screw loose, she couldn't hold her liquor and she drank like a fish. But before she chucked him out, screaming insults because she thought (quite rightly, though he never admitted it) that he had been chatting up some other girl right under her nose, they had spent a pretty cool summer together. They went to the movies every day. Céline was a projectionist and had a card that admitted her and the guest of her choice to any cinema. It was a sweltering summer, they looked for those with air conditioning. They liked the Gaumont big-screen theatre on the place d'Italie, but they did not show the best films. She loved Carax and Téchiné; he preferred Scorsese and De Palma. Vernon had never thought about Céline again. She had amazing tits.

He finds three private messages on Facebook from a journalist called Lydia Bazooka, who did not think it worthwhile to wait out an appropriate period of mourning before starting on a biography of Alex. Vultures start to circle around a corpse while it is still warm, grabbing the best places for the feeding frenzy. This bitch is scouring the internet looking for anyone who ever knew Bleach and Vernon is surprised that she has already tracked him down. He never appeared in any of the official portraits. Like a lot of people his age, Alex had been marked by the meteor that was Cobain. He would often say that, in the record industry, the ideal gig was working with a dead artist. That's why they are so eager to push them towards an early grave. Lydia Bazooka remembers that Alex often mentioned Revolver in his interviews. When the record shop still existed, it was a useful piece of publicity, albeit the benefits were very short-term. It is strange, in retrospect, to realise how much Alex tried to support him, and how he had not thought of it as generosity but as a way of affirming his power. The journalist is insistent. He feels like telling her to fuck off. Death has kindled a tenderness in him that he has not felt in a long time. Vernon decides not to reply, then changes his mind and sends a message: "I'll bet you're earning peanuts to piss on his grave." She is doing it to have her name on a book and considers it perfectly acceptable to exploit whatever comes to hand.

Vernon expects her to take offence, or try to justify herself. She replies instantly, "Don't worry, I'm used to being paid peanuts. But meet up with me for a chat and I'll buy you a coffee on expenses." And since it takes him a moment to react, she adds: "I love your eyes in the photos. I'd like to see them for real." She is funny. He googles images of Lydia Bazooka and finds only two. She is short-legged with a round, fat nose, downy hair and pale skin. But she makes up for it in her presentation: plunging necklines, long nails, short skirts. A geeky pin-up who makes the most of what she's got. Perfect. In her case, being passably ugly works to her advantage, the effort she makes is touching. He asks her where she lives.

Searching the web, he finds several articles she has written about Alex. Her approach is impulsive, but better than he had expected. She has been a genuine fan from the very beginning. As he searches, he comes across a multitude of eulogies in praise of the dead singer. People have already moved on, there are no recent mentions of him on social media. But in the three days after his death, every blogger seemed to have something to say. Alex was thrown to the sharks, their jaws snapping in the void, churning out words that nobody reads.

Then Vernon turns his attention to a series of friendly messages from Louis, a former customer at the record shop to whom he was never particularly close. Louis writes to him with a rather curious eagerness – Vernon remembers him as a cheerful, thuggish lad, these two traits not being mutually exclusive. He is disturbed by the number of videos and photos of Charged GBH, The Exploited and Kortatu, the guy has posted on his page . . . How old would he be now? Forty? When he notices that Louis still lives in Cergy-Pontoise, he decides to keep the conversation polite but distant and does not mention that he has nowhere to crash. These days, Louis works in a bookshop, he likes hardcore crime fiction and offering his opinion on the state of the world. He is obsessed with Syria; he is convinced that Bashar al-Assad is a victim of a sickening campaign of propaganda orchestrated in Israel and Washington by the infamous Judeo-Masonic secret coalition. He is a part of the virulent left-wing, and clearly sufficiently involved to embrace the dark side of the force. What fascinates Vernon about Xavier, Sylvie and now Louis – three people who have nothing much in common – is that they have no doubts about anything. They are perfectly aware that no-one agrees about anything, something that might prompt them to wonder what to do in the face of so many contradictory views. Far from it, any challenge seems to reinforce their conviction that they are right.

Facebook these days is nothing like the chaotic free-for-all Vernon was a part of ten years ago. No-one quite knew whether it was a love shack, a night club or a repository for the emotional memories of the whole country. The internet has created a parallel space–time continuum where history is written hypnotically at a speed much too frantic to allow the heart to introduce an element of nostalgia. Before it has time to take hold, we have moved on. Vernon hangs around on Facebook the way he might a cemetery, the few remaining occupants are rabid zombies who rant like guinea-pigs locked up in cells, flayed alive and having salt rubbed into the bleeding flesh.

The only person who is more or less amusing in this gallery of horrors is Lydia Bazooka. Vernon rips open a bag of crisps, pops a can of beer and browses for something worth watching on television. He knows he needs to keep Lydia on a slow simmer. If he replies as soon as he gets her messages the pleasurable sexual tension between them will snap like an old knicker elastic. He blocks Sylvie, who is sending worried, increasingly hysterical messages. He scatters crumbs everywhere as he munches the crisps, thinking about how Sylvie would shriek if she could see him now, how she would bombard him with insults and threats before nuzzling against him like a little girl and insisting he say I love you. It feels good, being on his own. He has enough money to pay for another night here, not counting the watch that he hasn't sold yet, he has enough to survive for several days. Little Lydia Bazooka will have to be patient.

I FINK U FREEKY AND I LIKE YOU A LOT – THE SOUND OF DIE ANT-
WOORD floats vaguely in the background. The bar is rammed. On
her smartphone screen – cracked because she dropped it even
though she'd only just got it back – Lydia is simultaneously keeping track of her Instagram, Facebook and Twitter notifications.
It is compulsive. Infobesity. Tonight, she's waiting for a message
from Vernon Subutex. It's a work-related thing. He's more or less
agreed to meet up with her. But there is nothing work-related
about her excitement. She wants him she wants him she wants
him and she's not imagining it: he is flirting with her. She has
spent the past forty-eight hours glued to her Facebook page –
every paltry "Like" is a pelvic thrust, every comment an orgasm,
and every private message drives her into a frenzy. There has been
nothing explicit about their exchanges, but she could swear he's
on the same wavelength: sex, sex, sex. But since Saturday, he has
only briefly logged into Facebook to drop a random "Like". She
stares at his Facebook page, wondering what the fuck he's up to.
She hopes he hasn't changed his mind. Apart from the fact he's
got her horny, she needs to see him for her book. Because right
now, workwise, she's not exactly off to a good start.

At her table, everyone is talking about telephone company call
centres, each has a disaster story, complete with the usual jokes
about the accents of the technical advisers. The line-up at her table

is not exactly ideal; Lydia doesn't like to be seen with people who are less than extraordinary. She does not believe in cosy relationships anymore than she would favour a pair of Nikes over stilettos. Trainers may be more comfortable and better for your back, but you make more of an impression in a pair of fuck-me heels. Friendships are the same: if people on the outside are not jealous, you're sitting at the wrong table. Right now, for example, she's just Ms Nobody sitting at a table with a bunch of badly dressed randoms. No potential kudos here.

Test message from Cassandre – they're at the Mécano. Since she knows that this factoid alone will not be enough to convince Lydia to shift her arse, and since Cassandre wants her to come because she figures that Lydia will either have some coke on her or, failing that, the number of a dealer, she sends a second S.M.S.: "Paul's just arrived. Alone."

Okay. Lydia clicks off her iPhone, slips it into the pocket of the Balenciaga bag she always keeps on her lap – her one designer handbag cost her a kidney, if it gets stained or someone nicks it, she'll immolate herself.

She doesn't have any coke. Her dealer is still on holiday. When he's not at some wedding in Normandy, he's visiting his mother in the south of France, shopping in Amsterdam, seeing a friend in Berlin or at a wedding in Toulouse. Not to mention the fact that he disappears over Christmas, at Easter and for six weeks during the summer. A hundred and ten euros a gram it cost last time. Hardly surprising that you never see dealers campaigning for decriminalisation. It would make it harder for them to triple prices in the space of six months. A hundred and ten euros a gram – she half expected the friends she was buying for to throw her out of the party. Actually, he charged a hundred euros a gram, but Lydia figured that since she had to trek all the way out to Saint-Ouen, and she was the one wandering around carrying ten grams of coke, it was only fair that the others club together to buy a gram for her. But at €110, eyebrows were raised. Especially as the coke wasn't particularly good. In fact, even calling it coke was a private joke; it was speed. By three in the morning they needed to dig out boxes of man-size tissues since everyone was on the brink of nasal collapse. Who knows what the hell it had been cut with. But the fact remains that, tonight, she has no dealer.

Lydia leaves the bar without saying goodbye to anyone, as though she is just stepping out for a smoke. Tomorrow no-one will be in a fit state to remember that she slunk away like a thief. Whereas if she mentions she is leaving, there is a risk she'll end up being forced to drag them all to the Mécano like a ball and chain.

It takes a certain dose of swagger to go from Bastille to Ober-kampf on foot in six-inch heels and a short skirt after eleven at night. All the arseholes in the city are on duty. Cops consider it their bounden duty to ruin the life of any girl walking by herself in the street. Avoid eye contact. Walk swiftly. Keep herself bolt up-right by imagining she has a sword in her Balenciaga, like Beatrix Kiddo. Keep her mouth shut; keep moving. The tongue clicks intended to attract her attention. The insults – hoe, slut, skank, cum-bucket, yo babe where you goin'? get yo' ass over here, racist bitch, I seen that big-assed booty of yours, be careful now babe, them lips would look real good wrapped round my dick. Never slow down. She loves guys, loves them pragmatically, energetic-ally, loves them with every inch of her skin and with what's inside her belly. But she would also love to kill a few of them. She wishes she had the licence – legitimate self-defence. There's a gang of you, following me around, threatening me, I whip out my sword and off with your heads. Lydia is used to it. You need chutzpah if you're going to be a hot piece of ass. You get no support from anyone on this earth. Not from the guys you hang with, not from the girls who are your friends and not from the guys you're not prepared to blow. One day on the boulevard Sébastopol, some fat guy grabbed her wrist and tried to force her to go with him, she pulled her hand away and said "Fuck off, freak", the guy flushed beet red and she could tell he was about to go ballistic and whack her. He forced her to apologise. She complied, and then she beat it. In all the time he had her cornered, threatening her, she saw not a single person slow down or even glance in her direction. He could have kicked her to death there on the pavement and people would have looked the other way.

She walks into the bar. Ty Segall streaming from the speakers. Lydia looks round to find Cassandre's table, Paul smiles when he sees her. There are no chairs free so he squeezes closer to his neighbour on the bench to make room. She slides in next to him, careful not to show her gratitude. He is not particularly buff. But he's sexy. You can never tell, there are some guys you just want to screw. She likes the cool swagger he has when he tries to pick up girls. He is not pushy, he's not rushed. But he gets straight to the point. Lydia blanks him, her upper body turned towards Cassandre, filling her in about seeing Les Chacals live, the piss-poor sound system, the gawky teenagers doing some sort of post-pogo that was pathetic but touching, the songs that all sound the same, the first song is a slap in the face because they can really fucking play, the groove is tight, but by the sixth song, the effects have worn off and you're heading to the bar to get a beer. Under the table, where no-one can see, her leg is pressed against Paul's, their thighs nestling together comfortably without their faces betraying the slightest emotion. Lydia glances around her, smiling, serene. She has butterflies in her stomach, she wants to take him in her mouth in a mixture of excitement and gratitude – and she thinks it is awesome that he wants to do the same thing. All the same, she checks her iPhone: still no word from Vernon. It's a pain. Paul sees her looking.

"You waiting for someone?"

"No. Just checking. Thing is, I'm writing this biography of Alexandre Bleach, and I'm expecting a message from a friend of his – we were supposed to meet for an interview but he's stood me up . . ."

Their ankles are entwined; their hands, above the table, play no part. God, she loves his eyes – the way he can smile with just his eyes. For months now they've been circling each other without ever finding the right time. She feels herself getting wet and that excites her even more. She never expected him to be so direct. She has a thing for geeky guys, she has techniques to help them make the first move, but when they know what they want, it's amazing. Cassandre is watching them, but nothing in their behaviour hints at what is happening outside the frame. She claims to think it's disgusting that Lydia is constantly cheating on her boyfriend, Pierre. But mostly it is that Cassandre is too pretty to sleep with just anyone. She is selective, it goes with her physique. But in the end, she feels as though she is being conned. In not making the most of life. She is right. If playing the unattainable icon means spending your nights bored rigid and alone in bed to be virtuous while your senior vice president executive-class boyfriend is constantly abroad on business, you might be better off being some random girl who can live it up and shag every available guy worth fucking. They won't be young for long, and they are at that perfect age when their hotness is not tinged with pathos.

Paul whispers in her ear in a neutral tone:

"Sorry I haven't messaged you on Facebook for a while, my girlfriend is completely paranoid about me talking to other girls."

"She's jealous?"

"Hell on earth."

"She's got good reason. My boyfriend is jealous too."

Under the table, their legs press together and slowly rub against each other, each millimetre of touching skin declaring that they plan to fuck like rabbits. This countdown to ecstasy is nerve-racking. Never before has Lydia been so keenly aware of her knee as she is now while it seeks its mate. Cassandre leans over the table and asks in a low voice:

"Got any . . . *farlopa?*"

Ever since she spent six days in Barcelona, she cannot bring herself to say yayo or Charlie, or even cocaine – only *farlopa*. Lydia leans in and shakes her head:

"*Nada.* You interested? I've a contact who usually hangs out in a bar near here. Want me to go check?"

Yes, Cassandre is interested. She has trouble getting through an evening without a line or three. She insists that she is a casual user. But when there's no nose candy, she would happily call up the whole world to get some. This is the perfect excuse, Paul grabs his jacket:

"If you've got a contact, I'm in too. You want me to come with?"

Cassandre is so focused on powdering her nose that she doesn't notice anything strange. Usually, she is more perceptive than this. And more pervy. But she's so desperate for a line she doesn't catch on.

Outside, they walk a little way, still talking about the last gig by Gossip, then turn the corner, Paul spots a couple going into a building and has the presence of mind to stick his foot in the door, still chatting to Lydia, as though one of them is heading home and just finishing the conversation before calling the lift. The couple barely notice, they take the stairs without looking back. Paul drags Lydia into the hallway, there is a nook behind the lift. This is their first kiss, and they are just drunk enough for alcohol to make their movements fluid, but not so drunk it makes them do sordid stuff. Tomorrow, she will remember each particle of this moment. Because this is the only thing that interests her in life, but it interests her deeply: the first time they kiss, the first time he pushes up her jumper and lays a hand on her bra, his fingers fumbling to unhook it, to get it out of the way, the first time she pressed her hand flat against his cock through his trousers and he was so hard that she thought she might pass out, the first time he flexed his wrist to press his palm against her pussy and immediately slipped two fingers inside her, that he took her, fingering her like she had never been fingered before and she came on the spot, standing behind the lift, pelvis thrust up towards him, staring into his eyes so he could see the effect he was having on her. She wanted to suck him off right here in the hallway, but he whispered "can we not go back to yours?" and she said sure, my boyfriend's not there. They went out to look for a taxi. The madness and the mundane begin to merge again. On the way there, Paul compliments her on her writing. She expected him to be more kinky. Not the sort to say nice things when you open your bed to him. He is adorable. This is confirmed when they get to her place, rip off their clothes and get down to fucking. He is gentle, patient and attentive. She is disappointed. Too much foreplay. It's not a total disaster, she likes the way he moves, his smell, their bodies are content to mesh and rub against each other. But if they were going to stick to kids' stuff, they might as well have snogged when they left the bar and gone their separate ways. What she likes about sex with guys she's not dating to is the sense of danger, the feeling of something that she cannot control taking hold of her. She is always nice to the guys she screws, she's not the kind to signal to let them know she's bored. She patiently fakes it, and sometimes when you fake it you manage to convince yourself, but sometimes you don't.

Luckily, he leaves pretty quickly. He was probably bored too. She had expected it to be more interesting with him. She rejects her itchy nightdress in favour of an old Ramones T-shirt and pulls on thick woolly socks. She sits down at her computer. No messages from Subutex. With nothing better to do, she trawls the web.

Turns out Gérard Depardieu is a Russian. Brilliant. The last straw. Okay, so France is a shit-tip, but to go trading in your passport for a Russian one . . . That said, in the interview, Depardieu doesn't sound particularly pissed off, he claims to be French, Russian and – coming soon! – Belgian. So, all sorted now, are we? Maybe he feels that forcing his whole family into the film industry didn't piss off enough people. You're right, Gérard, your junkie son would have got much better care in a dictatorship. Clearly, being part of the select group of French apparatchiks was not classy enough for him. Lydia would have loved to be the daughter of someone in the business. You see them everywhere – Guy Bedos' kids, Higelin's brood, the Sardous and the Audiards, then you've got the Lennons and the Coppolas – and now you've got the parents bitching that people don't make enough effort. She needs to click on something else before she bursts into tears. Okay, Putin is sexy. Putin is all the sexier because he's one powerful motherfucker, but even if he wasn't, he would still be sexy. Stripped to the waist, riding a horse, he's seriously buff. Thighs pressed tight against the horse's flanks. It conjures so many images. Lydia, like all women, is susceptible to spurious reasoning. She's never slept with a Russian. She has so much yet to achieve.

She is muttering to herself, as usual, bent over her screen. Paul has already sent her three texts. She would never have expected him to be like this. Clingy.

She gets up and goes to the cupboard. Milk chocolate, crisps, roasted salted peanuts, a *galette des rois* (serves six) from Día, a jar of ersatz Nutella. She spent half her salary on this. She needs fat. Even sweets and desserts have to contain fat. She starts with the chocolate. A whole bar while staring at her screen. She eats, without gorging, but without pausing either. She would be better off on crack than these bouts of bulimia. A month ago, she thought of these binges as unhealthy gluttony. A way of making herself throw up several times during the night was the only way to eat and stay thin. She is slim. She has no choice: she is not particularly pretty. She needs at least one thing that makes her attractive.

It was Sophie, a girl her age who works for *Grazia* who first mentioned the word bulimia in her presence. It was during a press junket to Seattle, they were staying in a swish hotel: they met over the buffet breakfast. Seeing Lydia refill her plate several times, Sophie flashed her a knowing smile: "You make yourself throw up? Me too." Surprised by the question, Lydia did not have time to deny it. Sophie giggled. "A couple of bulimics at buffet breakfast, we're going to have a wild time you and me!" And they organised a plan of attack, croissants, muffins, cold meats and cheese. They practically had to be dragged out of the restaurant – and between courses they would go to the toilets to throw up. Bulimia. Lydia had never thought to associate this word to what she did in private. Bulimia. Fuck. That's all I need . . .

Every thirty seconds she clicks on the rosaliethatslife tab, glances at her Facebook profile. All she can think about is the moment when Vernon Subutex will log on and overwhelm her with "Likes", maybe give her a virtual orgasm by leaving a couple of comments on her timeline. In the past four days, this is all she has been doing – checking online for something that might make her react. Radio silence. She is in agony.

Sulkily, she launches Word. She has to start writing this book at some point. Then she logs in to her bank, checks her balance, double-checks every transaction, gets up to look for a God Is My Co-Pilot C.D., follows a flame war on Twitter without knowing what it's about, has her cards read on tarot.com then remembers she has to send off a cheque for the rent, fills it in, slips it into an envelope and leaves it to one side because she can't be bothered to look for the address of the letting agent. She has the attention span of a jumping bean. She goes back to the blank Word document.

Most of what she has done since starting work on this book has been developing a work schedule. The editor who commissioned it has not got the first idea who Alex was. Lydia cannot understand how he came up with the idea. She googled the publishing house – not very Rock the Casbah, as it turns out – before heading to her meeting with the editor. He's got a fifteen-year-old daughter who has been banging on at him about Alex. He wanted to publish a book she would read for a change.

Over lunch, he freaked her out. He was wearing this really tacky suit, all that was missing was the tie, and his manners were like something from before the First World War. He had made enquiries before contacting her, meaning he had looked at photographs of her online. And he liked her. Lydia is not exactly backward in coming forward, but when he started coming on to her in his subtle, convoluted way, she had to wonder if it was a joke. People actually sleep with guys like this? She does not even want to think about what kind of socks he is wearing.

The editor is weird. He does not watch television, rarely uses the internet. He lectured her about e-book rights: "You're not prepared to accept the same terms for e-book and paperback? Authors always assume they can earn more on e-book rights, arguing that there are no warehouse costs, no shipping costs, no booksellers ... But do you realise how much it costs to develop bleeding-edge technology? We are a vital part of that research." Lydia was relieved that Apple and Amazon could count on the solidarity of editors and their authors. The idea of small businesses like his surviving on their own clearly terrified this guy. Brilliant. He had obviously never even heard of the music business. If he had, he might wonder whether he really wanted to be part of the carnage.

So, this guy who has never listened to pop, to rock, to funk wants a book about Alex Bleach. She managed to exploit the vagueness of the situation to negotiate an advance of three thousand euros on signature. The contract arrived by mail the following day. She signed in a heartbeat. And in that case, she did not leave the envelope sitting on her desk for two weeks. There is another three thousand due, when she delivers the manuscript. She needs to write fast.

It was Kemar who prepared her. Without him, she would never have asked for so much money. He popped by to give her a dose of courage the night before her meeting. He knows nothing about publishing, he works as an engineer for Numéricable. Lydia adores him. In her private top ten of lovers, he ranks third, no question. It's unusual for her to want to see a casual fuck-buddy for so long. Either you're in a relationship or you just screw each other senseless three or four times, anything in between eventually becomes complicated. And boring. Except with Kemar. He's got a machine-gun sense of humour, he comes out with two gags a second that are funny enough to make you piss yourself. He's built like a brick shithouse but his dick is no bigger than a Vietnamese spring roll, he's ugly as a troll but he's the best fuck in the world. He's so good in bed, you can't remember what you did with anyone else. She is not the only one who thinks so. The guys all wonder what he does to women. They've got good reason. The girls wonder too. Every time he leaves her place, she feels better than she does after two hours of Bikram yoga: her chakras are completely balanced. She is still floating the day after. He rarely drops round, but he never quite forgets her. And, aside from his gift for sex, he gives great advice. He did a coaching session with her just before her meeting with the editor: ten thousand euros. She is the expert on Alex Bleach, she has contacts no-one else has, the guy was a living legend, his fans are obsessive, they'll rush out to buy the book. Ten grand, minimum. She should ask for fifteen. Lying naked on top of the duvet, chin resting on her clasped hands, she listened to him, sceptical and bewildered, as he prowled around the bed, insisting that she ask for fifteen thousand and not accept anything less than ten. She got six. Without his valuable advice, she would have cheerfully settled for a thousand.

She sat herself at Pierre's desk. In the thirty square metres they share, they have managed to create two desk spaces. Everything else happens on the bed. They perch on the end and eat dinner in front of the television. Then they shuffle back two metres, prop themselves against the headboard, snuggle under the duvet, and watch some more. When they have visitors, they turn the two desk chairs to face the coffee table at the end of the bed while they sit in their usual spot. It is rare that they have more than two guests, but when it does happen, people sit wherever they can find a space between the desks.

She loves sitting at Pierre's desk. His chaos is inspiring. The weird plastic goblin with the red cap. The fat blue Ice-watch with the broken strap. The AC/DC zippo.

He is away for two weeks. Working at a dance festival in Dijon. Doing the sound. That's his job. She is often on her own. Well, often without him. She doesn't talk to him about what she does when he is not here. She thinks he probably suspects, and if not, it doesn't matter. Things work fine the way they are. Before, with other guys, it used to cause a lot of problems; there would inevitably be a night when she didn't come home and didn't let them know in advance. Pierre is often away for three months at a time, she has all the time in the world to be a dirty stop-out. When he is home, she is so desperate to spend time with him that she never dares to sleep around.

She is a freelance rock journalist. The print media is dying on its feet and the music business with it. She signs her pieces Lydia Bazooka. When she published her first article, she was high on life for months. She's over all that. A woman in the music industry. Whatever she does, whatever she writes, she is treated like a weirdo and a moron.

She never got to fuck Alex Bleach. When he died, she was devastated. That voice. Those chords. He was a god. She never thought about sleeping with Alex Bleach. It would have been blasphemy. He fills her with infinite gratitude. Before she listened to his records, she had no idea she could feel such deep emotions; Alex opened her up. It was someone within her that he summoned, some connection to mysterious spiritual forces whose presence she loved, even if the intensity of emotion could be painful. He opened a door onto the extraordinary. She had interviewed him several times, for different magazines. He seemed to like her. Until one day, on a music website, she published a particularly wild article – faced with a mood of general indignation she admitted it was a fantasy, and as far as she was concerned she had simply expressed her fascination with him. Alex Bleach read it – and vowed never to see her again.

Years of loyal, faithful service, sleepless nights spent making sure every article was faultless, hours spent hanging around in hotel bars, flights to go and see him play in Quimper or halfway round the world.

All so that one day *Match* would send her to cover the recording of his new album. Lydia was thrilled – in the print media, *Match* was a freelancer's wet dream. Then the *coup de grâce*: the magazine's music editor phoned the day before the interview. Bleach's manager had called to say: "anyone but Lydia Bazooka". She got the call while she was waiting for her treatment session at Body Minute. The world came crashing down. It is impossible to comprehend the anguish of a rock critic who has fallen out of favour with her idol.

It went on for two years. Having to read interviews with other journos, having to buy tickets to go to his gigs and avoid wandering like a lost soul around the dressing rooms. Two years of obscurity before a day came when the press officer put her name forward for the official webcam interview – the interview that would be posted on the artist's official website, and even though she was off-camera, it was her voice asking the questions so everyone could witness her readmission to the inner circle. Finally, they picked up their old conversation.

It was to be his last album. Lydia did not know this.

Among the people she hangs with, it's difficult to brag about the fact that she is writing a biography of Alexandre Bleach. It's too middle-class hipster for the baby fascists of her generation. Alex is old hat. She doesn't give a shit. She takes it on the chin.

In an interview with a journalist from *Vogue*, two years before his death, Alex said, "It gives me no pleasure to imagine boatloads of little white kids trying to reach Egypt because there are rumours of jobs in the United Arab Emirates, I don't get a hard-on picturing them being gunned by police as soon as they reach the shore, or stoned to death by Muslims who think blond boys stink and blonde girls are whores. But that's how it will be. Europe is finished, tomorrow we'll be the immigrants. I'd like to imagine we might try something else. But I don't believe it will come to that either. That's the one great advantage of contaminated water – a tumour doesn't give a fuck whether you kneel or stand to pray or whether you're broke or loaded. A tumour eats away at your brain, and that's that."

The interview was a big hit on nationalist French websites.

Lydia goes through every interview in detail. Unable to actually write, she immerses herself in her subject. She listens to Alex's voice on her headphones. She enjoys spending time with him. Every day, she reworks the list of people she needs to meet. Those she has contacted have all refused to cooperate. They claim it's too soon. What they mean is that, as a journalist, she's not famous enough. Lydia knows her subject, she knows that Vernon meant a lot to Alex, though they were only three years apart, it was at Revolver that Alex discovered rock music, a fact he never forgot.

She would like to track down the fuckwit who came up with the idea that every headline on the Yahoo! homepage should be a riddle – the "incredible discovery at Chicago airport" – the psychopath who came up with the most irritating clickbait formula imaginable by not telling readers what the article is about.

She clicks on the Facebook tab again. Yes! Vernon has left her a private message. If she's up for it, he can swing by for a coffee and she can tell him what she wants. Oh, she's up for it! She is *so* up for it.

PAMELA WENT BY THE RUE MARSEILLE TO PICK UP DANIEL'S favourite bread. The cold snap came on suddenly, she turns the radiators up full blast, the studio feels like a cosy womb. He makes the green tea, it is a ritual, before uncorking the Jägermeister and skinning up the first spliffs – they are having a body-pampering afternoon. Pamela Kant talks about her latest brilliant idea, writing a children's book, a guide to porn. Since they're gorging on porn on the internet before they even learn to read, she thinks it only sensible to tell them what it is.

"But it's true, though, you can't BitTorrent a series without seeing some babe sucking cock, someone's got to talk to kids about this stuff, am I right? When it comes to illustrations, I think we should go with something cutesy . . ."

"But what exactly are you going to explain?"

"I was thinking about starting with a brief history, the seventies, state censorship, the eighties, video recorders, the nineties, camcorders . . . up to the internet. That way, you can give them a list of the classics, so they can start out with soft-porn flicks . . . after that I'd explain how you shoot a scene, the make-up, how many people are on set . . . Take the mystique out of it."

Daniel carefully pours the dregs of his green tea into the bin and then rinses out the filter. He has always been a little O.C.D. But she knows that when he takes his time like this it is to avoid giving her an honest answer. Pamela has spent years trying to come up with the book that she should write. All the major porn stars have published at least one book. She refuses to be the only hard-core hustler not to swan around bookshops doing signings. For a while, she toyed with the idea of a biography of Gypsy Rose Lee but gave up on it based on the lack of interest on the project. Daniel points out:

"It's a brilliant idea. But I'm not sure the public are ready for it . . . The thought of a girl who's done hardcore porn talking to their kids might make them uncomfortable . . . you know what people are like."

"Yeah. That's the point. It's not like *they're* going to tell their kids about this stuff. People are all the same, the minute you mention porn, the light goes out, their minds glaze over, it's like their intelligence goes on holiday. Do you spend time on YouPorn?"

"Never."

"I'm not surprised. All you care about is pretending you've never done hardcore porn."

She feels like being aggressive because she finds it difficult to talk, even to Daniel. She spends a lot of time on YouPorn. She feels like the wicked stepmother in "Snow White": she goes onto porn-sharing websites to see if her films are still in among the "Most Viewed" website on the screen, who is the hottest babe on the scene . . . She stopped filming a decade ago, but people still remember her, she has held out much longer than anyone else in the business. But her star is fading. She is used to the idea. The golden era of true porn stars is over. These days, girls on Facebook call themselves porn stars when they've only shot three homemade flicks . . . The last time she was online, she came across this film.

The girl was probably Hungarian. She was tied to a bed. Some guy was pouring neat vodka down her throat. She was not consenting. She was begging, you didn't need subtitles to understand what she was saying. It was a gang-bang, the guys fucking her had put paper bags over their heads to remain anonymous. The girl was sobbing. She wasn't pretending so as to make the whole scene more exciting. Things had barely started when she realised she was no longer in control. Almost as soon as the filming started, she wanted to stop. Pamela would like to talk to Daniel about the film, if there is anyone who might understand what she feels and not try to humiliate her, it is him. But she felt so degraded by what she had seen. She cannot bring herself to talk about it. This is the nature of shame. It leaves you speechless.

She imagines the feminist sluts gleefully rubbing their hands: See? We told you, sex is always hostile to women. All the old biddies, the ageing grannies who only noticed their snatch when they were giving birth would have a field day, they always refused to distinguish between choosing to be a porn star and being raped. But Pamela knows it is not the same thing. This is the first time she has ever seen a rape, and it has nothing to do with what she used to do.

She got into porn in the early 2000s. She was lucky. She experienced the last glory days of the profession. She earned a good living – more than she ever dreamed of earning. There were a few arseholes, but you get them in every job – but mostly, it was a friendly environment. Back then, people still talked about porn stars. There was a lot of rivalry between the girls – though they got along well – they all wanted to be the best in the business. Pam wanted to make a name for herself. Not everyone could make it big, but it was not particularly complicated. Eliminate the competition, capture the biggest market share, maximise your competitive advantages – an economics teacher at school had left a marked impression on her, she had a clear idea of what she needed to do to be the best. It worked out pretty well.

Giving it up had been hard, as it was for all the girls who did porn. People still recognised her in the street, but she missed the atmosphere of being on set, she missed the photo sessions and the intoxicating feeling of being the centre of attention, of being able to deliver what is expected of you. She loved being treated like a legend, like a movie star.

Afterwards, the most difficult thing is realising that you never really give up. You are cut off from the business, you lose the friends, the easy money – but you are marked for life. While she was making porn, she only hung out with people in the business and disapproval was only a vague concept. But wearing the badge of 'Porn Star' every day among ordinary people is a different matter. She would rather die than actually say the words, but good guys always win in the end: they make your life so difficult that even someone like Pam is forced to finally face it – she would have been better off keeping to herself. Ten years on, she still cannot go shopping in a supermarket without being recognised by some stupid bitch who glowers at her – women are her harshest judges. Those who settle for what is expected of them despise strong women. If they could, they would burn their husbands' idols. They know their men get hard at the thought of Pamela Kant and it sickens them. The porn industry has become the dreary business imagined in their sick fantasies.

Two months ago, she took a job doing hair and make-up for

a film. She thought she might use the opportunity to take some photos of the girls. Shooting started at eight a.m., so the actresses had to be in make-up by six. Everyone was still on the set at three o'clock the next morning. Of the five actresses, two were gorging on laxatives to stay thin, they had vicious stomach aches all day and their skin was shot to shit. Another girl's boyfriend spent all day plaguing her with text messages asking for nude selfies from the set. And she sent them. One had a boyfriend who was constantly calling in a jealous rage because he worried that every guy on set had a bigger cock than he did, though as they talked Pam found out that *he* was the one who got her into porn, even set up her first shoot . . . and he was only thirty years older than her. The fifth girl was fine, but she has already been filming for five years, the porn industry is done with her, she's worked with every director, every producer, it's time for her to give up gracefully . . . In this business, it is important to manage your exit. This is something Pamela learned from Coralie, Ovidie, Nina Roberts and girls with names like Elodie . . . It is important to get out before you start accepting films you should not accept. What shocked her most is how freaked out all the girls were by anal. This is not a profession you can do if you hate sodomy. It's like saying you're allergic to flour but you want to be a baker. Listen up, girl, for pity's sake find another job.

Daniel tucks into the box of candied chestnuts. He eats like a pig and never puts on a gram of fat. She cannot live without him, they are constantly together, but she sometimes finds him exasperating. He knows this. Daniel has transitioned. F2M. Pamela had never heard of the term until Déborah, her best friend, decided to become Daniel. Even the choice of a first name can be very confusing. It came on her like an urge to piss. Déborah and Pam had got into porn at the same time and left the business together. They were good friends. They had been through a lot together – some hilarious, some not so fun. And then one day, wham. "I'm taking testosterone." Shit. At first, Pamela didn't even know what she meant. She thought testosterone was something you took to stop painful periods, or to lose weight – Déborah was carrying a few extra pounds at the time. Nothing heralded, or justified this decision. It meant – simply – transitioning to become a guy. Pamela read up on it, usually when people do this, it's been eating away at them for a long time – like "I've always known I was a guy trapped in a woman's body". In cases like that, fine – it makes sense. But Déborah . . . honestly, she was just doing it to piss people off. "Why are you doing this?" "I felt like trying. I've got tattoos, I've done porn, I've smoked crack. Why shouldn't I become a guy?" Because it's not the same kind of thing, you idiot . . . You don't give yourself daily testosterone injections for shits and giggles. Pamela immediately predicted it would be hell on earth – illness, depression, regrets, feeling out of place . . . not to mention the aesthetic aspect – for fuck's sake, woman, don't you realise how dumb men are? Do you really want people to think you're one of them?

But what is most annoying is how happy Daniel is being Daniel. The illness, the depression the regrets and so forth may come some day, but for the moment it's mostly . . . little bow tie, short-leg jeans, visible socks, impressive muscles, thin hipster moustache . . . Daniel simulates fulfilment so well that it is difficult not to be dubious. He had a mastectomy without a second thought, using the same absurd logic, "I had breast implants, why shouldn't

I have my breasts removed?" If you go around doing everything you could possibly do there is no end to it, but, okay . . . . Today, he is wearing a men's black Dior jacket over a little Fred Perry shirt. With the tattoos, the delicate features and the shock of dark slicked-back hair, he has a lot of style. And a lot of money. He managed to get a job in one of the first e-cigarette shops in Paris. Pamela would not have bet a centime on the fake fag business, who wants to smoke a fountain pen? But it was bigger than anyone could have imagined. And Daniel, rather than staying on as a sales assistant and taking home minimum wage, became regional manager responsible for expanding sales outlets in Paris. The job was a gold mine. It drives Pamela half-crazy: it would never have happened without the transition. As a former porn star, Déborah would never have got a job in sales. Or she would have been fired as soon as they found out, and you try taking a case for wrongful dismissal and arguing that your boss discriminated against you because everyone can go online and watch you suck off three guys in a row! And even if Déborah had changed the way she looked, let's say she got a nose job, changed her hairstyle, put on twenty kilos – so much that she was unrecognisable . . . no-one would have given the job of business development manager to a woman. Daniel told her every last detail of this meteoric promotion, shocked to discover that it was all based on backslapping, laddish jokes, being more comfortable around other men and evenings spent smoking cigars . . .

She finds Daniel's pragmatism depressing. But he is still her best friend. She cannot live without him. To cap it all, Daniel is attracted to women. It's the last straw. Déborah had a heart like an artichoke – "a leaf for anyone, but a meal for no one" – she loved every man, one at a time, she could even be infatuated . . . but Daniel evolved: you should see the way he has with girls. So when a cute little dark-haired girl offered to iron his shirts and do his shopping, he thought to himself – why not? I got fucked like a bitch by the finest stallions of my generation, I've got a good basic knowledge, I know what to do to fulfil a woman who likes that kind of guy. Self-confident, a macho dickhead. Pamela's pride as a first-class courtesan is wounded: she has never used a strap-on, it was never part of her artillery. And now she gets the impression that Daniel knows things about sex that she doesn't. The very idea is intolerable.

There's no knowing what will happen when you're with Daniel. He struts in the Métro, preens on café terraces, dances at parties – and no-one can quite work out why his face seems oddly familiar. That said, minus the breasts and sporting a little beard, a porn star, even a famous one, can be difficult to recognise. So while monsieur swaggers around town, Pamela is forced to go to the post office as soon as it opens when no-one is about, shop for groceries on line, and stream movies at home . . .

Pamela is not secretly jealous that he has made such a success of everything he set out to do in recent months: she is openly jealous. And it makes Daniel laugh, though he puts up with her even when her hostility becomes insufferable. Because one thing has not changed during the transition: they still need each other. Pamela curls up on the sofa while he attacks the washing-up. She never really cared about housework, whereas he cannot bear to spend the evening in a messy studio.

"Oh, I meant to say, I've got news. Guess who contacted me on Facebook?"

"When did you start reading your Facebook messages?"

"I don't actually read them, but from time to time I open them – just imagine, Booba tried to get in touch and I didn't know."

"Booba got in touch?"

"I said I've got news, I didn't say my world got turned upside down and I'm getting married."

"Who, then?"

"It's unbelievable. I'm looking through my messages and I see the photo of this girl in a veil who's written to me, like, forty-five times . . . at first I thought it was some pathetic little Arab girl looking to make halal porn and wanting me to give her contacts . . . I was going to block her, but I was so fucking pissed off with her bombarding me with chat requests, I decided to troll her. Guess who she is?"

"Pam . . . how do you expect me to guess?"

"She's Satana's daughter. Aïcha."

"Satana had a daughter? How old is she?"

"Just turned eighteen. Satana used to go on about her daughter all the time . . . the kid didn't live with her, the father got custody."

"You're right, that does ring a bell."

At the height of their careers, Vodka Satana and Pamela Kant were like Oasis and Blur, the Beatles and the Stones: twin superstars jostling for first place. One would turn up on Cauet's show, flashing her tits and badmouthing the competition and the next day the other one would be on the set of "Le Grand Journal" wearing an ultra-low-cut dress bitching about her rival. They had never done a scene together. If Satana heard that Pamela was working on a film, she would hike up her fee and keep hiking until the deal fell through. They had cordially loathed each other until, one summer, they found themselves in Los Angeles, flat broke, and were forced to share an apartment . . . at which they – briefly – became inseparable. Satana had had a remarkably short career. She was famous for her legs which were 1.20 metres, slender, perfect. She claimed to be Lebanese, but actually her family were *blédards* back in Oran. She was the only actress Pamela had ever seen be more of a diva on set than herself. Guys didn't like shooting with her, Satana was so rude to them that even the hardiest had trouble keeping it up. She could be emasculating or endearing as it suited her. She had her little favourites.

Satana had had a fling with the rock star Alex Bleach. She had appeared on the cover of *Voici*. Pamela thought she would never get over it. Their rivalry was over – Satana had made it into a different world. At the time, Bleach was breathtakingly beautiful. When he walked into a room, every girl felt the same thing – surrender. He had a high forehead, a firm jawline accentuated by meticulously trimmed designer stubble. On stage, he would quickly strip off his shirt to reveal banks of chiselled abs, bulging dorsals, a body for which anyone would sell their soul. Pamela rarely found herself flustered, when faced with her, men expected to be spurned. But Bleach had the beauty of a woman – too conscious of the effect he produced to be seduced.

Satana had stopped shooting porn, it was rumoured that these days she did private shows. Meaning she took advantage of her fame to turn tricks and charge a small fortune. Despite what amateurs might think, being a prostitute is very different from being a porn star. As an actress, you worry about the camera, the lighting, and your position, your partner is of no importance. As a prostitute, you are a lion-tamer. You have to get to know the beast, anticipate its reactions, know how to make it do what you want. Relinquish control, make the slightest mistake, and it will rip your arm off. Satana always liked wild animals, she was not afraid of them. Pamela, for her part, has never been particularly interested in men. They are too quick to humiliate themselves. She does not know a single one who is incorruptible. She hates them, not out of perversity, but because they're sheeple. She never understood how a woman as beautiful as Satana could still be obsessed with them. But something must have gone wrong – she was very young when she killed herself.

Daniel is cleaning the cafetière as though trying to make it look new – Pam pulls a face but says nothing – the coffee will taste of washing-up liquid. He asks:

"So what did she want from you, the daughter?"

"She said some girl came to see her father. Aïcha overheard the conversation. She was in her room, doing her homework, she wasn't supposed to be listening to what was going on in the living room . . . This girl was a journalist, she wanted to talk about Alex Bleach, and I don't know why, but my name came up in conversation . . ."

"Maybe because you and Satana were friends back in the day?"

"Anyway, the daughter googled my name, found out who I was . . . and she wrote to me and said 'I wanted to ask how you knew my mother'. Can you imagine how I felt?"

"So what did you tell her?"

"Do you get what I'm saying? The kid doesn't even know who her mother was . . . Her father never talked about her."

"Really? In his shoes, I'd be the same."

"I was outraged. The kid's a grown woman now, fuck's sake, she has a right to know. It's not like her mother was in the Waffen-SS!"

"You see, we're back to your idea of a porn guide for toddlers . . . if you'd written one, the father could have casually left it lying on the kitchen table and when the kid said 'Papa, what's a gang-bang?' he could have said, 'It was one of your mother's greatest talents'."

"You're cheerful this evening."

"I'm serious. It must be difficult telling your daughter that her mother was a porn star. Having to tell a kid: your mother committed suicide, that's bad enough . . . but having to go into detail . . . I can understand why he wasn't in any hurry to tell her."

"We must know, like, forty porn actresses who've got kids, and they're all fine."

"Yeah, but they're alive . . . Don't say you told this kid on Face-book her mother's porn name?"

"No. I looked at the photos of the daughter and I realised why I was upset . . . She looks like the sort of kid who stays up at night doing homework, she wears the veil, she's always sulking . . . it's not down to me to tell her."

"She wears a hijab? Satana wouldn't have been too impressed . . . That said, she always did have a sense of humour."

"Things have changed. In our day, if you wanted to shock people, you did porn, these days all you have to do is wear a veil."

"It's not the same thing . . . so you dodged the question?"

"Yeah, I told her I knew her mother because we both loved dancing and we'd often see each other at parties . . . The girl sounded disappointed that her mother went out dancing. So, she's definitely not ready. Fucking pain in the arse, this whole generation. Hope they all die from global warming, and soon."

She is often depressed by young girls who look like Mormons or wear stupid veils. When it's not religion, it's family, or managing to remain a virgin until you get married . . . fundamentalist storybook romanticism. It's like they're determined to spend their lives making *râgouts* and *tartes aux pommes*.

DANIEL WILL NEVER GET USED TO THE PIGSTY OF PAM'S APARTMENT. Every time he spends the night there, he tidies up but by the time he comes back, chaos has reasserted itself.

Pam chats to him while she watches T.V., cradling her games console, playing Tetris with a bunch of Koreans. She has been playing the game since he first met her, at dazzling speed.

They both behave as though the relationship has not changed recently. But for the important difference that, these days, they could be a couple. Now that he is sleeping with women, he sees her differently. He is careful to avoid mentioning that he does not quite see her as he used to. She would consider it a betrayal. He cannot tell her the effect it has, taking testosterone, he constantly feels the urge to fuck. And they spend half of their evenings together. They are bound to end up together. It wouldn't matter whether he was a guy, a girl or a two-headed kangaroo – he is the only person she can bear to be with for three days straight. All it will take is allowing Pam the time to realise that she has been single for years, and that Daniel will never let anyone take his place. It is taking Pam some time to come to terms with the choice he has made.

It came as a blinding flash. One night they were at a Lydia Lunch gig at 104. The sound was shit, it was freezing cold and Deb went outside for a cigarette. Whirlpool baths in the courtyard were steaming in the darkness. Films were being projected onto the walls. She spotted a group passing a spliff around and ambled over, as though to join the conversation, and stood next to the person holding the joint. She chattered to the person on her right, a cute, little guy sporting a lot of ink. She had heard the expression 'trans' used for a girl who became a guy but she didn't make a distinction between transvestite and trans, she didn't give a shit, she assumed it meant a girl who dressed as a guy. It didn't bother her one way or the other. Later that night – at least five blunts and three beers later – she was still chatting to him, seduced but circumspect since the guy's girlfriend never took her eyes off him. And one of the other girls said, as the guy was heading inside to see the end of the gig – I thought you knew her from before? When I first knew her, she wore her hair in pigtails and everyone called her Corrine.

She instantly knew: she would do this. She began searching on the internet that same night. Deb was almost twenty-seven. She had already had several bodies. She had been an ordinary little girl with no particularly vivid memories before the age of ten. Then she had filled out. At first, she was just a little chubby, but she could still go to the swimming pool without people teasing her. She felt fat in the way certain girls are: horrified by a hideousness that she alone could see. Then, with puberty, she ballooned to become obese. It went on for four years, and every day was hell. People can behave how they like with fat kids. They can lecture them in the canteen, swear at them for eating in the street, give them horrid nicknames, taunt them if they ride a bicycle, ostracise them, give them advice on diets, tell them to shut up when they try to speak, laugh if they confess they wish that someone fancied them, glare and pull faces every time they appear. They can jostle them, pinch their belly, kick them – no-one will intervene. It was perhaps at this point that she learned to give up on gender: male or female, fat people suffer the same exclusion. Others are entitled to look down on them. And if they complain about the way they are treated, deep down everyone is thinking the same thing: eat less, you fat slob, at least try to make an effort to fit in. Deb's relationship to sugar was the same as it was to coke years later: she was hooked. She thought of nothing else. Sugary foods called to her in the night. She used to say this as a joke, but it was true: from the kitchen cupboards she would hear a bewitching air, she had to get out of bed, had to gorge herself. It was not a decision, it was an overpowering urge. After school, she would get home as quickly as she could, her parents were working and she pictured herself as a cute, chubby panda, slumped on the sofa. She spent the whole time watching television, she would get presents of boxed sets and retreat into another world. "Ally McBeal", "Sex and the City", and "Buffy" were closer to her reality than school. Sitting in front of the T.V. screen, she was a slim, elegant American girl.

At seventeen, a tyrannical dietician railroaded her onto a draconian diet. Like someone who had been waiting in vain for a train for five years, this time – for some reason – it worked: she managed to catch the train and within six months she was a different person. At that age, you can melt away even as you exploded in a season. Another new body. She had become overweight while still a little girl, from that lump of fat a rather pretty young woman emerged and when she looked at photographs in magazines and compared herself to them Deb realised that she was a fine specimen. She had elegant shoulders, pert, finely shaped breasts, a shapely waist, long legs and slender ankles. Having spent four years shunning mirrors, she could now stand in front of them for hours, discovering herself. But still she did not recognise herself: the girl in the mirror never became one with Deb. In fact, in her whole life, the mirror had never given her a true reflection. She would gaze at the body in the mirror and, whether obese, moustached or big-breasted, it was a stranger.

She had lost eighteen kilos in the space of six months. It made her furious that people's attitude to her could so quickly change according to how much weight she was carrying. Fat, she was happy to take on the role of the poor bitch, the scapegoat, the girl who gets slapped or humiliated to make others laugh, the one people turn to stare at if there is an unpleasant smell on the Métro. Okay, that was her – the fat girl. She had adapted to the role of the girl who needs to have a sense of humour and focus on other people's stories. She was used to it. But the fact that it could change so completely in such a short space of time left her furious. Now, suddenly, she was treated like a pretty girl. Fucking arseholes. Choosing clothes had been a nightmare, she practically had to apologise to sales assistants when asking whether they had something in her size, now all she had to do was reach out and slip something on – and everything fitted her perfectly. It was the same with people. She was so used to being nicer than other people to avoid being slapped or shunned, she was friendlier than a girl at a perfume counter. Now everything had changed. She only had to appear and everyone was kissing her arse. Because she was wearing a pretty dress. Because she had come back into line.

She was invited to parties, people squeezed up to make room for her in cafés, boys asked for her number so they could send timid text messages. Meanwhile her rage was a tumour gnawing at her bones, the size of a walnut at first it bloated and swelled to the size of a clenched fist, septic, suppurating, threatening to explode. And then she met Cyril. He was a taciturn boy who rarely smiled but he lit up when she was with him. In hindsight, Daniel can see that the guy was such a self-centred hick he was almost retarded, but when she first met him it was like stepping into a fairy tale. He was handsome, admired, respected. He liked her to wear simple black dresses and dizzyingly high heels that cost a fortune. He would straddle her and massage her back while telling her about crime novels he particularly liked. He was a smooth talker, he talked to her in a slightly condescending tone, little compliments that turned her head. Her anger transmuted into passion. There was sunshine, rides in his car, weekends in the country, nights when he D.J.'d and girls swarmed round him but he was no player, he was with her. These slivers of time glittered like shards of gold, it was the polar opposite of what she had experienced before she met him. She repressed the image that came to her, of the bird in the fairy tale impaling itself, pressing its throat onto a thorn. She knew that this sunny weightlessness could not be real. He treated her like a princess. He was spending ten times what he earned. The hotels the first-class trains the seafood restaurants the taxi rides the champagne for breakfast. She knew that he lied from time to time, that he owed a lot of money to a lot of people. She could tell something was not right. He could not afford this extravagant romanticism. She tried not to think about it.

And so, when he mentioned filming, she quickly gave in. As a favour to him. The poor guy was in deep shit. He was sincere, when he asked her to help him out, he believed what he was saying:

just this once, babe, I'm really sorry, after that, I've got a plan, I'll make up my losses. Just this once. She had never felt particularly attached to the stunning body that was now hers, she saw no problem making use of it. Just this once. For him. Besides, they would be doing the scenes together, and it did not seem particularly complicated. He swore that no-one else would touch her. He knew a guy who rented out his town house in Saint-Germain-en-Laye for filming. They played poker together. This was how he had come up with the idea. But at nine a.m., when they were supposed to film the scene, Cyril did not have an erection. The verdict of the professionals was final: "can't get it up", a complaint the crew were familiar with, and one for which there was no cure. Deb did not yet know that in the porn industry there are guys who can get it up and guys who can keep it up, and those men who can do both are never likely to be out of work. She had to do the scene with someone else. The director was happy with the results. He said she reflected the light well. Cyril was no longer gutted, his girl had done the business, he was proud.

She did a second scene, feeling more relaxed, the crew complimented her, at the time she did not realise that she was slipping on the skin of a new character, one that she would play for years. To change invariably means to lose a piece of yourself. After a period of adaptation, you feel it falling away. It is both a sadness and a relief. This was her continuing journey.

In the car on the way back, Cyril was considerate. He turned the music up full blast – a mind-blowing techno mix. He let his hand rest on her thigh. He loved her. He said nothing that needed to be said. She stared out of the window and watched the world flash past. A week later, there was another shoot, and he really was up shit creek, there were guys who would smash his face if he didn't pay them back, he adored her, could she *please* do it, just for him. She had been expecting this. And it was true, he did adore her. In this moment, their roles were reversed – from now on she was the star.

In the porn industry, she could measure her success by how hostile the other girls were to her. Everyone wanted to work with her. Cyril negotiated a great deal on her first boob job. Another transformation. She could not walk into a room anymore without people thinking about sex. All they could see were her breasts. And yet she could not manage to shed the two kilos that, in her mind, still separated her from absolute perfection.

She could tell that a lot of people on set used coke, but at first she did not touch the stuff. They were constantly disappearing to the toilets, passing each other little wraps of paper. When she finally fell, it was head first. She became thinner than she had ever thought possible. She would gaze at herself in the mirror. She could not believe her luck at inhabiting this body.

Once she got her nose into the stuff, she dumped Cyril within a fortnight, she was done with masochistic romance: she could not stand him helping himself to her emergency stash when she went to sleep. He infuriated her. He claimed to be her agent, but he never did a tap of work. He didn't book the shoots, didn't negotiate her fees, he spent his time on set swilling beer and joking. Sometimes, he would be helpful, go and fetch something for her, but it would never occur to him to leap to her defence when a director suddenly sprang something on her at the last minute – no way, I didn't come here to do a gang-bang, you know that perfectly well,

I was told this was a straight vanilla scene, so don't fucking think I'm about to take four guys up the arse, no, I said no, do you take me for a rookie or what? Just pick one of these four fuckwits and I'll give you one blow job, one anal scene, one money shot and you'll have to make do with that. No, it's not the fucking same thing. Yeah, right, you'll fuck up my career good style – like I haven't heard that before. Cyril had become surplus to requirement. With a gram of coke in her bag, she didn't need anyone. Good riddance.

Then she had met Pam, at a "salon of erotica" down the country. It was just after Satana killed herself. They spent all night ripping rails and talking about her. As dawn was breaking, Pam announced:

"I'm done with coke."

"Me too."

"Seriously?"

"I'm in if you are."

They caught the train home together and, two days later, Pam called her: "I'm still straight. You?" "Me too." They kept the pressure on each other, at first it wasn't a struggle, they both assumed it was just a temporary break. Then it became a curious sort of competition: you're still straight? Me too. They would meet up to talk about it, at first to humblebrag about how amazing it was, and how easy. But all too quickly admit how tough it was. But neither wanted to be the first to give in. As much to show they were strong as out of solidarity. But there was no point shitting themselves: life was a lot more interesting with coke than without. This was their gift to each other – they had managed to quit. Though for both of them, it was a long shot.

Pamela held up well – she got into exercise, she bought fitness

D.V.D.s and would park herself in front of the television counting off press-ups crunches squats cardio work . . . She was radiant. For Deb it was harder. She found dealing with quitting the business and quitting coke very difficult. She piled on weight, it was all she thought about. She was wary of the men she met. She no longer had money to take taxis everywhere and refused to take the Métro on her own. She often felt like crying.

Then there had been this concert. Lydia Lunch. The little transsexual. So cute. Deb instantly knew that this was her way out. She quickly realised that the trans community would take a dim view of her starting a testosterone course just to be rid of her old body. She lied to the endocrinologist, she regurgitated all the stories she had read online and managed to dodge the question when asked why, if she had always felt that she was a man, she had had a breast augmentation. This was not an interview, it was the Inquisition. Luckily, the guy doing the consultation was not into porn. She managed to dupe him. Gel, injections. She had not reckoned on the fact that she would change on the inside too. Her personality did not change, but the intensity of her emotions shifted. More diffuse than the effects of the drug, the readjustment was radical. What at first she had seen as a means of escape, a desperate attempt to get out of a situation she could no longer control, turned out to be the most inspired decision she had ever made. She had lied to other people in the trans community online – cutting and pasting their comments and passing them off as her own. Daniel was such a cool vehicle that she sometimes wondered: how could I be so lucky? Being Debbie the porn star had been fun, but being Daniel, the cute little guy everyone loved – that was the Rolls-Royce treatment. The pleasure of walking into a shop and being taken seriously, of chatting to other men and knowing they liked you. Before now, she had never realised how much men liked each other.

And Daniel is in love with Pam. Maybe Deb was before him. From that first night they spent together. But Daniel can admit it to himself. The next step is to admit it to her. Right now, they are binge-watching "Game of Thrones" and he is having trouble following the plot. "Is it me, or is it really complicated?" he says. Pam, not looking at the screen, still playing Tetris, snaps back, "It's you being stupid. It's completely obvious." Daniel opens the text message that has just appeared on his phone. He says:

"What was the name of the journalist, the one who went round to Satana's daughter's house?"

"She didn't give a name. She wanted to talk about Alex Bleach."

"Because I've just had a message from someone who calls herself the Hyena who wants to meet up to talk about Satana."

"Really? Show me. I don't believe it – you've had a nose job, you've changed gender, and you've changed your mobile number a hundred times, how the fuck did she track you down? You think this is something to do with Alex Bleach?"

"They can hardly blame Satana – she's been dead for years."

"That would be so unfair. So, what are you going to say?"

"Some chick who calls herself the Hyena? Nothing. I'm not going to reply at all."

A BLONDE IN A FLEECE JACKET WITH A FUCHSIA-PINK SHOPPING bag tucked under one arm is hanging from a strap and reading the latest Stephen King. A dark-haired girl in glasses chewing gum is wearing a black and white polka-dot blouse with the top buttons open and pearl earrings in her ears. She has the look of a saucy *giscardienne*. A black teenager with a red hoodie, a skinhead crop and thick black-framed glasses is jabbing a message into his phone, he seems pissed off about something. A guy of about forty with a rucksack and a pair of fluorescent yellow headphones is sitting with his legs manspread, he is obviously not familiar with the city. Vernon rides all the way to the end of Ligne 5. The deeper he penetrates into Paris, the more diverse the population. Past the gare de l'Est, the platforms are heaving. He surreptitiously observes the passengers, careful not to stare. A woman pushes her way through the crowd wearing a brown wool cardigan and dragging a luggage trolley to which a small amplifier is strapped with a red bungee cord, she is singing flamenco in a beautiful husky voice.

Things ended badly with Lydia Bazooka. He still feels shaken. He had expected to be able to stay at hers for two weeks, no trouble, since her soundman boyfriend was touring with -M- and had no days off planned. The field was clear and Vernon quickly settled in. Lydia Bazooka was much nicer than he had expected. He had popped round to her place, as arranged, to talk to her about

Alex Bleach and found her listening to Kid Loco's "Here Come the Munchies" on repeat at full blast in a tiny studio full of stuffed animals. Women are weird sometimes: what possessed this girl to get into collecting toys? As he stepped in, he noticed that the couch was not a sofa bed and besides was piled with mountains of clothes. If he was going to sleep here, he would have to share her bed. She had a tiny, charming body, her skin, unmarked by tattoos, was so white that it looked fake. She had put some beers in the fridge in his honour. If Lydia had flirted with him shamelessly online, now that they were face to face, she proved charmingly timid, she blushed at the slightest thing, something that made her even more attractive. For the first five minutes, Vernon was on his guard, then he relaxed. He could read her like a book, he had met her kind before. She was into Jane's Addiction, the Pixies, Hüsker Dü, the Smiths and Oasis – an eclectic bunch of oldies, but nothing seriously off-putting. She was obsessed with rock, he knew the type – the misfit who takes refuge in music. Above her desk she had pinned various photos of Alex. She was a real fan. Vernon could hardly complain, that was one of the reasons that rock music exists. People say fans are not best placed to talk about musicians but Vernon has always disagreed, after all, the fans are the only ones capable of staying awake for forty-eight hours straight tomake sure they don't miss a single tour date out in the sticks.

He was hungry and fried himself some eggs; the kitchenette was teeming with cockroaches, Lydia gave them nicknames. She was curious by nature, she asked a lot of questions and had a talent for giving the impression she was listening. She found it completely normal for him to settle himself in a corner of the apartment.

He listened to her talk about her book project. She had the energy and verve of a writer who never manages to get their project off the ground. Vernon had spent a lot of time listening to people tell him about the book they planned to write propped up on the counter in the record shop – he was all too familiar with this feverish logorrhoea that was a substitute for getting anything done. She *aspired* to write something good. This is always a problem. Someone saying "I'm going to paint a thoroughbred at full gallop", does not mean they can. More often than not, they end up scrawling something that just about looks like a squashed rat. This girl wanted to create a book that would be like a cathedral in the sky, she would probably end up delivering a plywood shed.

He talked to her about Alex. He was surprised to hear himself setting aside his cynicism, and say, by way of preamble: "The last couple of times I saw him, it was blindingly obvious he was begging for help, but I pretended I didn't notice. Like most of his friends, I suspect. I liked the guy, but it would never have occurred to me to do something. He was in such a bad way. I never really understood why he was so depressed. In the end, he simply lost the plot. Physically, he was still there, but who he was deep inside had been hijacked – bodysnatched. He was done with himself. And I just listened and made as if what he was saying was perfectly normal." Lydia said, "That's still a way of being his friend, giving him space." She wanted him to start off by talking about Alex back when he was gigging with unknown bands. Vernon tried to marshal his thoughts, "He was always handsome. Girls fancied him. That's the one thing that made him different from the others. He was very self-effacing, he only came out of his shell when he was singing. The way we saw it, Bleach becoming famous was like

Nirvana suddenly making it big when we were expecting it to be Tad or Mudhoney – he wasn't the one we expected to make it to the finish line. The difference is that everyone was happy when it turned out to be Nirvana. It wasn't the same with Bleach. We didn't think he was the most talented, we thought it was unfair that he hit the jackpot. The fact that everyone liked him didn't help, it was like bubblegum pop. You wanted to listen to something else. But success is like beauty, there's no arguing with it, it is what it is. And it strikes where it strikes. Did the fact that he was black go against him, for those of us who knew him before? No. It went against him when he started banging on about it in interviews. A lot of people said he overdid it – here he was, hugely successful and still bitching about how tough it was being black . . . but in the beginning, it didn't matter any more than his haircut. Not to him, and not to us I think."

They talked about the videos Alex had recorded at his place. He hoped she would say that her publishers would pay to get their hands on them. He even told her the truth, that he had been evicted from his apartment and needed a thousand euros so he could get his stuff out of storage. Lydia had a hard job hiding the fact that she didn't give a flying fuck about him being homeless, but she was wetting herself with excitement at the thought of unseen interviews by Bleach. She couldn't believe he had not even listened to them. But on the subject of money, she was uncompromising: "They're not worth shit. Unless he confesses he was Hortefeux's lover in which case, yeah, maybe we could get something for them . . . But the publisher isn't going to shell out another cent, take my word for it. On the other hand, it would be a serious scoop for the book if I had access to interviews no-one's ever seen . . ."

He tried to calm her down by explaining that he couldn't very well call Emilie and ask for the tapes without giving her back her laptop. Lydia was disappointed, but convinced they could come up with a solution. She had called a friend who came by to sell her a gram of coke. Then she and Vernon spent the night talking about Alex, about the past. He was thinking about sex, they both knew the other was thinking about it. But he was put off by the idea that he had to fuck her to crash here for the night. Sometime in the early hours, they collapsed, fully clothed, on the bed. Within minutes she snuggled closer to him, he pretended he was already asleep.

He had spent the following day holed up in the apartment, in the placid euphoria of a coke come-down. Lydia was a really funny girl. She didn't sulk because he hadn't fucked her. She told him how she had first discovered Alex's records through a friend of her big sister and became so obsessed that she wouldn't talk about them with anyone. Listening to her talk about her first interview with Alex you would have thought she had met the Virgin Mary.

Then Lydia stopped and threw herself at Vernon. Literally, she jumped on his back and wrapped her arms around him, a gesture so clumsy it was touching. At first, he didn't like the way she kissed – she tended to get overexcited and bump her teeth against his. In less than ten minutes she was straddling him, tugging at his belt buckle with an enthusiasm that was more scary than sexy. She was one of the porn generation, she faked everything with a manic intensity and was happy to be fucked every which way. In the end, Vernon found it turned him on. Her little gymnast's body bent to his every whim. She was an exceptional cocksucker – it was impossible to tell what she did with her lips and her tongue that others missed – perhaps it was an innate sense of rhythm. But when he came, he felt nothing very much.

She was pleasant enough to live with. She had a little-girl laugh that was constantly erupting. He felt at home in her place. He spent time on his Facebook page, adding more bullshit posts – making sure he had a fall-back option, Lydia's boyfriend was bound to come back sooner or later. Sylvie had flown into a rage. This depressed him. In a fury verging on lunacy, she trolled him on his own page and those of his friends: liar, thief, fraud, psychopath, terrorist, child rapist, chicken fucker. It was not so much the things he had stolen but his sudden disappearance that angered her. Luckily, he could rely on the deep-rooted misogyny of most of his acquaintances to chalk up her diatribes to common-or-garden hysteria. But he was shocked to see the extent of her rage and worried that it did not seem to be diminishing. He blocked her access to his page and those of his friends and struggled to think of a casual message that might neutralise her fury. Gaëlle got in touch. "Hey, sounds to me like you got yourself a girlfriend, huh?" Vernon tried to explain "It was just a casual thing, but I think she's hung up on me." "Don't sweat it," Gaëlle wrote back, "I can't stand the bitch, she's always pissing people off. So, how you been, old man?" And when she heard that Vernon was looking for somewhere to crash in Paris, she gave him her number – there was a spare room where she was staying. Lydia, to whom he read these messages, was astonished that girls were forever offering to put him up. He slipped an arm around her, she allowed him to kiss her.

"Don't be jealous. I'm not likely to go sleeping with Gaëlle – she always claims she's bi, but I've never seen her with a guy."

"I don't do jealous. You can't have them all. But why is it always girls offering to put you up?"

"Guys with families aren't allowed to bring friends home. And the ones who have no wife, no kids, no job . . . well, they remind me too much of my own life. I'd rather stay with a girl."

One day, Lydia posted a photo of Vernon on Instagram. Nothing compromising. He was bent over his laptop, looking for a video of Iggy Pop doing a cover version of Yves Montand, the naked light making his face look gaunt, it was a beautiful shot, he had rarely seen himself look so handsome. In the background, a mirror dusted with coke and a neatly cut straw from McDo gave the scene a festive touch.

Who knows how Sylvie came to stumble across it. And how she tracked down Lydia's address. She must have spent all night searching online. She did a good job.

The following morning, Vernon and Lydia were lying slumped together, too tired to fuck, but too wired to sleep when the front door juddered under the force of a pounding fist. Clean and sober, it would have shocked them, but given the state they were into, it was like being plunged into a Scorsese movie, helicopters police raid bloodbath. And things did not get any better when Lydia opened the door.

It's amazing how much damage a skinny little thing can do, both sonically and in terms of sheer physical damage. For the first time since he got here, Vernon found a use for the hideous collection of stuffed animals: thrown against the wall they neither break nor make any noise. But that just seemed to fuel Sylvie's rage.

She destroyed both laptops, upended the bed, ripped the sofa, smashed the crockery and stomped on the C.D.s, it seemed clear she was about to attack the windows before starting in on the foundations of the building, she was howling like a thing possessed, a stream of abuse that was directed at Vernon but went far beyond the nature of their recent relationship. He had two decades of frustration and disappointment thrown in his face. He was the embodiment of every man who had ever humiliated her.

Vernon was forced to overcome his fear so he could creep towards her, whispering gently as though trying to pacify a wild animal, but as soon as he came close, Sylvie calmed down. "Come on," Vernon said, "let's talk about this over a cup of coffee. She's just some girl who gave me a place to crash, I don't see why she should have anything to do with the conversation. Come with me." Sylvie was still railing, "So what did you steal from her, huh? I'm betting you fucked her too, yeah? Do you have any idea who you've had living with you, mademoiselle? No, you don't. You've got no idea who Vernon Subutex really is." But she agreed to go with him.

Vernon was terrified at the thought of finding himself in a bar with her. Sylvie was shrieking that she had gone to the cops and reported him for misappropriation of funds, robbery and receiving stolen goods. He had no idea whether she was bluffing. It was so out of proportion to the situation that he would not have been surprised if she'd pulled a gun and put a bullet in his head. She was psycho. But very quickly he realised that all she wanted was for him to come home with her. After a scene like that. He made a show of being uncertain, then suggested she go home and wait for him. He had to go back to Lydia's to apologise and pick up his belongings. Sylvie believed him, but insisted on going with him, she was sorry for what she had done, she wanted to compensate Lydia for the damage. Vernon raised a hand: no, I'd prefer to do this alone. At that point, Sylvie knew he was lying and flew into a new rage. She threw herself at him, lashing out with her fists and seeing him shield himself without hitting back, she sank her teeth into his shoulder. He pushed her off and made a run for it. Sylvie, who was wearing high heels and could not follow him, screamed "Stop him!", but no-one paid any heed. He ran for so long that he finally collapsed, winded, beside Hoche Métro station.

He had to sit on the pavement for several minutes catching his breath before he could get to his feet. His legs were still trembling. He had come out without a thing, he did not have Lydia's address. All he had was an iPod in his back pocket, two euros, and Gaëlle's phone number scribbled on an empty pack of Rizla. He wandered around Pantin, unable to find the building he had just left. He was petrified of running into Sylvie, who was probably still looking for him, but even so he tramped the streets. He knew there was a Vélib docking station at the foot of Lydia's building. Every morning she would peer out of her window and survey the extent of the damage. "The black kids hate the bikes, I don't understand why", because every time she saw someone trying to destroy one of the bicycles, it was a black boy. "Would it even occur to you to try and set fire to a rack of bikes? But there must be some reason why they do it . . ."

Failing to find the street he was looking for, Vernon phoned Gaëlle. He gave his last two euros to a teenager so she would lend him her mobile, she handed it to him, pinning him against the wall so he could not do a runner with it. He was surprised that Gaëlle answered right away and said no problem, and suggested he meet her at a bar on the canal Saint-Martin so they would go back to the apartment together.

Vernon crosses the place de la République. A couple of Roma kids are sitting on a mattress propped against the wall of a bank, they look lovesick and anxious, they are not attempting to beg, they are leaning together, talking about something important.

Gaëlle has not changed. Tattoos have invaded her wrists and her neck, but her face has barely changed. Her thing is motorbikes, Hells Angels, anything that involves getting your hands covered in grease. She was just a kid when she first showed up at the record shop, Vernon had never heard the expression "butch". In the late eighties, it referred to any woman who looked like a truck driver. But Gaëlle was too blonde, too skinny for anyone to think of calling her butch. She didn't often smile. She used to listen to Crazy Cavan, The Easybeats and David Bowie. She would steal C.D.s by the handful, stuffing them up her jumper, she had seen kids doing it in the film "Christiane F.", but she had no aptitude for crime beyond a willingness to try. Vernon would lecture her but he could not bring himself to ban her from the shop. She was too like a scared kitten.

Gaëlle calls him my old buddy, puts an arm around his shoulder and introduces him to the barman, sticking her chest out, "See this guy? We fought in 'Nam together." She does not ask any awkward questions. She knew Alex well. As she talks about him, she painstakingly rips a beer mat to shreds that she stacks into neat piles:

"You know that sooner or later you're going to get the call 'Alex is dead'. But it's still just as painful when it comes. He was the guy I always dreamed of being. Shameless, handsome, talented, furious . . . seeing him onstage in the last few years, he'd stopped doing the wild acrobatics, he was in no fit state . . . but remember him in the early days? He was one of the most beautiful guys I've ever seen on a stage. Those last gigs, he'd leave the band alone out front because he needed to go backstage to take something. It was sad. You saw it too, didn't you? The dead don't all go the same way. Some fade right away, as if this is what they've been waiting for. Others hang around, they visit you in your dreams, they are looking for something . . . Alex wakes me up in the middle of the night – he blames me. He says you didn't even try to help me. I justify myself – fuck's sake, I'm too close to going under myself to be able to save anyone else. But it grates on you. It really grates."

"Did he talk to you about alpha waves?"

"You too?"

"He forced me to spend a whole night listening to them. Gave me tinnitus."

"He could be a complete pain with that stuff."

Vernon pretends there's a problem with his bags, that he slammed the door of the apartment and left his keys inside and that his friend won't be back until tomorrow . . . Gaëlle is completely chilled, she says, "We'll sort something out for tonight, you'll see, back at our place there's bound to be a spare T-shirt and a razor." When he tells her he's only back in Paris to get a new passport and sort out his social security, Gaëlle is sympathetic. Social security? That will take weeks, no point kidding himself it will be sorted quickly. "You know what they do when they've got too much work? They toss out a bunch of files. I swear, it's the fucking truth, a friend of mine who's a doctor told me. You're going to be stuck here for a while . . . It's obvious that you haven't been living in France in a while, things have seriously changed . . . no, I don't have a place of my own. Haven't had for a long while now. Don't have any social security these days either, but I'm never ill, so I don't give a shit . . . But you'll see, the crib I'm staying at is cool. It's fucking huge, it's up in the eighth arrondissement. I'm really pleased to be able to help you . . . given all the stuff I stole from Revolver. But there's to be no shit: you make the smallest cockup at this place and I'll track you down and smash your teeth. Are we clear on the rules? Don't make me regret my magnanimity. But, yeah, I'm really glad to be able to help out. Maybe you and me will finally get to fuck, since my girlfriend's not around at the moment. Only kidding, you're not in a Kechiche film. She's twenty years younger than me. She wants to party all the time, you wouldn't believe how much energy girls have at that age . . . when I was young, being a lesbian was tough. But kids these days, they've got a life, they've got parties every night, two thousand of them show up shaking their booties, and you can't imagine how much they fuck, the little sluts: they show up, whip out a harness and a huge RealSkin, and for them, that's normal. Stuff that took me years to get my head round, they're into it straight away . . ." She began to get Vernon aroused, pretending not to realise what she was doing, describing the soft detailed texture and the convenience of the newer models of strap-on dildo . . .

Vernon has never really worked out what it was Gaëlle does for a living, she has no fixed address, she never had children, her lifestyle has not changed since she was twenty years old. She looks fifteen years younger than her actual age, she claims it is because she never wears make-up. She was born into a well-heeled family, though she doesn't appear to have much money – she is as worried by the price of beer as Vernon. But she has the attitude of a princess. "Loser" is not something that exists in her psychology. People like her are artists, bohemians – their lives are profoundly intense. They are never "skint". They could be signing on for *securité sociale*, they could be banged up in jail, it doesn't matter – unless someone rips out their intestines and forces them to suffer like ordinary people, they are above mere financial concerns. Having nothing makes it easy to be frivolous.

Gaëlle takes him to an apartment ranged over three levels with a total floor space close to 300 square metres, it feels like a supermarket, just making the grand tour is exhausting. A terrace runs the length of the top floor. The rooftops of Paris, in an infinite palette of grey, extend as far as the eye can see, the sky does not open up, there are only a few hours of light every day. It is like a lid over the city. The terrace is too high to be able to clearly make out the people below, the eye is drawn to the empty sky and discovers that it is ceaselessly criss-crossed by planes. Vernon shivers with cold. Gaëlle opens a can of beer and the sound of the tab being popped and gas being released immediately reassures him. Gaëlle has a biker's way of performing even the simplest tasks. She makes them strangely sensual.

"Who would even think of building an apartment this big?"

"A large family. The floor we're on was staff quarters, the middle floor – well, if a family had four kids, every bedroom would be full, and on the top floor were the reception rooms . . ."

"How much does it rent for, a place like this . . . ?"

"You don't rent, you buy. On a whim, in this case. Given the neighbourhood, you're talking about three million . . . he was a cash buyer, so he probably got a discount . . . He can afford it. He's a trader, his girlfriend is studying. They're both out all the time, you'll see, the place is chill. One thing: don't go raiding the fridge, they hate that. If you're thirsty, if you're hungry, go downstairs and buy whatever you need."

"You been living here long?"

"I've had the room for a while . . . but I try not to spend too much time here. It's too tiring. For the first couple of days, it'll seem like fun, but after that, you'll see, coming down for your morning coffee and finding a dozen fuckwits in the kitchen who don't even know what they're talking about going on and on about the true message of Christ . . . well, it gets old fast. But for a couple of weeks, you can live like a king here."

"It's a real lifesaver, you've got no idea."

"All you need to do is spin a set. The master of the house is having a little party tonight. I'll tell him you're a D.J."

"I've got my iPod. I don't suppose you've got a Mac you could lend me? If I'm going to prepare a playlist it would make things easier . . . and I'd need to get online, I have to contact the friend whose flat I accidentally locked my bags in."

When he thinks about writing to Lydia to explain that he couldn't find his way back to her apartment, the memory of the scene that took place this morning makes his throat tighten and he feels his blood freeze.

THE MUSIC IS SICK! THIS GUY'S A GENIUS. ALWAYS TRUST GAËLLE. When they first saw him, everyone thought who is this ageing freak, then he hooks up his iPod – the man's a fucking God – it's like holy water in your ears. The Klipsch speakers are pumping out Rod Stewart – this guy is fucking crazy, he'll play anything, but it works. He's the Nadia Comăneci of the playlist. After tonight, he's going to be Kiko's D.J. in residence. Red Bull and fat rails of coke, clusters of girls start to show up. They're tipsy, slutty, up for it – just the way we like them after dark. Some dickwad throws up over the pot plants. Kiko grabs the guy's shoulder and spits in his ear "Get the fuck out of my house, go on, fuck off", the guy is mumbling something but Kiko shoves him towards the door, he's not listening. He hates losers who can't hold their drink. A diaphanous blonde, all skin and bones, is tottering on a pair of freakish heels. She looks like she's walking on a tightrope. Her shoulder blades stick out, he feels the urge to shatter a bone. Neurons fried. For a second he considers clambering over the terrace rail and throwing himself off. Just for the buzzkill. This morning when he got up, Kiko said to himself: tonight I'm gonna be chilled. He needs to rest, eat Japanese, catch a movie, sleep it off. He'd forgotten he was having a party at his place – he could have cancelled, but that would have taken more effort than letting things ride. Claudia shows up. She's in Paris doing a cover for *Vogue*. He likes being surrounded by people who are successful at what they do. They radiate positive energy. She's brought some of her girlfriends from the photo shoot. Supermodels are "so" last decade. Has beens. There are a dime-a-dozen. Disposable. Even a dog can snag a catwalk model and get her into bed. He finds this thought amusing and immediately tweets it. He's in a twitter war with Jé, who's in Shanghai – what time is it there, what is he doing posting at this hour: "I'm studying the green of my vomit", with twitpic evidence. Sick. Who knows what the fuck he's doing over there. Other than making himself sick. Ever since the last Bond movie, Kiko's been planning to go to Shanghai. Not for work – he wants to have time to get out of the hotel. Get a feel for the city. But he doesn't have the time. Story of his life. You spend your time working your arse off to earn serious cash, but to spend it you need some sort of work–life balance. And in his line of work, there's no such thing. His job is speed. People outside the business don't understand. They think he analyses companies, but he's a sprinter. He reacts in a hundredth of a second, moves at the speed of the technology. Black holes. A stock market crash lasts a second and a half. Generating billions in profits. Or losses. And it's all down to you. It's hyper-instability. No time to touch ground, he's attuned to the wavelengths of algorithmic trading. He responds to an underground rhythm ordinary mortals cannot hear. Makes pivotal decisions at the speed of sound. We're talking billions, we're talking nanoseconds. He is constantly alert, an exceptional warrior. Britney Spears, "Work Bitch". Subutex is his bro, the guy can read his thoughts, he knows what to spin to get people dancing. Gym workout music.

Jérémy is pestering Marcia to cut his hair right now. Kiko can't stand the guy anymore. He used to be funny and charming. Used to be his best bro. These days, he's pathetic. They've known each other since they were kids. But Jérémy never realises when he's not wanted. He outstays his welcome. He's broke, his father cut off his allowance when he found out how much he was putting up his nose. Kiko managed to get himself fired from the board of directors, it had to be done. He trashed the C.E.O.'s office, just picked up a chair and started swinging. At the time it made them all laugh. But afterwards, well . . . It was pretty loserish behaviour. You've gotta be able to draw the line. Keep the wild and wasted shtick for the night-time. Daytime, you have to keep your nose clean and not make waves. The guy pisses him off. Ever since last summer when Jérémy insisted on coming to Calvi on the Rocks. Turned up without a fucking cent. Leeching off everyone. Embarrassing. Kiko had made it clear that there were ten of them staying in the house and it wasn't exactly an Olympic pool either. But he showed up anyway. No respect. This is one thing Kiko cannot abide. If you can't handle your drugs, go into rehab. For years, they were inseparable, they agreed on everything. But it's over now. Jérémy has lost his touch. These days, he is part of the crowd Kiko dismisses as roadkill – he is not about to feel guilty for being a killer. He knows not everyone is as lucky as he is. Always hustling, always on the move. Most of the people he knows are already past it. It's a long game, a tough game. They shoot horses don't they, Kiko would be the last man standing on the dance floor. For Jérémy, it's game over. His father won't let him fall through the cracks, but he's finished. His brain probably looks like a wrinkled Chinese pot sticker. Fried and cold. He won't climb back into the ring. Kiko is hacked off to see him drooling over Marcia – Marcia still makes him horny. Jesus fuck she makes him horny! Past her prime and not really his type. But she owns it. It's something about the way she moves, she fucks with every breath. She reeks of sex. A real woman is one of the guys. He types this into Twitter and jabs "send". He's leaning over a bridge above a motorway. The tweets keep coming, Boule2Kriss is on this crazy riff about the "human Barbie", some girl who's had surgery so she could look like a doll. He's coming out with some sleazy porn shit. Depeche Mode – this Vernon guy is a genius. You never know what the next segue will be, but he's spinning a blinding set. He's got B.P.M. burned onto his cortex. The party cranks up another gear, you can feel it, it's buzzing, buzzing, buzzing. Janet Jackson, "All Nite". There's a lot of sucky-fucky going on in the corners, it's cosmic and it's crass, just the way he likes it. Chicks can be dry when they're blitzed on gutter glitter, so mind those foreskins, boys. He tweets this. Too bad for the guys who've been cut and whose pricks can't feel anything. He could have any girl in this room tonight. That's why they're here, just seeing the size of the apartment gets them wet and they're gagging to suck off any guy who can afford it. He can see everything. He is a surface, attentive and alert. It's the yayo, but it's not just that – his mind is a single, giant interchange. Like downtown Tokyo. Information courses through him; he classifies. He spends all day simultaneously watching eight monitors while barking orders down the phone. He is multiple. Through training, his brain works a hundred times faster than that of some bumbling C.E.O. The average bank manager is like some guy scaling a mountain on the back of a donkey while he is riding a rocket – three times round the world every day, and his giant strides don't just take him round the world from market to market, they take him to its core – sifting information, finding points that match, connecting them. Transmitter–receiver. Inter-galactic sorting office. Plugged into world time. In a Sicilian village or an Indian megalopolis, in the frozen tundra or the Amazon rainforest, everywhere functions on Market time. Our advantage is speed, ubiquity is our gift. The meteor moves too fast for anyone to alter its trajectory, it's all about intuition. Kiko can sense time, he is the big hand on the watch. In global time. He is the swiftest, the strongest. It's nothing to do with the drugs. He is in control. A quick bump first thing in the morning and he's off and running, no more hits until he takes a break at two p.m. – his first line. He is in control, during the day he takes only what he needs to keep riding the gnarly wave. He never spins out. He is an exceptional surfer. He's worth this apartment, he's worth all those honeys shaking their asses in the living room, he's worth the drugs. He's worth the Berlutis. He's a fucking wolf. His concentric part is rising – anyone would give anything to be in his shoes. Shit! A Trentemøller remix of Presley – at this precise moment, it's the perfect piece of mixology. It's savage, the babes love it, they can swivel their hips. This guy is a genius. Kiko loves him. They are kindred spirits: in his business, Kiko is a virtuoso – he rides the comet, the comet is his own body. He hears the blood pumping in his temples, the sound of his blood, throbbing, throbbing, it's good. Powerful. Even the people who pretend to be modest do it because they're bitter, because they can't be like him. If they don't get to taste the soup, they try to spit in it, but if someone passed them the bowl they'd change their tune. No-one likes a loser. He nearly tossed that old bastard Vernon out on his arse – it's one of his pet hates, when people bring someone round who has no business setting foot in his place. He nearly lost his rag when Gaëlle showed up with this fucking tramp, with his piss-poor excuse about not having his gear – he had to lend the guy a T-shirt. Kiko had glared at Gaëlle but she shot him that look that always gets to him, the look of an old hand knows what she's doing. And she was right. The guy is sick. He may not have looked like much standing in the living room in the cold light of day, but bent over his playlists right now, the look almost works. He hardly moves – tough guys don't dance – but he's at one with the music. The fucker does a 180-degree swerve into music that's hot and kitsch, and it works. Kiko glances at the track on iTunes, Candi Staton "I'd rather be an old man's sweetheart" how the fuck did he have the balls to spin this now? Exactly the right tune, just the thing to get the babes warmed up despite the coke. Top night, never met a guy like this. How did a guy like you end up poor, how come you're still a filthy bum. The guy probably grew up eating peanuts off paper plates, a life fuelled by frozen crêpes and meat pumped full of antibiotics. The cultural habits of the poor make Kiko want to puke. He imagines being reduced to such a life – over-salted food public transport taking home less than €5,000 a month and buying clothes in a shopping mall. Taking commercial flights and having to wait around in airports sitting on hard seats with nothing to drink no newspapers being treated like shit and having to travel in steerage, being a second-class scumbag, knees jammed against your chin, neighbour's elbows digging into your ribs. Screwing ageing cellulite-riddled meat. Finishing the working week and having to do the housework and the shopping. Checking the prices of things to see if you can afford them. Kiko couldn't live like that, he would rob a bank, put a bullet in his head, he would find a solution. He would not put up with it. The fact that they do means that they deserve it. Guys like him could not live like that. What have the rich got that the poor have not? They're not content with what they're given. Guys like him never act like slaves. He stands on his own two feet, come what may – he would rather die on his feet than kneel. People who allow themselves to be subjugated deserve to be subjugated. This is war. He is a mercenary. When you fall on the front lines, you don't run crying to someone. You're here to fight. Three days ago when Kerviel was asked in an interview on telly "Did you realise what you were doing when you were speculating on commodities?" – the kind of bullshit question that comes from a guy who doesn't realise that that's the job – Kiko fell about laughing. Do you really think we have time to inspect our own arsehole to check whether it's clean. Who is the strongest. The fastest. That's the only question. As soon as you know the answer, you go for it. You've got guys bellyaching about the markets, they bring Kerviel on and they want him to say it was all his fault. Why don't you ask the real questions: who sells these shows? They are the masters of the universe. Ask yourself what Google is doing instead of bleating that you don't understand the industry. Twelve trains late, gentlemen. Who comes up with the algorithms, that's the only important question. The little people worry about the rise of the far right. That won't change the markets. Whether it's the far right or any-one else, the markets will barely notice. There is no going back. These people are still living in the '30s. Kiko is connected to the universal flux, the pure source of power, money may thrash, it shies, it rears but Kiko stays in the saddle. Would anyone think to ask a bomber pilot to examine his conscience? People are still worrying about threats to education and social security. Retards. Do the unemployed need to read in their free time? The old world is done and dusted. Why bother educating people who are surplus to the job market? The next time the peoples of Europe are called upon, it will be for war. You don't need to learn about literature and maths to fight. Now *there's* somthing that could kick-start the economy. A war. But well-read welfare scroungers – honestly, what a ridiculous notion. People think that on the trading floor we give a shit about protest movements – do they really believe that it makes a trader's heart bleed to see a bunch of guys without the cash to buy bread? Life's always been like this. It's hard. It's war. When Kerviel crashes and burns, no-one rushes to defend him. When it comes to Kiko's turn – he will face it alone. He is a mercenary, he knows he can count on no-one. In a war you have to win. To survive. To have the proper tools. The right algorithm. The rest is poetry. Empty promises. Of course there is the thrill. Yo, shitwank, you think I don't get a hard-on for a bonus trailing five zeros? If he walked over to Subutex and said, you know today I added hundreds of thousands of euros to my capital, he'd know that made him hard, right? He's got a full-on robot chubby. He is a bull in the ring, he fights. He sees people who've retired at forty. Palaces, big cars and high-class hookers, they move to countries where no-one gives a shit about human rights, where people are progressive, where they don't hassle you for income tax. He's never seen one of them with tears in his eye because little black *bamboula* hasn't got enough to eat. Try doing what I do, you'll see. I hedge, I speculate, I double, I anticipate, I short. Always on the alert. Bad news for the people of France: the party's over. Move along, there's nothing to see here. We've sold off the fridges the laptops and now we're restocking to fuck off and sell elsewhere. And you'll do what? Apart from whingeing, what are you going to do? Kill each other? Good idea. We've got arms to trade. His countrymen are dumb, ungrateful, arrogant arseholes. They take to the streets shouting bullshit slogans and thinking they're all that. They're nothing. Up where we are, we don't even hear. Not a whisper reaches our ears. It's all done and dusted. It's over. Wave your little pamphlets. We can't even hear you.

He needs to get to bed early tonight. One more line, one last drink and then beddy-byes. Albert King. "Breaking up Somebody's Home". Vernon is shit hot. Kiko yells D.J. REVOLVER IN DA HOUSE. He knows it's lame but he doesn't give a shit, this is his place he'll trip how he likes. It's wild, the guy's got like a sixth sense. He's at the controls and the spaceship is about to lift off. It's tight, the people the bodies the lights the sounds – it's too tight. He goes over and grabs Vernon's shoulder. Fuck dude, props on the set, it's awesome, the sound is banging. You're a badass motherfucker. The baddest. You got everything you need in your room? Just ask, yeah? Want me to hook you up with a babe? I've had, like, a million D.J.s here and maybe they've got a style but you . . . you're one savage mofo. Look at them bitches, look what you're doing to them, any minute now the whole room will be one big fucking orgy. Actually, Kiko decides he likes the guy's face. He's not shy, he's mysterious. At first sight, he assumed Vernon was a loner. He hates that. Motherfuckers are savage or at the very least they're loudmouths. They're up for anything. Shyness is a sign of subterfuge. Of middle-class hipsters. The fucktards who think they're someone. Timidity is the sign of neurosis, neurosis is the sign of treachery. You've got to be careful who you let in if you want the atmosphere to stay fluid. You have to filter. An apartment is like a country. You've got to keep out the undesirables, you've got to be ruthless, only let in people who know how to party. I'm paying so I get to choose. This Vernon guy is brooding and mysterious, ever since he started spinning the tunes he's been transfigured. An artist. He's an artist. It's always useful to have a couple around. Tonight, for example, he's short of actresses. They always add a little something. Not actresses of the telly. They're boring. They're depressing. They drag you down. Like stand-up comedians. "So weit wie noch nie" – old school techno. Everyone's up, everybody's pumping, it's like trance. Truly, this guy's got mad skills. It's something you can't put your finger on, but when a D.J .brings a little soul, everyone senses it. Just when Kiko was about to hit the sack, the perfect tune. There's been a dark-haired girl circling him for a while now, she thinks he hasn't seen her as she gets more and more obvious. Give it a few minutes, she'll be dancing naked in front of him, desperately trying to make eye contact. Her nose is so skinny he wonders how she can get coke up there without it disintegrating on the spot. Maybe it's a prosthesis, maybe before she sucks him off, she'll take off the nose and show him her zombie face. Shake that body, baby, shake it. I'll take care of you. Tonight I'm not going to fuck you, I'm too shattered, but I'll take you to bed. We'll fall asleep next to each other. Biancha is dancing with her eyes closed, Marcia is pressed against her back. A little lesbian performance, go on give us some girl-on-girl action, set this room ablaze. It's hell in here. Tribal, tribal. I love it. He takes the dark-haired girl by the hand. She looks like she's sixteen. I'm going to fall asleep with two fingers in that shaved little pussy of yours, but I'm not going to fuck you, I don't have the energy, maybe you could blow me, but I don't think I can even manage to come. In his apartment, porn is what happens in the bed. He's a god. His bedroom is far enough from the living room that he can leave the others to amuse themselves. He is a prince. He doesn't say goodnight, he beckons for the girl to come with him and she complies. They're all the same, and the ones who think they're too good to come when he whistles can go fuck themselves, there's always some girl shrewd enough to want to keep him warm. Because tomorrow, who knows, maybe I'll remember you, maybe well enough to give you a little present. It all depends on you, on how good you are.

THERE'S NO COKE IN THIS COKE; WHEN YOU RUB IT ON YOUR gums, you feel nothing. Her head is aching and a vicious come-down is already sending twinges through her back despite the fact she's still flying, so tomorrow morning is not going to be pretty. Marcia has a photo shoot at three p.m., leaving her enough time to get some rest. The party was nothing special, she would have been better off going to bed. The same faces as always. The same conversations played over and over. She opened her pack of ciga-rettes when she got home and it is already empty. More than the booze and the drugs, it's the nicotine that wears her out, in the morning, she can hardly breathe. She needs to quit. Her complex-ion was being ruined by smoking too much, so she switched to tobacco that contained no texturising agents, Gaëlle told her she could really feel the difference, but Marcia feels nothing. This headache. She has been rooted to the same spot for more than an hour, sitting next to Framboise who is chain-rolling pure grass blunts. An hour that she has been promising herself she will go to bed. White noise in her gums, super gross, it is all too familiar. Tomorrow, she needs to get some rest.

With the first notes, her mind splits in two: *Construcción*. Viglietti's Spanish cover version, a series of shifting images, of smells and sounds, what his body felt in that precise moment. Like flicking through a book at random, she cannot choose what will happen. *Amó aquella vez como si fuese última.* Back then she was Leo, with a hairstyle copied from Isabella Rossellini. Belo Horizonte. Trees towered over the city, luxuriant, that vivid green of countries in the south where life pushes up even through concrete and in a single movement climbs towards the heavens. Bairro Foresta, a low-roofed house, a record player in the Silvio's house – his parents were away – and this song, played over and over for days on end like an obsession. They went to see "Betty Blue" at the cinema. They went several times that day and came back again the next. They drank beer in the streets, breathed in the heady perfumes of the *damas da noite.* Leo in a favourite pair of Radley sneakers. The city was jammed with Volkswagens; they had no car. Always the same gang, just the five of them. They wore faded blue jeans. *Besó a su mujer como si fuese última.* Not one of them had stayed in Belo Horizonte. The dawn was so dazzling it hurt your eyes, gorging on *pão de queijo,* the taste of cassava, their boyish bodies, tireless. The blue Sony Walkman she was so proud of. Listening over and over to Cazuza's "O tempo não para", the horror of AIDS that was yet to come. Lula being defeated in the elections, she had been too young to vote, she was barely sixteen. Her country's first direct elections. And already, Europe was beckoning. It had to be Europe – not the U.S.A., Europe. She was in love with a teacher who taught literature at the most exclusive school in the city. "*Sus ojos embotados de cement y lágrimas.*" She was crazy about this song. Listening to it in Spanish was pretentious. The gang would hang out together on Broaday (no "w"), go to hip-hop gigs, Racionais MC's, not a white person in sight, the excitement of being there, the bodies of the boys, the bad boys. There were "Free" cigarettes, the elegant white pack criss-crossed with two waves, red and blue. All the accessories that made them who they were, the props in their game. No-one in this room with its vast terrace in this eight-floor apartment in the *triangle d'or* of Paris, no-one here experienced being fifteen the way she did. She split herself in two. She wanted to leave for Europe. If someone had told her then, if someone had told her how wonderful everything would be – would it have made the slightest difference to the impatience gnawing away at her. "*Por esa arpía que un día nos va a adular y escupir. Y por las moscas y besos que nos vendrán a cubrir.*" She had been spellbound by this song – its tragic spiral. Her whole country – striving towards tragedy and swaying.

Ever since the party started, Kiko has not stopped raving about the guy spinning the set, "The guy's amazing, isn't he? He's fucking awesome", Kiko has his whims, he loves to love somebody. Now and then he is a loyal friend. Marcia has not had a good night. She found the atmosphere depressing – people sick to death of seeing each other compelled to corrode their sinuses so they can fake a half-hearted hilarity. It is not quite dawn, but that curious moment when darkness drains away before the sun has risen. In twenty minutes the sun will rise, the moment when the city smells most exhilarating. The song ends, her every bone trembles at the impact of this random access memory – she whirls around, raises her arms in the air. "Hey! D.J. Revolver, you've just given me my first orgasm of the night." She looks at him, she hasn't noticed him until now. A subtle smile, he gives her a wink and puts on Prince – "Sexy Motherfucker". Well played, Mister D.J. Other images flood back. By now she is in Paris, no-one here calls her Leo, she wears microshorts, glossy black Lycra leggings, cherry-red stilettos she buys at Chez Ernest near Château d'Eau – she has started training to be a hair stylist. Her life is like a vinyl disk, several tracks have already been cut. The images unfurl, she is back there. In Paris, in those early years, it rains every day, which is exactly how a South American girl pictured the city. Paris in the early nineties is bewitched by the sounds of Brazil, the French long to be able to dance, they sway as best they can to music they cannot understand. They move their feet, they move their shoulders, their hips are lifeless. When she first arrived in Paris and saw Johnny Hallyday on television, she realised there were a lot of things she would not understand. Things you had to be born here to appreciate. But Paris was besotted with Brazil, and the fashion world wanted girls like her, they wanted that accent, that sexy swagger, they wanted the exotic. Most dirt-poor Brazilian trans women headed directly to Nation, it was almost compulsory. It was not exactly signposted, but almost. When Marcia told the other girls she met "No, I didn't come here to turn tricks", they would shoot her a pitying look. The street was not an option, it was her place, it was written. H.I.V.+ Brazilians arrived en masse, they knew they would get better health care in France. But Marcia was obsessed with Scarlett O'Hara and decided that Scarlett would do things differently, she would go on the game. The fact that Scarlett was not poor cast a different light on things, but Marcia tried to ignore this fact. If she had no money, at least Marcia had luck on her side. One evening in Gibus, she made friends with a girl from Bogotá who, like her, was taking oestrogen. The girl was a hairdresser-cum-drug dealer, people were constantly traipsing in and out of her place for a hair cut and two or three grams. This was how Marcia learned. Hairdressing. In the beginning, she did the colour rinses in the bathroom. It was easy. She was sub-letting a room from Fabrizio, the only screaming queen she ever met who claimed to be in the mafia. And Fabrizio adored her – he used to say she was as beautiful as Dalida – and he introduced her to the scene. She was learning to style hair. And she had her first fashion shoots. She would make everyone laugh, it was what people expected of her. A sense of humour. The girls she had met when she first arrived began to die, some killed themselves before AIDS could utterly destroy their looks. The epidemic was also killing off the Parisian queers. For once, there was a sort of fairness. The disease treated everyone alike. It was a strange sensation, this feeling of belonging to the same caste. All of them. And life went on – all around death continued to strike without pause. And people didn't give a shit. ACT UP Paris organised die-ins but people didn't really start thinking about AIDS until they, too, were affected. When straights got sick, that's when the disease became real. Marcia dodged between the raindrops. She had work, and she still did not have AIDS. There was a feeling of guilt that came with time, survivors' guilt, and with it a fierce gratitude. Life was so good to her, and there was no end to it. Then came the lovers who pampered her. The trips, the palaces, the jet-set. In the fashion world, the nineties were utterly magical. Evangelista, Campbell, Crawford, Schiffer, Casta, Alek Wek, Herzigova, Banks . . . She grew accustomed to luxury, to being part of a world in which she would never belong. The little mermaid: the girl for whom each step is agony, who walks gracefully, who always smiles. She has never thought about going back to Brazil, even when she heard about the economic miracle. She loves Europe. The richness of the old world, the opulence of its lower classes, the heedless attitude of these people who were capable of forgetting the humiliation of poverty, dictatorships, convinced that they are safe because they are more deserving, more hardworking, more intelligent. She likes the fact that everywhere is heated, even the post offices are clean, anyone would love to be born French. The French are the only ones who do not realise it. Or perhaps this, like so many things that seemed immutable, will change eventually.

This is the first time in years that she has thought of Belo Horizonte and felt the desire to go back in time. Take the young boy-girl she was and whisper in his ear don't worry you'll never believe all the things that will happen to you one day you'll see you'll be so jaded of opulence and easy living, so sated by life you'll complain that you're bored. Like a real princess.

Subutex. Kiko has been screaming his name all night. She scarcely noticed him, but now that she looks at him, she too sees something in him. He has beautiful hands. Vernon is calm. He is middle-aged. The wrinkles around his mouth are those of someone who has laughed a lot. He has obviously made the most of life. She goes over to him. "What's that you're playing?" She whispers the question, her fingertips brushing the inside of his elbow. He looks up at her, stares into her eyes without smiling. The look is hard. It catches Marcia in the pit of her stomach. "Freddie King," he says. He has a rich, deep voice, he whispers the title of the song into her ear: "Please Send Me Someone to Love", for a Frenchman, his English pronunciation is excellent, he doesn't overdo it. He is self-assured. She finds him attractive. A little. He is engrossed in the music. He changes the groove. Noir Désir's "Tostaky". A grey dawn spills a little light into the room. She raises her hands above her head, follows the guitar, her eyes half-closed. She has always been able to get anything she wanted from men by dancing.

"Tostaky", she recognises that pulsing French rhythm. Hips pitched to the guitar, back to the drum kit. Vernon is probably a total bastard. It is something she feels in her belly: if she is attracted to a guy, he must be dodgy. She has drama in her blood, she can only come with brutal men. Guys who want to kill you always make the most attentive lovers, otherwise you wouldn't let them do what they do. No-one accepts that first slap unless it is followed by a torrent of apologies, of promises, by a desperate desire not to lose you, not to imagine losing you. The ones who might well kill you are invariably the ones who care most. When she really wants them, it means she knows that they could kill her. She does not need to look at his eyes to know that he is watching her. When she dances, she has to hold back, she is too old to make an exhibition of herself, she curbs her energy. Her wrists flex, she plucks at the air, fingers tensing at every note then, hands behind her head, she gestures dropping something on the floor. "Tostaky". The extraordinary beauty of that French singer – the most Latino of them. Crescendo, her heels gently hammer the floor – restraint is important in Paris, even when dancing, you don't seek to lose yourself in a trance, you remember to smile. No frenzy, no carnal passion. In Paris, the body is a mask. Vernon segues into Rihanna – other forms, moving around her. She ignores them. She dances for him, he ignores her, taunts her. This excites her. She likes guys of every kind. Every age, every build, every race, every creed, every means, and every temperament. She likes them all, but it is even better when they are immune to the way she sways her hips. She will have him.

She goes out onto the terrace to smoke. The icy air whips her skin, a pleasant sting. She takes a deep breath – at last she has come up on the drug. Only now does she feel it, a dawn burst of energy. Jérémy and Biancha are talking about the problems faced by the U.M.P. since Sarkozy's departure. Snatches of arguments, they repeat the same things a dozen times, blowing hot air. Early-morning conversations. She hates that. She is coming down off the speed. She should have popped M.D.M.A. It's back in fashion these days. She hasn't had enough to drink, she feels in no fit state to deal with this. She goes back inside, Vernon has not moved, he is locked into the music, he is self-sufficient. She likes him. She brushes against him as she leaves and says, "See you tomorrow, Mister D.J. You do realise no-one here is going to sleep, you can go up to your room whenever you like. They're not listening any-more." He smiles without responding. She likes him more and more. He is her story for the night, he is the one reason the party did not totally suck.

She does not run into him the following morning before head-ing off to the photo shoot. Gaëlle hasn't slept, she's still doing lines, sitting on her own in front of the television, drinking bowls of Genmaicha tea. She doesn't ask what time he went to bed. Coming out with the question point-blank would arouse suspicion and Gaëlle has never been able to hold her tongue. Kiko would not like the idea of her prowling around a guy who is staying with him. They haven't flirted for years now, but she would never bring a lover back to his apartment. It is a tacit agreement – she has a pied-à-terre in Paris, she does her fucking elsewhere.

It's weird seeing Gaëlle trying to gauge the right distance to read a text message. Like an old woman. For parasites like them, presbyopia is a scourge. Preserving one's charm while losing one's looks is an equation that rarely balances. Although people like to feel useful and magnanimous, they have a terror of ageing bodies, weathered faces, the poignancy of faded glory. One day the two of them will be ruins – something that was once sublime and is now no more than a pile of rubble. As though reading her mind, Gaëlle adjusts her aim, languidly stretches then flashes Marcia a malicious smile that particularly suits her. Taking all the time in the world, she lights a cigarette with graceful insouciance, then looks into Marcia's eyes.

"You looked good on the dance floor last night."

"Yeah, for a bit . . . I was shattered, I really should have gone to bed early."

"Take me for an innocent virgin all you like, babe . . . but don't talk to me about Subutex. It's not like it wasn't patently obvious that you were doing your slutty best to hook up with him."

Marcia makes an effort to remain impassive. She is jubilant. She is in love. She longs to hear his name, to know things about him, she longs for Gaëlle to tell her that it was painfully obvious that he was into her . . . For her, there is nothing more exciting than these days – the days before it happens.

Gaëlle rolls her eyes to heaven, she feigns disappointment:

"How long have we known each other? Do you really think I can't read you like a book?"

"I don't know what you're talking about."

"Not a bad choice. He's a decent guy. If I was into men, I'd want to sleep with him too. One snag: you'll break his heart, babe."

"He does have beautiful hands, but it stops there."

"Where exactly do his hands stop?"

"I get off on love . . . is that a crime?"

"Love, love . . . I'd be more inclined to say you get off being

fucked rigid like the latent sleazy bitch you are. Well, I say latent
. . . But, at the risk of repeating myself: you'll break his heart."

Marcia wants him. A door has opened and she wants to see what's on the other side. "It may be wrong but it feels right to be lost in paradise." She didn't find him particularly handsome, she wants him to want her, wants him to take her and destroy her. She wants him. It is a caprice, or a compulsion.

ON THE BUILDING SITE NEXT TO MERCAT DE LA BOQUERIA, A HUGE crane is hoisting a cement mixer above the heads of passers-by. The Hyena has spent too long sitting in front of her computer and her lower back is stiff and aching. She is walking off the tension.

Two girls in shorts and wedge heels, backpacks slung over their bellies, cross the Plaça de Sant Agusti, studying a map of the city. Their shoulders are tattooed and they are speaking in a language so strange that the Hyena cannot help but wonder if they are making it up. A bearded man is pushing a meat trolley. Tourists cycle past wearing brightly coloured helmets. A group of homeless are sitting around a fountain. They are all about fifty and sporting mohicans. Taxis honk at every intersection. Catalan flags blossom from every building with banners that read "We want a respectable neighbourhood". On a patch of pavement out of the way of pedestrians, a seagull is eviscerating a dead pigeon.

She arrived in Barcelona last night. On the television, there were news reports of a woman in her sixties throwing herself from the window of her apartment when bailiffs came to evict her.

Gaëlle calls her from Paris. She is livid.

"What do you mean you can't come round right now?"

"I'm not in Paris, girlfriend."

"Why didn't you let me know before? What the fuck am I supposed to do now?"

"Keep him distracted. I'll be back in three days."

"Come back tonight."

"Can't be done."

"Are you taking the piss? I did what I said I'd do. If Vernon fucks off tomorrow, you still have to pay me what you promised, agreed?"

"What did I promise you?"

"Two hundred euros."

"We never talked about money."

"Alzheimer's is eating your brain. You offered me twice that, but I'm giving you mates' rates."

It seems fair enough. The Hyena protests for the sake of form, thanks Gaëlle and promises to come back as soon as possible. After she hangs up, she holds on to her mobile phone. She thinks about telephoning Dopalet. She could tell him she has traced the guy he has been looking for. He'll say "Already?", he'll congratulate her, he'll be relieved. He'll tell her to come back right now.

She slips the phone back into her jeans pocket. It has been a long time since she got away from Paris. She had not realised how much she missed it, having a change of scenery. She does not feel like being an asset to the team. Dopalet is taking this business very seriously, he checks every day for updates. The Hyena says as little as possible.

She has found no mention of a collaboration between the two men on the internet. Dopalet is a vicious little creep by nature, but ordinarily, a little searching will turn up a link between him and the object of his fury. Not in this case.

When she found out she was expected to track down someone who had known Alex Bleach when he was young, she immediately thought of Sélim.

*

They lived in the same building for four years in the quartier des Lilas when they were younger. What Sélim never knew was that the Hyena often visited his apartment because she fancied his girlfriend who had a fondness for cocaine, something the Hyena always had on her in those days, so she would offer the girl a little toot before her husband came home. It was not strictly honourable, the girl wasn't even twenty at the time. No-one wanted to bother her with lectures about hygiene, people wanted to pleasure her. She was very young. It was not so much a matter of age – Sélim and the Hyena were barely seven years her senior – rather a question of inexperience. She had arrived from the sticks and knew nothing about life. She was a little rough around the edges, yet so slight that she seemed like a sparrow trapped in a kitchen. It was this energy that made her so charming. It's impossible to imagine any boy who was cooler than Sélim at the time, but he was still a boy: he was not exactly subtle. He had married this kid he was hopelessly in love with and could not understand how she could be bored with the life he had made for her. He loved Roland Barthes, Russian cinema and the songs of Barbara. She was twenty, she wanted to go out, to dance. He thought that if he gave her a baby, everything would be fine. She completely freaked out. Then one day, she disappeared, she was infatuated with the *caïd* in the neighbouring tower blocks. Sélim was the only one who found this incomprehensible – everyone wanted to say, did you not notice how bored she was in the kitchen. Sélim took care of little Aïcha with a tenderness redoubled by maternal abandonment. It was now that he found himself alone with the child that he and the Hyena became closer – when he needed to go on an errand he would take the Moses basket upstairs to his neighbour's apartment. He felt comfortable in this world composed exclusively of women and, at the time, he was funny enough and engaging enough to be accepted.

A few months after his girlfriend left, in his local video rental shop, Sélim stumbled over the cover of a hardcore porn flick. The Hyena never dared ask what he was doing in the Adult section. His little Faïza was now Vodka Satana. The Hyena would not set eyes on Vodka Satana again until her affair with Alex Bleach, when her picture was everywhere.

After the meeting with Dopalet, she immediately called Sélim. He was not exactly thrilled at the idea of having coffee with her. Nonetheless, he invited her round to his place; his tone was chilly.

He has changed. The ebullience that characterised his personality has drained away, his exuberance has been transformed into bitterness. He makes no attempt to hide this fact, quite the reverse. He is determined to make it clear that his life is miserable, with the same eagerness that, as a young man, he used to seduce all those who crossed his path. Because Sélim was a brilliant boy, and it was impossible to take him anywhere he did not end up hogging the limelight, monopolising the conversation, stamping his particular brand of madness on the evening. Once slender, handsome, stylish, he had become a bald, pot-bellied little man who wears hideous, mismatched clothes. The sort of guy you avoid engaging in conversation, his anger has become rank.

The Hyena took a seat in an identikit Ikea living room that looked as though it had been deliberately denuded of all appeal. She was waiting for the sign that said we share so many happy memories, I'm really glad to see you, then she shrank back –

deciding that thirty minutes was the minimum period before she could politely slip away. She did not really know what she expected to find at Sélim's that might help her decide whether to accept Dopalet's assignment or let it drop but, sitting here facing him, she knew that coming here had been a mistake.

Sélim was now a professor at Paris 8, something she would have expected him to take a certain satisfaction in – university professor is something one can admit to at dinner parties without blushing. At least this was what she believed. These days, according to Sélim, everyone despises academics. Intellectuals. People like him.

Sélim, whom she remembered as someone interested in other people, asked no questions about what she had been doing, nor why she had come to see him. She tried:

"I thought about you when Alex Bleach died . . . We never talked about it at the time, it must have been awful for you, seeing her with him . . ."

"Of all the decisions she made, that's not the worst I had to stomach."

"It doesn't bother you, me talking about this stuff?"

"No. I thought about it a lot after he died. She was in love with him. At the time I felt humiliated, obviously, but I was relieved . . . I thought maybe he could help her rebuild her life. I think he loved her too."

"But not the best person to help anyone try and rebuild their life . . . Such a waste, that guy."

"I didn't know you were so interested in French pop music."

"I liked him."

"If you came to see me to talk about Alex and Faïza, you've

had a wasted journey. You'd be better off talking to some of her girlfriends from back then, Pamela Kant or Debbie d'Acier – I'm no good to you . . ."

"Pamela Kant . . . I'd forgotten her name . . . Were they good friends?"

Sélim had leaned forward, stared hard into her eyes and paused. He was giving her his best film noir pose.

"I asked if that's what you came here to talk about."

"Absolutely not. I didn't think you'd be so bothered by me calling to see how you've been . . . I didn't realise we were on bad terms. But there is one question I wanted to ask – since you know a lot about the film industry . . . I'm trying to track down a French screenwriter whose first name is Xavier . . ."

He raised an eyebrow, clearly surprised by the incongruity of this question, but he did not have the time to answer. Aïcha came into the living room looking sulky, she did not bother to say hello, but simply asked "Do you think we could order pizzas tonight?" Genetics had done her no favours. She had the sturdiness of her father, and a wonderful nose that she did not inherit from either parent but clearly ran in the family which, while it gave her face a certain character deprived it of any possibility of harmony. Aïcha wore the veil, something that did not really add to her charms – all one could see was her nose.

Sélim said no to the idea of pizza, no white flour tonight – it seemed to be an established principle in the family since the young girl did not even protest, she puffed her cheeks to signal she was unhappy, but did not insist. Sélim introduced her to the Hyena:

"You won't recognise this lady, but she used to live upstairs from us when you were little. She used to babysit you."

And the Hyena nodded and looked at the girl with the eyes of an adult who has powdered your bottom when you were a baby and refrained from saying "I knew you when you were this high", or "It's been a long time, you've grown so tall!" though her expression said all of these things, because it is an enduring mystery to adults that things that crawl around on the floor sucking on dummies can so quickly mutate into semi-monsters with size 42 shoes. Aïcha dragged her sullen mood around the living room for a few more minutes before heading back to hole up in her bedroom, "I've got work to do."

"Is she at university?"

"Tax law."

"Does she study hard?"

"On that score, I can't complain."

"You're lucky. A lot of kids don't know what to do with themselves."

"The Prophet is the problem."

"Sorry?"

"She spends all day banging on to me about the Prophet. Drives me insane."

"You have to move with the times."

"It's pretty obvious you don't have a daughter."

"Yeah, I can imagine . . . I can just picture having a daughter and her turning out straight. It would be a total nightmare, I don't know how I'd live it down."

Sélim smiled, for the first time, at something she had said. For a while she listened to him complain about how difficult it was to be a parent, to bring up a daughter alone. Then she made her excuses.

Sélim had called her back the next day.

"We were interrupted yesterday. This screenwriter you're looking for, it wouldn't be Xavier Fardin?"

"Never heard of him."

"Remember that early nineties movie – "Ma seule étoile est morte" – it hasn't aged well, but back when it was first released everyone was raving about it."

Her mobile phone sandwiched against her shoulder, she typed Xavier Fardin and Alex Bleach into Google – bingo, they knew each other. The Hyena gave a low whistle:

"Good call."

"When you don't know something, always ask daddy. So, tell me: do you know much about the psychology of girls?"

"Hey, that's my specialist subject."

"Cut the shit. I'm talking about my daughter here. Can we meet up?"

"Again? Yesterday you didn't even want to go for coffee with me and now you're talking like you want us to get married."

In fact, he simply wanted her to join his daughter on a week's holiday to Barcelona. "For assessment purposes." The Hyena found it hard to believe he was really suggesting something so unlikely. But he was serious. He sucked on his e-cigarette like a crotchety old baby and wouldn't let it go.

"Your daughter? In what sense exactly do you want me to assess her?"

"Terrorism. Jihad."

"Has she been googling plane tickets to Iran?"

"No. I don't know what she does. I don't want to spy on her. Even if I did, I wouldn't have the first idea how to go about it. Okay?

But I've got a feeling something is not right. I'm afraid she's living a double life . . ."

It was difficult to blame Sélim for developing paranoid fantasies. It's a symptom of the times. And when a guy marries a supercute, shy, funny little *beurette* and she leaves him overnight, takes a Russo-Satanic stage name and floods the world with hot, double-penetration porn videos . . . well, he has a right, later on, to suspect the female of the species of being capable of anything. The Hyena keeps this line of argument to herself and tries to reassure him:

"I spent, like, five minutes with her but honestly she didn't come across as the suicide-martyr type . . . so you're freaking out just because she wears the hijab, is that it?"

"No. She's obsessed with religion."

"It's better than being hooked on crack."

"I'm not so sure. Seriously. I wonder how far it goes. We barely talk."

"Okay. You know she'll get over this? She's young, it's a phase . . . How do you expect me to follow her around Barcelona? I can hardly shadow her . . ."

"Of course not, you go there with her. Actually it was Aïcha's idea. I didn't want her to go on her own. Last night, after you left, she suggested you could babysit her. She said 'That way you won't have to worry.' And it's true . . . after all, you've done a lot of bizarre jobs . . . and obviously, in your own way, you know a lot about women . . . Once you've spent a couple of days with her you'll be able to tell me what you think . . . It's just a case of observing her."

"How on earth did she come up with the idea?"

"She doesn't have a lot of female role models."

"As female role models go, I'm hardly typical – Does she know I'm a dyke?"

"I'm not exactly planning to go into the details of your private life with her . . ."

"All due respect, Sélim, what you're suggesting is totally lame."

"I helped you out with Fardin, didn't I? Please, as a favour to me."

The Hyena would be incapable of explaining how the details were ironed out, but in less than an hour, it was settled: she would go with the girl to Barcelona. Often, the craziest decisions can seem coolly logical.

And it was true, he had helped her track down the screenwriter. Xavier Fardin. It had taken Sélim only a couple of calls to find his phone number – and she met up with him the same day in the bar opposite his apartment. Hetero douchebag type, smug, confident in his opinions, spewing hoary old clichés yet convinced he's just invented the wheel, cocksure for no reason she could fathom – she felt his bovine, lecherous eyes brazenly undressing her. He was all excited that someone was taking an interest in him. When she told him she worked for a producer, he instantly reeled off his whole C.V., he made it very clear that he would love to work on a film about Alex Bleach. But he could not tell her where she might find this guy called Vernon Subutex who had the footage – she could try searching on Facebook, but he seemed to be in hiding, he was having problems with a particularly vengeful ex. He was a decent guy who, for years, had run a record shop in Paris.

When she got home, the Hyena had called Gaëlle – yes, she knew Subutex, the guy who used to run Revolver, a nice guy as it goes, sure, no problem, she could try and get in touch with him.

Her search had not just taken off, it was soaring like a helium balloon. The Hyena had said nothing of this to Dopalet, when he phoned she kept him on tenterhooks – "It's pretty complicated, you know, but I've got a couple of leads, I'll keep you up to speed." If you tell the client that the job is easy, it's difficult to tell him later that it is going to cost a fortune. And besides, she enjoyed seeing him in meltdown – it's always nice to see dictatorial C.E.O.s squirm from time to time.

The Hyena crosses Plaça de la Universitat and heads up calle Aribau towards the apartment. Barcelona is still a charming old whore, smiling whenever she gets a tip, it seems that nothing can ruin her beauty, not the tourists, not the shop signs, not even the blocks of modern architecture. Rubbish bins line the pavement, at regular intervals men open them and peer under the lids. No two are the same. An anti-globalisation activist finds a pair of jeans in his size, an Eastern European guy pushing a shopping trolley salvages a roll of electric cable, an elderly man can find nothing that takes his fancy, an African digs out a wicker basket which he fills with books and newspapers.

She had met Aïcha in the café at the gare d'Austerlitz – which was little frequented after 9.00 p.m. – to take the night train. The Hyena does not take planes. Aïcha was worried about arriving exhausted.

"It means leaving a day earlier and getting there shattered. I'm attending a seminar, it's not like I can relax."

"You do know Islamists always take this train? It's famous for it."

The girl looked away, appalled at the turn the conversation was taking. But it was true, the train was always full of bearded men, foreheads marked with brutal prayers.

Aïcha's suitcases were so heavy that it would have been reasonable to wonder whether she were transporting weapons. But they were filled with books and documents. She had obviously thought to herself, I'm going to Barcelona for a week, why not take my whole library with me.

She is not like her father. She has his studious side – Sélim had been gifted and assiduous, a combination that tends to make for happy students. It was after university that things became complicated. He perfectly understood university rules and regulations whereas the chaos of real life bewildered and demoralised him. Aïcha has not inherited his whimsical nature. She is a single-minded girl whose serious expression and frequently knitted brows make her look permanently angry. Not frenzied, I'm-going-to-smash-someone's-face angry, but so focused that she seems harsh.

She is obdurately polite, reserved to the point of being chilly; from the second she set eyes on the girl, the Hyena liked her. She is not pretty, in the classic sense of the word. Too stout, too sullen. But this is precisely her charm. An impression of intelligence allied to strength without a trace of feminine gentleness. Despite her veil, Aïcha does not seem very modern, she has the face and the expression of a girl of long ago. She has the face of a girl from the seventies. Probably something to do with the nose. Which, it turns out, you get used to.

The two women scarcely spoke to each other before boarding the train. The station platform was deserted at this hour, the few passengers were like ghosts. The Hyena had taken this train a dozen times, she liked the anachronistic feel of it. The carriages were something from another century, and had not changed. She was happy to be taking it one last time. Soon, the night train would no longer exist. Too expensive.

"So, how do you feel about your father being worried enough to send someone with you to Spain when you're almost twenty?"

"It's sad, isn't it?"

"Are you angry with him?"

"No. He's my father. I love him as I will never love another man."

She said it simply, everything seems very clear in her mind. The Hyena suddenly understood why her father was worried, she had rarely encountered someone so strong-minded. Her words were tinged with a deep sadness – Aïcha seemed already resigned to the fact that the love she speaks of is not something to be taken lightly.

"But doesn't it make you want to rebel, your father having someone constantly keeping an eye on you?"

For the first time, Aïcha seemed surprised and she smiled and looked away.

"No, I don't feel the need to rebel."

And the way she turned her head away said it all: maybe people still rebelled against authority back in your day, long ago. See where it got you? My generation goes about things differently.

They were sitting side by side in the tiny two-person compartment. Then the ticket inspector came and asked them to wait out in the corridor while she made up the couchettes. The space was reduced, bags and suitcases had to be carefully stacked. Aïcha took out a file of course notes – L.L.M. modules in Corporate Tax – she said this as though talking about something commonplace like an English course. She buried herself in her notes. The Hyena scanned the news headlines on her mobile phone before striking up a conversation.

"What exactly are you studying?"

"I'm in second year tax law."

"Is it what you wanted to do?"

"No-one forced me."

The Hyena made the most of the silence to wonder what the hell she was doing here. While feeling happy to be aboard this train – it had been so long since she had last travelled.

"So, you knew my father back in the days when he and my mother were still together?"

"I lived just upstairs from your place."

"Did you know my mother?"

"We were neighbours. I used to pop in for coffee, she'd come by to borrow cooking oil . . ."

"Before you came around last week, I didn't know that my mother was a whore."

"I'm sorry?"

"No-one ever told me that she had done porn. I heard you mention the name Pamela Kant when you were talking to my father. I looked her up. It was grim. I wrote to Pamela Kant to ask if she knew my mother, she wrote back some rubbish. I looked up some more photos of her. It took a while before I recognised my mother."

"You didn't say anything to your father?"

"It's too embarrassing."

"So you were waiting to talk to me?"

"Yes. It's because of you that I found out, so I thought you would tell me what I wanted to know."

ZBLAM. ZBLAM. THIS IS THE SHITTY SOUND OF REALITY BANGING at her door. *Zblam*. But no everyday reality, not yesterday's reality. *Zblam*. Not familiar reality. Nor something horrendous some unbelievable news an earthquake an event demanding some reaction some swift decision. *Zblam*. *Zblam*. It is more like madness, light as a shadow but beneath a blazing sun. It is the past that is past, something that cannot be changed stuck right in the middle from now on nothing will ever be as it was before.

Aïcha is a room in which the contents of every wardrobe have been ransacked, tossed onto the floor. Nothing can hold back the past. It is inexorable. Her mother was a prostitute. Everyone knew. No-one told her. She was the daughter of a whore. A "public woman". Like a public toilet, but slutty. Her father was the husband of a whore. Her father outraged that she found out. Shit, Papa. Shit, shit, shit. Why didn't you kill her?

She loves her father. Loves him so much it hurts. Like razors in her veins. Loves him enough to spill her own blood. She knows it is unfair, this thing that has driven them apart these past two years. When she first discovered Islam, it was another way of saying that she loved her father more than anything. She had never been taught about religion at home. Her grandmother had died too soon. At the school she went to, there was no-one she could talk to. One day, she had been fortunate enough to listen to the imam and everything he said seemed familiar. Everything, finally, made sense. It was a matter of thinking about life differently rather than sacrificing it on the altar of consumerism. Everything her father had taught her, she rediscovered, magnified, in every grain of Islam. Everything he despised, those things he fought, the Qur'an said was wrong. Everything he respected, his regard for other people, his striving to do good, the Qur'an said was right.

The first time she got up from the table, one evening in June, "I'm going to say prayers", her father had turned pale, he had said "You're what?" Aïcha had not expected him to dig his heels in. She thought that they would discuss the matter, that he would welcome her faith, that he would be proud of her, because he would realise that it was a right and necessary choice. He did not let her speak. He clenched his teeth and turned his back, leaning on the sink and jerking his head towards her room, "Get out of here, I can't even look at you."

It was not fair. She does not hold it against him. She is sorry that it upsets him. She is patient. She knows that one day he will understand that being devout is her way of being worthy of him.

After her grandmother's death, they had packed her things away in cardboard boxes. In these boxes Aïcha discovered photographs she had never seen before showing her father as a young man, in several he is laughing. His head is thrown back, his eyes screwed up, laughing with his whole body. She has never seen him laugh like this. In the boxes, Aïcha found his master's thesis on the films of Bergman, articles by Claude Julien carefully clipped from *Le Monde diplomatique*, an outline for a thesis on

Victor Serge. All the girls in the photos of him at university are French; they wear their hair short like Jean Seberg, they are slim and wear clothes that show off their bodies.

Who is this young man? His expression is different, it is confident, determined. There is no sign yet of that wound, that sadness like a fissure through which all his joy would trickle away.

France persuaded her father that if he embraced her universal culture, she would welcome him with open arms as she would any of her children. Fine promises, but empty; Arabs with university degrees were still the *bougnoules* of the République and were kept, discreetly, outside the portals of the great institutions. For a daughter, nothing is worse than to see that her father has been conned – except perhaps discovering that he fell for it. Her father had been duped. He was told that in France everything is based on merit, that excellence is rewarded, he was taught that in a secular state, all men are equal. Only to have doors slammed one by one in his face, with no right of appeal. No communitarianism here. But there always comes a moment when you have to give your first name – that "Close Sesame" that magically means that apartments are already taken, job vacancies are already filled, a dentist's schedule is suddenly too busy to accept an appointment. "Integrate," people said, but to those who tried they said "See? You're not one of us."

She stared at her father's hands in the photographs, the hand of an intellectual, clean, well cared for, toying with a cigarette holder, the hands sketching ideas in the air. Faith alone is capable of holding back the rage that gnaws at the daughter's insides. She refuses to be a slab of hatred, a wounded, dangerous animal. Just as she refuses to sell her body. She refuses to give up her humanity. And faith alone affords her serenity and a sense of structure, offers her dignity.

Her relationship with her father became fractious and Aïcha could do nothing to prevent this. He says, "You're only doing it to piss me off", referring to her faith. He refuses to discuss things. And yet, he used to adore her.

She was not annoyed that he refused to let her go to Barcelona on her own, even for her studies. She knows that he worries. She wishes that someone would reassure him. The Islam she practises has nothing to do with what the newspapers lap up when they want to sell their lies.

When she heard the old lesbian talking about Pamela Kant, she had no idea who she was, she remembered the name because it sounded funny. Then she googled it. She was outraged at the point at which she contacted Pamela Kant on Facebook, but she decided it was best to focus on other things. It nagged away at her and she overcame her disgust and did a little more digging into the case of Kant, this woman her mother liked to go dancing with. Vodka Satana. She did not immediately make the connection. She would never have made it but for the tattoo, the eye of Isis on the shoulder blade.

She should have been chary of her curiosity. She does not need to know the truth about sins she had not committed. She does not have to answer for censurable acts that are not her own. Allah in His wisdom knows every thing we do. Shit. She would rather have sewn her eyes shut than see what she has seen.

She knows that life was difficult in France for women of the previous generation. They were blown up on their way here. Men told them they were beautiful and encouraged to expose themselves to lustful eyes. Turn away from Allah and trample their heritage. They did not realise where it would lead them. The washing machines, the well-paid jobs, the unseemly clothes and the promise of an easy life. Some of her girlfriends' mothers dye their hair blonde, show their buttocks and hang out in bars. Aïcha was more pragmatic when it did not concern her own mother. Now she has hit the jackpot. Why is this happening to her?

Aïcha will not even kiss a boy on the cheek when saying hello. Her conduct is always modest. She shuns all closeness because she knows that, once it begins, it can quickly get out of hand.

She is grateful that the Hyena does not try to evade the issue. Aïcha told her what she knew. The woman said nothing for a brief moment, then she turned the night-light on again.

"You're a pain in the arse, kid. Don't you think you'd have been better off taking this up with your father?"

"I would never dare talk about this with my father."

She would never dare talk about it with anyone. Not her girlfriends, not the imam. It does not touch her, it does not sully her – she keeps her distance, and that is the end of it.

What is it she finds most repulsive? Herself. Her mother. The filthy bastards she hung out with. A culture that pushes women to do such things. Not just sanctions them but actively encourages them. These are the same tarts who sneer at her for wearing the veil. What is it she finds most disgusting? Why did her mother not turn to her father for refuge when she realised she was in danger? Did she despise her own family so much? Her father would have saved her. Why did she not protect herself? Who is it speaking within Aïcha? Who is arguing? Her thoughts are fleeting, conflicting and inconclusive.

The Hyena is completely deranged. This makes it easier to dare to ask blunt questions.

"Your mother was a brilliant girl."

"Brilliant girls find other kinds of jobs, don't they?"

"You have to take these things in context . . ."

"I would kill her. If she were still alive, I would have killed her. I would have done it to avenge my father, I would have done it for myself, and for her."

"Yeah, right. You would have hugged her, you would have adored her. Everyone adored your mother."

Aïcha sneered at her flippancy, her cynicism. Entirely dedicated to pagan glory, to the almighty monotheistic cult of money, the woman did not realise what she was saying, she blasphemed every time she opened her mouth. But Aïcha also felt a certain pleasure at someone insisting "your mother was adorable" and refusing to budge an inch. This was something no-one had ever told her. It was unbearable and at the same time pleasant.

They talked for much of the night. Aïcha was in the top bunk. In the berth below, the Hyena would savagely kick the mattress whenever the girl said something she didn't like. The old lesbian was stark staring mad, but she was funny. She was defiant when it came to moral considerations, and had the extravagant exuberance typical of certain heretics who call themselves hedonists and think they can take pleasure without regard for the law and without facing the consequences. But if, during this long conversation, Aïcha refused to listen to anything that might suggest her mother was a woman to be respected, she had enjoyed having someone who was prepared to stand up to her.

They were shattered by the time they rolled into the Estació de França, the sun a dazzling screen. They have not mentioned the subject since.

Today there is a general strike in Spain. No radio, no television all morning, they sit out on the balcony, the traffic on the street below is like a Sunday. Most of the shops are shuttered, the tobacconists, the bars, the restaurants. Only the Orxateria is open, though the metal blinds remain half-closed. Aïcha does not go to lectures, the university is not open. The Catalan students advised her to do any shopping she needed the night before, since everything would be closed. Even those traders who wanted to stay open have changed their minds, fearful of reprisals. Previous protest marches have left the city in flames – mopeds dustbins cars, everything that could burn was set ablaze.

A heavy atmosphere hangs over the streets, heightened by the leaden sky. Aïcha wants to go out for a walk. The Hyena suggests they go to the cinema, but the cinema, like everything else, is closed. At about ten o'clock, police officers take up positions at the intersections, black armoured vans roll along the street. The Hyena suggests perhaps Aïcha might use the time to do homework. "I don't really think it's a good idea for you to go out today, your father is counting on me to look after you." She sits on the sofa, laptop on her knees, writing comments on the websites of Parisian restaurants and spends the rest of her time following today's events on the homepage of *La Vanguardia*.

First explosion, a long way away. The police fire rubber bullets.

A bus moves down the street and is quickly surrounded by demonstrators. In less than thirty seconds, the windscreen is plastered with stickers. Passengers stream off, grumbling blasé supportive amused uncertain. The police appear and order the bus driver to move on, the bus empty, her visibility non-existent.

A helicopter sets down to the west, over what must be the Ramblas. The whine of the rotors fills a city empty of cars. Down below, pedestrians go about their day, an elderly bald man wearing slippers and a tracksuit stands smoking his pipe and talking to himself, a couple walks a baby in a buggy. American-style police sirens hurtle past at regular intervals, yellow paramedic cars rumble up the street. A blind man walks along dragging a rolling suitcase with one hand and gripping his white stick in the other. Foreigners with wheeled suitcases search for taxis.

Aïcha says she wants to find a pharmacy, that she needs artichoke juice. The Hyena looks up from her laptop. "Artichoke juice? But didn't you buy black radish gel capsules when we got here?" Yes, but Aïcha can feel her gall-bladder is not responding well to the oil-rich food she has been eating over the past few days. The Hyena groans. "I've never come across a kid so obsessed by her digestion. God knows what you'll be like when you're forty."

She rubs her face with both hands as though wiping it clean. "You really want to go out, do you? You realise there's not a soul anywhere in the city, yeah? The march is not until six this evening, everyone is having a siesta right now." "Just to look for a pharmacy." "I'll go with you."

They walk in silence. It is not a hostile silence. It is something that suits them both.

As they pass Starbucks, Aïcha stumbles as someone roughly

pushes past her. Before she even realises that he has snatched her bag, she sees him being slammed into a wall and hears the dull crack as the Hyena snaps his knee with her heel. A second man charges towards the Hyena, Aïcha grabs his shoulder, spins him round and lands a punch on his jaw. He reels. The Hyena bends over the thief, growling in rapid, heavily accented Spanish. "Sorry 'bout that, you gave me a bit of a fright – can you walk?" She pats him on the back, then glances around worriedly. He grunts angrily, the Hyena turns to his friend who is still staggering. "Get him out of here quick, there are cops crawling all over the place and we're starting to attract attention. What are you waiting for? You want to end up in hospital?" The guy who came to the rescue stares at Aïcha and spits on the ground, a passer-by asks in French "Is there a problem?" and the Hyena smiles but her jaw is so tense that the rictus grin is terrifying. "No, it's nothing, we just bumped into each other." "They didn't steal anything?" "No, it was an accident, it's all fine . . ." She turns to the man still lying on the ground whose friend is heaving him roughly to his feet.

Aïcha and the Hyena walk off without waiting to find out how the story ends. Aïcha knows that she should be ashamed of what just happened. But she feels a thrill of excitement in keeping with the day, the helicopter, the sound of explosion. She whistles: "You're pretty quick for your age, I didn't even realise he'd snatched my bag before you'd walloped him." The Hyena stops. "For my age? Are you looking for a smack in the mouth, Mike Tyson?" She raises an eyebrow, clicks her fingers to indicate they should move on. "Shift it, there are Feds everywhere." "Are you worried they'll ask to see your papers?" "No. Why d'you say that?" "Then why are we in such a rush? And why did we come by train?" "You can never tell what will happen with the cops . . . if we end up in custody, how am I going to explain that to your father? And would you care to explain where you learned to land a right hook?" "Boxing lessons." "You took boxing lessons?" "When I was little. But later on, one of my father's girlfriends decided it didn't do much for my femininity. He suggested I give it up." "Your femininity?" "Yes, when I was a kid I was pretty . . . tough. I'm more demure these days. But I've still got the reflexes. I saw the space open up, I took a second to think and – bam! It's the first time I've raised a fist to anyone since . . . well, primary school, I think." "Isn't it sinful for a girl to fight?" "Absolutely not. If she's attacked, it's perfectly fine for a woman to defend herself. We don't know those guys." "Would it be different if we knew them?" "Yes, maybe, it depends whether we owed them respect. But I don't owe them any respect, they're thieves. It's not my fault that his mother gave birth to a feeble little fucker, honestly, he'll never make a career as a delinquent." "I'm glad you're more demure and less tough. I'd hate to see the uncensored version."

Something happens between them in that moment. They are walking towards García, passing people waving Catalan flags and others carrying yellow protest banners, small groups before the protest itself.

"You want to carry on walking or should we go back to the apartment and I'll make you something to eat."

"You do know that you're a terrible cook? It takes me an age to digest the muck you serve up."

"No-one's ever told me I was a terrible cook. That said, I rarely cook."

"Maybe that's why."

That evening, Aïcha is rereading her course notes and the Hyena has decided to simmer vegetables without any fat so they can drink the broth. She claims it will be good for Aïcha's "liver function". The Hyena approaches the table, waving for the girl to shoo: "We're about to eat, shift that paperwork, you can go back to it later," and when Aïcha does not immediately obey, she takes a step back and raises her foot, brandishing a tatty slipper with the sole hanging off, "Hello, I'm Ms Slipper, hurry up, I'm hungry for vegetable broth". Aïcha bursts out laughing because it is so stupid that it's actually funny. They sit down to eat and, after the first spoonful, they both fall about laughing. The broth is absolutely disgusting.

Afterwards, Aïcha feels self-conscious. She clears the table, checks the time, eager to say the evening prayers, to re-focus herself. She does not say a word, but the Hyena comments aloud: "Oh quit it, just because we've had a laugh doesn't mean we're suddenly B.F.F.s. What are you afraid of? Don't worry, lesbianism isn't contagious." And Aïcha stares at her – can this witch read her mind? But she somehow cannot get worked up because it's obvious that the Hyena is cool and she has no intention of brainwashing her or leading her off the strait and narrow.

PATRICE'S NOSE HAS BEEN STREAMING SNOT FOR THE PAST TWO days. The skin around his nostrils is so red raw it is painful to blow his nose. He takes magnesium chloride at €1.90 a sachet. Diluted in water it tastes revolting and instantly triggers diarrhoea, but twenty-four hours later you're cured. He feels his intestines spasm and shudder, he finds it pleasant to evacuate despite the pain. Especially since the bog is the only nicely decorated room in his place – he has plastered the walls with posters of all kinds . . . naked girls especially, which means stepping into a cave full of tits, flat stomachs, bronzed skin, bee-stung lips. It is restful. This is where he keeps his magazines. He spends much of the day in here, especially when he is alone and can leave the door open and listen to the music in the living room.

When he wakes up, he still feels sick. Forgetting that Vernon is sleeping on the sofa bed, he nearly headed to the bog bare-arsed with his wedding tackle hanging out. Facing the toilet, he pauses for a moment, which is more pressing – throwing up or diarrhoea? He has to choose. It has often occurred to him that, in a more civilised world, it would be possible to sit and lean forward, thereby reliving yourself in both senses without having to change position. People who design toilets clearly do not drink enough, they don't take account of crucial everyday situations.

The night before, Vernon showed up with a bottle of rum, they drank like there was no tomorrow, and now his every organ is protesting at the evils inflicted on it. The morning after a drinking binge with a dose of flu, he is out of commission. For some time now, his body has been gradually falling apart. Less than a year ago, he was admitted to accident and emergency with pyelonephritis, he showed up a raging fever, delirious and hallucinating about animals, imagining giant turtles, alligators lying on his belly, his skin felt hot and viscous, he could see huge snakes coiling around his legs. It reminded him of tripping on shrooms in Mexico. It took more than a week for the fever to break. He was in a room with an old man who moaned and ripped out his I.V. lines during the night, the old codger kept trying to run away but by the time he reached the end of the corridor he would forget his own name and the nurses would calmly escort him back, eventually they strapped him to the bed, but he kept complaining. The doctors were stunned that Patrice had waited so long before he began to worry – didn't you realise you were ill? He said no, in the mornings, I'd just assume I had a vicious hangover, I'd have a beer and it would go away. A young doctor with pale eyes and an accent that was probably Lebanese or something like that told him he was suffering from delirium tremens, from alcohol withdrawal. He advised him to stop drinking. Why? So he would wind up in hospital later rather than sooner? So he would sleep better? The booze is destroying his liver, the cigarettes are attacking his tongue, his throat, his lungs, the greasy food is clogging his arteries – surely he can get one thing right in his life and die young.

Lying on his side, Vernon is snoring. Coming back to reality isn't going to be easy for him either. Patrice fills a bottle with water, his temples are pounding as though there is major demolition work going on in his cortex. Shit, when they were young, they'd be skipping around the morning after a booze-up.

Patrice flicks on the radio and turns on his computer. This is what he does every morning. He knows it drives him mad. Back in the eighties, when he started buying newspapers and listening to the radio, things were different. There were moments when he got angry, but there were also journalists he enjoyed reading, correspondents he liked to listen to. There were artists he was happy to see become politically engaged. Relationships with the media were not entirely defined by defiance and hostility. The moronic comments about the fall of the Berlin Wall, about Tiananmen Square or Scorsese filming "The Last Temptation of Christ" were heard over the bar – between people who were physically present, could see each other, respond to each other, get confused. People didn't just spout gibberish, anonymous and angry, condemned to come out with highly polished turds only to be met by the deadening silence of their own powerlessness. Today, he feels like tidying up but he does not have the strength. He visits the websites of newspapers he would never have bought when he was young. Poisonous tentacles insinuate themselves into his brain prompting no deliberation, only rage. The urge to fight, anything and anyone, a morbid sickness. He does not want to add his voice to the throng, he does not want to start a blog to pour out his bile, he does not want to add his pathetic little turd to the torrent of shit. But he cannot bring himself to look away. Every morning, he has the feeling that he is staring out of the window, watching the world go to hell. And no-one among the governing elites seems to realise that they urgently need to backpedal. On the contrary, the only thing they seem to care about is heading for rock bottom as fast as possible.

He reads the story of little Adam who burst into an American elementary school and shot twenty kids and a dozen adults. He wishes he had the balls to do something like that. Not in a school – his generation doesn't go around killing toddlers, it lacks a certain level of nihilism. Or senselessness. When it happened, like any parent he pictured the school his children attended. His two kids go to the same school. If anyone so much as touched a hair on their heads . . . last night on television, one of the American fathers was saying that he had already forgiven the killer. It was simultaneously heartrending and revolting.

The day Patrice became a father was not the best in his life. It was the most terrifying. He was temping at the time, working night shifts in Rungis, Cécile sent him a text message to say she was on her way to the clinic. She was in too much pain to phone. Text messages were a new thing at the time, this was one of the first he ever received.

The foreman was a pathetic Portuguese guy who walked with his toes turned in, he was a bastard but, being a father himself, for once he was decent and allowed Patrice to leave without busting his balls. No-one tells you what it's like, a woman giving birth. No-one ever talks about it, it's only when it happens that you realise you don't know shit – and thank fuck for that. When he got to the clinic, there were howls coming from the delivery rooms. It was a full moon. The midwives said this with a knowing smile. There was screaming from room to room and every woman was saying the same thing: I don't think I can do this. And: for God's sake help me I'm dying here. Cécile was just like the others. He arrived two hours after he got the text, traffic on the *périphérique* was already choc-a-bloc. No sign of the kid's head yet. Nothing but his wife who could no longer hear him, she was streaming with sweat, her feet, which had swollen up like bruised balloons three days earlier, hanging in the stirrups, she no longer had the strength to push, she had been through too much pain. She had already shat herself copiously. And this was just the beginning. Her labour lasted five hours. The medical team decided it had gone well. Luckily people don't know anything about giving birth. Afterwards, women are fine: they forget. Not men. Before going at it again, men seriously wonder – is it really a good idea? A year after their first kid, Cécile was already talking about the next one. She had erased the memory of five hours of hell, of the grisly bloodbath; she remembered only a single image: when the baby was laid on her belly and, in her own words, she "understood for the first time the meaning of the Other".

But he had forgotten nothing. Watching someone he loved suffer had been the most terrible experience of his whole life – he had asked whether, for their second kid, she was sure she didn't want to adopt. She wouldn't hear of it. If he gave her a slap – a little love tap – she would still be sulking six months later, here she was, having had her belly ripped in two, she was up for doing it all over again. So don't go telling him that men and women are the same, deep down. It makes a cracking sound, the pelvis, when it opens up to let the kid out. Crack. No-one tells you this stuff, no-one mentions the crack. The second time, he stayed in the waiting room, he refused to be present for the birth. Cécile understood. It wasn't about the shit and the blood, or the fact that when it comes out the kid is a howling monster. It was seeing her suffer. Everything else was fine, he was happy to show up to cut the cord. When the thing opens its gob and screams . . . The child is breathing, it's all good. The midwives were knowledgeable, they talked to him like he was retarded, which was exactly what he needed. They were good with Cécile. Which was just as well. One of them had pressured her along during labour, she had felt things were going too slowly and made her toe the line, "I need you to push now, go on, go for it" while Cécile was in tears. He had almost said something but then remembered that she spent all day doing this for a living while he did not have the first clue. His wife was dying, they had conceived the child of Satan, a cloven-hooved infant, a baby whose skull was armed with fearsome horns, only that could explain why she was in such pain giving birth.

They were shattered. When he looked at the clock, it was nine o'clock and they had not slept a wink, and he realised how exhausting the experience had been. Cécile had fallen asleep, her hand in his. He loved her so much. He cannot bear to remember. How much he loved that woman. His wife. Her eyes. Something in her eyes made him surrender, he gave up the ghost and a feeling of ecstasy coursed through him from his heels to the roots of his hair. She had fallen asleep and he had gazed at Tonio. There had been a brief moment of disbelief, and then his life had changed forever. Fear. He had never understood it before. Now it wrapped itself around his entrails and refused to budge. The fear that something might happen to this tiny creature. A second had been enough to conjure the full extent of that *something*: illness, injury, attack, accident, infection, aggression, torture, starvation, abuse, molestation, penetration, kidnapping, disease, fire, terrorism, bombing, warfare, epidemic, tsunami, typhoon, asphyxia . . . "The apple of my eye": the expression is a poor description of the bond between parent and newborn. His eyes could be gouged out but that would not kill him – "the marrow of my bones" might be more accurate, describing that it is something that inhabits the whole being, that this bond appears before you can even distinguish your baby from another. The child had barely been born, and already Patrice was filled with terror.

After Tonio, Patrice felt centred. Despite the fact that Cécile cried all the time. During the pregnancy, after she gave birth, when the baby took his first steps . . . he remembers only Cécile, desperate, swollen with tears, gasping and spluttering. The second time, the medical team eyed her suspiciously when the two of them arrived for the birth. A Sunday. This time he had been there to drive her. They noticed the bruises on her, he felt them looking at him askance. The tension quickly faded, they concluded that it was not what they feared, they became more friendly. Patrice has always had a way with people. He sets them at ease. It's complicated, his relationship with Cécile. It was not just "a violent guy beating his pregnant wife". It was more complicated than that. He loved her with all his heart, treated her like a princess. But every now and then, he flipped.

It had been a nightmare, when she had left. When she had started signing statements other people had written saying that this was how it had been between them. Spousal abuse, that sort of bullshit. She had betrayed him. Court injunctions, vile letters. She had betrayed their love. She was surrounded by prying, prissy old biddies. Not to mention her mother, her sister, her friend Mafalda, a fat retard who was only too happy to destroy a passionate relationship when she herself would never experience so much as a decent fuck. Witches who patiently bided their time and then threw him out.

It has been seven years since Cécile left him. Tonio had been three, Fabien two. It never gets easier. Sometimes he thinks it might, he does not try to stop it, he is tired of suffering like this. But then it starts up again. He thinks about it, is constantly tortured by it, even when he is with people, even when he is working, all he can think about is this. Booze doesn't help. Staying sober is worse, because of the insomnia.

He quickly worked out that Vernon was lying when he claimed he was just back from Quebec to sort out his papers. For the past three months he's been pissing around chatting with his French friends on Facebook, and now suddenly he lands up with a guy he barely knows who lives out in Corbeil? He's obviously homeless. Everything about him says he's on the streets. When Cécile left him, Patrice spent six months couch surfing. He wound up staying with people who had him do the cleaning and the shopping in exchange. Or left him to babysit their kids every night. Then there are women who can't understand why you won't sleep in their bed since, after all, they're putting a roof over your head. There are those who are so filthy that eating off their plates, drinking from their glasses gives you heaves you have to hide. He was sure Cécile would change her mind, he was in no hurry to get his own apartment. It had happened once before and they had lost a fortune. For nothing. He thought she would change her mind, but after six months he could no longer stand sleeping on couches in other people's living rooms. He knew a guy, an old friend from school, who worked at the public housing office in Corbeil. He phoned the guy, embarrassed that he was asking for a favour, for an apartment, like, now. But instead of telling him to fuck off, which is what he would have done, this guy was happy to do what he could to help. Within two months it was all arrranged. He was living in Corbeil. A pretty decent apartment. In an area that made you want to buy a shovel dig a hole and bury yourself alive so as not to have to see it. The problem isn't the scumbags, it's the feeling of living in a vast open prison. But once inside the apartment, everything is fine. He's high up, trees outside the windows, he can see the sky, a patch of green, the apartment has floor-to-ceiling windows. It's comfortable. If he weren't so depressed, he could get to like living here. The neighbourhood is a dump but it's mostly inhabited by old biddies and old codgers, even the local thugs can't bring themselves to be violent. They live their lives a couple of streets away where it doesn't feel so much like an old people's home.

After the sixth message on Facebook, Patrice twigged that Vernon was asking him for a place to crash and he said sure. He was still wary, Sylvie had complained about Vernon stealing stuff. Serve her right, the bourgeois bitch. She got what she deserved. But even so, he let Vernon know the minute he opened the door: I'm happy to do this, but I can't stand being fucked over, you take anything from this place without my permission and I'll rip out those pretty blue eyes of yours.

Patrice has the right build for this sort of speech. Though the only thing that remains of his youthful persona are the tattoos. Even when he wears a suit and a turtle neck, they show. He has stopped wearing his team colours, got rid of the motorbike, these days he listens to Coltrane and Duke Ellington. He got fed up with trying to be a Marxist Hell's Angel. Too many contradictions to handle. He's still a Marxist, he packed in the Angels. But he kept the look. He had no choice. However much he changes his clothes, he still looks like an ex-con. He is inked from his neck to his wrists, and not the kind of faggoty tramp stamps girls get these days. He is used to buttocks clenching when he enters a room. He has kept the long hair, the chunky rings and the collection of metal bracelets. He still has all his hair, which is now a gentlemanly white, just like Gérard Darmon's. When life gives you a gift like that, you don't go cutting your hair.

Vernon still has all his hair too. And those blue eyes really pay off at his age. There is something about his face that is not tainted. Vernon always was a modest kind of guy, never caused any trouble, happy to help out. Not the sharpest knife in the drawer, like most guys in the music business, brain the size of a pea, but he's not the kind to stab you in the back.

Unlike everyone else, Patrice feels no nostalgia for his years as a musician. He ended up playing bass with the Nazi Whores when the original bassist left, the official reason being that his girlfriend didn't want him touring anymore. The real reason was that he was sick of the drummer stealing his girls, including his long-term girlfriend. Patrice learned to play the three notes he needed to stand in, it was Alex's idea. He never became a good musician. He had the vocation but not the talent, no matter how hard he practised, he never learned. But he enjoyed putting on a show when he was on stage. His apelike prancing made up for his lack of emotion. He enjoyed playing the wanker. It was his age. For two years he had a blast, touring endlessly in the G7, warming up spouting shit. They could sometimes drive 800 kilometres between two gigs, their manager was resolutely impractical and thought it would be rude to insist they eat something other than tabbouleh and sleep on some guy's floor. It was all part of being on the road, you had to just suck it up, otherwise there would have been no scene. It was all fine by him, until he got sick of it. Minimum three rehearsals a week, rock is a serious business, with guys who had fuck-all else to do but showed up an hour late, took thirty-minute breaks and made a racket in between songs. He quickly got tired of the lack of discipline. And spending his weekends playing gigs out in the sticks or in sleazy Italian dives with a thick haze of dope and no-one coherent enough to listen to a gig . . . The first year was a buzz, the second exhausting and the third year, he quit the band. A few months before it broke up. There are three ways that a band can break up. Boredom leading to natural death, open warfare, or a traumatic incident like the death of one of its members.

In Patrice's case, as he was heading down into the cellar to rehearse one day he realised he wasn't enjoying it anymore. He wanted to spend Saturday nights in watching telly, find himself a regular job where he didn't need to get time off on Fridays to drive to Bourg-en-Bresse for a gig. He announced his decision to the others. I'm done here, you'll need to find a replacement. Alex was the one who was most upset. It simply confirmed what he already knew – that his experience was different to the others'. Alex had no choice. He had nothing else. He had no family, no j ob, no other ambitions. And he was the only one of them who had an ear, with an idea of how to write a song.

Patrice didn't miss it. The relief he felt trumped any regrets. He was sick of the music industry, the hardcore scene, all that shit. There's a reason it's called a subculture. Half-wit douchebags who could spend the whole night discussing different amps, fuzz pedals or shirt collars. The real eggheads could hold forth about audio cables. Like a bunch of junior mechanics who've never qualified. He rebuilt his life around more adult passions, and when he ran into people he'd known back then he was always struck by how little they had changed.

Vernon might have been dumb as a sack of spanners. But he had charm. Easy going, good company. Too few neurons circulating to get worked up about anything. When he offered to put him up, Patrice hadn't been expecting a particularly fascinating evening. He did it because he wasn't yet bitter enough to refuse an old friend hospitality just because he would have been happier sitting on his own in front of the T.V.

Vernon had showed up with a bottle of rum, he looked like shit and seemed determined to get hammered as fast as possible. They settled down to watch "Koh-Lanta", each with a packet of crisps in his lap, and Vernon turned out to be the perfect foil when watching reality T.V. On the island, the arrival of the "survivors" played out as it did every season: badly for the minority group. Patrice and Vernon vented their bile on the various contestants. Around the camp, all the men were hunting for the Hidden Immunity Idol. The girls stayed around the fire, making food.

"I'd be only too happy to be a feminist. But can you explain to me why they don't even try to save themselves? Have you seen much of 'Koh-Lanta'? Have you ever seen one of the girls find the Hidden Immunity Idol?"

"I know, I've watched the programme. Have you ever seen the guys gang up against other guys in the tribal councils?"

"No."

"Cards on table, if you were a girl, would you trust the guys to make a deal? I know I wouldn't."

"Says it all, really."

*

And "Who Wants to Marry My Son?" which came on just after "Koh-Lanta" did little to radically change their atavistic views on the female of the species. They came to the same conclusions: in theory, they are prepared to accept sexual equality. But they cannot help but notice that girls don't seem in any hurry to develop a little dignity.

If Cécile had been there to listen to their maunderings, she would have wrinkled her nose, that hamster-like twitch that sent them into helpless giggles, she would have called them "foremen". Among working-class children, this is an insult that means what it says.

Patrice has always knocked his girlfriends about. Every one of them. He can pick up a girl, have a one-night stand without feeling the need to hit her, but as soon as it becomes a relationship, the first slap looms on the horizon. Obviously, it hurts him more than it hurts her, that first slap; the girl doesn't yet realise that it has started. Even when they've been in a dozen relationships where they've been abused a dozen times, girls refuse to admit that they know how it works. They need to believe that it's an accident. Love will prevail over brutality and turn their boyfriend into an attentive partner. People look for their identity in these relationships, they look, and they find themselves. Patrice isn't a kid any longer. Whenever he meets someone new, he hears himself open the floodgates to big promises, to gifts and compliments. He dupes himself and she allows herself to be duped. This time it's different, he has changed. He need only wait. The first slap. A pair of eyes, wide with fear, tell him he cannot succeed, but he manages to convince himself otherwise. Anger has shown up uninvited. She knows the routine, she can come back when she likes. He will discipline her. She will believe him when he swears it will never happen again. He will be sincere. He will back her into a corner, beat her, break her down until eventually she leaves him. And if she does not leave, he will kill her. And every time he says that he is sorry, he is telling the truth. He is frantically looking for the switch, something that will allow him to control himself.

With Cécile, the first slap came after they had been together ten months and he was convinced that he had finally found the right girl, the one for him. With her, things were different. The love he felt for her was a mixture of trust and excitement, tranquillity and intensity – she calmed him without boring him. He didn't see it coming. Even though he recognised the pattern. It begins in the morning with angry tirades about everything Cécile does wrong, in their relationship, in life in general. Ludicrous arguments that seem justified at the time. Things that go round and round in his head until he is convinced he is being conned. One day, it all comes out, she breaks down and cries. She is shocked that a man who spends his time telling her he adores her can harbour such resentment. She sobs and he apologises. Because when he sees her in tears the very reasons for his fury no longer seem valid, he no longer remembers believing they were true. But something has been set in motion, a pattern of negative thinking that he can see no way of stopping.

One night, when he came home, he suggested they order in pizza and Cécile started going on at him, oh sure, why not go out and have Vietnamese, yeah, he said, why not, and she said we could have sushi delivered, it's more expensive but if you really fancy it why not, if it comes to that why not go down to the Japanese restaurant, still she kept on and on, he was right, pizza would be fine but if they really wanted to save money she could heat up some pasta, she had the makings of a sauce, maybe but if they had Bún bò Huê there would be no washing up or anything, and he fancied Vietnamese. This was something she often did, take a simple possibility and turn it into an unintelligible muddle. It was something that had always bothered Patrice, but had never made him lose his cool. That night, he had let her blether on for ten minutes, then barked, "Give it a rest, you're doing my head in. Order a couple of pizzas and shut your hole." Cécile, unintimidated, because she did not really know him, flew into a rage, "Don't talk to me in that tone of voice, no-one talks to me like that do you even realise how aggressive you are towards me?" And at that point, bang, wallop. Not a slap with the flat of his hand, no, his fist clenched, aiming for her temple. And another one before she had time to realise what was happening, to make it quite clear that this was not the start of a discussion. People who never lash out don't understand how it works. It is a beast crouching in the belly, it moves faster than thought. And once unleashed, it is like a wave: all the good will in the world cannot stop it from breaking. It has to come crashing down. The crucial moment comes earlier, this he has realised – he needs to listen for the rumble of the wave, learn to deflect it before it swells. But by the time he feels himself getting angry, it is already too late. He doesn't have time – as pissant do-gooders suggest – to put on his trainers and go walk it off – it would be like asking a volcano to postpone an eruption . . . He must carry on, must go all the way. The other person must shut up. Must capitulate.

*

Later, in group therapy – because he ended up going to one of those fuck-me-gently-with-a-chainsaw shrink sessions, because he was so desperate to hang on to Cécile, he would have done anything – they tried to make him say that he was simply acting out what his mother had done to him. And it was true. She did batter him. And his brother. A single woman with two sons, they were out of control. They were soundly disciplined. This was back when taking down the strap didn't cause a moral uproar. She would beat them with a strap. Patrice never believed there was a connection. If every boy beaten by his parents grew up to be a violent man, people would know about it. His mother wasn't an alcoholic, she never hit them for no reason, she didn't go round changing the rules. His mother demanded respect, no more, no less.

It is a viper in the breast, it is something in the blood. It's got nothing to do with the past. He was born this way. If he had ever known his father, he might be prepared to accept that there was a biological explanation. In the moment, all you want is that rush of power. To look into the woman's eyes and see respect. Fear. And if the girl isn't completely terrified, you go on punching. Only when she demonstrates that she is utterly submissive does the violence end.

Immediately after these bouts of rage, he would feel drained. He would look at his wife, huddled in a corner, and long to erase what had just happened, to take her out walking in the sunshine, have a good time, act as if nothing had happened. No words growled through clenched teeth, no punches that could smash a door in two, no raised hand, no trembling body as he stared her in the eyes demanding that she take him seriously, because for as long as there remained even the slightest flicker of defiance, he had to go further.

At first, it's nothing. A couple of quick slaps and it's over and already you're making up. It escalates gradually. All the players need to know their roles. If the girl resists, if she isn't instantly petrified, if she doesn't immediately cower, things can turn very nasty. The essential is to instil terror, to make the woman submit. Unreservedly. He acknowledges his fault. He is a void, a wrong that can be righted only by lashing out.

Cécile was not made for such things. She didn't leave and slam the door at first, because she was in love. When the brute inside him was at peace, they were so good together.

He hated to see her cry, to see her body crumple. Becoming the opposite of what she was: a happy, light-hearted, vibrant woman. Exactly the type of girl he went for. He had watched, devastated, as she transformed into his girlfriend: drained of life, dark rings around her eyes, bitter lines tugging at the corners of her mouth. It was almost as if destroying them was part of the pleasure.

Cécile is much better now they're not together. You can see it. Even her hair is more lustrous. She is no longer afraid. She is still in love with him. But she will not come back. He will never get used to it, but it is better this way.

For a year after Tonio was born, he did not raise his hand to her. They both thought it was over. When it started again, she warned him: not in front of the baby. But the cycles had begun again. Violence was a demon that kept its distance just long enough for Patrice to believe he had changed. Then the demon coolly reasserted itself. Some nights, Patrice would beat her. In front of the kid. Before he was two years old, the boy had learned to crawl under his bed and curl into a ball. He never cried. He withdrew into his shell like an oyster and would stay that way for days. Nothing brought home to Patrice what he had become more clearly than the sight of his terrified son, huddled, hands clamped over his ears so as not to hear. With Cécile, there was still a part of him that managed to find excuses – it wasn't really that bad, she was laying it on thick just to make him feel guilty, it was one of those feminist things that meant women wanted a real man but not the beating that comes with him . . . he never said these things aloud, but it was what he thought – if it was as bad as she said, she would have left him. But when he saw his son, that fearless, giggling little colossus, huddled under his bed like a terrified animal, it would take him days to calm down after a violent outburst. What kind of bullshit excuse could he come up with to let himself off the hook – that the kid hadn't learned to be a man yet, that he would get used to it? At two years old? No, at the age of two, his son was not man enough to watch his father batter his mother with his fists. When he was man enough, he would get a rifle and put a bullet in the head of the fucker who had put him through this hell.

But still he could not stop it happening. Cécile joking with the fat lump of a waiter. What was he supposed to do? Let this bastard imagine he could fuck his wife right in front of him and he would say nothing? Cécile thought that women could flirt and joke with men without it meaning anything. It's obvious they've got no balls, if they had they'd know what men were thinking when they laugh and joke. Cécile was wonderful, but there are some things that women just don't understand. They want this utopian thing: friendship and closeness with guys. It doesn't exist. Guys want to fuck, otherwise they would be talking to other guys. So Patrice would thump the waiter and, when they got home, he would carry on and beat his wife.

They had a second kid – they were determined to believe that by bringing so much love and joy into their home, the rage would subside out of a sense of shame. But rage is a whore, it is shameless, Patrice carried on exactly as before. Except that, while she was knocked up, he was careful not to punch her too hard in the stomach.

One day, Cécile waited for him to go to work, then she packed her things, took the kids, and walked out. Patrice was furious when he found out that she had gone to stay at some home for battered wives. Their relationship wasn't like that, it wasn't some cliché of domestic violence. But, as it turns out, it was. Their story is just like every other. He is a caricature.

He loathed group therapy – he is nothing like the other guys who go there. His father didn't fight in Algeria, his mother didn't abandon him, he is perfectly capable of talking to his girlfriend – but the worst thing about listening to them was their phoney self-awareness. You could hear it, the group moderator was a big fan of childhood stories. He would swallow any old shit. But Patrice was not so easily fooled. All the guys who came to the group were liars. They said what they thought people wanted to hear. Some of them were smooth talkers. The devil is a hell of a dancer – why else would anyone join him on the dance floor? The guys sitting in a circle were old hands looking only for excuses and explanations, pretending to be relieved that they could finally express their emotions. But the only time these scumbags cried real tears was when they were feeling sorry for themselves. Patrice could see into their souls.

He had done the "anger diary" thing. Every time he raised his voice during the day, every time his rage became too much to handle, he would write down what had just happened, like an idiot, noting the time and the severity of the outburst on a scale of one to ten. He would find himself reaching for this fucking diary every day. It came as something of a shock: he could suddenly see with his own two eyes just what a bastard he was. The neat tally of his rages and the reasons for them made him seem more of a pathetic loser than even he had imagined.

Group therapy was all bullshit. It never got to the heart of the problem: without his rage, what would he be? A guy who keeps his trap shut when someone steals the parking space he's waited ten minutes for? A wimp who doesn't say shit when some fifteen-year-old arsewipe disses his girlfriend in the street? A pushover who says nothing when a colleague lands him with a sackload of shit that isn't even his responsibility? He spent all day being fucked over. What was he supposed to do? Just let it go, knowing that he was part of the social class of punchbags, doormats and pissant pussies? The guy leading the group would say that it was important that you didn't lump everything together – politics, feelings and petty frustrations. You try sorting them out.

One day during group therapy he spoke up: if I give up violence, what have I got left? It's not like I'm a fucking dentist – he used this example because among them was a prosthetist, a bastard who was sickly sweet and full of remorse here in group when it was blindingly obvious the guy was low-life scum. I've got no professional status. I've got no professional future. If I quit being violent, when do I ever get to feel like I'm the master? Come on, who's going to respect a submissive pleb?

He enjoys bar fights. He likes a punch-up, has done ever since he was a kid. Last year, in the Métro, he was sitting next to this skinny, puny black kid. When the doors opened, two other kids about the same age, but well built, came into the carriage and went for the kid, intending to take his money and administer a savage beatdown. Two hulking brutes against this scrawny kid, Patrice had not even tried to make sense of it. He had grabbed them and punched them out. Slick job. That day, in the Métro, he had been the hero – his fellow commuters were happy to have a psychopath in their midst, no-one was thinking he should be in group therapy. They were congratulating him. The whole carriage was ecstatic. When would he ever feel alive, feel happy, if he did not have his rage?

The sons of bitches in the group were all dirtbags who beat their wives, but most of them would never dare to beat up a guy. Patrice might be guilty of a lot of things, but not of being discriminatory. He would punch anyone. He enjoyed it – he was not afraid of anyone. When things kicked off, everyone else had to back down, he was perfectly happy to die rather than admit defeat.

Luckily it is a Saturday when he wakes up with this horrendous hangover. He would not be able to go to work today. He has managed to hang on to this job for four months. Usually he doesn't make it past three. Fixed-term contract working for the post office delivering mail. It's hard fucking work. He is sorry he has always been so down on postmen. First off, it's hard not to steal stuff. But the main problem is all the walking. And it's an obstacle course, working out where people mount their letter boxes . . . If it were left to him, he would have regulations in place like a shot – the fuckers already get their mail delivered for free, the least they can do is have standard-size letter boxes situated in the same place. Make things move faster. People take public services for granted – they've been spoiled. People need to make sure they have their letter box in the right place, that there are no vicious dogs barring the way, they need to realise how lucky they are to have a postman come by every morning. Otherwise, it's a mess, and people are forever shouting the odds.

It's long, a postal route. The old-timers are devastated to see what the postal service has come to. It's like everything else. They're witnessing the systematic dismantling of everything that worked, and to top it all they get told how a mail distribution system should work by wankers straight out of business school who have never seen a sorting office in their lives. Nothing is ever fast enough for them. The skeleton staff is too expensive. Tearing down a system that already works is quicker. And they're happy with the results: they are good at wrecking things, these bastards.

Vernon folds away the sofa bed, keeps his things in a neat pile in a corner, leaves nothing lying around the bathroom, folds his towel and rinses down the shower. He's a guy doing his best not to get in the way. He knocks back two coffees then pretends that he is off to see some friends, asks what time he can come back. You want to have dinner here? Why not come back for a drink before-hand, whaddya say? It's raining. If there is nothing to do, he spends the day in the cinema and wandering round a shopping centre. Let him sort out his own fucking problems – just because the man's crashing here doesn't make Patrice his mother.

Patrice likes to do the cleaning on Saturdays. He has binge-watched every series of "The Walking Dead". He cues up Season

Two on the video projector. Wherever he is in the apartment, he can see a section of the living-room wall. The video projector is something he got through Sandrine, a girl he worked with when he was temping doing the inventory at Muji. Her sister worked for a computer company, she would walk out with video projectors and flog them for a hundred euros – a sixth of their retail price. So, anyway, he likes to do the cleaning on a Saturday, usually he will put on the original soundtrack to keep his English up to scratch. When he was young, he took a master's in English. He enjoyed university. The classes, the canteen, the students' union, the parties, the exams.

Now, there's another example: how would he have managed to get a room in the halls of residence as a student if he hadn't been violent? It was only by scaring the shit out of people that he got what he was entitled to. Otherwise, he would have been trampled over, the way so many people were trampled over, and he would have given up. In therapy, the little gayboy running the group didn't like it when he said that if he'd been rich, he wouldn't have been violent. Yada, yada, yada has nothing to do with social background because yada, yada, yada has no bearing on the position one holds in the economic matrix. And my fist in your face you lying fucking retard, I suppose that's got nothing to do with me being a full-time, working-class, underpaid lackey? You think it wouldn't make any difference if I dragged my arse out of bed every morning without having to worry about some piece of fucking registered mail I'm going to get landed with or having to rush around wondering how I'm going to sort out this, to pay for that, you really think it wouldn't improve my mood? I'd still feel vulnerable if I was minted? You sure? I wouldn't be any less afraid? Are you taking the piss? If I didn't have to spend all day keeping my trap shut, with my body aching from the hell I put it through and still not make enough to send my sons on a school skiing trip, would I be the same person? I don't think so! On the contrary, I think I'd make the effort not to jump out of my car to pound on the window of the driver who tried to cut in front of me. I'd calmly let him be an arsehole, I'd think about my plans for the weekend, I'd think about my new suit, I'd think about my kid on the tennis court, I'd think about my ex-wife living in the hundred-square-metre apartment I gave her when we split up, I'd think about the contracts I was negotiating. I would have less time to think about cutting the throats of rich wankers who only get to live well because they've taken everything from me. From me and mine. Taken everything.

He had watched a documentary about Africa at some point during the holidays. An oasis, all the animals drinking together. Zebras, giraffes, ostriches, hippopotamuses, the whole lot. Until a gang of lions shows up. All the animals make a run for it, sharpish. The bully boys have entered the oasis. As far as he is concerned, he would rather be a wolf. Lone. But he likes the feeling it produces – the good guys hightailing it, running for help. If he had money, he wouldn't compare himself to an animal. He would be eminent in his field and on days when his self-esteem is low he'd go hang out in a bar in a fancy hotel where the staff would remind him that he is someone, that there is more to life than the place reserved for him: time, luxury, people to pamper him. He was a parking valet, years ago, at Closerie des Lilas. You had to suck up to the customers. He used to look at them, before climbing into cars that stank of farts, dirty feet and cold cigarette ash.

Drive them into the car park so that they didn't have to walk two hundred metres unaided. Tips at the customer's discretion. From tight-fisted to extravagant – the important thing was that it was according to their largesse. What they chose to give according to their mood. Whatever they felt like: their largesse. A fat slab of hate would have been obvious. The thought that bastards who paid tens of thousands in tax every year might feel the urge to punch *anyone* seemed extraordinary to him. They could just fuck off and get massaged by whores in Mauritius, give everyone a bit of peace.

He would like to see these vultures forced to pay back all the money they've stolen to the people before he dies. See Mélenchon in power. The result of a revolution. He would like to see the suburbs in flames, but not so someone could hoist a green-and-white flag, he wanted to see black flags flying. For his rage to have meant something – if there were barricades in the street tomorrow, a civil war against the profiteers, he would be seen as a hero. He is getting old, his strength is declining. But he's still a fine figure of a man. He so wishes he had seen blood spilled. Bankers, C.E.O.s, billionaires, politicians . . . Fuck's sake, in time of war guys like him are heroes. That's why he is so pissed off with people busting his balls for being violent. He is convinced that if there were a half-decent riot, he would never have to hit a woman. Cécile would have made a fine soldier's wife. She's tough, she's got a good head on her shoulders.

He did his weekend cleaning, grateful that Vernon had picked up on the fact that it was best to give him some space on his day off. Having to see his face all the live-long day brings back a different world. He has a sneaking admiration for rockers, the way they manage to go straight from juvenile to senile without pausing at mature. It's obvious that Vernon – like a lot of guys – has never had doubts about anything in his whole life. Group therapy, sessions with a shrink, the responsibilities of fatherhood, he sailed past them, piece of piss. He's exactly like he was at twenty, it's like he's been preserved in formaldehyde.

When Vernon shows up again, he looks shattered. He insists on making gratin dauphinois, he has calculated the shopping down to the last centime. Patrice will never understand people's obsession with food. The only dish whose poetry he understands *steak frites*.

"You remember Xavier? We had coffee together just after I got back to Paris. He's doing pretty well for himself – you know he's a screenwriter? He lives in this huge apartment – every parents wet dream – in the centre of Paris."

"Xavier was always a wanker, wasn't he?"

"You mean right-wing?"

"Among other things. But mostly he's an idiot. Always was, wasn't he?"

On the T.V., Patrick Bruel, Garou and Raphäel are singing an old Brel tune. At the end of the song, Johnny Hallyday walks onto the set, his back to the camera – Patrice and Vernon simultaneously dissolve into giggles. His master's voice, his master's legs, his profile like some prehistoric beast, strutting like some ballsy bitch. The stentorian voice booms out, he's determined to make the other singers look like a delegation from the society of casual crooners. The singers laugh good-naturedly, saluting the man nothing has been able to kill, not heavy doses of class-A drugs, not ridicule, not success. The beast. Vernon finishes peeling his potatoes, there is something working-class about his gestures, the way he holds the knife, the flick of the wrist, the skill – like a son of the soil come to live in the city. It's not just his eyes, the guy has charm, always did have. It's pleasant, spending time with him. He makes things easier, more interesting – he never complains. How is it that a guy like this hasn't found some babe to take care of him? What can he possibly do to screw up their lives and make them run a mile given that most women will put up with anything rather than pack their bags?

Vernon gathers up the peelings, tosses them in the bin and wipes down the countertop. He has decided to play the good guy. Patrice is grateful, he is incapable of peeling a potato without leaving the kitchen looking like a bombsite for ten days. Vernon feels a wave of depression, his expression changes suddenly. He says:

"The last girl I was with was Brazilian, she used to talk to me about Johnny, she'd say that if you're not French you can't understand the effect he has on us."

"You have to have grown up with him to like him. It's the daddy principle. My sons will never love me like a real father, they don't see me often enough . . . How come a guy like you didn't settle down years ago? By now, you should have kids and all that shit . . ."

"I always fall in love with women who only find me entertaining for five minutes."

"So this Brazilian, she ditched you?"

"She wasn't as free as I had thought. Just my type. Already in a relationship. With a guy who's filthy rich. She didn't need to think too hard to work out which way her heart was leading her . . ."

"You still raw?"

"Yeah."

"Not a tranny, was she?"

"Yes, she's transgender. Really beautiful. Really classy."

"You're joking?"

"No. You asked, I'm telling you . . ."

"Yeah, but I was just taking the piss – you said a Brazilian so I said a tranny, but it was only a joke, it wasn't a real question."

"I got the wrong end of the stick. Her dick was bigger than mine. At first, I was pretty surprised that it didn't bother me. You're not going to believe this, but I came to the conclusion – and believe me I was as shocked as anyone, but I had to face facts: we don't really care about pussy. We don't care. There's more to a girl than her pussy."

"Unless you want to have kids."

"I'm talking passion here, not pre-school."

What unsettles Patrice is not so much the fact that Vernon might fall in love with a Brazilian babe with a boner. It's the fact that he's prepared to admit it. He's forty kilometres from Paris, he's got nowhere to crash, and rather than keeping his head down and dodging the question, he's shouting it from the rooftops: I slept with a tranny. Patrice doesn't know how he should take it. He feels himself tense up. This whole thing since Vernon moved in, feeling relaxed around him, enjoying his company, is starting to take on a significance he doesn't like.

"Why did you have to tell me? You've made me uncomfortable."

"I'm not ashamed. She's the most beautiful girl I've ever been with, the most feminine, the most elegant, the most sophisticated

. . . Walking down the street with Marcia, I tell you, I realised what it feels like for a guy to drive a Porsche. We think they're dickheads, but that's only because we don't drive a Porsche. And when you're a loser like me who can't even shell out for a Jack D. in a bar, and you think to yourself this girl holds me like I'm the most precious thing in the whole world and all I can give her is love and sex . . . I swear you feel like a billion bucks in the sunshine. But it's not just about showing her off . . . I mean, I don't care if I'm shallow. She's got class. She drives me crazy."

This changes the atmosphere between them. Patrice doesn't know what to think. He wishes Vernon hadn't said anything. He is shocked. So shocked that it surprises him. And makes him think. What the hell does he care what Vernon does in bed . . . He doesn't want to imagine what precisely it might be. He remembers certain images of Brazilian girls, some of which raise minor issues of masculinity . . . Brazilian girls are stunning – he has to admit it. On T.V., Rihanna is singing something about diamonds. They listen in reverential silence. Vernon carries on cutting the potatoes into thin slices. Eventually it is Patrice who breaks the silence, after all he has no reason to feel awkward:

"I have a thing for Rihanna, I really have a thing for her. She could sing anything, do cover versions of Carlos or Annie-fucking-Cordy and I'd still be glued to the T.V."

"For all the favours she's done battered women: try telling some young girl that she shouldn't let her boyfriend hit her when that dumb bitch is still running around saying how much she loves Chris Brown. Did you see the photos of her that time he beat her? She's beautiful, yeah, but that's no reason to be stupid, don't you think?"

"That's why my wife left me. Took the kids. I used to beat her."

Tit for tat. Not that it was premeditated. One–all, buddy. You tell me you fuck guys in dresses, I tell you I used to beat my wife. There is another lull in the conversation. During which Patrice realises that he is wavering between rage and gratitude. He remembers the atmosphere of the rock industry, the studied superficiality. Sarcasm, scorn, and serious conversations about record sleeves. Never any closeness, never any intimacy. Even when talking about politics, no-one made an effort to be sincere. Macho little boys playing at being tough guys. It unsettled him, Vernon telling him about the Brazilian girl. But in a way, he was glad. There is something ballsy about allowing yourself to be seen naked.

"You beat your wife? Was she cheating on you?"

"You don't batter the mother of your kids because she did something wrong. You do it because you're violent."

"But you knew it was wrong?"

"Some guys drink, some gamble away the rent, some are unfaithful . . . me, I lash out. I put her in casualty more than once. Not every day, obviously . . . it's not like it was a hobby."

"Did you hit the kids?"

"Never. Cécile said that sooner or later I would. I'm not sure. There were times I shook them, there are some days when you get wound up . . . but I never lost control. Not that it makes any difference. The kids could hear what was going on with her. Of course. My son Tonio was still pissing the bed at the age of five. I didn't need to take him to a specialist to know what was wrong.

My problem is that I've never been suicidal. Otherwise, I would have known what to do."

Vernon listens attentively as he piles the potato slices into a large white dish Patrice would never have thought of putting in the oven, but thinking about it, it's obvious, in fact it's a gratin dish.

"You're too sensitive. Violent men are always so sensitive."

"Spoken like a woman."

"We never realised we'd fuck up this badly, did we?"

"If we had known, what difference would it have made?"

Vernon sets the timer on the oven, takes a couple more beers from the fridge and finally sits down in front of the television. Patrice realises that he is not as bored as he expected to be in his company. He is starting to like Vernon. After the series of big names, TF1 promotes a number of younger singers contractually tied to the channel and the variety programme goes downhill. Some girl standing in a weird posture is singing, Vernon maintaining she's handicapped. Patrice says she's a hunchback, and that doesn't count as handicapped.

Nolwenn Leroy and Patricia Kaas duet on a cover version of Piaf – for once Vernon and Patrice agree that they are pretty classy, and both have a middle-aged crush on Patricia from back when she used to sing "Mon mec à moi" and they actually liked the song, not that they would have admitted to it publicly. She had the same sort of beauty as the women they slept with, but slightly more sublime.

"These days, even the really famous singers have to sing in pairs just in case we'd see one singing solo and reach for the remote."

267

"You're right, it's a bit harsh, they could at least let them sing solo."

The gratin is sputtering in the oven. The T.V. presenter gives the answer to a question so idiotic that it feels insulting that he asked it in the first place. The name of the winner appears at the bottom of the screen. Then, without any segue, the presenter's expression changes and he starts bleating tearfully about a dear friend who recently passed away before his time. And a vast black-and-white photograph of Alex Bleach is projected onto the back-drop of the set. Vernon pitches forward, as though he has taken an invisible punch:

"Oh, Jesus fuck no . . ."

"'Fraid so. Into the whores' graveyard like every other celebrity . . . Did you see much of him?"

"Yeah. You?"

"A lot, in the early days. When his career took off, he never stopped calling, I felt like I was his brother."

"Likewise. But he couldn't be arsed to show up when he arranged to meet, he was a pain."

"I was still with Cécile. I'd make sure to see him when she wasn't around. Alex would happily fuck your girlfriend in your bed while you were asleep and not think twice. He was a danger to any happy couple, the bastard. Have to admit, though, women loved him . . . At the funeral, I heard some people saying that women wouldn't give him a second look when he didn't have money. But it's not true, long before he cut his first record, he only had to show up at the door and I'd get my girlfriend to hide. Go home, I don't want to argue, tonight you can do your own cooking. He was a real case, that guy."

268

"You went to the funeral?"

"The whole band was there. It's only when someone dies that I'm still considered part of the band. We'd been talking about the band re-forming, didn't he mention it?"

"No. Whenever I saw him he was shitfaced and he'd ramble on about weird stuff, but never about work . . . He paid my rent for a whole year. Two, probably. But we didn't see that much of each other . . ."

"Your rent in Quebec?"

"By bank transfer, yeah."

"I'm just joking. I'd be glad you don't feel obliged to tell me everything, otherwise I really would get worried . . ."

"I couldn't bring myself to go to the funeral. Too many people. And not really my people."

"It was pretty grim. There were a few celebs, and every loser in the world was there pretending to be sad when all they really cared about was sitting next to Vanessa Paradis."

"I think the gratin is probably ready. Should I make a salad? Are you hungry? Why didn't it work out, the band getting back together?"

"Personally, I thought it was a dumb idea, especially given that I don't listen to that kind of music any longer . . . but when someone told me how much money was involved, I felt a sudden urge to pick up my bass again. I'd have performed pirouettes in a fucking thong for that kind of cash . . . and I'm not saying that to wind you up. Alex was up for it but we had one rehearsal and after that he never had the time. I can understand. I was disappointed because of the cash, but in reality the whole thing felt squalid. Dan had his tongue so far up Alex's arse it was embarrassing. Vince was constantly bitching at him. Pissed off that he wasn't the star. None of us could play for shit by then, but still we all had to pile into Alex, make sure he didn't get to be the front man, etcetera, etcetera . . . he never came back."

"You like lots of vinegar, in the dressing?"

SOPHIE DOES NOT ENJOY THE SUNDAY LUNCHES AT THE RESTAURANT with her daughter-in-law, her son and their daughter. Seeing them leaves her sad as a lump of lead. As usual, the little girl's pushchair is parked right next to the table. The girl is five years old, what does she need with a pushchair? And a baby's bottle of chocolate milk to boot! They tell her it's a generational thing, but all around she can see other children who are better behaved. When the little girl whines during lunch, Marie-Ange puts a hand over her mouth and carries on talking. She doesn't ask what's wrong, doesn't teach her not to interrupt grown-ups when they're talking, she reaches out a hand and muzzles her. Xavier knows that this is no way to treat a child who has already learned to walk and talk. But he simply avoids his mother's eyes, stares down at his plate. His father was a coward too.

Their daughter-in-law is touched by a vague madness that is anything but charming. Her gaze scorches everything it touches. Marie-Ange was in love with Xavier. But not anymore, not for a long time. When she is with him, she makes no effort to hide her boredom, or her contempt whenever he speaks. She has recovered from the fairy tale of the little princess who marries a humble commoner. She is probably remembering what her father said when she announced that she was engaged, "For a woman, there is nothing worse than to marry beneath her station". And the old bastard had the nerve to say as much in front of the bridegroom's mother. Marie-Ange refuses to leave the girl alone with her grandmother. Here again, Xavier did not have the courage to tell her straight out, but Sophie understood. She must have done something wrong. Her son furtively leaves her to mind his daughter for an afternoon from time to time. Doubtless he lies to his wife when he gets home, tells her he was with the two of them in the park all the time. He prevaricates, he beats around the bush. She is not the only woman among her friends to be disappointed by how her grown-up son has turned out.

It is something you never get over. There are some people who can survive anything, each to his own character. There was that December 13, 1986. Before that, a slow agony – two years of sheer hell, but still life clung on. There were solutions to be found, there were reasons to believe. That they would come through this. Their eldest son was a drug addict. They put their faith in everything, though they were at the end of their tether, still they never gave up. For as long as Nicolas was alive. Prayers, herbs, psychology, pharmacology, sport, cold turkey. They put up with the insinuations of therapists – when there is an addict in the family unit, all the family play a role. Nicolas did not want to die. It was a cry for help, he wanted to get well. Then came December 13 the police at her door. They did not telephone. They simply appeared. As soon as she opened the door she had known. The sun was dazzling, it was a Saturday, she was not working, her husband was on business in Toulouse. She had got up early and was washing the windows with rubbing alcohol, they had invited the whole family for Christmas and she was getting the house ready. They no longer travelled, it had become too complicated. Xavier had spent the night at a friend's house. They allowed him to do more things than they had his older brother at the same age. A therapist had warned them, it's complicated for the younger boy, you need to give him room to breathe. And this was what they were doing. Allowing their younger son room to breathe away from them. Xavier was her favourite. Her little baby. He was calmer, more affectionate. He knew how to make his mother happy. She bitterly blamed herself later. Perhaps this explained everything. She had been so much more comfortable with her second child.

She knew what they had come to tell her. But the words, one by one, stabbed into her and there was nothing she could do to prevent them forever changing the course of things. Nicolas' body had been found in an abandoned car. The officers said "overdose", but at the autopsy it was discovered he had injected drugs mixed with battery acid. In her little boy's veins. Battery acid.

The curtain came down over their lives. What was surprising was how easily everything disintegrated. A fade to black so brief that for years afterwards she clung to the absurd conviction that, if she persisted, it might be possible to go back to that instant, that all it would take was one thing done differently and everything would carry on as it had before. A magical thinking that she would never shake off – it must somehow be possible to go back to that day and to change it.

All that was required was for Nicolas to buy from a different dealer, for them to decide to scour the whole city and bring him home by force as they had done a hundred times. But they had not known how to protect him from himself. Sophie never understood how it had begun, through what narrow chink misfortune had slunk into their home. They had had a wonderful family life, no money worries, no health problems. When the children were little, it had been a happy house. They had been loving, caring, she could not imagine what had driven him to despair. Though she went over the past again and again, dissecting the lives of every uncle, each grandparent – she found no history of depression or dependency . . . Nicolas had been an unruly boy, not particularly happy at school, but good at sports and successful in everything he undertook. He was curious and forthright.

She had come to the conclusion that it was chemical – his individual chemistry could not resist heroin. He had been doomed from the first line he snorted. Thousands of teenagers did a line, threw up and moved on to something else. Others got hooked and decided to quit, and though it could be tough, she had met many young people who managed to quit during the period when they were trying to help him, she knew that it was possible. Politics, girls, studies, sport, music . . . other people's children found other passions. Nicolas had only ever known one: powdered death. The pale spectre of heroin had chosen her son. And there had been no other life than this, with the needle, the constant checking for dilated pupils, the sallow complexion, the dark rings round the eyes, the lies, those looks at once evasive and filled with rage, the hair plastered to the temples, the hazy smiles, the cigarette burns on the bedsheets. This was life on smack. It had ended only when the boy died.

Xavier used to call his brother Houdini and his parents could not help but smile. My brother is Houdini, when Nicolas managed to escape from his bedroom on the sixth floor, bypassing the locked door, and taking with him two gold bracelets that had been hidden in a safe and which he sold to pay for his next fix. My brother is Houdini.

They buried Nicolas and the sickly young man faded from his mother's memory. She remembered the little boy. So belligerent that she was known to every head teacher in every school where he was enrolled. He loved Candlemas crêpes, the old westerns he watched with his father, climbing on top of the wardrobe in his bedroom and pretending to be Goldorak, he collected Rahan comics and loved to make spaceships out of cardboard boxes. He also liked to grab his brother by the hair and drag him across the garden on his back.

Sophie lives with that little boy. She talks to him, she goes back into the past every day to tell him she has not forgotten him.

After his death, everything imploded. At first, the protagonists remained standing. Dried husks filled with ashes. Things crumbled slowly. Her marriage. Xavier's cheerful temperament. Her job. Sophie despised the pain that was etched into the faces of her family. She is not one of the elite who are ennobled by suffering. She did not wish other people to be happy. She was astounded by how faint the echo of her catastrophe was in the outside world, dumbfounded to see that, for other people, life goes on as though nothing has happened. She gritted her teeth when she saw beaming mothers gazing lovingly at their children, clenched her fist when she encountered happy people in the supermarket. She wanted each of them to go through what her family had gone through, she wanted everyone to experience a world divided in two. Before the loss, and after. She wished she could believe in God so that she could ask: why them?

Everything in the house fell into one of two categories: things that were there when Nicolas was alive and those they had acquired since. Every lightbulb changed was another handful of earth tossed onto the coffin of her son. She dissolved into tears when the coffee machine stopped working. This machine that he had touched. A cup that broke as it was being rinsed tugged at her insides. This cup that he had rinsed so often after he'd had his morning coffee.

Her husband left. At first the tragedy brought them together, like Siamese twins joined by a burn scar. Later, he could no longer bear it. He had the courage to admit as much. He could not stand it anymore. The atmosphere in the house. The furious guilt mingled with denial. He started a new relationship, with a woman who was not damaged. He left her there. He literally fled. She never heard from him again.

She is convinced that Xavier still sees his father. But he does not want to talk to her about it. The break-up is something else that she never got over. She does not count herself among the strong. In the faces of people she knows, she can see the impatience – still suffering, after all this time, is that really normal? She wishes each and every one of them might live through what she has.

It is out of the question that she will ever recover. She does not want to. This is probably why Marie-Ange does not want her little girl spending time alone with her grandmother. The old bat is crazy. She is still in mourning.

She could have done more to take care of Xavier. She senses his hostility, she knows he bears the guilt of having been the favourite son, and the guilt of having survived, and she knows she did not do enough. She was unable to protect him from the chill that swept over the house, after. Now he is a grown man. She is shocked by each new wrinkle she sees on his face. They no longer have much to say to each other. These Sunday lunches are a chore for all concerned. Chinese food does not agree with Sophie. She makes up a dentist's appointment so that she can leave early. Marie-Ange, who believes that these few hours with her family are the old woman's only happiness, is surprised – a dentist, on a Sunday? – her eyebrow arching into a circumflex. Xavier understands. As always, he prevaricates. Sophie insists – yes, the dentist is a friend, he is happy to see me at weekends.

She has no desire to go back to their place, to watch the child play without being allowed to go near her. Marie-Ange is wary of her mother-in-law, she thinks the old woman is morbid and half-mad. She may well be right. If she were allowed to have a closer relationship with her granddaughter, the little girl would not warm her heart, she would poison the child's. Has she become toxic? Was she always this way? Is she to blame for everything that happened? Does she contaminate those close to her? Perhaps.

It is a day of radiant sunshine, such as February affords from time to time. It is bitterly cold but the light is dazzling. She has a beer on the terrace at Rosa Bonheur. In the daytime, even old ladies can sit on the terrace without being stared at. Paris is wonderful in this respect. She drinks too much, she drinks like an alcoholic – starting early in the morning, small doses, in secret. Gently. Her face bears the marks of the booze. Another expression of defeat. Her son pretends not to notice. He is afraid of her. He is afraid he might have to listen to her talk about something other than her lung X-rays or delays in the Métro. Besides, she bores him.

She usually avoids the parks, because of the children. It has never faded. He is there. He is always there. Climbing the wrong way up the slide, clinging like a demon to the sides, and arriving at the top, he gives a vicious kick in the solar plexus to the boy climbing up the right way. The boy was like a thing possessed, he could not be let loose among other children without making several of them cry. His eyes crackled with mischievous malice. His mother would call his name and he would turn away. God, she did so much running. If she had known, she would have relished every one of his stupidities. Nicolas is still here, the past is frozen, her two sons are playing on the slide, she is worried that they might hurt themselves, might hurt another child. It is here forever, the noise of their squabbles, of their laughter – in her life she had a moment of joy, it is still intact. Nothing happened. She is insane. It is easier to get used to than you might imagine.

But this afternoon, she wants to see the trees in Paris, to have a beer on a terrace far from the roar of traffic. She forces herself to go into the park. She passed the slumped figure of a homeless man on the first bench. She pays him no heed. She thinks of Prévert's poem: "Despair is sitting on a park bench." Like so many city dwellers she is immune, accustomed to the hardship of others, yet still ashamed to turn away. She takes a few steps, unable to dismiss the image from her mind. Poor lad, he is young, and judging from his appearance he has not been on the streets long, though he is clearly homeless. And so she slows her pace. She knows that face. She cannot place him. She hesitates. It is preposterous. Impossible. She retraces her steps.

"Vernon? Is that you? Don't you remember me? I'm Xavier's mother. You remember? I used to iron your frilly shirts when you slept over at our house."

She should not have stopped. The sadness now cleaving her chest is worse than all the rage she has accumulated. My boy, my little boy. My darling, my treasure. Poor child. He too has grown up to be a man. She would not dare take him in her arms. As if the ravages of time were not enough. Your little face. His eyes are just as beautiful as ever. His cheeks are hollow. My little boy. She often thinks about it, Nicolas would be a middle-aged man now, his face lined, his body already sapped. Sophie sits down next to Vernon, who says:

"Of course I remember you. You haven't changed a bit."

She smiles. He always was a charmer. Even before he turned twenty, there was something chivalrous about his manner. A real little gentleman. She had been so happy that Xavier had a friend he brought round to the house. Vernon's family lived in the provinces, she treated him like a second child. He would bring her flowers when he came to dinner. It was some time before Sophie realised that it was not at his parents' insistence; he bought the flowers himself, with his pocket money. He would help her clear the table and force Xavier to do the dishes. He lit up the house. She used to check his pupils, the way she checked the pupils of all the young people she met. He was fond of his beer, but he was not into hard drugs. She approved of his influence on Xavier, the snatches of excited conversation, the whispers, the squabbles and the laughter of young boys roughhousing in the bedroom as they listened to endless records. The sounds of a normal house, a house that has not been ravaged.

"I saw Xavier just a little while ago. Are the two of you still in touch?"

"Of course. I looked after Colette not long ago . . . he didn't mention it?"

"No. He must have forgotten . . . the little dog died, didn't you hear? He was devastated . . . I was sorry to see him in such a state."

"I'm sorry to hear that. She was a lovely dog. I'm really sorry."

"Cancer. He was very upset. What about you, Vernon, what have you been up to?"

He does not really want to talk to her. She thinks she knows how he feels. When you find yourselves among the plague victims, there is a clear divide between you and those who have been spared. You do not want charity or empathy. Deep down, you would rather be spared all human contact. There are barriers on every side, words no longer have the same meaning.

His hands are red and chapped from the cold. He is hunched. His clothes are in good condition. He is clean. She cannot leave him here.

"What's happened to you?"

"I've been going through a rough patch. But you don't need to worry about me, honestly . . . you might think, seeing me like this . . . but it's just temporary, it's only a matter of days . . ."

"Why don't you come back to my place? I have a spare room, you wouldn't be putting me out . . . and if, as you say, it's only for a couple of days, that's all the more reason. And I'm used to living alone so don't worry, I won't insist on making conversation all evening."

"That's very kind of you. But I'm not actually living on the streets . . . last night was, well, it was complicated, I live way out in the suburbs and I didn't manage to get home and today . . . well, it's a long story. I don't want to bore you. But I'm fine, don't be upset by how I look, I'm fine, honestly."

Some men do not really change past the age of fifteen. She recognises this curious little habit men have of telling foolish, bare-faced lies, probably based on the principle that women are too half-witted to distinguish between a plausible assertion and a story that does not make sense. Vernon lies the way he did when he was fifteen when the bedroom reeked of stale tobacco in the morning and he and Xavier would claim the smell was coming from outside and refuse to budge an inch. When it came to twisting the truth, Nicolas had inherited all the family flair. Xavier had always been a terrible liar.

Vernon is lying to her, she can tell from the state of his shoes, from the smell when she first sat down, from the rucksack on the bench, from the haggard look he cannot quite mask, even as he tries to reassure her. He is hungry.

"I look like death warmed up today, but you really don't need to be concerned about me . . . Give my regards to Xavier, tell him I was really sorry to hear about Colette. Don't worry."

What can have happened for a boy like him to end up in such a tragic situation? When people see a homeless person, they always say there but for the grace of God, that could be me, that could be my son, but Sophie realises that they never truly believe it. They think there must be something, a mental health problem, some explanation. God knows she is better placed than most to know it is a lottery. She is still an expert at examining someone's pupils, this boy does not have a drug problem.

She rummages in her purse, slips Vernon the only twenty-euro note she finds – forces him to take it and when he shies away, firmly stuffs it in his pocket. She finds herself treating him the way she did when he was just a young man who brought a little healthy excitement into her son's life.

"I won't miss it. Please, take it. It's nothing, it's all I've got on me. Stop lying to me. Would you like to come and have something to eat with me? I was just about to get a little snack . . . my treat?"

"No, madame, it's really sweet of you. I don't have time."

"Vernon, listen to me: if you want to come back to my place for a few days and you don't want Xavier to know, I'll be silent as the grave. I'll ask you no questions."

Seeing that he will not be persuaded, she makes him promise to wait. She dashes to the Société Générale outside the park gates and takes out a hundred euros. It is all she has until the beginning of next month. She will make do. She does not want to spend tonight wondering whether he is sleeping rough, what with the weather being so cold. She wishes she could find the words to convince him to go with her, to let her take care of him. She remembers this feeling – wanting to help someone who turns away.

But already she can imagine redoing the little room where she does the ironing, so that he could move in and she could help him with the official red tape. She is not afraid of queuing in offices, of filling in forms. She can do something for him. She needs this as much as he does. To be useful for something.

When she comes back, the bench is empty. She is distraught. She wanders the park looking for him. She encounters people out walking who stare at her in alarm. She knows that she looks like a madwoman. She is used to it.

SITTING AT EYE-LEVEL WITH THE BAGS AND THE SHOES, VERNON is forced to look up to see faces. He is sick of watching a parade of arses. There is a constant flow of people waddling past his stretch of the pavement. Time was, he was careful always to look homeless people in the eye, to say I see you you are there I am aware. What he did not know is that, once you are sitting on the pavement you don't give a flying fuck whether passers-by look at you. Do they put their hand in their pocket, that is the only thing that matters. Awareness can't be eaten, it doesn't keep you warm, so they can keep it.

It has taken him three days to resign himself to sit down and beg. He spent the first day entombed in the Métro. Riding the lines from one end to the other. He rode them all. He dozed, he read the newspapers people left behind when they got off, he watched the stations flash past, he made connections, he listened to buskers. He got off at a random station, let several trains pass, then got on again and rode all the way to the terminus. To throw people off the scent. Not that anyone noticed what he was doing.

He came up to the surface when the Métro gates closed. He was somewhere near Passy. He spent his first night sleeping rough sheltering in an A.T.M. booth. The weirdest thing was finding himself scouring the darkness for cardboard boxes to insulate him from the cold floor. It felt oddly as though he were playing a role.

He could not quite believe what was happening. Taking advantage of a drunk from the sixteenth arrondissement staggering up to the A.T.M., he stepped in behind, pretending to wait his turn, cool, laid-back, three cardboard boxes tucked under his arm. Then he nipped inside, settled himself on the ground, head propped on his rucksack, and waited for dawn to break and the Métro to reopen. A blanket wouldn't have gone amiss. He is still not properly equipped. The following morning at five, he was waiting for the Métro to open, he had a nap on Ligne 8 then got off at République, still determined to pretend he was a guy who was going some-where. He sat for a few hours – or a few minutes, time had lost all meaning – on uncomfortable benches staring at the wall opposite like someone preoccupied by minor everyday concerns. This time spent moving from station to station had left him covered with a film of black grime. Needing to get some air, he had come up to the surface. He walked for a long time, looking into shop windows like any other pedestrian. When he reached Opéra, he went into the Apple Store to get warm. The staff in their blue T-shirts didn't notice him, there were too many people clamour-ing for their attention. He logged in to Facebook to see whether Marcia had left him a message. He saw that she hadn't and closed the page. He tried to read the news but had a hard time finding a story that interested him, he watched a few videos with girls in them. Then he went on his way. He walked as far as Pigalle
and then went down into the Métro where he stayed until evening.

This time he was fortunate enough to sneak into a building behind a couple. While he waited for them to disappear, he pre-tended to be looking for a name on one of the mailboxes. Always pretend you belong in the city. He went up, taking the stairs, all the way to the top floor. On the ground floor, the stairs were wide and carpeted with a threadbare red runner, but by the top floor the stairs had narrowed and were bare wood. He lay on the floor, the polished floorboards felt warm after two days on the street. He was woken by a jangle of keys, someone leaving their apartment, who stepped over him without a word. He waited for someone to chase him out. When nothing happened, he fell asleep again for a while. Dealing with the cold has become a full-time occupation.

He doesn't feel sad, or desperate. What he feels is different, a mood he doesn't recognise. White noise. The static of a T.V. screen at night when he was young. A blizzard of tiny dots, a soft hiss. On the third day, he walked all the way to Père Lachaise before going into the Métro, ducking through the turnstile behind an elderly woman who glared at him when he pressed against her. He followed the crowd heading for the platform for a few steps, then he slowed, stunned to realise that his legs would no longer hold him up. Hunger gnawed at his stomach. He sat on the platform. Perhaps he blacked out, perhaps he dozed. Someone came and sat next to him. A young guy with a protruding chin, his face deeply lined, his fingernails black with grime, filthy with a dirt ingrained by years, almost a tattoo. He was clutching a beer in one hand and a fur-lined jacket that was clean and in good condition. His shoes, on the other hand, had had their day and should have been replaced long ago.

"Having it tough?"

Vernon wanted to say something but could not form a single word. Laurent proffered his beer:

"Take a swig, it's good for you. You hypoglycaemic? You want a sugar cube? Not long on the streets, yeah? It's pretty obvious just looking at you."

"It's just temporary."

"Always is. Me, it's been temporary for nineteen years. Name's Laurent . . . yours?"

"Vernon."

"What kind of name's that? Where's it from?"

The beer had perked him up, Vernon felt a little better, but not enough to feel chatty. Laurent had no problem holding a conversation all by himself. The tone in which he talked about his nineteen years on the streets left no room for doubt: it was a badge of pride. He had dozens of stories to tell. Fights, arrests, trips, squats that were bricked up . . . he began to recount in detail his various heroic feats. Vernon felt as though he'd known him all his life – rock concerts are teeming with guys telling their life stories in multiple episodes. Laurent was a loudmouth, who proclaimed to the assembled passengers on the platform that he had chosen to live free of the hassles and humiliations of being a wage-slave wanker.

He dredged two more beers from his pouch and launched into a frenzied diatribe – this encompassed management working hours expenses invoices banks codes employers landlords pressures degradations case files surveillance . . . everything that exemplified voluntary slavery. Vernon was cheered by his company. Laurent offered him a crash course in begging – "If you really need money, like to pay for a hostel, you stand, you don't sit, you smile when you ask, and if you can think of a little joke, all the better, the people you're talking to, their lives are fucking shit, never forget that, if you can make them smile they'll put their hands in their pockets, they spend their lives crying so you're a distraction – they *love* the notion of the poor fucking beggar who keeps his spirits up." His garrulousness was refreshing, and he spent the day producing beers from his pouch though Vernon could not work out where they came from. That said, he got drunk pretty quickly. According to Laurent, Vernon had potential. "You've got amazing eyes, you'll see, the handsome beggar always does well. You find a pitch, you show up every day, that's important, yeah? You pick a spot and you get them used to you. I mean, with your eyes, you'll get enough to pay a hostel, easy . . . Try and cadge a couple of books, yeah, put them next to you and pretend like you're well into them. They love that shit. A fucking homeless guy that reads. Or you can do the crossword, they go for that too. You'll get your bearings and you'll be minted, I'm telling you, just keep your spirits up . . ."

Night had fallen, they had emerged from the Métro and Laurent had chaperoned him as far as the soup kitchen at Saint-Eustache where he managed to sort him out a blanket before leaving him, though not before telling him to drop by and see him in the Parc des Buttes-Chaumont. "You need anything, bro, just ask for me."

Vernon had collapsed in a doorway of a boulangerie sheltered from the wind and had woken up – in the middle of the night this time – shackled to a brutal hangover and without the first idea where he could find water. He had headed up towards Pyrénées Métro station only to stop at Goncourt, dead on his feet. He had been having trouble breathing for a few days. He had sat down by the church, thinking that maybe he could pass for some suit out on the tiles waiting for someone in the cold. Then he had held out his hand. It had not been premeditated. He had simply made the gesture – once again feeling it was not quite real. Despite

Laurent's advice, begging while sitting down worked out better than he had anticipated – maybe, given that he still looked like a relatively normal guy, people could identify. In the first three hours, he managed to pocket twenty euros. Beginner's luck. Shadowy figures slowed, fumbled in their pockets and dropped coins into his cupped hand. There were the tightwads who came on like good Samaritans and stumped up five cents, the spendthrifts who never gave less than two euros. There was no correlation between the apparent wealth of the passer-by and the size of the donation. This was when Vernon lost all interest in their faces. When he got up, he had pins and needles in his legs, he invested in a kebab and a beer and wandered around looking for a bench where he could eat in peace. As he walked, he came across a young man sleeping on the pavement guarded by three huge dogs, a mixed-race girl with frizzy hair sitting talking to herself in a telephone box among dozens of plastic bags. He passed an old man sitting on the pavement outside a building listening to his radio, surrounded by so many curious objects it was as though he had re-created his apartment on the street. He had never noticed there were so many people in his situation. When he reached Jourdain Métro station he sat down again, giving a wide berth to the other homeless people pitched outside the church and the Monoprix.

Once you get over that first hump, the rest is a breeze, everything moves effortlessly and disturbingly fast: he is through the looking glass. Already, the lives of working people seem remote. They are in a desperate hurry to be somewhere, ashamed of their fear that they might end up like him if they don't slog their guts out. Laurent is right, their lives are shit. Some grunt as they pass by. Vernon ignores them. He is dazed. He has begun to feel a strange satisfaction at having fallen so low. Instinctively, he knows he must be wary of this tendency. This revelling in his own misery. In the meantime, what preoccupies him most is the cold and he is only too happy not to be able to focus on his racing thoughts.

The hardest thing is recognising people. It is something he recently experienced. Until he met Madame Fardin, Xavier's mother, none of this felt entirely real. When she came and talked to him, he thought he could pretend he was just sunning himself on a bench. Instead, he broke her heart. Because what is happening to him is patently obvious. When he was a child, Madame Fardin was like Mamie Nova, the little woman on the yoghurt pots – always in the kitchen making something, but a widowed version of Mamie Nova, unhappy and inconsolable. When you stepped into the house, it smelled of death. Grown-up tears had drained the atmosphere. Madame Fardin was so desolate as a young woman that twenty years later she barely seemed to have changed. He had forgotten that he used to go round to have dinner with Xavier's mother when they were twenty. She made Vernon feel important and he sometimes wondered whether she wanted to seduce him. No-one talked about cougars back then, but "The Graduate" had made its mark on young impressionable minds. He was at the age when boys still believe that if he fucks her properly a man can restore a woman's passion for life. In the lobby of their building in Colombes, Vernon used to stop to look at his reflection in a mirror before getting into the lift. Check his hair, his teeth, stand up straight, adjust his jacket collar. And he would always find an excuse to leave Xavier's bedroom to look for something in the kitchen, share a joke with Madame Fardin as he passed. Make her laugh. She was very fond of him. She was happy to meet one of her son's friends. He had just begun working at Revolver, and Madame Fardin congratulated him on his seriousness and resourcefulness. Not many adults had ever paid him a compliment and he liked to fish for hers, trailing in her wake. He had been tempted to go with her, when they met a few hours ago. But he could not bear to disappoint her. She'd had enough shit to put up with in her life.

Vernon decides to take a break from begging. He stretches his legs in front of the C.G.T. offices on the avenue Secrétan. In the smokers' area, he spots a pile of cigarette butts and hunkers down to pick out the longest stubs. Immediately, a figure approaches and, rather than sending him packing, gives him three cigarettes from his pack. Vernon smiles, thanks the guy and gives him a wink. Vernon is a novice. He could have sworn that the guy who just helped him out looked like a wanker.

It will come. Laurent has warned him that in a month he'll see things differently. You can get used to anything. He is surprised that what bothers him most today is not having a toothbrush. He left his at Patrice's place. He is embarrassed by his own mouth. His situation reminds him of being in prison. Without the visiting room and the right to a lawyer. In the thick fog that has slowed his thoughts these past few days, he feels, more and more, as though he is in someone else's skin. Only Marcia continues to obsess him. She is at once a happiness that is in his blood, radiant and reverberant, and a blade planted in the middle of his chest.

That first night, he had barely noticed Marcia. The girls were stunning, a smorgasbord of prime poontang so listless and bemused it felt as though you could have any one of them just by favouring them with a look. Marcia had been part of this job lot.

Though she did not particularly stand out when she began to dance, by dawn, he was admiring the elegant thrust of her hips, her way of flaunting herself while remaining discreet. He was not excited when she stared into his eyes – he had been through the wringer that night. He felt amazing, his head buried between the speakers like some foolish kid, that night was a bubble of gentle sweetness that distracted him from his gaping wounds.

It was only the following morning, in the cold light of day, that he had been struck by Marcia's beauty. She had been cradling a cup of tea in her hands, her face turned towards the light, eyes closed, sitting facing the picture window. The neat line of her chin, the flawless curve of her lips, that face like a queen in exile. In an instant, she became all the women he had never had. In the rock business, he had hung out with models, debauched debutantes, porn stars and masochistic intellectuals . . . the granddaughters of Patti Smith and Madonna. But the others – the daughters of J-Lo and Beyoncé, the young Rihannas and Shakiras – they had no use for rock music. They played in a different playground. Vernon could not imagine what a girl like her might see in a guy like him. But in the apartment, Vernon always knew exactly where Marcia was, he would wander into the room she was in by chance, careful to appear casual, and it seemed to him she always needed to pop into the kitchen to boil the kettle when he was there, to look for her scarf in the living room when he happened to be there. They circled each other, they did not say a word, joined by a taut, invis-ible cord. Gaëlle, aware of their little game, managed to slip into the conversation – "No, Marcia wasn't born a girl, I thought you would have guessed", and Vernon took the blow. He was so unsettled he did not know what he thought. He had never watched transsexual porn. Not that it bothered him – it did not relate to him.

On the cover of a coffee-table book, Marcia was using her Gold Card to cut a series of impeccable, neat, precisely spaced lines. Vernon asked her how she managed to create such symmetrical lines and she explained that when she first arrived in France, in the south, she had played a lot of pétanque and that had given her an eye for precision. Vernon watched her, wondering whether she had studied every gesture of femininity so she could mimic it to perfection. The way she threw back her head after she snorted her line, the way she ran her fingers through her hair, the way she crossed her legs in mid-sentence, everything about her was bewitching. She was talking to him about cocaine while taking cocaine.

"With every line, you have to remember you are inhaling *o narcotráfico*, the bloodiest form of capitalism you can imagine, you are snorting the corpses of the farmers who grow it and have to be kept in poverty so they do not raise their prices, you are snorting the cartels and the police, the private militias, the atrocities committed by the Kaibiles and the prostitution that goes with it . . . men who cut people's heads off with a chainsaw. Cocaine dollars is what bailed out the banks, the whole system is set up to launder drug money. You know where cocaine was invented? Austria. Don't tell me you can't see where I'm going with this. Coke is the only drug that is not spiritual. That and its little cousin crack. Even M.D.M.A. brings you closer to God. Coke is the only drug that winds you up and leaves you more stupid than you were when you started."

At no point did Marcia make a single gesture, give a single look that made you think – there, that's something a real woman would not do. Quite the opposite, she was the embodiment of femininity at its most arousing. She headed back to bed and did not reappear until evening. Vernon noticed her in the hall, getting ready to go out, she was exquisitely elegant. He was the first to be surprised by what he felt – a twinge of jealousy, sharp as a sucker punch – who had she made herself so beautiful for? This searing flash brought him face to face with the obvious: he wanted her. He didn't give a shit about being the guy he had always been – a guy who only sleeps with real girls. In fact, the expression "real girls" suddenly seemed ridiculous: who was more deserving of the epithet than this unlikely creature?

That night, he stayed up late talking to Kiko. They talked about music, Vernon was taking his new role as *D.J. de salon* very seriously, getting girls to dance was a vocation that might interest him, and one he might prove to have flair for. After all, choosing the perfect track to play next had been the principal occupation of his life.

When Marcia came downstairs to dinner the following day, she was wearing an incredible white silk dressing gown, or perhaps it was a kimono – she had looked at Vernon and, running her hand over his head said "What is with that haircut?" Everything in him that was broken, aching or vulnerable faded away.

They sought each other out. They would manage to pore over the computer at the same time so that their shoulders touched, to run into each other in the hall so they had to brush past each other, to listen to a song together using the only pair of headphones so that their knees were pressed together. And the more they touched, the less Vernon questioned things. They had downed a bottle of J.D. between them when they first kissed. Marcia was simultaneously demure and depraved. Her hips were narrow, her slender thighs powerfully muscular, she could keep her balance in any position. Were it not for the booze, Vernon would probably have thought to wonder whether he was turning queer given that he was sleeping with a girl equipped with a prick. But he was too entranced by Marcia's arse – never had he encountered anything so perfectly erotic. And he felt so comfortable between Marcia's breasts, on Marcia's belly, against Marcia's arse, between Marcia's lips – that the most distinctive thing about her body immediately became the most adorable thing about her body. Vernon could not remember desiring other women before her. A curtain had parted, everything that had come before Marcia had been a childish game, a rehearsal. Inconsequential.

And from the very beginning, she warned him. "Kiko mustn't find out. He's very jealous." They had their orgy of sex in a tiny little room under the eaves of the hotel opposite, which Marcia seemed to know well. Back in the apartment, Gaëlle looked at him differently. Half-sardonic, half-suspicious. Vernon was in love. He was transformed into a little pack of marshmallows. He had forgotten how life without Marcia had been possible. And he realised, though he was almost fifty, that he had never been in love before. Loving Marcia was something so obvious he surrendered himself to it recklessly. Even as his life spiralled into a disaster area, he felt more privileged than he had ever been.

One morning, Kiko burst into Marcia's bedroom unannounced. Vernon had come to bring her a cup of coffee and had slipped between the sheets. At the time, Kiko simply said Subutex I'd never have believed it of you in a tone of surprise that said you're nothing but a fucking peasant and it said and Marcia what the fuck are you doing with this guy can't you see you're demeaning yourself. He had walked out without saying another word. He was off his head – for four nights he had been sleeping too little and drinking too much. After he left, Marcia had panicked. For five days they had been utterly love-struck you and me it's magnetic the effect we have on each other a single life won't be long enough to satisfy this desire all the time every moment being with you talking to you making love to you. He felt her emerge from that state. Like a door closing. She had kissed him, saying "See you tonight" and Vernon had not wanted to understand what was happening.

Gaëlle already knew by the time Vernon found her in the kitchen. She had seemed upset on his behalf, it looked serious. He had said "Why is Kiko taking it so hard? It's not like she's his girlfriend. He never told me not to go there", and Gaëlle said "Sometimes he can be a pain in the arse". In a tone that said but when you're loaded like he is don't expect me to hold it against him. All that matters is that I don't get caught up in the fallout. Broadly speaking, it was the truth, she did feel upset for him, but since she was the one who had introduced him, she felt responsible – she wanted him to pack his bags straight away. She wanted them to keep in touch, she took the forty euros she had in her jacket and her jeans pocket. She wanted to know whether he had anyone in mind or if he wanted her to hook him up with somewhere to crash. Vernon had said: "I'll have to talk to Marcia." Then he had joked "I didn't realise I'd be nominated so quickly" and Gaëlle was grateful to him for taking it gracefully.

But he was stunned to discover he had been evicted. He felt so at home in the apartment. He was a long way from the stage where you get sick of seeing drugs around every night. After all, drugs had been an essential part of the best years of his life. Besides, he'd slipped easily into his role as resident D.J. He had said, "I'll have to talk to Marcia" and when he saw Gaëlle's expression he felt the ground fall away beneath his feet.

He had opened a beer, rolled a spliff and stood in front of the computer. He scanned through his list of Facebook friends with a new eye – he needed to find someone who could put them up, him and Marcia. Things were getting complicated. In that moment, he had chosen not to believe that Marcia would dump him. Gaëlle was wrong. She didn't get it, what they had. She hadn't been there, these past four days.

In the early afternoon, Kiko had burst into the kitchen, seething. He had slammed Vernon against the wall. "Get the fuck out of my crib, I don't want to set eyes on you again." Then, he had shoved him hard and given him a kick in the arse to send him on his way. The apartment felt deserted although Gaëlle was there, with one of her girlfriends. While Vernon was packing up his few belongings, Kiko was constantly behind him, throwing a bitch-fit, head-butting doors, knocking over tables, trying to kick a wardrobe to smithereens. "Move it you fucking lowlife skank I shoulda never let you in the thought of you even touching her is disgusting get the fuck outta here you make me sick."

Gaëlle had reappeared in the hallway, she was upset and a little anxious about her own fate – after all she had been the one who brought Vernon back. She slipped him a bag into which she had crammed a bottle of beer a bottle of rum a flash drive with some of his playlists a razor and shaving foam, and a new bottle of Hermès perfume that didn't belong to him. Vernon had said to her: "Tell Marcia that I'll wait for her to message me on Facebook I'll sort myself out a computer" and Gaëlle had shaken her head again "She's not going to write to you, you know. She can't afford to be in Kiko's bad books. But I'll tell her. I'll write, Vernon, let's keep in touch, yeah?"

In the street he had asked passers-by for directions to the nearest library, no-one could tell him, until a helpful teenager looked up directions on his iPhone. When Vernon had logged on, he had been relieved that Patrice had said yes. Vernon crashed at his for a week. Marcia had not replied to any of his messages. His every breath was painful. It was difficult to drink and not burst into tears, to collapse on Patrice's sofa and howl, curl into a foetal position and carry on sobbing and whimpering. It was hard to fall asleep though not as hard as staying asleep. He would wake up in the middle of the night to a split-second of respite during which he remembered nothing. Then it would all flood back. His situation was easily summed up. Marcia didn't give a shit about him. He still could not believe it. How could someone give up on something like this? The worst of it was that she was right. What would a girl like her be doing with an ageing loser with no home no money no friends no job? Patrice had been an impeccable host. The guy didn't talk too much, didn't pry too much, he liked to chill and watch T.V. They got along well. On the eighth day Vernon realised it was time to split. An old mate who these days sold books on the banks of the Seine had told him to drop by whenever I'll give you the keys to mine, I'm never really there. But when Vernon got to the river, he wasn't there, his stall was closed and fastened with heavy padlocks. And this was how his first night sleeping rough came about. His friend was not there the next day either.

And so Vernon found himself on the streets. He had finally reached the destination where his path had been leading for weeks. He was only sorry that the damage wasn't fatal.

Vernon finds himself a scrap of pavement. Laurent had recommended begging outside *boulangeries* because people pay cash and come out with small change. But most of the good pitches are already taken. Vernon settles himself in a little square, sitting with his back to the wall until a woman comes along and politely asks him to move, "It's a school exit, you see, they'll be coming out soon and you'll be in the way – if you wouldn't mind moving a little that way?" He sits a little further away, between a bookshop and a florist's, a few metres from an organic grocer's. He holds out his hand, arm resting on his knee, back leaning against the wall. His thoughts are racing. His cheeks itch, he is not used to having a beard. His own smell is overpowering. It is not unpleasant. The bags that parade past his nose are all different – handbags, wicker baskets, briefcases, little leather pouches – the same is true of the shoes, threadbare trainers, platform heels, creepers, leather boots . . . He watches them approach, slow down and stop, four pairs of men's shoes that now circle him. He is paralysed with fear. He does not even dare look up. He suddenly feels the urge to cry.

"Good morning, sir, what's your name?"

"Vernon."

He answered too quickly, he should have given his official designation, his French name. But they do not hit him immediately. Three shaved heads, faces like inbred students, like vicious thugs, and a young blond guy, a boy who is smaller than the others, his features fine, regular, as handsome as his classmates are fear-some. Seen from below, they look like giants. It is the blond who is speaking, he kneels so that they are at the same level, stares at him attentively:

"My name's Julien. You know, Vernon, if you were a Romanian migrant you'd have somewhere to sleep."

Julien lays a hand on Vernon's shoulder. The three acolytes who are still standing nod in agreement, all of them super sad that he's not a Romanian migrant, because if he was he wouldn't be reduced to freezing his arse off on the pavement. Vernon is bathed in sweat. Never has he been so relieved to be French – all he wants is for these three morons to be satisfied by his responses. For them to fuck off. From his bag, Julien takes a packet of biscuits and a carton of milk, hands them out and asks:

"Have you got the number for social services? Have you tried calling them today?"

"They told me they're full. But I'm coping."

"Too many monkeys in the shelters, yeah? Africans causing trouble, yeah? Someone beat you up?"

Vernon says to himself that there is no danger, that these guys are racist militants who are not planning, with the steel toecaps of their perfectly polished boots, to give him a good kicking. Yet he is trembling from head to foot. He is on the ground. He is terrified that this will tempt them to lash out. He wants them to go away, to let him catch his breath. It is at this point that, in a howl of unintel-ligible screaming a redheaded giant appears, her arms whirling like windmills, shoves them aside and splutters:

"Go fuck yourselves you dickless little turds, leave him in peace, don't you see you're scaring him witless, you stupid skinhead shitwanks?"

She clears a path, jostling and throwing punches. She is frenzied. And for the second time in as many minutes Vernon thinks
why me, Lord, why me. Because she won't be the only one who
gets thrashed, he will be caught up in the mêlée.

"You fuck everyone's heads up with your pathetic bullshit, get
out of here. Go tell your skanky mothers they'd have been better
off sewing up their cunts than giving birth to scum like you. You're
radioactive pollution, you bunch of moronic losers."

Vernon remembers the woman on the old hundred-franc
notes, the bare-breasted bitch waving the flag who looks like she's
four heads taller than the guys next to her scrabbling over the
barricades. The redhead is wearing a long khaki parka that is much
too small for her, and huge, brand-new, trainers that are fluorescent green and yellow. But Vernon is not about to criticise her fashion sense. Any more than he plans to make conversation with the
four thugs she is shrieking at. The girl is probably not big enough
to take on four guys single-handed, but she is certainly scaring the
shit out of them. Has to be said, she's got bottle.

The four guys are bewildered: what has this deranged harpy
got against them? One of them shrugs, sniggers and turns away
pretending to let it go. The giant whirls around and kicks him
in the back with all her might, he stumbles forwards and falls on
all fours. The cute blond guy pounces on the madwoman, but he's
so puny that, as he clings to her, he looks like a marmoset trying to
climb a coconut tree. The woman dispatches her assailant with a
quick jerk of her elbow. Vernon would never have thought she
could keep control of the situation for so long. The four guys close
ranks intending to give her a thrashing, but once again she takes

them by surprise, she starts pounding her chest with both fists and screaming at the top of her lungs. Hard to tell whether she's channelling Scarface or Tarzan, but this display leaves her adversaries stunned. It is impossible to say what has stopped them in their tracks – fear surprise disgust respect for such extraordinary energy . . . the whole neighbourhood can hear her, several people slow to see what is going on.

The boys quickly confer with furtive glances, the blond spits on the ground, "Come on, let's leave the mad bitch to it, should be locked up the fucking lunatic". And they walk off, heads held high, and before they reach the corner they turn around, giggling, and, from a safe distance, give her the *bras d'honneur* from a safe distance, one of them twirls a finger at his temple to indicate his diagnosis. Vernon watches as they disappear and thinks that it's a bit much that they have left him here since, all things considered, he would feel safer surrounded by a group of neo-Nazis than he does under the protection of this "madwoman".

Gasping for breath, the giant slumps down on the pavement next to him. Her hair is very fine, a shock of orange-auburn, probably the remnants of a dye job, her face is round and flat, her eyes set far apart, something about her features brings to mind a child with Down's syndrome. It is impossible to guess her age.

"Someone needs to kill those fuckers. Pick them off, one by one. It's unbelievable, we're in fucking Belleville, what are those wankers doing here? They think they own the place. Last week, they beat up two kids who were pick-pocketing. They hang around the Red Cross and hassle the Africans who come for something to eat. What the fuck has it got to do with them, huh? Is it any of their business? Do they have to sleep on the streets? What do they think we are? Shit, that's what they think we are. Because we're excluded from the system they think they can come round here and lay down the law. But we're the real tough guys, yeah? If we don't give them a kick up the arse, then who will, huh? Who?"

She wags her finger as she says this, as though lecturing. Vernon is thinking, there you go, I wanted company, I've got company. Always the same with answered prayers. The woman heaves herself to her feet and announces:

"This isn't a good spot. C'mon, let's go sit outside Franprix. That's my pitch."

It is more of an order than a suggestion and Vernon, unable to imagine disagreeing with her, obeys.

"Haven't seen you round this way before, you're new, yeah?"

"I was evicted a while back but I managed to find a place to crash here and there. Until last week."

"Last week? You're a rookie, man. I thought I could still smell soap on you."

She settles herself outside the supermarket and says to the first person going in:

"Monsieur, monsieur, could you buy me a Coke, please?"

And then, patting her belly, she adds "It's for the baby", and turns to Vernon "What do you want?" then she calls back the guy as he is pushing open the supermarket door and he turns, wryly amused, and takes her order "And a beer, please, for my friend".

"You pregnant?"

"No, ugh! But my public like the idea. I'm starving, I haven't had lunch yet."

She hails another shopper, an elegant woman in a hurry, "Hello madame, could you bring me out some crisps please? It's for the

302

baby." When she is talking to strangers, she becomes sweet and childlike. Vernon notices that her voice, when she is calm, has a pleasant huskiness. She smiles innocently at passers-by, rubbing her big belly, she has a face like a clown, round as the moon.

"Do any of them actually bring you what you ask for?"

"Often. It doesn't cost them much to give me something to eat, I only ever ask for peanuts, crisps, Coke . . . chocolate sometimes . . . Obviously, since I'm here every day, a lot of them know me, they're used to bringing me stuff. They're happy to help. After all, they are human, you know."

She pauses. A young man heads into the supermarket with a baby strapped in a sling over his chest, she tilts her head to one side, "I love fathers, it's so nice seeing a papa with his baby", then calls after him, "Hey, m'sieur, can you get me a bar of chocolate? It's for the baby".

As he comes out, another man hands her a Coke and a beer, she smiles and passes the beer to Vernon.

"If there's anything you particularly want, let me know and I'll ask."

SALTED PEANUTS AND DARK COOKING CHOCOLATE IS OLGA'S preferred diet. She is wary of alcohol. If they weren't bladdered all the time, her fellow vagrants might make for better company. She might even be able to turn them into respectable revolutionaries. But these idiots keep knocking it back until they can't stay upright. You're in the middle of talking to someone and suddenly everything stinks of piss, the guy has just wet himself. Or they turn to you, glassy-eyed, you think they're about to say something and they puke all over you. I'm no hygiene freak but, seriously, that really sucks. It's impossible to hang out with them after dark anyway, when they're not snoring they're spoiling for a fight, or something worse. You have to be wary of the shit they come out with when they're hammered. They'll fuck you up the arse like a goat and then swear blind they can't remember a thing. If you beat them up, they bleat about it, a bunch of them will go at you and then call you a lying bitch. When guys are together, they close ranks. This is why Olga likes rookies, they've still got basic manners. This one is really handsome, he's tall, super thin, the sort of guy she's always fancied. His hands are still white, unblemished. They'll be disfigured before long. Everything gets disfigured on the streets.

She had spotted him last night, talking to Georges, one of the fat winos camped outside the church. She and Georges aren't exactly on good terms, she kept her distance. At first, Georges comes across as a laid-back kind of guy, but pretty quickly you find out what he's really like: a tyrant and a manipulator. If you don't do what he asks, he flies into a black rage, he's given her a few beatings in his time and, old as he is, the guy has the viciousness and the tenacity of a jackal.

This morning, when she saw him surrounded by skinheads, she decided to go get him. She wants him as a friend. Now, she is sharing her food with him. He eats hungrily, it's a pleasure to behold. She can teach him lots of things, where to go for a shower, the best days to go to the *Secours populaire* for decent clothes, she can give him advice on homeless shelters. He doesn't have a dog, so that makes it easier. She likes taking care of other people. When they let her. She tries to get him to laugh. That's how she makes friends. She makes them laugh, and she listens. When she was younger, she saw a doctor who advised her to drink less, he told her she had no self-respect, that she was a trash can of confidences. You'd have to be a doctor to be dumb enough to sneer at empathy. She asks a passing kid to bring them a packet of Curly and the boy tells her to piss off "Get yourself a fucking job, you fat sow". She curses him, giving him the evil eye "for ten long years you will suffer for what you just said", she knows they don't like that, they don't know whether she's really a gypsy, she might be a powerful witch. Vernon giggles. She likes his name. She would like them to hang out all the time. They could be a team. It's been a long time since anyone wanted to hang with her. She says:

"That's the way it is . . . They all serve the interests of big money and they're surprised that we flake out and don't want to be part of their bullshit system. Just look around you – in this neighbourhood, whenever a shop closes a bank opens. Or an optician, I've never understood why there are so many shops selling glasses. My father was a communist. So when I read the newspapers, I get the message: praise be to big business. Woe betide those who do not submit unconditionally. Never has a dogma been so well observed. It's a stroke of genius, their invention – debt . . . like whores who've been trafficked they'll spend their lives slaving to pay back what they owed at birth. Oh, when it comes to work, they work . . . you know why they tolerate us in the city? They've ripped out the benches, they've fitted shop fronts with spikes to make sure we can't sit down, but they haven't started rounding us up and sending us to camps yet, and it's not because it would be too expensive, no . . . it's because we are a foil. People need to see us so they remember to unquestioningly obey. I worked – ten years I worked. Developing photos in a lab. All day hunched over developing tanks with skimpy little gloves for protection, I ended up with eczema. They said it had nothing to do with the chemicals and they fired me. I don't regret it. I had a shit life. My whole salary went on the rent and the car, I had to check the price of everything I put in my shopping trolley. They make me laugh, the whole lot of them. Marxists these days make me laugh as much as the rest – the worker and his factory, creating employment and all that shit . . . Me, what I want is not to work anymore."

"But I thought your father was a communist?"

"Yep. I'm like the daughter of Zeus. If you'd known my papa . . . now there was a real man. When he was angry, the ground trembled. He wasn't a pathetic domestic tyrant screaming at his dumb wife and terrorising her. I'm talking about righteous anger. When I was little, we couldn't go into town with my father without him raining down justice. He didn't often do the shopping, but when he did – I've seen him empty supermarkets without anyone paying at the checkout because they were understaffed on a Saturday, it took him five minutes, he'd march out with the security guards, the checkout girls, the other shoppers, fists raised. I saw him rip down parking barriers because we had been waiting too long for a space. Longwy, let me tell you about Longwy – my father could trigger a factory walkout with nothing but his big mouth. He would take on the riot police, the C.R.S., try to persuade them to make common cause. He knew the enemy was never going to be minimum-wage workers. Terror, he imposed a reign of terror wherever he went. My father's wrath, I swear, that was something to see . . . And you should have seen him with women. He wasn't a ladykiller, he wasn't some lounge lizard squirming like an eel to seduce some hot babe, but he had a way with women, they flocked to him, they were so smitten they used to faint. He couldn't help it, poor bastard. It was his character. And when you've got a father like that and you hear someone say of other people's fathers "They're men too", I swear you have to hide your face and laugh. You think, have you *seen* that thing you call papa who spends his whole life doing what he was told . . . weaklings, cowards, pussies, nonentities, invertebrates, incompetents . . . that's men in general. But my father, yeah, one look at him and you know what a 'man' is. Looks at other men's wives – they spend their time bitching, they don't get what they need, it's obvious. Poor bitches marry some moron when they're twenty and two kids later they finally figure out they're playing nursemaid to a complete loser. It's not men they've married, it's rags full of shit. They're Diet Coke men, like in the billboard ads when we were kids, they roar like the real thing, they stink like the real thing, but all they know is how to knuckle under and take orders. Their wives are furious. That's why they turn out little fascists like the ones you ran into earlier. These are kids who never had a father. They grew up seeing their mother not getting any and bitching all day long, and it broke their hearts. Par for the course. So they try to imagine the kind of man who'd be able to make his wife come. But they can google all they like, the formula isn't on the internet. It's in the genes. If you'd seen my mother: radiant, chic, satisfied, always happy. When they're well fucked, I swear, women are so different. All those fatherless wimps born from a pussy by a flaccid dick that stinks of piss. They search all over the place for father figures, they can hardly see a beard without blubbing *papa*, they get themselves adopted by losers . . . poor fuckers don't know what it is to be a man. They churn out the same shit – they knock up pathetic little girls, leave them unsatisfied and breed more arseholes who don't know how to stand up straight. A limp dick in a fusty cunt, that's the problem, mark my words . . . what can you expect of a nation of sexually frustrated flunkeys."

"Couldn't your father help you out?"

"No. He remarried. His new wife already had kids. I'm surplus to requirements. I serve no purpose in his new life, I just cause him trouble . . ."

"Don't you miss seeing him?"

"Not as much as my dog Attila-the-Fun. They stole Attila-the-Fun from me three months ago. You should have seen him, a handsome dog, so gentle, a real teddy bear. An American Staff built like a truck, a real beauty . . . and those bastards stole him from me. It's not like he'd done anything . . . you see the way they treat humans, so it's no surprise that they go round nicking dogs, especially from homeless people . . . sometimes they try to get them adopted. But Attila-the-Fun fucking freaked them out. We sleep in the park, you know, up in the Buttes-Chaumont."

"You know Laurent?"

"Everyone knows Laurent. We're not exactly friends, him and me. When he's drunk he winds me up, he's like a war veteran with his dignity and his moral decency and all that shit . . . let's face it, we're sleeping on the streets, let's not compete for who gets a gold star . . . But we sleep in the same place, yeah, and we're part of the same gang – we're not part of the press-ganged poor, we're happy not to be working. The rich hate us because we're smarter than they are. And they know it. That's why they want to kill us. When we're starving and riddled with tumours and have to kill to eat, they'll be able to point at us and say – See? At least we rich people are more refined."

"Don't you ever get sick of living on the streets?"

"No. I do miss Attila-the-Fun, though. He used to sleep next to me, he was my buddy, I loved the smell of him, dogs aren't like people, they never wash but at the end of the day they smell like a cake factory. Anyway, one morning, he goes off for a walk and I'm not awake yet – this is why I don't like booze, if I hadn't been drinking the night before, I would have felt him getting up. Anyway, he was wandering around and the bastard fucking cops and some guys from the dog pound, they hunted him down. The park wardens knew him, all they ever said was to put him on a lead, that's all . . . So obviously the dog, he panics, he bares his teeth – that's all the excuse they need, a dangerous dog, have him put down. He was chipped and everything, but I didn't have the paperwork to get him back and by the time I sorted it out they'd killed my Attila-the-Fun. He was all I had. Dangerous dog my fucking arse . . . If a bunch of strangers jump you and try to drag you from your master, of course you defend yourself, it's normal. That's what they call a dangerous dog. Bullshit. They treat dogs the same way they treat people: they pick you out, and those that try to defend themselves when they're hunted get eliminated. You're not supposed to defend yourself, you're supposed to let them fuck you over. Nine years, nine years Attila-the-Fun and I were together. Can you imagine the void that leaves? I miss my dog. And I miss music."

"What kind of music do you like?"

"I love Adele. I could listen to her James Bond song all the time."

"I used to be a record dealer. A long time ago."

"Yeah? Vinyl and old school photography – so you and me are both castaways from jobs that were shipwrecked."

She would like to slip her hand under his arm, just to touch him, as though he were her best buddy.

XAVIER HAS JUST BEEN THRASHED FOR THE THIRD TIME STRAIGHT at Zynga Poker. Some pompous twat who hesitated to go all in when he had quads confused him and he went all in with two pair. Some days go pear-shaped. He shouldn't spend so much time playing the game. It's harming his work. The other players' avatars are so horrendous they're mesmerising – sports cars, side arms, some wanker in shorts on a yacht, guard dogs, hot babes trying to get picked up – like they're really using their own picture – and photos of kids.

When he's not frantically playing dumb games, he's working on a biopic of Drieu la Rochelle. He sees Magimel in the title role. Or, if he needs to go younger, that little blond actor, Vincent Rottiers. He's got amazing eyes. He'd make a decent Drieu. He knows it's a good idea, it's the perfect time. When he was young, he used to laugh at the idea of writer's block, the whole fear of the blank page thing. Well, now, that's him. He's blocked, bunged up, like some middle-class mediocrity with constipation. He has to get his arse in gear before some card-carrying director comes to the same conclusion and gets in first. Now that it's okay for people to be on the far right, it wouldn't surprise him if lefty directors went round appropriating leadership figures that don't belong to them. It's all about subsidies – if there's money for the taking, they'll be queuing up with their hands out. He has to work fast.

But he is freaked out just by the very thought that he's come up with a good idea.

His mother's panic made him uncomfortable. Usually, the two of them just stick to superficial chatter, insincerity has always been the hallmark of his family. They have always been terrified of outbursts in his family, they know the damaging consequences of truth. They generally use words to ward off any subject that might be upsetting. Conversation entails discussing schedules, meeting places, sums of money, ages. Everything else is avoided. When his mother called to tell him she'd seen Vernon, she was distraught. Xavier promised to go and check out the park. She says she can't sleep. She has already told him that the co-owners downstairs have voted to have the two benches outside the building removed because tramps were sleeping there. The owners said it was driving down property prices. She has good reason to complain: given the posh neighbourhood she lives in, a couple of tramps aren't going to devalue anything. They should be thanked for agreeing to move into such a miserable area. She had a showdown with the other owners about the benches, they argued that it was the concierge who got lumbered with the dirty work, she wasn't the one asking the tramps to move so as to mop up the piss, and it was the concierge who had to make sure they didn't empty the contents of the rubbish bins all over the pavement. Xavier listens to her tell this story for the fourth time, not daring to tell his mother that, honestly, he thinks it's a good idea to rip out the benches. The tramps aren't the worst of it, hoodlums could have set up home there. He doesn't like to think of his mother running into hoodlums every time she leaves the house. We all have our own shit to deal with, maman. But she's obsessed with this affair – it drives her crazy to think they're using the concierge as an excuse so they can deny the destitute a place to sleep. In politics, as in so many things, his mother is still living in the 1980s.

It makes him livid that she is suddenly so worried about Subutex. It's always the same old story. You just have to let yourself go and his mother gets out her nurse's outfit. Xavier is careful not to mention that her beloved Vernon robbed the apartment of a friend who was putting him up. Xavier has never much liked Sylvie, she's a dumb, lefty, trust-fund bitch who's never worked a day in her life, a jumped-up apparatchik, forever preaching to people on subjects about which she knows sod-all. But even so. It's the principle of the thing. He's always hated guys who don't keep their word. If Xavier were to wind up on the streets some day, he is convinced he wouldn't turn into a scumbag. You only become what you allow yourself to become.

That said, it's convenient, having news of Subutex. The woman who was looking for him was very clear on that point: anyone who helped her track the guy down would be rewarded. No spring chicken, but classy enough that he didn't just tell her to take a hike, I don't know anything. She had said she was called the Hyena. The sort of nickname you get stuck with at twenty that becomes difficult to live with later. She had said she was working for a producer, she didn't give any details, but she seemed serious. And at least she wasn't a slut. Not the sort of skank who gets on her high horse talking about a woman's dignity but walks around half naked and acts all surprised when all you can think about is fucking her. She was a lady. She had heard about the interviews Alex did. Xavier could not work out how she had traced him. Respect.

The Hyena had left her number so that he could call if he had any information. He let it be known that he would love to work on a posthumous portrait of Alex and that, if he ran into Vernon he would talk to him about it. Actually, he would rather rip out his fingernails than work on a posthumous portrait of some piss-poor crooner for suburban housewives, but everyone's got to eat.

Alex Bleach, Jesus Christ, like we haven't heard enough of him. People asked Alex for his opinion about everything, whether it was climate change or Tina Turner's menopause, they wanted his take. He had absolutely nothing to say. Or if he did, it was no more interesting than the next guy. He wasn't risking his job when he said he was anti-racism, anti-nuclear, anti-rape, anti-road deaths, anti-cancer, anti-Alzheimer's. He never rocked the boat, when asked all he ever said was "It's not my job to do interviews". Like his job was being a musician. Bullshit. But he was good-looking, and not the worst performer on stage. If Vernon hands over the interview tapes – and Xavier has a couple of persuasive arguments up his sleeve – there would be a concise portrait in there somewhere. Who knows, it might even put him back in the saddle. It would be tough to swallow, but given what an S.A.C.D.-accredited director makes when his film is show on T.V., he'd be prepared to swallow it and smile to boot.

He types "leave table" and quits the poker game. Marie-Ange finishes early, she's the one who picks up the kid. She is spending a lot of time with her daughter at the moment. Marie-Ange is going through a rough patch. It reminds him of the movie "Quiet Chaos". They don't talk about it, but the truth is the dog's death has been devastating for both of them. He knows this, but Marie-Ange is less in touch with her emotions, she doesn't know how to express her feelings. He wishes it had brought them closer, but for the moment they are each dealing with their grief alone.

He would never have imagined that people could be so shaken up by the death of a dog. Marie-Ange won't let him talk to their daughter about it. Xavier thinks that it's important to talk to children about death. During the weeks of cortisone treatment, the dog was pissing all over the apartment. He would pull on a pair of blue rubber gloves, dip a red sponge in warm water and clean up after her. By the end, she could not even manage to stay standing while she relieved herself. She would flop on her belly into the puddle of urine and had to be wiped down with a face flannel. He'd say to her, you're getting old, girl, you're not much longer for this world, it's over. There is no cure. Then she started to wheeze nonstop. He slept next to her, she snuggled against him, she was terrified. There was nothing he could do for her. One morning, he called the vet to have her put down, it was a beautiful day though they were still in the depths of winter. The little one left for school, he told her to give Colette a cuddle, then he made the phone call. He didn't want to take her to the surgery. Marie-Ange thought it sounded too expensive but he was adamant. He refused to go. For more than a month, the dog had been unable to walk unaided, he had carried her around the apartment and for as long as she could still stand he would take her outside to do her business and get some fresh air. He never said anything, but she did weigh thirteen kilos and there were times when he was exhausted. He did push-ups every morning to strengthen his lumbar muscles. To carry her for as long as she needed, he got himself fit again. He would take her in his arms, that huggable little body, because he knew that it was over. It was terrible, knowing that she was dying, she trusted him and he could do nothing to make her better.

The vet took the body away in a black plastic bag. Xavier asked if he could have the ashes. He lied to Marie-Ange about how much it had cost. He didn't give a damn. When he went to collect the ashes from the vet and saw the name "Colette" on the box, he realised that it was done. He put the box on a shelf, between the biography of Lemmy and a book about Mesrine. He still cannot get used to how quiet the house is when he comes home. He has never known the apartment to feel so empty.

When he opens the front door, it is freezing outside, a deathly cold. Okay, so Vernon got what was coming to him, but even so it would be weird to find out that someone he hung out with for years had died of cold, alone, at night on the streets. If he does find him, he'll keep his promise to his mother: he'll take him to a hotel. That way, she will know where he is, she will be able to look after him keep him warm feed him and all that shit.

He changes trains at République. On the platform, Xavier counts: three white guys, ten black guys, five Chinese, eight Arabs. Paris as usual. Only you're not allowed to talk about it, otherwise the politically correct start screaming you're a racist. Who's going to protect the little old white woman who gets mugged coming back from doing her shopping at Tati, that's what he wants to know. Don't try telling him the Chinese would step in, as soon as they settle here, they wash their hands of anything French.

Another tramp begging at the foot of the stairs. A kid with a cat in his lap, the cat is obviously on drugs otherwise it would run away. It's easier to drug a cat than it is to learn guitar, that's for sure. Xavier thinks about the heft, the weight of his dog, this thing that he will never feel again. The most difficult thing to accept is the fact he will forget. One day, he will look at a dog and not think of Colette.

He hasn't gone two hundred metres from the Métro before he spots Vernon in the distance. He is outside the supermarket sitting next to some hideously ugly, XXXL-size bag lady. All the same, it's a vicious right hook to the solar plexus. He makes the most of the fact that Subutex hasn't seen him to slip into the McDo opposite. He joins the queue; at the counter, some teenager about three metres tall is ordering dozens of burgers, in the adjoining room he can hear the screeching of kids celebrating a birthday. Xavier orders a beer and a KitKat McFlurry, then posts himself next to the window. He hadn't expected to be so disturbed at seeing Vernon. In fact, he hadn't expected to see him.

His brain randomly regurgitates images of him and Vernon when they were teenagers, it's always pointless images that resurface at times like this, the colour of a carpet with a Stooges album lying on it, Vernon's ankle-boots sticking out from under the shop counter, the hassle of getting home after the last Métro and the two of them, tripping on acid, walking all the way back to the suburbs, the relief, when they got to Zurich, of seeing H.R. on stage with Bad Brains doing his dangerous back-flip. Other memories get caught up in the net – seeing his brother in the street, unconscious, at a bus stop, drooling over himself, head lolling on his chest surrounded by passers-by. His father pretending to read the newspaper in the evening, and never turning the page because he was waiting for Nicolas to come home. His mother lifting the clock up to her ear to check that it was working, or picking up the telephone to make sure the line was free. His fucking brother who only cared about himself, his dope, his dope – all warmth consumed by his vice. Xavier said nothing. Catching Nicolas with his hand in a drawer, stealing their dead grandparents' wedding rings to buy a fix. He had wished his brother dead a dozen times. And when it finally happened what little remained of the family stability crumbled into squalor. His mother never set foot inside a church again. While his brother was alive, she prayed constantly, utterly consumed by fervour and by hope. Xavier still believes. He takes his daughter to mass on Sundays, faith is the most precious thing his father left him. Everything else was reduced to ash. Like the body of his dog. Frankly, he doesn't need to see a shrink to work out why it freaks him out to see his old friend in this state. He wishes he could save him. He wishes he would drop dead. He wishes none of this were happening.

The creature Vernon is hanging with outside the supermarket is an indeterminate female, she waylays passing strangers with ape-like gestures. She is filthy and degenerate. Xavier wishes she would wander off, but they look like they're shacked up together. Next to her, Vernon looks frail, his back is hunched to ward off the cold, his face is grey, the beard makes him look haggard. He deserves all the shit that's coming to him, like all the fuckwits of his kind, but that does not make the slightest difference to the heartache the spectacle arouses. Xavier has always loathed pity, that sickening emotion, he would rather kill a man than pity him. But these protestations are at odds with his gut.

Xavier hesitates for a long time. Behind him, a wide range of people come and go carrying trays that smell of fried grease that is not exclusive to McDonalds, a nauseating smell that simultaneously makes you want to throw up and makes your mouth water. He could go home, spare himself this shit, let his mother take the R.E.R., let her come and comb the neighbourhood herself, given her fondness for tragedy, she'd be thrilled to see Vernon like this, she could fall to her knees and play out that primitive scene so crucial to his family, the scene where the mother helps her grown-up child get back on his feet. She can wallow in her pity until hell freezes over as long as she leaves her son out of it. Xavier wants nothing to do with this emotional blackmail, he doesn't want his stomach gnawed away by grief because someone else could not be arsed to save himself. The notion of trying to get back the Alex tapes seems absurd. That poor fucker Vernon probably had his rucksack stolen ages ago. It is his mother Xavier is worrying about. He cannot do this to her. She has him in a bind. He gave her his word. He walks out of McDo's, crosses the streets and stands in front of Vernon. Seeing him approach the female flashes him a hideous smile, "Oh, monsieur, you wouldn't have a spare ciga-rette?" Vernon lays a hand on her arm to shut her up. Without a word, the two men stare each other down. There is fear in Vernon's eyes, but hatred too. This is not the welcome Xavier was expecting. Then the man sitting on the pavement speaks, in the tone you might use if you casually bumped into someone in a bar:

"I ran into your mother the day before yesterday. She told me about the dog. I'm really sorry."

Xavier, nonplussed, replies in the same tone:

"Brain tumour. We found out too late. It was very quick."

"You lost your dog too?"

He refuses to speak to this pig. Christian charity is all well and good, but extending it to the far-flung suburbs of outer fuckwittery is out of the question. The fat female's eyes fill with tears and he doesn't have time to tell her to shut up before she starts:

"They stole my dog three months ago. Hurts like fuck, doesn't it? When you're with them, you know that you're going to lose them someday, you know it will probably be tough . . . but that's nothing compared to what you feel when it happens. What breed was yours?"

"French bulldog."

"They're so cute. There's a lot more of them around these days, hipsters love them. Mine was a Staff, they're bigger but it's the same principle, they're huge hounds. There is no body as perfect as the body of your dog. Mine had these amazing little eyelashes, I could spend all day looking at them. It's details like that . . . my dog was a magnificent animal."

From a distance, Xavier would have sworn that this giant communicated only in grunts. He is surprised to find her so effusive, so articulate. She's not as drunk as he thought she was. The most surprising thing is her voice, which doesn't fit her tubbiness or her appearance. She has a voice that deserves to be on the radio, a beautiful voice. He knows exactly what she means. Colette had beautiful eyelashes too. You have to be a true dog-owner to notice these things. He can't tell her to fuck off after what she has just said. It's the basic principle of owning a dog: you talk to people you wouldn't give the time of day in ordinary circumstances. He nods.

"It must have been terrible for you."

"The list of all the little things you used to do that you'll never do again. I'd give anything – I can't say everything I own, I don't own anything, but I'd give a kidney to be able to kiss his slobbery lips. To stroke his belly. I want to see him there when I wake up. Attila-the-Fun. You know what I'm saying, yeah? I keep expecting him to turn up, wagging that big arse of his. He liked to sleep under the duvet, he'd snuggle up against my belly."

"You named your dog Attila-the-Fun?"

The fat slob has a sense of humour. Either that or she's psycho. If she weren't so filthy, he'd say she belongs in the category of people where you can't decide if they're brilliant or barking. He crouches down next to her, never mind keeping his distance.

"Towards the end, my dog would piss all over the kitchen floor every morning, and I'd mop it up, hose it down, get out the Cif and scrub, making sure to clean between the tiles. Now every morning I get up and I see the dry floor and I remember that she's dead and I can't cry. I've got a daughter, I've got a wife, I'm a man for God's sake. I can't go crying just because my dog is dead but there's nothing sadder in the world than making breakfast in the morning and not having her nosing around for crumbs."

Tears trickle soundlessly down the woman's face, and he knows she is not faking it to get him to put his hand in his pocket. She shares his grief.

"Eleven years I been living on the streets. Attila was ten – he wasn't even a year old when I got him, his master got himself banged up leaving the dog with his mother, and she was out at work all day, she couldn't look after him, so she gave him to me. The son did five years and even then he fucked up, ten days after he was released he was back inside I found out later. When they took Attila, I thought to myself that if I lived a normal life they'd never have taken my dog. But if I had a job, I wouldn't have been able to spend all my time with him, we wouldn't have been as happy . . . a dog whose master is homeless is the happiest dog in the world because he's the only thing you've got, and since the homeless shelters won't take you if you've got a dog, you never leave his side, you eat with him, you sleep with him. I never go to social services, they won't let you in with a dog. So I don't go in. You can't leave a Staff tied up outside. And I'm not going to leave Attila-the-Fun with some wino who's likely to lose him. Or sell him – you never know with the vermin I have to deal with . . . But I can't help thinking that if I'd had a normal life, they wouldn't have taken my dog. So I feel guilty, I feel guilty. I can't stop thinking about him in that kennel, I'm sure he knew what they were going to do, I think about the vet's steel table, and I wasn't even there for him. Someone came to fetch him and he must have thought I'd abandoned him. I didn't look out for him. Were you there, when your dog died?"

"Yes. She was relaxed, lying on the sofa. But if it's any comfort, I feel guilty too. Afterwards I thought I should have killed the vet when he rang the doorbell."

And for the first time since it happened, he knows he is about to cry. People can stare, they can think what they like, they can fuck off, the lot of them. Olga's tears trace grime over her cheeks. Vernon listens to them, making no attempt to join in the conversation.

"I DON'T GET IT – WHO'S 'THE STUNNER' – HER?"

"Check the photos, check 'em: who'd want to climb on top of that? Amirite? If that sleazy crack-whore found a half-decent guy to give her a good rooting, you think she'd even say thanks?"

"I don't know, if she asked me nicely I'd fuck her in the arse for free."

"Fuck's sake, is there nothing that turns you off?"

"One of these days you should give us a list of the one girl you wouldn't bone – save time."

Loïc smiles, he enjoys the pressure. Noël is sitting awkwardly. By the time he arrived, the only seat left was the skankiest armchair in the place. He is annoyed. He has assumed Loïc wasn't coming. He doesn't look at him.

The whole situation is a pain. If he'd known, he would have gone straight home. He's shattered. He's been on his feet for three days straight, without a glimpse of daylight, putting hangers back on rails, re-folding jumpers and rushing around various departments tidying away the clothes abandoned by customers in the fitting rooms. Saturdays are a full-scale riot. All the emos, queers, hipsters, niggas, fashion-fags, losers, students, ragheads, posers and pretty boys in Paris pile in through the glass doors to try on the latest swag – the shit made by kids in the third world that Jew bankers are trying to flog – and these douchebags *pay* to wear this stuff. Before he worked here, it wouldn't have occurred to him to think of buying a jumper or a pair of jeans in a place like this. Certainly not on a Saturday. Someone should lock the doors with everyone a couple of times a day and gas the fuckers. Seriously. The freaks that hang out in this shithole. You should see the girls spending all day posing like hookers in front of the mirrors, you'd never imagine how a bunch of ugly hoes preen and pout when they see themselves in here. Fat slags who haven't exactly been blessed by nature, but here they are squeezing themselves into bush-league brands – and yakking non-stop about "The Bachelorette". The guys are not much better. They should try spending their Saturdays off pumping iron, the puny little fuckers. They've got all the musculature of earthworms. They're twenty years old and they've got love handles that look like rubber rings under their trendy T-shirts. Why don't you do a few ab crunches before you start thinking about what to wear, you tub of lard. You've got your Saturday free, you could be hanging with your mates, having sex with your girlfriend, seeing a movie or just vegging in front of the T.V. with a nice cool beer, but no . . . You have to come here. And the idiot who has to clear up after you is yours truly. Noël. A dozen times a day, the department manager whispers in his ear – smile, please. There's crappy muzak blaring from the speakers all day long. Smile, please. Sure thing, boss. The shop is swarming with people. They elbow Noël in the ribs, stamp on his feet, barge into him and never apologise – everyone knows shop assistants are there to be trampled.

*

He should have gone home as soon as he finished work. A ready-meal in front of "The Voice", a little trolling on Twitter, a couple of hours playing "No-Man's Land" and then bed. Would have done him good, a quiet night in. He needs to find himself a girlfriend. How long has he been single – six months, more? Well, there's no danger of meeting anyone tonight, there's never any girls round J.P.'s place. When they're not talking sex, they're talking football – it's hardly likely to bring in the babes. Besides, these days his luck is shot to shit, every time a girl is into him she turns out to be sweet but not beddable.

Loïc is constantly trying to suck up to him. Making jokes, looking over at him, taking a beer and offering him one. It's making Noël uncomfortable. Last night he and Julien had a long conversation about Loïc. Julien is right. You have to decide where your loyalties lie. Noël is generally the sort to live and let live. Loïc is a funny guy, gotta give him that. Okay he's a cocky bastard and a real shit-stirrer, but when he's not there, their evenings are a lot less fun. Julien is hacked off with him. It's been brewing for a while now. He can't stand Loïc's sarcasm. He's not wrong. It's getting to the point where it's embarrassing. When Noël showed up tonight, Loïc was taking the piss out of the dweebs who designed the flags for Génération identitaire, because they look like party banners from an M.J.C. rally in Fontainebleau in the early eighties and then he started mocking the website guys for publishing photos of members of Projet Apache with long hair to prove that the lefty feminazis were lying when they called them skinheads. The post on the site was pretty funny, it was ironic, there was no reason to trash-talk the guy who wrote it. But Loïc would sell his own mother for a decent one-liner, and by now everyone was pissing themselves laughing so he wasn't about to stop. It's funny. But it's snide. You can't sign up to a cause and then snigger at everything it stands for. The problem with Loïc is he thinks that talking smack about everything proves he's astute, when actually he's showing his weakness by refusing to take the cause seriously. If you want to be in politics, you have to learn self-discipline. You never know what Loïc really thinks. On the important issues, he's systematically evasive. He always needs to prove he's the smartest, that you can't get one over on him. Julien has him sussed: he's winging it. He tried recommending stuff for him to read, tried to help him improve his mind. But Loïc just pulls a face. He's got no conviction, no insight. Action doesn't preclude a sense of humour, but you can't do what he does, spend your time mocking everyone and everything. One of the values they are sworn to defend is solidarity. No mercy for the enemy. It was mimicking poor Soral, sitting on the sofa in his apartment in the Marais filming himself babbling non-stop bullshit about his heritage as a good *rouge-brun* Marxist sensitive to the complexities of patrimony and private property, that Loïc first made Julien laugh and they became friends. The take-off was enough to make you piss yourself. Everyone knows Soral is a joke, it goes without saying. But you don't say that to your friends on the internet. This is about propaganda, it's important to have strategic alliances otherwise the enemy gets to watch us tear each other apart and laps it up. "The Association of Former Faggots Converted to Catholicism" is hilarious. But it adds nothing to the debate – quite the opposite. His imitations of Frigide Barjot would have you rolling on the floor – "Is the junkie jezebel turned papist poodle going to the dogs?" But the problem is Loïc has no boundaries, he's capable of doing his impressions in front of anyone. And being a militant is a serious business, not an ego trip.

The three of them got along well initially. With Loïc as court jester and footy expert and Julien with his gift of the gab, his culture and his intelligence, the two of them galvanised the troops. But for a while now, Julien has been distancing himself from his acolyte whose limitations he can keenly sense. Recently, he went up to Rennes for Génération identitaire's first charitable initiative. He militates on the ground. He passes on information, makes speeches, he gets involved. If it comes to choosing a camp, Noël would rather side with those who dare to commit themselves.

Noël has less ego than the other two. That's the reason they like his company so much. He's got enough personality to be a good mate, but he doesn't have a pressing need to monopolise the conversation. He is a comrade, you can count on him, he has only one loyalty. But he knows he doesn't have the makings of a leader. His thing is bodybuilding. Ever since he got his T.R.X., he's been bodyweight training and following a strict high-protein diet, he has managed to develop his lower body. Something he was having trouble doing. He hates guys who only work on upper body strength – because it's easier and not as painful. But he's working to develop his hamstrings. Tonight, he brought along a little cargo of Napalm, an adreno-muscular stimulant that will give them some pep. He's already giggling to himself at the thought of seeing his friends flush red, pretty soon they'll be all hot and scratching themselves and straight after they'll feel wide awake. Napalm is like drinking molten lava straight from the volcano.

His mother worked at a checkout. Noël watched her slave and get fucked over her whole life. She votes socialist. Even now. She does it but she's got no illusions. When *Le Nouvel Obs* runs headlines about the former director of the I.M.F. paying for whores, they're spitting in his mother's face: it's just us, we can do what the fuck we like, just make sure the money doesn't leave the room. And these people, when it comes to allocating H.L.M. apartments in the housing projects, they're open-handed and they give it to immigrants rather than his mother, to foreigners and friends with long arms. For people like him, it's always come back tomorrow. When the middle classes have had their pound of flesh and there's nothing left for anyone else, and still they come on like they're good Samaritans and great minds at the expense of the dumb bastards who really work and no-one ever gives a stuff about. Health insurance that costs an arm and a leg. Commuter trains that break down every other day, but you've still got to pay. You have to pay for everything. Disgusting meat that you thought tasted off because it was halal but it turns out it's horsemeat from some old nag hopped up on hormones, or chicken that's got rabies, just shut up and eat, you fucking pleb, and before you go home after your forty-five hours slaving in some scuzzy shopping centre remember to donate some of your money to the Romanian meat industry. And remember to save up for when you have cancer, you fucking prole, the public hospitals are overrun by illegals from all over the planet who know France is the place to be. When it's not North Africans being used to drive down working-class salaries, it's factories moving abroad to countries where people are starving. And why wouldn't they? What's the downside? Who has ever told them that lack of patriotism is a crime? Meanwhile, the country is being sold off to the Russians, the Qataris and the Chinks. The mother country flogged off to the highest bidder like some tenth-rate whore, open to anyone with the money to pay for a hole. And they're supposed to just accept this shit? The Jews run the banks and all they care about is how much they can make off other people, and the masons have politics sewn up and all they do is give each other cushy jobs. Spending public money, that's all they're there for. And meanwhile the middle classes get all politically correct because a couple of Romanians get insulted. You can tell they don't live near a gypsy camp. No, they shell out on organic meat, certified organic French meat because they have to protect their spoiled rich bodies from disease. Tough shit for the proles and losers. And when they have to send their kids to school, they move house because they don't want their little blonde angel being called "chalk-face" by jealous hordes. When a Jewish banker rapes a hotel maid he just gets out his chequebook and every whore in the République lines up to impale themselves on his prodigious prick. Women love bastards. All those parasitical bastards who hold their nose when the proles vote and think that by lying in newspapers, on T.V., in magazine articles, they'll get to fuck them over again. They've forgotten the Paris Commune. The people care more about the state than its leaders. The difference is honour. *Viva la muerte*. The people are prepared to die because they're desperate, because they've got nothing to lose, but because they can see the future. We *are* the state. The future of France depends on our determination. One people, one language, one future. Contrary to the bullshit they're constantly being fed, the people are not condemned to be powerless. He is trembling with excitement at the thought of abolishing the impunity that protects the great and the good of this world. They would cut their children's throats without a second thought, stick them on a pikestaff and parade them through the town. He will die in a hail of bullets if need be to defend his country. He will stop at nothing. He refuses to let his native country fall apart and just sit worrying about how he is going to pay his taxes. In interview after interview, the pillars of society claim that only Muslims are motivated enough to die for a cause. Demoralising the people. They plan to prove otherwise. They are ready. They are preparing for war. Honour, homeland. He feels it echo in his chest, feels it surge through him, drag him in its wake. The vision it stirs is a powerful steed he joyfully saddles. Together, they are invincible. They will overthrow every-thing.

And that is precisely Loïc's problem. He is bitter. He's resent-ful. He has no vision. Once, when he was ruinously plastered, he said to Noël: "Overthrow everything? I'm pushing forty. I know the human race too well to have any illusions. There'll be three days partying and years of hangover. The only thing that'll change is that four jerks who didn't amount to shit will get cushy jobs. It's only about replacing the ruling party, but the game will be the same. They'll behave exactly like the people they've replaced. Lying, trafficking, cheating, making sure their brothers-in-law get all the privileges." This, according to Loïc, is what politics boils down to. Nihilism. When Noël heard him say this, he realised it was over. Julien is right: there is no time for cynicism. They have to be ready to fight. And you don't go into action armed with big talk.

Third beer, Noël still has all his wits about him, but he feels a wave surge through him. The Napalm is spreading its black magic through his body. A feverishness, a furious joy. A rush of energy. Loïc comes over to him. "You avoiding me?" "No. I need to get something to eat, otherwise I'll be legless." "Wanna go down and get a McDo?" Noël cannot see how he can refuse, and now that he's had a drink he feels like a laugh and at least with Loïc he's guaranteed a laugh. "You sure you haven't been avoiding me? You've been really evasive. Did Julien tell you not to talk to me?" The question is caustic, like he's saying you're only a kid who takes orders from grown-ups. Noël is irritated, but now he is more irritated with Julien. It's tough being caught between the two of them. But fuck it, he's not some punk bitch. He shrugs, grabs his woolly hat, "Yo, we're heading down for a McDo's", and the little group gets to its feet to follow. There is a lot of shoving and banter as they head down the stairs, that awesome early-evening buzz. They're jostling, getting excited, high on alcohol and Napalm – they're ready for some fun.

Outside, he feels good. They take up the whole pavement. With all of them, you'd have to be crazy not to step aside and let them pass. Without doing so consciously, Noël exaggerates his macho swagger, he feels nervous, it's a blast. Strutting through Belleville, with the hipsters and the Chinks and the *bougnoules*, it's good to see them step aside. This is *their* turf. They exist. Despite the mosques invading Kebabcity, everyone remembers and steps aside – they're playing at home. It makes a change from being at work where they make him dress as neutrally as possible, make him wear the shit they sell. Obviously not the sort of stuff he'd choose or bring home in the evening, no, fucking faggot clothes he's forced to wear and has to turn in at the end of his shift. He smiles at the black guy who frisks them before they leave. Fuck's sake, like I'd want to take dreck from this place home with me . . . On

331

that point he and Blacky Chan understand each other. The old security guard used to bring a hand up to his shoulder, do the *quenelle* then flash him a wink and a pathetic little smile – like: we understand each other, we're on the same side. Yeah, right Snow White . . . but as any of your black colleagues will tell you "Respect yourself, don't expect me to do it for you". Relief when he was fired, it was such an embarrassing situation. Noël has nothing against the Blacks. But why can't they look after their own countries instead of scurrying away like rats lured by French breadcrumbs.

During the day, in the shop, it's not him slogging away. His body is present, his actions are automatic, he shuts himself down and turns off his brain. At night, on the town with his mates, they are lords of the street. No more slaving away. An easy rubbing of shoulders, the sounds of boots on paving slabs, the simplicity of being in the gang, the banter, the knowing looks. It is a sound, a common energy. The pride of being part of it, and the satisfaction that people notice them, avoid them, respect them. The nation's future, in battle formation.

When they reach McDonald's, J.P. slows, something on the other side of the road has caught his eye.

"Don't tell me it's not true! Madame Fat Arse!"

The way he whistles, smiling maliciously. Loïc moves closer to him – what has he seen? J.P. drones something by Napalm Death in a voice from beyond the grave as he stifles a snigger. Then he explains, this morning, with Julien, the kicking he got, the mad bitch, that fat filthy slag whose only claim to being female is having a cunt, how what that *thing* deserves is to be gutted alive. The world has no business tolerating a piece of shit like her. And she's aggressive to boot. So she likes a good fight, does she? Sniggers here and there. Noël remembers Julien's advice to them. It's important to support the destitute, to do what the French state refuses to do: our own people come first. First feed our own, then we'll talk about the plight of those who didn't love their own country enough to stay there and fight together to climb out of the shit. But it also means you don't go looking for trouble with the defenceless – it's an image thing – especially not if they speak our language. It winds Julien up, posts on websites in shoddily spelled French. It's called a mother tongue for a reason, it's what makes us a nation. Noël makes a lot of mistakes. He never leaves a comment on a site unless he can check the spelling. It drives him mad, seeing the typos and the epic fails some guys come out with. Even he can tell that they're riddled with mistakes. It's just not good enough.

Tonight, in this moment, it is mostly the beer and the Napalm talking, the lithe movement of the gang as they slope over to this girl who screwed with their mates – just to give her a piece of their mind. Let's face it, even blind drunk, they're not going to gang-rape an ugly slag like her. And even if it was a pretty blonde, they wouldn't do it, it's not their style. Julien doesn't need to worry – it's just a bit of fun. A little walk-past, let her know they're in the area. Maybe ask her, just to make sure: who's the boss round here? Who do you take orders from?

The woman's eyes are red and swollen, the old guy next to her looks shitfaced drunk and panics when he sees them coming. With these two, it's going to be a formality. The problem is the two-bit thug chatting to them. A local hipster buying himself a clear conscience, he's crouched down next to the tramps to show he respects them, but don't worry, he'll be sleeping in a warm bed tonight and they can go fuck themselves. Go on, papa, go home. You know you're not up for this. But instead of realistically assessing the situation, showing them some respect and heading home without causing a scene, this mad bastard stands up and faces them, hands in his pockets, jutting his chin. This dumb fuck has no street smarts, one more idiot who hasn't had his share of beatings, so when he sees a herd of bulls bearing down, he waggles his lilywhite arse and tries to lecture them:

"You got a problem?"

"You sad fuck, you've been watching too many action movies."

"Yeah, dickwad, you a cop? No? Then fuck off, we want a word with your girlfriend."

"Outta the way, we've got a score to settle with your woman here."

"Get lost, boys. Go play somewhere else. I'm sure you'll find someone your own size to pick on. Move along!"

"Did she think about it, this fat slag, before going apeshit on us this morning? Thing is, bro, there has to be law and order in a city. We just came by to tell her that: there has to be order."

Usually, when Loïc gets like this, with his psycho scowl right up in some guy's face, they don't argue the toss. They just want it to stop. If the hipster wants to play hero, it's going to end badly for him.

"Go sleep off your beer somewhere else, you're getting on my tits."

Noël glances around him, makes eye contact with his mates, a big grin on his face. They know it doesn't look good for this guy. He's been working on his leg muscles so much he can climb five flights of stairs and not even feel it – it's like he's being carried. He wouldn't like to be the guy who takes the results of his T.R.X. reps in the face.

"Do I look drunk to you, you bourgeois faggot?"

A quick slap, a love tap. If the guy had a flicker of common sense, he would consider himself warned. He'd let the fat slag take the abuse and the beating she deserves, it would all be over, they'd move on to McDonald's and the rest of their evening. If they have to fight, they prefer to go up against big black gangstas – it's tough to big it up later if it's six of you against two pussies and a psycho bitch, so it would be better to get this over fast.

And then this guy spits in Loïc's face, staring him right in the eyes.

It's not Queensbury rules, it's Cage Warrior rules. Noël knows his kick is lethal, he gives three kicks, head belly head. In that order. Textbook, perfect reflexes, every shot right on target. "That'll teach you to shut your big mouth you fucking bourgeois bastard. Hey, hobos, tell him from me: next time you bow your head and beat it. Let this be a lesson to him."

AN ICY DRIZZLE SOAKS HIS BACK. THE TOUCH OF THE CITY. VERNON simply trudges on, without thinking. He passes a cinema with its lights out, there are few cars at this time of night, he crosses place Gambetta without stopping at the edge of the pavement, he wouldn't mind feeling the brutal impact of the bodywork shattering his bones. He cannot remember ever feeling such an emptiness inside. The signal is detected, and triggers nothing. He sees the closed shutter of the florist's, the three drunk kids are staggering along, a figure sprawled on the bench at a bus stop. The events of the previous night unreel inside his skull without producing the slightest reaction. He has turned himself off. He is a spectator, a fare dodger in his own life, a stowaway. It has finally happened: the void has engulfed him.

The worst of it was the minutes when Xavier was lying on his side, motionless, eyes half-closed, a thin stream of blood trickling from his nose, a red line that stopped in the groove above his lips, seemed to hesitate then followed the curve of his mouth and flowed towards his chin. When Vernon looked up to ask someone to call an ambulance, none of the passers-by would meet his eye. They rushed in and out of the supermarket oblivious to the scene. Though several people had watched the brawl from the other side of the street. Then Olga had pressed herself against Vernon's back, tugged at his sleeve, a childlike gesture, clumsy and insistent: "We can't stay here, big guy. The police are coming, we can't stay here", in a gentle stubborn whisper, never letting go of his arm. Vernon was calling out "Someone needs to call an ambulance", but, as in a nightmare, he had become invisible. It cannot have lasted more than a minute, but he plunged into that moment, it was almost as though he slipped inside and disappeared, his mind, at least, was swallowed up. Then the bouncer at Franprix appeared and took out his mobile phone. Vernon had noticed the guy looking daggers at them all day, as though they were contaminating the entrance to his place of work, and he had found the guy's ugly mug all the more unsettling because it radiated an exceptional stupidity. As it turned out, despite looking like a first-class moron, the guy had a decent knowledge of first aid, he manoeuvred the body confidently, rolling Xavier onto his side, bringing one leg up, cautiously lifting the head, and the paramedics showed up quickly, in a wail of sirens that seems surreal when it directly concerns you.

In the meantime, Olga had disappeared. A police car parked across the street next to the paramedic van. They asked Vernon a few questions, distractedly at first, as though any information he might give was already known to the police, then their manner abruptly changed when they realised this was not a couple of drunks settling old scores. The man on the ground had an address and a credit card. From being friendly and easy-going, the men in uniform were suddenly transformed into busy, anxious professionals. Vernon had to go with them to the station to make a statement. He was insisting on going in the ambulance with Xavier but this was out of the question. "You know him?" in an insolent tone as though they suspected Vernon of trying to cadge a free meal from the emergency services. Vernon said yes I've known him for years, he gave the name, the address, but no, I don't have his wife's number so you can let her know. "Only family members are allowed to accompany the victim." The unconscious body was loaded onto a stretcher, Vernon asked again to go with him but the request went unheard. There was no hostility. Now that he spent his days sitting outside the supermarket, he was less real than he had been before.

Then suddenly there was a new development, Pamela Kant stepped out of a taxi. Vernon recognised her immediately. He saw her hesitate, scan the street, look in his direction. When she marched straight over to him, he did not react. He did not know that what interested her about this scene was him. He was not the only one to spot her. He noticed the paramedics elbowing each other, still going about their business, whispering to each other, and two of the cops literally froze, an incredulous smile on their lips.

"Vernon Subutex? I've been looking for you for a week . . . What's going on? Are you in trouble?"

The circumstances did not lend themselves to joy. Reeling from the shock, Vernon was unable to savour the moment . . . He remained silent. Wild thoughts hurtled towards him like blazing meteorites, and frankly he had no idea whence they came, nor what he was supposed to do with this hot mess. But Pamela was waiting for an answer, and finally he offered one:

"A friend of mine just got beaten up in a brawl. He's lost consciousness."

"Xavier Fardin?"

"You know each other?"

"Of course, I watched "Ma seule étoile", like, a hundred times when I was a kid . . ."

338

*

The appearance of Pamela Kant in itself was pretty implausible, but Pamela Kant talking about Xavier's film as though it were a classic, surrounded by dumbfounded cops and paramedics – Vernon thought, wake up Xavier, for fuck's sake, you can't miss this shit.

And so Pamela took matters in hand with disconcerting ease, as though the role of gang leader was hers by right – she insisted on going with Vernon, fine, she needed to talk to him, a statement, of course, could she leave her mobile number with the paramedics so they could let her know where she could reach Xavier once she and Vernon had finished at the police station? Nothing now posed any problem for anyone. If she had asked them to turn on the lights and sirens and take her window shopping at a department store the boys would have said sure, do you want us to fire in the air while we're driving? The most annoying thing about the whole incident was witnessing this exaggerated display of male solidarity and finding himself completely excluded. It was something that had never happened to him – but a homeless guy, even one who personally knows Pamela Kant, remains a curio in the eyes of working men, Vernon was no longer a real man, he was a creature apart, and when his eyes encountered those of a paramedic there was no sense of complicity, just a puzzled curiosity. So Pamela Kant's little kink was getting screwed by a tramp?

No-one asked his opinion, but he had no particular desire to go and make a statement. Once in the police car, it was all about Pamela Kant, who played the role of the slut with zeal. She gently insulted the men, they were utterly charmed. He left her feeling completely at home at the police station reception desk and followed a young officer into a bleak cubicle.

"White guys, young? Did they mention the name of a faction?"

"No. We didn't talk much . . . I wouldn't have recognised them, I'm not even sure that it's exactly the same group of guys we ran into this morning. To be honest, I didn't get a good look at them."

"And they had some grudge against this woman?"

"I don't really know her. I was only evicted recently, I'm still in shock . . ."

"I understand. I'm sorry."

The police station was in such an advanced state of disrepair that it felt ironic for someone who spent his life working here to feel sorry for someone living on the streets. Like a hospital pitying a charity.

The cop was just a kid, he can't have been more than twenty-five, which heightened the sense of unreality engulfing Vernon that was growing increasingly unsettling. He answered randomly, not quite knowing what it was prudent to hide or reveal. Fairly quickly, the man sitting opposite him dropped the mask of wary suspicion that characterised the beginning of the interview. There was nothing shady about Vernon. In fifteen minutes, the statement was done – all that interested the inspector was the race of the assailants, once this was established he had a slim dossier of photographs of far-right militants for Vernon to look at, no, none of the faces were familiar. Before letting him go, the officer wrote on a Post-It note, in a clumsy, careful scrawl, the phone numbers of various emergency shelters and the addresses where he could go to ask to have his case assessed. He was sorry, times are tough huh, what did you work at before, a record dealer, wow, shit, can't be easy to find a new job. No, here in the police things are fine for the moment, but my brother's in the state school system, I don't think he'll make it to retirement . . . Did you see, in Greece they just shut down the state broadcasting service? And you know who gets sent in to do stuff like that? Us, the police . . . and you know why nobody is talking about it in France? Because the same thing is going to happen here, it's inevitable. We don't like to boast, but the police is about the only thing that's not likely to be privatised any time soon.

Then he had had to wait for Pamela in the waiting room, men gathered round her as though she were a blaze of joy, none of them did anything inappropriate, but they were like kids in hospital when a princess comes to visit, lots of autographs and selfies. Pamela was firing on all cylinders and, watching her, it occurred to Vernon that you had to be very beautiful to carry off a hideous tracksuit, a hoodie and a pair of Eskimo boots that looked like carpet slippers. But Pamela Kant could pull it off, it was her eyes, her slim, impeccably proportioned body, but mostly the way she radiated. He had had to wait for ten minutes in a crowd of cops who took no notice of him, because the *commissaire* wanted to speak to Pamela Kant in private.

In the taxi, she dropped the act. It was a different person sitting next to him. The driver, a Chinese guy listening to France Bleu, did not even recognise her. Once the mask slipped, Vernon noticed the worry lines, the signs of exhaustion. She talked very quickly, avoiding his gaze, as though simply making eye contact might make him flip out. Vernon had asked what the *commissaire* wanted, she had shrugged and said dispassionately:

"He wanted to tell me what it would have been like if he'd been a girl . . . He'd be a stunner, obviously, all the right curves in all the right places and a total slut, he'd drive men wild, lead them around by their dicks, he'd have them by the balls, he'd get anything he wanted, he'd be rich, famous, he would have absolute power . . . The classic douchebag fantasy . . . what are you supposed to say to that? Where did he come up with the idea that sluts have it better than everyone else? On what planet do whores have power? In any case, if he'd been a woman, he would have been ugly as shit. What is he thinking? Anyway . . . I kept my lip buttoned."

"I still don't know why you're here."

"You mentioned you had interview tapes with Alex back at your place . . . Is that true?"

"It can hardly be at my place, I don't have a place. But the bit about interview, yeah, that was true. Are you a fan of French music?"

"Have you still got them?"

He was weary of being asked questions and not knowing whether he should tell the truth, avoid the question or blatantly lie.

"Why are you interested?"

"Am I the first person to ask about them?"

"Yes."

"*Yesss*! First dibs! I am totally shit hot. I may not be the only one looking for these tapes. But I'm first in the queue."

"Have you gone completely insane? There's nothing interesting on the tapes, you know. He was monged out of his tree when he recorded them. He barely knew what he was saying . . . I was just trying to be scam someone when I mentioned them. What I don't understand is . . ."

"Did you listen to him when he was recording them?"

"No."

"Why not?"

"I was asleep. I've always found lady coca relaxes me. Not Alex. He was jabbering nineteen to the dozen when he showed up. The fucker was always talking. I was hardly going to listen when he wasn't even there."

"Can I get my hands on the tapes?"

"Why are you busting my balls about this?"

And then he stops. It's obvious: Vodka Satana. Of course. They must know each other. Maybe they weren't exactly besties. Two porn stars of that calibre, it would strain any friendship. At the top, there can be only one Number One. But this is it, he says the name "Vodka Satana?" and Pamela stiffens, smiles, turns and stares at him. She is trying to seduce him. And although he knows this, although he wants to refuse, although he loves someone else, it is a hundred per cent effective. He would like to pretend he is just a little thrown but in fact he feels like a worm showing off on the end of a hook: she has only to decide and he will be enslaved. He has an idea of what she might do to thank him, but he is too overcome to speak clearly. He wants to know more:

"Who told you about the videos? It's crazy shit . . ."

"You're the one who talked about them."

"A little bit. At first, I wanted to sell them. Did Lydia Bazooka send you?"

"No. It's complicated. But there are several people involved. And I'm the first to track you down. I deserve a little advantage, don't you think?"

The tart – when she wants, her voice softens to a caramel that melts in your ear, when she says "advantage", it's not that he got a hard-on, he *became* a hard-on. Not the best thing when you need to think clearly.

Was it at this point that the rain began to lash harder or was he slipping away, sliding towards the shadows, he did not know. Pamela Kant laid her hand on his, she apologised.

"I've only been thinking about myself. I can see you're dealing with some serious shit, what with your friend in hospital and your personal problems, and here I am like it's all about me. I'm not always like this."

He almost said, yes, I know, I've watched your porn films, and you're not at all like that the rest of the time, you're better dressed and you do amazingly interesting things, and she is probably the type of girl to smile at a bitchy remark. But he had a lump in his throat. Xavier lying on a stretcher, even Pamela's charisma was not enough to erase the impact of that image. Then he was hit by the memory of Alex, never having taken the time to listen to the testament he'd been given, because until now he hadn't thought about it but maybe if he had taken an interest in the tapes when he got them, he might have been able to do something for him. Change the course of things. He had let himself sink, not even thinking to react. He had listened to the dead depart, he was already on their side. Tonight, he felt a terrible regret for having abandoned Alex. And guilt at having dragged Xavier into this whole thing. The two emotions intertwined – what kind of friend have you turned out to be. And just as suddenly, the violent feeling faded, and there was nothing left. For a long moment, Vernon had stared at Pamela Kant in silence, unable to utter a word. He was no longer sufficiently concerned by things. A bottomless gulf was yawning between him and reality – he felt so tired. They had driven endlessly through the hospital grounds, passing ambulances, patients wheeling I.V. drips smoking cigarettes, nurses imitating the Hindu dance. Before getting out of the taxi, he had said:

"I left the bag with the tapes at a friend's place, her name is Emilie. If you managed to track me down, I'm sure you'll find her too. Well, anyway, good luck . . . you can drop me here."

"Out of the question. I'm not leaving you on your own."

He wanted to say "I would prefer not to" and pull it off but at the last moment he remembered that, without her, he would probably not be allowed into the hospital. It was only too apparent what he was, they would take him for a guy who has seen the lights and come in to get warm.

The hospital was a historic building from a time when hospitals were built to look like convents, the façade radiated calm, but when you stepped through the door, everything was ugly. Seventies furniture, fluorescent strip-lights, staff in white coats with faces even more haggard than his own.

Pamela took care of everything, she leaned on the reception desk and waited for someone to come and talk to her. From time to time, Vernon recovered some semblance of rational thought.

"But how did you know where to find me?"

"You've got a hashtag on your head, at first it was that girl who gave you a beating, calls herself Simone du Boudoir on line but I don't know her real name . . ."

"Sylvie?"

"You went to crash at her place, fucked her like a bitch on heat then fucked off and left her. I don't know, maybe there's lots of women like that in your past . . ."

"Sylvie."

"Well anyway these days loads of people are using the hashtag. You've become France's Most Wanted on Twitter. But me – and I don't like to brag – I've got more followers than all the others put together. So, one of my fans spotted you at the public baths in the nineteenth arrondissement, you better believe it, I've got a fan who works there. And he recognised you from the photos I posted . . . I don't know if you know but Simone du Boudoir posted like a million photos of you on Facebook . . . You fucked with the wrong girl, man . . . You shouldn't have dumped her like a bag of trash . . . well, anyway, none of my business, okay, but seriously someone as famous as you are shouldn't be sleeping on the streets. To my mind, you lack ambition . . . because, I tell you, you're a star on the internet, everyone is looking for you."

A haughty black guy immune to Pamela's charms was eventually persuaded to tell them the hospital wing where Xavier had been admitted. In the corridor, Vernon had spotted Madame Fardin, handbag in her lap, shoes scuffed, body slumped, head resting on her clasped hands. He had felt as though his mind and heart were anaesthetised, felt exactly as he did before having a tooth extracted. His body was there, moving forward, registering information: from her face, when she looked up, he knew that the news was not good. But his emotions had switched off. Marie-Ange had appeared, visibly distraught, she had gritted her teeth when she saw Vernon, "What the fuck happened", and it was Pamela who had answered because no words came from Vernon's lips. He had assumed that Marie-Ange did not recognise Pamela, unlike several male nurses and doctors, the men in white coats, who were starting to congregate to trade information. A coma. And Vernon had managed to ask where are the toilets. He had taken the direction indicated. He had found the exit. There had not been a moment when he decided to flee into the night into the rain, he had just started walking, in the darkness, in a straight line, noting incongruous details. The weight of his arms, for example. He had his hands in his pockets and would have been unable to take them out – his arms seemed to be filled with lead.

Vernon was incapable of taking hold of the reins of his own machine. The urge to end it all, a fierce rage, a visceral self-loathing, a terror at what is happening, suffocation, despair and confusion all jostle for attention. He is burning up, his lungs are burning, he is streaming with sweat and his cheeks are ablaze. He walks like a zombie for hours and hours. He feels dizzy. But he remains standing. He climbs steps in the darkness, climbs them breathlessly, he climbs faster. He remembers the words of a song, "It's the story of a guy who couldn't stop dancing", he carries on, panting for breath, straining. He runs through the alphabet, he has never forgotten the name of a band in his life and now for the first time tonight he has to concentrate. Liaisons Dangereuses. "It's the story of a guy who couldn't stop dancing and in the end it killed him, that's just how it goes these days." Trivial facts of absolutely no use to him continue to pile up, always the same shambles, a cacophony, 1981, German band, D.A.F., Einstürzende Neubauten, "Mystère dans le brouillard". Still he climbs, the steps are never-ending, he feels as though he is climbing the side of a building, leaving the city far below. He does not slow, he strains, his head pounding. He hears the opening bars of "Los Niños del parque", a synth loop, a drum machine and female voices in the background.

Crumpled on a bench, he cannot catch his breath. He can no longer hear the traffic, the rain lashes more viciously, tiny leaden fists pummel his upturned face.

Day has broken yet he does not remember falling asleep. Though he did dream that Robert Johnson was sitting on the bench opposite, he was playing harmonica. Vernon does not recognise the street where he has collapsed, when he tries to sit up his body refuses to obey and he rolls onto his back and slowly turns his head. The rain has given way to a chill as sharp as a razor but he must have caught a fever because beneath the biting cold his skin is literally burning. A sane thought nags at him: how long has it been since he last ate? If only he could shut down, just like that, within the hour – he imagines a candle flame as it quivers and gutters, the black wick, the glowing pinprick, then nothing. But you do not die of despair, or at least not that easily.

The presence of a cat scrabbling for space between his legs wakes him with a start. In the dark of night, the rain returns and the cat scarpers. His thoughts are sickening. He can taste the smell of them in his mouth. Rotting corpses. He wishes he could throw up, but he can spew only bile that tears at his throat, he's too weak to turn his head and vomit on the ground, it spatters his chin, it is washed by the icy rain, he can see lights in the windows, they are dancing. He closes his eyes. He drifts, incandescent forms flickering on his eyelids, and once again his breathing becomes laboured. Has he just come to at this bench? He cannot sit up. He needs to do something. He is dragged down into sleep, unable to resist.

Later in the night, some hours have passed, or a minute, he does not know, he is shivering with fever. He is woken by the opening chords of "Voodoo Chile". Jimi Hendrix coughs, actually it's the intro to "Rainy Day". Not the version from "Electric Lady-land", Vernon has never heard this version but it is as clear as if he were listening through headphones, or he was in the best seat at an open-air concert. Opening his eyes is a painful effort. The sky is strewn with stars. It will be fine tomorrow. The music does not stop. He knows he is delirious, but it does not worry him. He closes his eyes again, returns to the chimerical patterns projected on his eyelids. The intro to "Voodoo Chile" is longer, he hears Eddie Hazel getting into a groove, he finds this surprising, then he distinctly recognises James Jamerson hooking a classic bassline, finally Janis Joplin's voice breaks through, perfect in its purity. An arc of sounds curves above his body. Steve Winwood's Hammond organ warps space, all that remains of Vernon is a fabulous tension, towards pleasure, a dilation in the darkness, the is the whole city, he is gazing down, Jimi and Janis are playing an unlikely concert that he alone can hear. Above him, the stars glitter with peculiar intensity in the Paris sky.

Later – he fell asleep for a time – he hears a torrent of light rolling over a guitar riff, Janis' voice pierces the pain like a scapel lancing a festering sore, he unravels. Deft, unseen fingers slide beneath his collar bones and pull, he breathes more freely, the heat spreads, his ribcage splays. Pleasure suffuses every particle of his skin, the song lingers.

When silence returns, he is surprised to find himself still alive. Everything he is wearing is sodden, he is weak but able to sit up. He has no idea where he is. It takes him some time to realise that the sense of strangeness owes more to the silence than to the setting itself. There is no traffic. His head is spinning. He has never felt such pleasurable calm. It permeates his whole being.

Even heroin cannot do this. Even mushrooms or L.S.D. or Datura could not produce auditory hallucinations as perfect as the one for which he has just been the conduit. He is not dead, indeed a nagging pain in his throat lets him know that he is very much alive. And ill. But happy, oh fuck, happy as a madman, happy as a lunatic. Facing him, he finds an open aspect, he is looking down on Paris from above.

I am a single man, I am fifty years old, my throat is like a sieve since my cancer and I smoke cigars as I drive my taxi, windows open, not caring what the punters look like.

I am Diana and I am the kind of girl who giggles all the time and apologises for everything, my arms are smudged with the ghosts of cut-marks.

I am Marc, I work with the R.S.A. and my girlfriend works to support me, I look after our daughter every day and today I taught her to ride a bike for the first time and I thought about my father, when I was a kid and he finally took the training wheels off my bike.

I am Eléonore, the girl I fancy takes photographs of me in the Jardin du Luxembourg, I know that something is going to happen and that it will be complicated because we are both in relationships but it will be worth it anyway.

I am in bed when I hear that Daniel Darc is dead, I think of his number stored on my mobile phone, I feel the urge to dial the number and the fact that it is now impossible makes me tremble from head to foot.

I am a teenager obsessed with the idea of losing my virginity and the redhead I have fancied for months has just told me we can go to the pictures together, I don't think she is making fun of me and looking at myself in the mirror I realised that my acne has completely disappeared, the Roaccutane worked and a new life is unfolding before me.

I am a young virtuoso violinist.

I am the arrogant whore flayed alive, I am the teenager indivisible from his wheelchair, I am the young woman having dinner with the father she worships and who is so proud of her, I am the stowaway who slipped through the barbed wire at Melilla I am walking up the Champs-Elysées and I know that this city will give what I have come to find, I am the cow in the abattoir, I am the nurse made deaf by the cries of the patients and by dint of powerlessness, I am the undocumented immigrant who smokes ten euros worth of crack every night to work as a cleaner cash-in-hand in a restaurant at Château Rouge, I am the long-term unemployed who has just found a job, I am the drug mule pissing myself in fear ten metres from customs, I am the sixty-five-year-old whore delighted to see her longest-standing regular show up. I am the tree, its branches bare, manhandled by the rain, the child wailing in his pushchair, the dog tugging at her lead, the prison warden envious of the prisoners' carefree lives, I am a black cloud, a wellspring, a jilted bridegroom going through the photos of his former life, I am a hobo perched on a hill, in Paris.

A New Library from MacLehose Press

This book is part of a new international library for literature in translation. MacLehose Press has become known for its wide-ranging list of bestselling European crime writers, eclectic non-fiction and winners of the Nobel and *Independent* Foreign Fiction prizes, and for the many awards given to our translators. In their own countries, our writers are celebrated as the very best.

With this library we mean to make the books you would not want to overlook harder to overlook. The landscape for literary fiction in translation is expanding; we will go on looking beyond our shores and making it possible for readers to share in the most exciting and most renowned international writers.

Join us on our journey to **READ THE WORLD**.

PUBLISHED IN 2017

1. *The President's Gardens* by Muhsin Al-Ramli

TRANSLATED FROM THE ARABIC BY LUKE LEAFGREN

2. *Belladonna* by Daša Drndić

TRANSLATED FROM THE CROATIAN BY CELIA HAWKESWORTH

3. *The Awkward Squad* by Sophie Hénaff

TRANSLATED FROM THE FRENCH BY SAM GORDON

4. *Vernon Subutex 1* by Virginie Despentes

TRANSLATED FROM THE FRENCH BY FRANK WYNNE

5. *Nevada Days* by Bernardo Atxaga

TRANSLATED FROM THE SPANISH BY MARGARET JULL COSTA

6. *After the War* by Hervé Le Corre

TRANSLATED FROM THE FRENCH BY SAM TAYLOR

7. *After the Winter* by Guadalupe Nettel

TRANSLATED FROM THE SPANISH BY ROSALIND HARVEY

8. *The House with the Stained-Glass Window* by Żanna Słoniowska

TRANSLATED FROM THE POLISH BY ANTONIA LLOYD-JONES

www.maclehosepress.com